HOST

SYSTEMIC BOOK 2
CHRIS LODWIG

ISBN-13: 979-8-218-12033-7

Cover design & Typography by T.A. Lubsen

DEDICATION

To Amy Lodwig for beta reading, offering strong opinions, supporting my writing, and being my partner in everything I do in life.

And to Christy, my cousin, friend, and editor, who became my teacher, coach, and therapist during our collaboration, and without whom this book could not have realized its potential.

ACKNOWLEDGMENTS

While it may be true that writing is a solitary act, creating a book is a massive collaborative undertaking. I would like to thank the following friends for their generous support:

- *Christina Scheuer – Editing and general collaboration*
- *Todd Lubsen – Cover design and artwork*
- *Ashley Powell – Copy editing*
- *Carly Jayne (Love Like Salt) – Materials textiles and dyes*
- *Shannon O'Meara Hamilton – Microbiology and vaccines*
- *Amanda Kost – Medical information*
- *Beta Readers:*
    - *Todd Lubsen*
    - *Carly Jayne*
    - *Ashley Nathan Feniello*
    - *Ashley Powell*
    - *Namita Sheokand*
    - *Gail Lee*
    - *Janieka Gan*
    - *Carrie Seeronen Hart*
- *Everyone who helped promote Systemic and encourage me, especially Holly Ward and Joanne Ryan who have always been outspoken supporters.*

CHAPTER ONE
Day 64, Year 290, New Era

The snow arrived before the professors that year.

In all of Reyan's thirteen years, it had gone the other way round. But two days ago, the air had grown unseasonably cold. A shin-deep blanket of snow had rolled down from the craggy peaks of the surrounding mountains and covered the small town of Orloton.

Townsfolk say professors only bring their caravans around during the warm, easy months when the hardroad is clear and safe. Reyan was afraid the snow would keep them away. But then the air warmed, the snow turned sodden and sloppy, and her hope returned.

The other kids whined and moaned about the tedious and dull professors. Most adults did their best to keep their distance, as though the professors were horses who were liable to kick. But Reyan liked the professors. She found their sessions informative and useful, if not terribly exciting. And she appreciated the structure and civility that settled—like snow—upon Orloton when a caravan arrived. But she knew that, every moment the professors remained, the town would grow more and more precarious and tense—like a held-back branch—and would snap violently back with scorn and abuse the moment the professors were gone.

So, even though Reyan looked forward to the professors' visitations, she sometimes wished that, if they could not stay forever, they'd never come at all.

When word spread that the professors' caravan had been spotted on the hardroad, everyone seemed taken by surprise. With Leader Rolf gone, a panic overtook the town. Everyone began rushing about making last-minute preparations, washing windows and children's faces, and clearing a place for the caravan in the town square. Reyan tried to help, but no matter what she did, Lyessa shouted at her for being underfoot. So, overwhelmed by the chaos, Reyan did what she always did: she slinked away to seek out the high ground of her tree.

Reyan's tree was a young redwood that stood a dozen crow-flaps from the edge of town. To passersby, it looked like any of the others that bordered the hardroad. But behind its shroud of needles were limbs worn to a dark, shiny polish by the girl's hands, bare feet, and the rough weave of her pants. Broken bits of scavenged metal and glass dangled in intricate constellations from branches and twigs on frayed and rotting bits of string. Golden beads of pitch dripped from symbols and figures she'd carved into the trunk with her knife or thumbnail.

She liked to believe that her sanctuary kept her well-hidden. But anyone who knew her could have found her if they bothered to look. If she had her way, she would stay here until her mind settled. But she knew she could not hold out for more than a few hours. Even the most obstinate girl needs food, water, and sleep.

Reyan perched on her favorite branch. From there, Orloton was obscured, and she had clear views of the mountains, forest, and part of the stream. But she could not see the hardroad. For that she had to climb up two more branches. From this new, shakier spot, she could clearly see the professors' caravan as it lumbered up the hardroad toward town.

Steam poured from the horses' nostrils. It hung in the still air for a moment before the beasts lurched forward to reclaim the swirling clouds of their own exhalations. The horses' hooves churned the snow into an icy lather speckled black and brown with grit and bits of newly fallen leaves. The trucks' hammered metal tyres pushed up a bow wave of slush that curled over and sloshed into the tracks left in the snow by wheels that had traveled the hardroad before them.

A group of children erupted from their hiding place in the brush. They advanced through the slush, stomping and cheering, until they were alongside the caravan. Reyan shook her head. *Little kids can't ever contain themselves when they see a caravan*, she thought. *It doesn't matter if the trucks are full of sweetroot, scab, or a bunch of dreary old professors.* Even when she was little, she would never have run with that gang of soggy, cackling children stabbing their noise into the calm forest. Even if they

2

had thought to invite her, which they never had.

The lead truck in the caravan was almost under her now. She inched out toward the end of the branch until it began to sag under her weight. From there, she could see the broad eye painted across the roof. Similar eyes decorated the front, rear, and sides of every professor's truck. But while the slicing angles of the lower eyes were severe and meant to ward off danger, the eyes on the roofs were open and round and skyward-gazing. People who stayed on the ground did not know about the upper eyes—only Reyan, up in her tree, knew.

She counted four trucks. Usually there were only two in the professors' caravans; one for each professor. These professors must have a novice with them. That would explain the third truck, but a fourth truck was unheard of. Stranger still, this final truck had no Eye.

I know those horses. That's Rolf's truck.

Ten days ago, Rolf had busied himself in the sunshine, readying his horses and loading his truck. Reyan had hung in the dark corners of the stable. She wanted to be near her benefactor but was afraid to get in his way. He kept drawing her out to hold a thing or tie down some other thing or to see to some detail he could just as easily have seen to himself. When he was ready, he crouched down and looked Reyan in the eye. "Try not to get into too much trouble while I'm gone," he said, but his eyes smiled. Rolf seemed to cherish the sort of trouble Reyan was always getting into. He tousled her dust-brown hair, messing it up even more than usual. Then he climbed into the driver's cab and disappeared down the hardroad.

He was headed east over the pass to the town of Pesh. As Orloton's leader, he acted as the town's emissary at Gishken ceremonies. No one knew how long the ceremony would last, but even the most austere exchange of gifts and honors involved days of celebration. Between the Gishken itself and the travel—which would involve visits to other towns along the way—no one expected Rolf to return for at least a few more days. His early return was a surprise. She smiled.

But then she looked at his horses. No reins reached out from beneath the windscreen to guide them. Instead, they were lashed to the rear of the truck in front of them. Their heads drooped at the end of their long necks, watching the road move past their hooves.

The cab of Rolf's truck was empty.

The cycle of her breath grew short and shallow, and panic flared in her chest. *Why would Rolf's truck be empty?* She dug her fingers into her ears and shut her eyes so tight they squeezed out tears. She wanted to smash her head against the tree trunk just so she could be in control of her own pain.

Look for facts, not fears, she scolded herself. She took a few breaths. *Rolf is a leader. He's very sociable. Perhaps he's riding in one of the other cabs, keeping the professor company. He loves being a benefactor. He's probably in the third truck right now, trying to mentor the novice.*

The noise from the shouting swarm of children faded. She opened her eyes and saw the caravan and the throng disappear into town.

4

Rolf had told her many times not to let her fears imprison her. And the professors were fond of saying that fears were just questions needing to be answered. All she had to do was figure out what the questions were, then start answering them one by one.

She tried to come up with some structure, some Systemic process, like the professors taught. She pictured a vast field. Next, she considered each thought she had about Rolf: that his horses were not reined and seemed sad; that he was not in his cab; that he was injured, ill, or dead. Things she'd seen with her own eyes she placed on one side of the field and labeled "facts." Things which were only thoughts and fears she placed on the other side and labeled "questions."

She was halfway through arranging her questions by importance when names began bubbling up from town as fathers called their children home. Rolf was not Reyan's father, but caring for the unwanted was part of his role as Orloton's leader. Rolf took his responsibilities seriously. If he had been in his truck, he would call for her. She held her breath and stared at the leader's house, willing her name to rise into the air with all the others.

She waited for a very long time.

CHAPTER TWO
Day 64, Year 290, New Era

It had been at least an hour since the caravan had passed into town, but Reyan could not bring herself to go home.

The sun began to set. All the colors—the bright green of the trees, the berry-colored tunic of a little girl running between houses—were converging toward the same shade of deep blue. Objects in the forest and the town lost their texture and depth and stood against the uniform blue-gray of the snow and the sky, stark and flat as the shadow puppets in the shows that came to town in late spring.

As the temperature fell, the snow began to harden. A cold mist rose and drifted through the needles of her tree and soaked through her roughly woven tunic. Her gloveless fingers felt fleshy and slow, and the branch she sat upon pressed a dull throbbing line across the backs of her legs.

Rolf always left his mate, Lyessa, to stand in as town

leader while he was away. Lyessa performed the role to the letter, always making sure Reyan was fed, clothed, and sheltered. But as she often pointed out, there was nothing in the Book that demanded she harsh her throat calling home idiot girls who didn't have the sense to come in from the cold.

In the end, it was hunger that finally sank its hooks into Reyan's stomach and pulled her home. She dangled from one of the lower branches and dropped down to the soft cushion of needles below.

The snow mist filled up the spaces between the trees and carried a muffled silence with it. As she made her way to the hardroad, all she could hear were the chortling of a raven, the steady drip and trickle of melting snow, and the sheesh-SHAUWK of each step resting for a moment on the grainy crust before breaking through to the slop beneath.

The hardroad spilled into Orloton and pooled into the town square in front of the leader's house. At the far end of the square, the caravan was curled into a half-circle that reminded Reyan of a sleeping dog. Rolf's truck had been unhitched and parked beside the house and his horses led to the stable.

The front windows of the stores and homes on the main street were dark except for the leader's. Through those bright and blazing windows, she could see grimacing people moving gingerly around the room as though trying to avoid something that had shattered upon the floor.

Reyan entered through the front door, then guided it shut behind her, lifting the latch so it would not make a sound. She wanted food, not attention. She tried to disappear by pressing herself against the side of the archway that led from the foyer into the large room where much of the town had gathered.

The sound of whispered conversations filled the room like the wind blowing through tall, dead grass. The air was humid and smelled of something foul that wasn't quite flatulence or stale breath or old sweat. Whatever it was, the smell was so strong she feared it would spoil the food.

Someone had moved the leader's chair from its place at the head of the table to a spot next to the fire, which was pulsing and spitting in the hearth. Lyessa sat in the stout wooden chair and stared past her knees down at the floor. A plate of food sat untouched on her lap.

At the other end of the woman's steady gaze was Rolf. He was laid out on a thick woolen travel blanket in the middle of the room. His face had the white translucent look of a smear of tallow melting in a pan. Rusty scabs had blossomed around his nose and lips. Reyan searched the room for something else to see.

Her eyes followed the three professors from the caravan as they floated into the room, still dressed in their long brown traveling robes. They huddled together for a minute and whispered like school kids hatching rumors, then broke apart and each headed to a different part of the room.

The eldest professor approached Lyessa, bending his tall, thin body and briefly pointing his sharp nose and bright blue eyes at Lyessa's feet. When he straightened and smiled at Lyessa, his intelligent, disquieting eyes did not smile with him.

The lesser heads of the town—the butcher, the waterman, and Leonid the Systemic Keeper—were gathered around Lyessa, holding their near-empty plates in front of themselves like shields. One by one they worked their dolorous faces into welcoming smiles and greeted the professor with words like "pleasure" and "honored" and "certainly." The townspeople always offered the professors too much food, drink, and laughter. But Rolf wasn't like that. He treated professors with a familiar disinterest, the way old farmers greet each other on the street and talk about their fields or the weather.

The old professor's thinning gray hair was combed straight back in an effort to keep it tidy, but as he talked and nodded, hairs fell out of place and wisped about. As he reached a hand up to smooth them back into place, his sleeve pulled back, and Reyan noticed the metal bracelets on his right wrist. One steel, one bronze. She knew that a karaband marked someone as a professor. What could it mean that this old man wore two?

The second professor was a few inches shorter than the first. His black eyes jumped around as though continually measuring the dimensions of the room and the distances between everyone and everything within it. He made the rounds, speaking briefly and gravely with one distraught townsperson, then the next. When he and Teacher Hewitt found themselves near the old professor and the clutch of town leaders, he touched the woman's elbow and guided her to a quieter place.

Reyan could not or would not let herself hear what he was saying, but as he spoke, he held his expression perfectly neutral. Most of his coal black hair had been pulled into a tiny ponytail and tied at the back of his head. He nodded intently while he listened. Strands of hair that were too short to be collected spilled like a river around the stone island of his face. No wrinkles framed his eyes or mouth to give a clue about his age or disposition.

He had a stiff-back yet benevolent formality, which struck such a perfect balance between concern, deference, and competence that Reyan guessed it was taught at the university as part of a professor's practice and art. She caught herself trying on his peculiar posture and expressions. She looked around, suddenly worried that someone might have seen her. Luckily, no one was so much as glancing at her.

Now it was Harut the baker's turn to corner the dark professor. As Harut expounded upon daily life in the bakery, the professor crossed his arms over his chest and Reyan saw light glinting off the pair of bands that he also wore.

The youngest of the three professors had dusty blond hair that brushed his shoulders. Reyan guessed he was only a few years older than herself. He made his way to a group of bored, pouting children sitting in chairs along the wall and called them to him. A scar warped the line of the young professor's mouth, so when he smiled it looked like his upper lip was stuck to a dry tooth. Unlike the older professors, his robe bore a broad white stripe. He pulled something from one of its folds and held it out for the children to see. The thing fit in the palm of his hand and consisted of an outside ring of polished steel, a dozen loose metal balls, and an inner ring of brass. It was beautiful and clearly ancient. He spun the outside ring and held it up for the children to see. It whirred and spun for an impossibly long time and reflected firelight into the children's widening eyes.

He began half-leading, half-following the group of children around the room, doing his best to steer them wide of Rolf, who still lay motionless on the floor. The young professor made a game of pretending to be ignorant, pointing to different objects and asking the children to explain them. Soon the children were waving their raised hands and shouting out answers. The noise elicited glares from the old professor and subtle smiles from the dark one.

When the young professor pointed to the scythe and axe hanging over the mantel, Reyan noticed his naked wrists held no karabands. So, this one was not a professor at all. Not yet. Though everyone in town would certainly call this novice "Professor" out of deference to or fear of his future station.

One of the girls pointed out the tools' handles. "Look. Those were carved to show us working hard in the woods and fields." A boy interrupted her and said, "See those pretty ribbons tied to the handles? The way the glass and metal beads are strung shows the year the tools were given to us at Gishken." Then he added, a bit embarrassed, "But I don't know how to read them."

The young professor pointed at the large seashell sitting on the mantel beneath the tools, "And what does that one mean?"

Rolf always made sure to put the shell away during the professors' visitations, but in all the hurry and chaos, Lyessa must have forgotten.

"Look at that," the old professor said with wonder. He walked over and picked up the shell. The room fell quiet, and all eyes snapped to the shell and the old professor who was holding it aloft.

Reyan loved the shell. On her first day in the leader's house, Lyessa had pointed at it and said, "This shell is one of the most valuable things in the world. Do not touch it." Out of respect and gratitude for her new benefactor's mate, Reyan made sure to not get caught on the many occasions she ignored the warning.

The shell looked like one of the tiny snails in the nearby pond had lived and continued to grow for a thousand years. Spikes like a castle's crenelations erupted along its ridges, growing as the shell's chamber swelled. Its surface was a chaos of artistry and beauty. In one area there were inlaid jewels, in another, polished stones. Across the lid of the eye-like opening was a lightning-forked crack that had been repaired and filled with aluminum. The lip was leafed with gold. Fine-lined symbols were etched into each surface.

She never tired of running her fingers down its curling spine and trying to find the very place where the line of tiny rough granules near the tip became the lumps and spikes near the base. She would close her eyes and pass her thumb across the borders between the natural shell and the various inlays.

Inside the shell was a rolled-up strip of leather with letters and numbers burned into it. She spent hours trying to parse their meaning.

One spring morning, Rolf and Lyessa came home and caught Reyan laying on her back on the floor, holding the shell up into a beam of sunlight and gazing at it. Lyessa yelled and threatened to beat her. But Rolf saw how lovingly she had been handling it. Laughing, he told his mate to give Reyan peace.

He sat down beside the terrified girl on the floor. He took the shell from her and held it in the light for her to see. "This shell is very special. It is not special because it is beautiful. Rather, it is beautiful because it is full of meaning. It is a symbol of unity and good faith. I used to carry it with me when I attended Gishken ceremonies. When I visited a town, I would give this shell to their leader. While they had it, they made repairs or added decorations as they saw fit." He turned the shell slowly and let the light jump off the different facets.

He pulled out the leather strip and opened it. "This is a list of all the leaders who have received the shell. The dates when they held it and the adornment their town provided."

"Is it really one of the most valuable things in the world?"

Rolf looked at Lyessa, smiled, turned, and offered the smile to Reyan. "I think it is. Everyone recognizes it. It's been touched by every leader in every town as far as the trade routes have carried me."

"Even across the River?"

Lyessa's eyes grew wide. Rolf's eyes twitched toward Lyessa so Reyan would get the hint that his worried mate was listening. Then he winked at Reyan and said, "By the Eye, I would never *think* of crossing the River."

"Put it down," Lyessa whispered. The old professor smiled and shrugged and put the shell back on the mantel, but with the point now facing the wall.

A cold tickling drip hung at the tip of Reyan's nose. She sniffed it back more loudly than she had intended, and all the heads in the room turned to her. She cast her eyes to the ground, approached the table, and began spooning food onto a plate. The townspeople quickly lost interest in her and turned back to their conversations. But the professors kept their gazes fixed on her, no doubt trying to interpret everyone's complete lack of interest in this wet, sniffling child who had walked in from the cold. The tall professor with the thinning gray hair began blinking more than necessary, and his smile became twitchy and forced. Finally, he spoke. "And who might you be?"

"That'd be Reyankaiya," Lyessa answered, spitting out Reyan's full name like it was a curse. The woman looked at her, eyes squinting, mouth screwed up as though she had sipped something spoiled. "But we just call her 'Kaiya.'"

"It's good to meet you, Kaiya," the tall professor said, smiling. When Reyan didn't react, he cleared his throat. "My name is Professor Sevv. This is Professor Parr," he said, indicating the dark-haired one. "And this young man is

Kavianhar. We're all very pleased to meet you." Sevv stepped forward with his hand out but stopped short when Reyan winced and shied away from him, shrugging her right shoulder as though the professor had touched her neck with a cold hand. Sevv looked at Lyessa with a question in his eyes.

"That's as close as Kaiya gets to being pleased to meet you," Lyessa said. Sevv lowered his hand, and the karabands slid into a clinking stack at the end of his wrist.

"What's wrong with Rolf?" Reyan asked Sevv.

The old professor looked around for the right person to answer, but everyone else's faces had hardened toward the girl, leaving the task to him. "He caught a disease, dear, Sevv said.

"How?" Reyan thought this question was important. Perhaps knowing how Rolf got sick might help others avoid his fate. But the room remained tense, and when she saw the look of bewildered disgust on Lyessa's face, she knew it had been a stupid thing to ask.

She looked again at Rolf's supine body. Her breath jerked in her chest, her throat tightened, and she wanted to turn away, but she made herself look.

The fire cast deep and shifting shadows down his face. As she focused on the rises and hollows and lines that defined him, the light stopped flickering and the shadows lessened until Rolf appeared lit within by a steady golden warmth. Rolf's glow intensified until it overwhelmed the candles, lanterns, and fire. She was within it.

Rolf had always drawn pleasure from being kind. She imagined the light of his benevolence radiated out into the cold darkness until it became a golden dome encompassing the whole town. It expanded like an inflating soap bubble. It enveloped the snowy caps of the mountains and reached down the other side of the pass. It stretched out to encompass all the towns on the northern spur of the circuit until he seemed to illuminate the entire world.

Then it burst.

She felt something that was not quite pain. It did not poke or pinch. It was the feeling of a collapsing void, like the moment a rock punches a hole through the surface of a pond and the water comes flooding back in. She felt the blow of the rock and the emptiness and the rushing drowning feeling all in the same moment.

Her mind flew back to the reality of this cold and joyless house and the gray waxen man lying still before the fire. His chest did not rise and fall. The lumps of his eyes did not lurch behind their lids. His fingers did not twitch to grasp whatever his dreaming mind had placed within reach.

Rolf was dead.

Lyessa drew a deep breath and made a stuttering sound when she let it out. "We'll hold his Last Day ceremony early tomorrow."

Sevv looked at Parr, who nodded with his black eyes more than his head. Parr moved over and slowly lowered himself on one knee next to Lyessa, facing Rolf's stiffening corpse. "I'm sure that would be best, Leader." He used the peculiar, practiced tone of one well-versed in dealing with grief. It was a mixture of sympathy and firmness that, until now, Reyan had only witnessed in doctors, veterinarians, and Rolf himself, when he had to tell a father that his child had been swept down river while tending a fish trap.

Lyessa forced herself to look steadily at the kneeling professor. She managed a single firm nod before sorrow weighed down her head and she stared once again at the floor.

Sevv snapped his fingers, and Kavianhar approached with a pencil and paper in hand that he had pulled from somewhere deep in his robe.

"Where shall the event take place?" Parr asked.

Sevv answered before Lyessa could, "This room is too small. I know that it is cold, but I think we should consider the square out front." When Lyessa didn't react, Sevv looked at Keeper Leonid, the waterman, and the butcher, who each nodded in turn. Sevv then glanced impatiently at Kavianhar, who dutifully jotted something on the pad.

Parr turned to the butcher and asked, "And the food, will you be helping with that?"

"I'll dress a pig this evening." The butcher looked over to Kavianhar, "You'll need to work with others to get the rest of the food. Talk to Manisha. Blue house, third on the right on the road south of the square. It's late, but you should go to her tonight." Kavianhar nodded and wrote it all down.

"As for the ceremony itself," Sevv began. There was a tip-toeing lilt to his voice. "Who will be…"

"Keeper Leonid will do it," Lyessa declared. Her eyes came up from the floor and focused on the keeper. Leonid nodded. She turned back to the professors. "I understand that you and Rolf have a history, but Orloton's leader will have his final day in Orloton's town square, faired-well by Orloton's keeper. And then all our people will show their respect and receive his gift."

"His 'gift,' Leader?" Sevv's question was tense.

Lyessa straightened her back and frowned. "Partaking of the gift has been a custom in Orloton since the time of the scab. During the worst of it, Rolf brought a woman from the east to help. We thought she was a professor at first. She seemed wise and just as foreign." She looked at the professors and her lips tightened into a smirk. "But she wore no robes or bands, and when she left, the scab left with her. So, I suppose, she wasn't much like a professor after all." Her voice cut like a blade. "She told us that, for the dead and dying it was too late, but within their blood they held a final gift that could save everyone they loved. She collected their blood and extracted their gifts. Our keeper at the time watched what the woman did. He did his best to write it all down later so we would not forget how to make the gift for ourselves."

"You were able to replicate her processes?" Parr asked.

Lyessa looked away. "We make do."

"And does it work? Does it help?" Parr asked.

"It worked when she did it, and it's never caused us harm."

"But Rolf just died of *scab*," Sevv said, stammering. "I don't know what other diseases have plagued Orloton over the years, but scab lives in the *blood*. Surely a wise leader, such as Rolf, would not have wished to be honored with anything so ill-advised as sharing the blood of a man infected with *scab*."

"If you'll forgive my saying so, Professor Sevvran, this has nothing to do with you or what you feel is well or ill-advised. You professors roll into town for a few days every year, armed with whatever secret knowledge you have buried deep in your minds. You tell us how to be Systemic and proper." She swept her arm, indicating those gathered in the room. "We, for our part, listen closely and show our respect." Her eyes narrowed. "But do not for a moment think that we do not respect other things as well. In Orloton, we show respect to our beloved dead by letting them bestow a final gift of protection upon us. As professors you are honored guests. You are welcome to partake of Rolf's gift. If you choose not to, no one will be offended. No one would even notice or care." Her words turned hard. "But by the Eye, if you have a mind to disrespect our town's greatest leader, I suggest you consider how far from your university you are."

"I've heard about your 'gifts,'" Sevv said, his jaw stiffening. "How are we ever to improve life in the nodes if we have to accommodate hysterical, heretical Erynite nonsense?!"

Lyessa turned and spoke directly to Kavianhar, and her attention startled him. "So, you want to be like one of these men?" She smiled wickedly and waved a dismissive hand at Sevv and Parr. "Be careful what you wish for, boy. There's something about that second karaband that makes professors even more arrogant and inflexible."

Parr stepped forward calmly. He whispered something into Sevv's ear that soured the old man's face. But Sevv stepped aside and let the dark-eyed professor speak to Lyessa. His voice was deep and quiet and clear. "How many are you, Leader?"

The flame left Lyessa's eyes, and she became businesslike. "Orloton has a population of four hundred thirty-seven."

"Thirty-six," Reyan said under her breath.

Lyessa lifted her chin to give the impression of strength. "Thirty-six as of today."

"We have seen many children playing in your streets," Parr said. "It is a testament to Rolf's leadership that you've been able to keep so many." This seemed to soothe Lyessa a little bit, and she offered him a sad smile. The professor continued: "It is late in the evening now, and the ceremony will be early tomorrow. Will the butcher have time to prepare a meal for so many? Will there be time for your people to forage and boil and bake enough to feed them all?" Parr's face betrayed no emotion. His voice was calm and quiet, but relentless. "Of course, it is up to you and your wisdom, Leader," he conceded. "They are your people now. It is for you to help them choose how to best fulfill the Governing Assert, how best to improve their lives. Still, perhaps it would be better—less disruptive to your town—if we selected a representative sample of adults to receive Rolf's final gift."

What tranquility Professor Parr had managed to impart upon her vanished, and Lyessa turned to him with cold, calm anger in her eyes. "Anything less than the town's full measure would be disrespectful, Professor," she snarled. "My mate was a leader among leaders."

Sevv chimed in, "I believe Rolf would have wanted you to do as Professor Parr suggests. He was one of our own, after all."

Lyessa raised an eyebrow. "Was he?"

"What Sevv means, is that Rolf was a Systemic man," Parr said. "He performed his role with dedication and skill. The System in Orloton flourished under him."

"I'm glad to learn that the professors finally approve of my mate." Her voice wavered, and she paused for a moment. When she continued speaking, her firmness was restored. "Rolf was loved by his people. He turned our enemies into trade partners." She paused and an idea lit up her eyes. "Perhaps we should wait another day or so. We could send word to our neighbors in Bar and Rowe and invite them to come pay their respects."

"No, Leader," Parr said quickly. "I'm afraid there will be no time for that." An apology was folded into his words. "You said the gift is in Rolf's blood. Blood will thicken beyond extraction within a day. Rolf has been gone for hours already. Orloton's neighbors will not have time to come. You should not wait for them."

Lyessa appeared to be searching for a trap in his words. Not finding one, she agreed. "Then we must drain some blood tonight before it thickens and prepare it for tomorrow. Butcher, sharpen your knives."

CHAPTER THREE
Day 3, Year 0, New Era

Three days after the System shut down, Lem sat on a rotting log on the shore of Lake Armory. When he arrived, the sun had been a white-hot spot near the center of the sky. Since then, he'd watched it roll to the far rim of the expanse, swell, soften, and cool. Now he could stare at it for two full seconds before his eyes involuntarily squeezed closed, leaving its memory to throb and kaleidoscope in the aching dark.

In all that time, no planes had flown overhead. There had been no rumble of tires or whispered breath of cars driving on the nearby highway, and no trains had cantered rhythmically down the nearby tracks. The only streetlight in the campground was gray and cold, its head bent over the road like a surgeon who had fallen asleep in the middle of an operation. But the insects still whined. The great blue heron's golden eye still kept watch over the smooth, polished surface of the lake. The lake still reflected the charcoal silhouettes of the trees and the fading flames of the sky.

Lem felt a soft tap on his shoulder. He turned and saw Eryn standing behind him, shielding her eyes against the glow of the setting sun. "How are you doing?" Eryn asked.

He turned back to the lake and didn't answer. She tapped his hip with the back of her hand, and he moved over to make room for her. Sadie the dog lay on the ground and rested her chin on Eryn's right foot. Ever since her master, Thomas, had died, the dog had slunk along at Eryn's heels, never straying more than a few feet from her side as they hiked from Prower to Lake Armory.

"I want to buy something," Eryn said.

"Like what?"

"I don't know. Candy bar. Coffee maker. Anything. I just want to see some new thing, decide I want it, and buy it one last time. Everything is just so quiet. It's terrifying."

They watched the sun slide like a copper coin into a slot in the valley's western ridge. The night's first planet appeared.

"You've been out here half the day," Eryn said, "You figure anything out?"

"No. You?"

Eryn closed her eyes and shook her head. She sighed. "Right after everything shut down, I was in shock. But now the shock is wearing off, and I'm looking around at this big lake in the middle of nowhere and I'm trying to figure out which of my past selves I should blame for getting me into this mess. Was it the self who was hyper-lethargic, crying on the couch and eating junk food, or the made-up self who was so confident she thought it was a good idea to hike through this valley alone in the middle of summer? I'm pretty sure I know which version of myself was dumb enough to follow Thomas into that bunker, but which one was too weak to stop him from shutting the System down? Trying to sort it all out gets confusing pretty quickly. I feel like I'm going crazy."

"It's a total mess in here, too." He tapped a finger on the side of his head. "But I think I've figured out a way to tell my pasts apart. The System made our lattices to help us overcome our misery. So, if I have conflicting memories, and one is terrible, and the other is nice and nostalgic, I figure the happy one is probably the one they composed and added to my lattice. I trust the sadness."

"That's a cheery thought. What about Thomas? Thomas was good. He was a friend. Real or fake?"

"No, Thomas was real. The bit at the end sort of gives it away."

They watched the molten glow slowly fade into the ridge. "So, what do we do now?" Lem asked.

"Get home."

"Home?"

"Well, Thomas' place. It's the closest thing to a home for a thousand miles. Plus, it's Sadie's home." She reached down and scratched behind one of Sadie's ears. The dog groaned and leaned into it then rotated her head to offer up her other ear.

"After everything this poor girl's been through, getting her there seems like the least we could do."

CHAPTER FOUR
Day 65, Year 290, New Era

"Where you going, Reyankaiya?" Tom's familiar eager voice hurried along behind her.

"Away," she said, over her shoulder. She knew it would be more kind to let the boy catch up and walk beside her, but she couldn't bring herself to slow her pace.

"Away from the house? Away from the town?" She didn't clarify. "Why?" Tom could be exhausting. He was young and silly and needy. But he was also curious and never judged her. And, now that Rolf was gone, Tom was the only person left in Orloton who showed any interest in her at all.

He jogged up beside her and struggled to match his smaller strides to hers. She felt bad about making him work so hard to keep up, so she slowed. Tom smiled gratefully and took a deep breath.

"Rolf died yesterday," she said

"Yeah," Tom spoke quietly, his head turned down toward the ground.

"Today will be his Last Day. Today, they'll share his gift."

"That doesn't sound so bad."

"'Gift' means they're going to take some of his blood, do whatever they do to it, and then *gift* it to everyone." She stopped and turned to face Tom. "Look here." She rolled up her sleeve to show three raised and neatly spaced scars on her right arm. "Those were just a couple of babies and an old lady. As a member of the leader's household, I had to partake, and even then they had to hold me down. But this is *Rolf's* Last Day, and Lyessa's in charge. Plus, with the professors in town, Lyessa has something to prove. The whole town will take the gift. The butcher's sharpening his big knives. I'm not sticking around for that."

She couldn't help enjoying the way Tom's eyes grew wide. Tom was fun that way. "But you can't just skip Rolf's Last Day," he said. "What about the Eye?"

"I'm not hurting anyone. The Eye won't care."

Tom considered this for a moment. "So, what are you gonna do then?"

She shrugged. "Hide until it's over."

"Where?" The boy sounded panicked and desperate.

"If I told you, it wouldn't be hiding."

"Can I hide with you?" he pleaded.

She wished she could take the boy with her, but she knew he would pay for that moment of avoided pain. If he hid through Rolf's Last Day, he would be forever associated with selfishness, cowardice, and—worst of all—*Reyankaiya Estermet*. His interest in her already earned him the smirks and teasing whispers of his friends. A sin of this magnitude would brand him forever. And not just in the eyes of the other children. Any parent would be ashamed of a child who hid from his responsibility like a frightened bird. Like *Kaiya*. Knowing that one of their children—not just that idiot girl—had refused to mourn a beloved leader would fray the weft and warp of the very social fabric Rolf had worked so hard to strengthen.

She considered the sort of leaders such an unraveling town would produce. Selfish, cowardly, factional. And if towns like Orloton sent forth fearful, partisan representatives to Gishkens, it would not be long before the world returned to chaos and war.

Reyan weighed these considerations on the broad scale of her mind and did what she felt was best. She said, "But what about the Eye, Tom?" The boy's face flushed. She felt bad teasing him. "Besides, you'll give me away."

"But I don't want to get poked or stabbed or cut!" The bottom rims of his eyes were beginning to glisten.

"I don't blame you." She heard Tom sniffle and knew it was the beginning of a full-fledged panic cry. She knew how he felt. She wished she could help. "Come on. Don't be scared like me. I would take the gift if I had the guts." She stopped and turned back to face the town and he stood beside her. "Go home," she said.

He took a few tentative steps, then turned to look back at her. "Go home," she repeated. He began to slowly walk up the hardroad into town. She called after him, "If you do decide to hide out, don't tell anyone I told you to, because I didn't."

Reyan headed in the opposite direction. She crouched through a gap in the green cloud of branches and needles and stepped into the waiting arms of her tree. Under the cover of the boughs, it was dark and dry and still. The air was laced with the dusty smell of rotted wood and the sharp turpentine taste of pitch. She climbed the smoothed branches until she was a dozen feet above the ground. From where she was perched, she could see Tom through a break in the needles. He had stopped again and was standing still and looking down the hardroad from town. He wiped his nose on his sleeve, then turned back toward town to face his fate.

That was the other thing Reyan liked about Tom: he was a brave little guy.

A half hour or so after Tom had returned to the village, she heard the panicked cries of children. She replayed her memories of the stone-faced butcher walking down the line of their outstretched arms making small cuts on each. Then of the keeper putting a drop of gift into each tiny wound. The adults made no sound as a show of respect. The older children stayed silent to prove that they were adults.

The cuts didn't really hurt. The butcher kept his knives so sharp he could slice through a fly in midair. Nor was it the sight of her own blood that bothered her. She'd certainly seen enough of that in her life. It was the *anticipation* she couldn't stand. Watching a kid down the line get a slit, and then the next, then the next. Watching them wince and cry out one after the other until finally the butcher came to her. She had been told many times to just keep her eyes and mouth shut, but that just made it worse. She felt certain it was now, then now, then now… And each time she misjudged the moment, her terror grew.

No. Hiding was all there was for it. Still, she wished she could have been there for Rolf's Last Day. She understood that taking in unwanted children was part of a town leader's role. But Rolf took the role seriously and worked hard at caring for Reyan. Most days he made it look more like a joy than a job— like she was his first born not his ward. Or so she let herself believe in secret. But accepting his final gift was more than she could endure.

Within twenty minutes, the cries had stopped, and the town grew silent. But goats needed to be milked, chickens fed, and things had to be moved about from place to place. So, within the hour, the normal sounds of life began to furtively creep out from Orloton's houses and shops. Normal children, with their maddeningly brief memory for fear and trauma, started running and playing again.

The gifting ceremony safely behind her, Reyan couldn't

bear to miss any more of Rolf's Last Day. She climbed down from her tree and headed back to Lyessa's house. When she slipped silently through the front door, the great room was arranged just as it had been the night before. Lyessa was in her chair near the fireplace. Keeper Leonid was standing stiffly beside her. He held his straw hat to his chest with his left hand, and his right hand rested on Lyessa's back.

Everyone was silent, their eyes cast down toward the void in the middle of the room where Rolf had lain. The professors were also missing. Masters of manners and good grace, they must have decided to leave the locals to their grief.

Reyan stepped cautiously into the room. "Leader…" Reyan had to concentrate on her lips and tongue and force her jaw to form the word correctly.

Lyessa's head snapped up. Her wet, bleary eyes were suddenly acute and dangerous. Reyan felt she was staring down the points of porcupine quills. The girl looked down at the ground. "Lyessa. Leader. I'm sorry."

Not wishing to bear witness to what was to come, the remaining guests quickly exited the room. They bobbed their heads in quick awkward goodbyes, leaving only Reyan, Lyessa, and Leonid, who stood at Lyessa's side like a sycophantic jester.

Once the room had emptied, Lyessa straightened her neck and back. She gathered herself upon the leader's chair like a storm brewing atop a mountain. "You're sorry?" Lyessa scoffed. "I don't think you know what the word means."

Lyessa was wrong, of course. It wasn't that Reyan didn't understand the word "sorry," but rather that it meant so many things. "I'm sorry he's gone," she said. "I'm sorry you lost your mate. I'm sorry Orloton lost our leader." *I'm sorry I lost my benefactor,* she thought but did not say. "Sorry" also meant shame. She was ashamed that the idea of Rolf's gift had filled her with a rushing terror. She was ashamed that her own cowardice had kept her from singing the drop of Rolf's kind and generous soul back to the Great Gray Sea. "I'm sorry I couldn't be here," she managed.

Lyessa reflected none of Reyan's sorrows back at her. If anything, she honed her quill-tipped eyes to even finer points. "And where were you all day while you perfected this show of sorrow? In that tree of yours, by the look of you. Off playing squirrel while the rest of the town paid their respects to your benefactor."

The wind began to blow. It was not strong. No one else probably noticed. But it was enough to start a tree branch moving. Reyan stopped crying and listened to it ticking against the window.

"You have always been spoiled and ungrateful," Lyessa hissed. "Always underfoot, always out of control, always demanding his attention, then running away in a panic when you got too much of it. Nothing was ever right for you. You came into our home and sapped all the joy from our final years together."

Reyan wasn't sure what to say to Lyessa. She hadn't chosen this life. It was a leader's role to be the benefactor of their town's uncared for and unwanted. But it didn't matter. Lyessa didn't want anything from Reyan but her deference. So Reyan kept her face turned to Lyessa to show that she was paying attention, but her mind turned toward the window and the tapping branch.

It felt like shards of glass were jutting up between Lyessa's words. "You will never have the chance to make it up to him, or to our town. You'll never be able to make it up to *me*. Rolf had an overdeveloped sense of responsibility. He did his duty by you, but I feel no compulsion to keep up his pretense." A snarl warped her face, then slowly flattened into cruel indifference. "Keeper," she said flatly.

Leonid's head snapped to look at her, obviously not expecting to be addressed. He brought his other hand to the brim of the hat he held to his chest and stepped before her. "Yes Leader?"

Now the twig was tapping out a steady rhythm. This meant there was a perfect balance between the pressure of the wind and the tension in the limb so that it recoiled just after contacting the glass...

"Keeper Leonid, I am no longer able to adequately provide for the child, Reyankaiya Estermet."

Reyan's attention snapped away from the twig, as she heard Leonid stammer, "But...But...*Fear The Eye*, Leader. Are you sure?" He asked weakly.

Reyan understood what Lyessa's words meant. She'd heard them before, when her mother had given her up. Those words meant chaos. They meant upheaval.

"I'm older now. I get to have a say this time," Reyan said.

"She's right," Leonid whispered.

Lyessa's face shifted through several annoyed shapes on its way to a beatific smile. "Yes. Of course. So tell me, Ms. Estermet, now that you are so grown up, what do you think should happen to you?"

She didn't know what to say. She hadn't wanted a specific result; she had wanted a choice. She began thinking about what the possible outcomes might be. Lyessa wanted to be rid of her, that much was clear. But where would she go? Who could care for her? What other option was there? If Lyessa kept her, she would have to live in this house for several more years, drinking and bathing from the woman's bottomless well of disdain. Or…Or what? What other choice was there? The branching limbs of her possible futures vanished into a black uncertainty. She faltered. She was silent.

"Noted," Lyessa said coldly.

Reyan wailed with inarticulate frustration. She turned to flee the room. But before she could leave, Lyessa stopped her. "Kaiya. Stay where you are."

Sobbing, Reyan froze.

Keeper Leonid stuttered, "Leader, perhaps I should retrieve the professors."

Lyessa stared at Leonid. The buds of several derisive

expressions threatened to bloom across her face, but she managed not to speak until she had nipped them. She blinked twice and said, "Go and get them, then. This will affect them too."

The frazzled keeper stepped past Reyan and out of the front door, putting on his hat as he went.

Once they were alone, Lyessa said, calmly, "Does this seem cruel, Kaiya? Is it painful for you? I think it's best. When you've had some time to think it over, you will see I'm right."

Reyan's lips quivered as she fought to control her contorting mouth, and her whole body heaved with the effort to contain her sobs. Her mind was flailing, grasping. It felt like trying to snatch leaves from the air in an autumn storm.

Keeper Leonid returned with the three professors in tow. Sevv led the way. "We've come to be of service," he said.

Leonid gestured stiffly to Lyessa. "Our new leader has just asserted that she cannot care for her ward, Reyankaiya."

The professor looked grave. "Is that so, Leader?"

Lyessa frowned and looked sadly down at her hands. "It is."

"But," Sevv stammered, his attention switching from the leader to the keeper and back as though hoping one might prove reasonable, "it is Systemic for children to be brought up in their communities."

Lyessa smiled slyly. "And what are the System and the

university if not our greatest manifestation of community?"

"But a girl her age? One who grew up…" Sevv held out his arms and swept them around the room struggling for something to say before deciding on, "…in a node this far east."

"When did Orloton become so undesirable? Or did you mean to say, 'under Rolf's roof?'"

"I don't believe the professor meant any offense, Leader," Parr said, his black eyes fixed on Sevv.

The old professor blinked rapidly for several seconds as he recovered himself. Finally, he managed, "Could you help us understand why you've decided this?"

"Reyankaiya is a wonderful child," Lyessa answered, the lie syrupy in her mouth, "But she's not like other children. She can be difficult to predict, and if you miscalculate, her reactions can be hard to manage. It is beyond my abilities—or anyone in the town's ability—to comprehend. Leader Rolf had a way with her, but I do not possess his gifts of patience and tolerance. Nor do I share his fascination with the peculiar workings of the girl's mind. I am simply not capable of caring for her in my current state of grief."

"We are truly sorry for your loss, Leader," Sevv said. "We understand that the burden of leadership was thrust upon you unexpectedly. But these hardships are temporary. Within a few weeks, your Systemic keeper will draw up a selection matrix, and Orloton will choose a permanent leader. At that point, the girl will become the new leader's ward. Wouldn't it be best for the child if you could continue to care for her until then?"

Lyessa smiled as though someone had just whispered the cunning answer to a problem into her ear. "Who's to say I won't be that new leader?"

Sevv's head made a subtle jerk of surprise. "But you just admitted that caring for your ward, one of the most solemn responsibilities of leadership, is too burdensome."

"Did I?"

"Well…yes. You have just stated quite clearly that you are not willing to support…"

"Am not able to support," she corrected.

Sevv stuttered as he recovered from the interruption. "Leader, if you hope to be selected for the role permanently, it is all the more important that you show your ability to persevere in the interim." He chuckled uncomfortably. "By declaring that you are overburdened by a single ward, you demonstrate that you do not possess a leader's qualities."

"You think so?" she asked.

"Well," he huffed, "it certainly will not help you in the preliminary scoring."

"Of course, as professors, you are the authorities on these matters, but my understanding is that the scoring reaches across many dimensions and the weight of each score can vary greatly based on context. Keeper Leonid tells me that it can be difficult to know the impact of any single consideration before the final calculations are run. Which would be the greater strike against me? A lack of strength in a single dimension of leadership, or a willingness to pass my burdens on to my successor unaddressed? I don't pretend to know."

Lyessa turned a self-satisfied smile to Reyan, then waved her hand in a theatrical dismissal of Sevv's concerns. "But honestly, my future role is not important. My chief concern is the girl's well-being. You professors wouldn't understand— you're so rarely here—but I have known Kaiya for all of her short tragic life. I was there on the sorry day when her mother could no longer care for her and she became Rolf's ward. And now I am forced to make a similar choice. It pains me. But the girl," Lyessa couldn't be bothered to lift a hand; instead, she pointed to Reyan with her chin, "has needs which are greater than I, or any leader but Rolf, could fulfill. I am willing to risk my score to give the girl a better life. In the end, perhaps that will prove decisive in the tally."

Sevv looked appalled. "Surely, Leader..." He turned to Parr looking for some help, obviously annoyed to be fighting this battle alone.

Parr looked at Reyan, his expression maddeningly calm. She had learned that this sort of non-expression generally meant someone was furious. His eyes rested on her a while. They seemed to stare deeper and deeper into her skull by degrees, until she wanted to squirm away and hide. At last, he broke his gaze.

Professor Parr put a hand on Sevv's arm. "Sevv. You and I both know that this would not be the first time the university has taken on a ward." He nodded in Kavianhar's direction. Parr stepped forward and whispered something to Sevv that Reyan did not hear. Sevv grunted in reply and flashed a quick smile at her before leaving the room. It had been a pained and pitying sort of smile, but it had been a smile. That gave her some hope.

Next, Parr placed a gentle hand on Kavianhar's shoulder and whispered into the boy's ear, "Take care of her." Reyan watched the boy warily as he came across the dining room to her. He did his best to reassure her with a smile, "Reyankaiya," he asked. "How about you and I take a walk. Maybe you can show me around the town?" He reached out a hand and gently touched her arm.

"No!" she yelled. She yanked her arm away and collapsed onto the floor. She pulled her knees to her chest, covered her head, and shielded her face as though the boy was going to attack or punish her. She knew how she looked, but she was unable to control herself. She wasn't rejecting Kavianhar or the professor's help. She was rejecting the horrible ambiguity of the future looming in the darkness just out of sight. Through a gap between her fingers, she saw Kavianhar glance around, looking for guidance. The baffled look on the poor boy's face made her humiliation burn all the brighter.

"Well, young man," Lyessa said, her voice full of cruel bemusement. "Now you and our Reyankaiya have been properly introduced."

40

CHAPTER FIVE
Day 65, Year 290, New Era

Reyan wanted to stand and face the professors. She wanted to prove Lyessa wrong. But she could not will her back to straighten nor her legs to lift her. The shame of it made her sob with self-loathing. Lyessa was right about her.

Professor Parr sent Kavianhar aside with a flick of his eyes. The professor approached Reyan. Reyan pressed her eyes shut and curled her body tighter, the way they had found Korwyn Ableman's boy in the corner the morning after the fire. She expected to hear the angry roll of Parr's thunderous voice or feel the lightning crack of his slap. Instead, he placed a heavy hand on each of her shoulders. He firmly but slowly pressed her down into the floor. It was exactly what Reyan needed—to be smaller, to disappear. Her muscles loosened a little, and Parr was able to uncurl her just enough to let in some air.

She pulled her face away from her knees and looked

briefly into the professor's dark eyes. The professor whispered in a deep rumble like a cow's low. The sound seeped through and soothed her. "Reyankaiya. Kavianhar is kind and good. Follow him. He will not touch you again."

Reyan began to slowly uncurl like a fern. She sat up and looked around the room. It was as though she had been underwater, drifting downstream, and had resurfaced to find that the world had changed while she'd been under.

Kavianhar turned to leave. He stopped and looked back over his shoulder, wordlessly inviting her to follow. The gesture reminded her of someone leading a wild creature into a pen. But Reyan stood and followed him anyway. Whatever cage these professors had made would be better than the one from which Lyessa was expelling her.

Kavianhar and Reyan walked in silence across the square to where the professors' three trucks were parked.

Because he was a novice, Kavianhar's was the oldest and most worn of the caravan's trucks. Over time, its wooden frame had begun to slouch. The corners had grown slightly obtuse and the sides a bit out of plumb. Which wasn't to say it was shabby. The side walls were constructed of a lattice of blood-red crossbeams and daffodil yellow panels. Green vines and decorative curly queues were painted into the corners of each panel, as though the truck had been swarmed by artistic spiders. Since the truck was currently set up for lodging, the forest-green driver's canopy was raised high and pegged in place to form an awning over the front porch, and curtains had been pulled over the canopy's glass panes to provide shade.

Kavianhar walked to the front of his truck and pulled on a knotted rope that dangled from the underside of the small front porch. A step ladder that hinged in the middle slid out and unfolded to the ground. He put one foot on the bottom rung, then turned back to look at Reyan. He smiled. "You're welcome to come in if you'd like." When Reyan didn't move or speak, Kavianhar shrugged. "Okay. I'll just pop in and grab some things to eat."

"I'm not hungry."

"That's okay. I am. I'll get you something just in case." She remembered Rolf explaining that eating isn't just about being hungry. Sometimes, food is a way to plant the seed of friendship. She knew adults sometimes used food in this double way, but she'd never known another young person to do it. It made her hopeful. But still, she couldn't bring herself to smile at Kavianhar. Instead, she began excavating a hole in the dirt with the toe of her boot.

He pulled down two wooden stools from the assortment of odds and ends lashed to the rack on the side of the truck. He made several trips in and out of the truck's skinny green door and returned with a folding wooden table, then dried meat, smoked fish, and a lump of hard cheese on an old, chipped plate. Finally he brought a clay pitcher and two mugs.

Steam curled around Kavianhar's nose into the cold air as he silently chewed a piece of fish. He swallowed, took a sip of water, and asked, "What was your name again?"

Conversations were hard for her—especially with strangers, not knowing where it might lead. She pulled off a tiny bite of jerky and forced it down with a sip of water. She looked up at the sky, painfully aware that it was rude not to answer him.

After waiting for a couple of minutes in silence and blowing on his pinkening hands a few times, he tried a different tactic. "I thought I heard that woman, the widow, call you 'Ray' and 'Kyah.' Is that right?"

She took a sip of water and whispered, "*Reyankaiya*. It's all one name." Then, with more ferocity than she'd intended, she added, "Don't call me that."

This seemed to startle him. "Is there something else I should call you? I heard her call you Kaiya."

"No. Not Kaiya." The word soured her stomach. "They call me 'Kaiya' because it means 'chaos.' They think it's a joke. I hate it. Sometimes, they call me 'Reyankaiya' when they want to sound fancy, like when there are professors around. But mostly they just call me 'Kaiya.'"

"What about 'Reyan'? Does that mean anything?"

"'Rises above,'" she explained.

Kavianhar smiled. "Should I call you 'Reyan' then?"

"I don't want you to call me anything."

Though he tried to hide it, she noticed his face fall a little. It had been a mean thing to say, and she wished she hadn't said it. He crumbled a bit of cheese off the lump and tossed it in his mouth. By the time he had swallowed, he had regained control of his smile and pressed it into service.

"I'll tell you my name," he offered.

"Your name is 'Kavianhar.'"

"You *could* call me 'Kavianhar.'" He shrugged. "That's fine. The professors call me that. It doesn't mean 'eater of rats' or anything awful like that." Her own lips surprised her with a smile, which she tried to hide by holding her mug to her mouth. "It's just that 'Kavianhar' is a lot to say. I think of myself as just 'Kavi.' It's not especially interesting or secret, but if you wanted to call me that, I would answer every time."

"What happened to your lip?"

It took Kavi a second to work through how to answer. "It's always been that way."

"Does it hurt?"

"No. It never hurts. Not really."

"Okay." She shrugged and picked up a sliver of dried meat.

As they picked at the rest of the food, Kavi kept his movements slow, careful, and precise. She kept expecting him to ask her why the people in Orloton didn't want her, but he never did. The longer he smiled and didn't talk, the more she found she liked him, and enjoyed sitting with him in the cold town square in the shadow of his joyful truck.

She put down the mug, her nascent smile flickering out.

She forced herself to ask the next question: "Kavi? Am I going to come and live with you and the professors?"

"I don't know," he said thoughtfully. "I honestly don't. But I know that's what Parr is talking to your leader about." Kavi tried to reassure her. "Don't worry, Parr is amazing at figuring out optimal outcomes. I don't know what's going to happen, but whatever it is, I know it'll be the best possible result for everyone."

"You aren't a professor yet, are you?" Reyan worried the question might have been rude. But he laughed.

"No. I'm not." He brushed his hand down the front of his robe, indicating the broad white stripe. "But I'm well on my way."

Kavi picked up the now-empty plate and carried it to his truck. When he returned, he said, "Hey, help me put this stuff away."

He lashed the stools to the rack on the side of the truck, while Reyan collapsed the table. He opened the skinny green door at the top of the folding stairs, and she followed him in.

It was hard for both of them to fit inside, especially with Reyan carrying the table. "Here, let me take that." He slotted the tabletop into a bracket attached to the ceiling. Then Kavi turned a latch, and the table was stowed up and out of the way.

"Well, here it is—a professor's home-away-from-home. What do you think?"

Every surface inside the truck was made of old polished

wood. A small desk, scarcely shoulder-width, was built into the left wall. A tall chest of drawers stood near the back of the truck. Footholds were carved into the spacers between the drawers to form a ladder that led up to the feather mattress that lay across the top. A cast-iron pan hung from a nail on the wall; a leather strap kept it from swinging while the truck was in motion. Reyan ran her hand down the side of a small shelf crammed tight with books. It reminded her of the well-worn limbs of her tree. "I like how everything has a special place."

"Well, we're out on circuit for months at a time. Everything we need has to fit into this truck, including us. There's a bit of an art to it. I must say, I haven't missed a thing from home." He smiled at her. "Except for my friends, of course. Hey, would you mind showing me around Orloton? This is my first time on circuit. I've never been here before."

"What do you want to see?"

"I don't know. Show me whatever the kids do in a place like this."

"Most children do little versions of their parents' work."

"What do you do?"

"No one in Orloton will apprentice me, and when I try to do odd jobs, everyone tells me I'm always underfoot. So mostly I just try to stay out of the way."

"What do you do for fun?"

"Most of the kids run and yell. They shove each other a lot. Sometimes they throw rocks and try to hit things, or they sit together in small groups and whisper."

"And you? What do you do?"

"I don't do any of that." She picked at a callus on her palm. "I do have a place I go."

"Can I see it?"

"No."

"Oh. That's okay," Kavi frowned and shrugged.

"Well, you might be able to see the very top of it, but it's hard to be sure with the buildings and houses and other trees in the way."

Kavi smiled. "Would you take me to see it?"

She shrugged. "Sure." They walked through the town square and down the short stretch of hardroad until they got to her tree. "You need to duck a bit so you won't hit your head."

It wasn't until they were inside the tree's petticoat that Reyan wondered what Kavi would think of it. She looked down at the ground and bit her lip and waited for him to say something. Lots of people had been to her tree over the years, but she'd never invited anyone in.

"Did you do all of this?" He looked around at the constellations of flashing spinning flecks of litter. She nodded. He walked over and rubbed a hand over a worn spot on the lowest branch. "You come here a lot?" She nodded again. He surprised her by quickly shooting up the branches like a squirrel; like her. About six branches up, he stopped and ran his hand over the golden drips oozing from the trunk, careful not to break through their thin skins to the sticky pitch inside. "I like this place, Reyan."

She followed him up and stood on the branch just below his and pointed out through the gaps in the branches. "From here you can see down the hardroad pretty far. That one up there," she pointed a few levels up, then cricked her finger to show she was pointing around the trunk, "lets you see the town square. You can actually see all the way past the town from there." She pointed to other branches as well. "Then there's the mountain view, and the bit of river."

They climbed to the branch with the view of the town, and she began to point to the tops of buildings. "Over there is the bakery. It smells like woodsmoke and yeast. The butcher's has dead animals hanging in the window." Kavi nodded thoughtfully. "Daruum the sewist lives there, and Michael the glazier over there. Neither of them likes holes in the things they make, so they can be pretty mean. The schoolhouse. Let's not go anywhere near that place. And way way over there, on the other side of town, there is a large grazing field overlooking the bluff and the bend in the river.

"So, that's Orloton?" he asked. Reyan bobbed her head. "I can see why you spend your time here."

"It's quiet," she said. "And hidden."

CHAPTER SIX
Day 4, Year 0, New Era

When Eryn, Lem, and Sadie arrived at Thomas's house, they found the porch and most of the walkway buried beneath an enormous pile of boxes. Eryn checked the delivery dates stamped on the labels. "Five days ago, just before the System went down."

Lem looked up and scanned the cloudless sky. "The air must have been thick with delivery drones," he marveled.

The air inside the house was sweltering and stagnant. In a bowl on the counter, a single mango slouched into a sticky puddle of its own juice, smelling over-sweet and foul. A cloud of fruit flies expanded around it as they passed. But there were hints of far worse smells in the room. Their eyes drifted to the dead refrigerator.

"First order of business, one of us should go dig a hole somewhere, and…" Before he could name the other task, Eryn quickly touched her nose, smiled victoriously, and walked out the door. Lem looked at the refrigerator with apprehension.

He gagged as he filled a delivery box with the refrigerator's rotting contents. The smell burned his eyes and coated his tongue like warm rancid gravy.

Lem carried the reeking box a couple hundred yards downwind to where Eryn was digging a hole. She had gathered her hair into an explosion of curls on top of her head and had tossed her protective overshirt across a nearby sage bush. The muscles in her shoulders rolled and flexed beneath her dark sweat-slicked skin as she worked. Eryn was powerful. Thrilling.

She stopped and rested on the shovel's handle looking out across the expanse of the valley. Lem watched a single drop trace a path from her hairline, down her neck, through the furrow between her shoulder blades, and disappear behind her dark blue top.

Sadie the dog raised her head when she noticed Lem and made a single lazy "woof." Eryn turned around and smiled. "You can't just sneak up on a girl like that." She nodded to the box. "At least you brought a gift."

Lem dropped the box in the hole, took the shovel from Eryn, and began backfilling. When the whole was filled, Eryn made eye contact with Sadie and pointed at the mound of loose dirt and sternly said, "No!" The dog's ears drooped, and she slinked away.

Guess I'm not the only one who finds her intimidating. That dog would never have listened to me.

Back at the house, they moved their packs into what Eryn referred to as "her room." They were hot and sticky and tired, but Eryn had a vital and lovely glow. Lem considered rekindling the apocalyptic fervor they had been acting out over the past few nights and smiled mischievously. She pretended not to notice him. She lifted her mass of dark curls and held it up so that the breeze from the open window could reach her grimy neck. "I'm disgusting," she said, letting her hair fall. "I'm going to see if the shower still works."

When Lem heard the bit-back curse of Eryn stepping into the cold shower stream, the idea of being in there with her instantly lost its appeal.

She emerged clean and naked a few minutes later. Her hair was up in a towel, leaving the distracting curve of her neck exposed. Her radiant pink flush had cooled to a more natural brown, the sweat replaced with drops of clean water. She was beautiful and he wanted to be with her. But he was still smelly and salt-streaked and dusty from the hike. She had already rejected his advances once, and he worried she would do so again—leaving him feeling awkward and disappointed. Lem decided to head outside and direct his efforts into work.

By the time Eryn and Sadie found him, Lem had moved four of the boxes to a space he'd cleared in the garage. "Food," he proclaimed, and wrote the word on the side of a box with a fat black marker.

They worked for hours opening boxes, labeling their contents, and moving them to the garage. When the garage was full, they cleared out and filled the tool shed as well, then started a final small pile in the living room.

Most of the boxes contained food, but others held seeds, medical supplies, sewing kits, extra water filters, even ammunition that matched the old hunting rifle that hung on the wall over the potbelly stove.

Near the bottom of the stack, they found a box full of pens. They exchanged a curious look. Lem cut open the next box and found it full of hundreds of journals. "I guess the System wanted us to take up writing."

Eryn picked up a notebook, opened it, felt the paper, and whistled. "They're archival paper, just like the big book. Fancy. And those are delible-static pens. They start off erasable like a pencil, but over time, the ink sets and becomes molecularly bonded to the paper. These boxes are basically full of stone tablets and chisels."

Lem passed his thumb across the side of the journal flipping through the empty pages. "Then I guess we should be careful what we write."

CHAPTER SEVEN
Day 65, Year 290, New Era

After a few minutes—far too short, by Reyan's estimation—Kavi grew restless in the tree. They climbed down and began walking back to the caravan. As they crossed into the town square, Sevv came loping across the cobbles toward them. He pulled Kavi aside, and they had a brief whispered conversation. Reyan didn't understand why people bothered whispering; she usually heard everything they said, no matter how softly they said it. In this case, Sevv said, "Parr and I have worked out what to do with the girl. Why don't you head inside? I need to have a conversation with the poor thing in private." Kavi smiled sadly and nodded, then left her with Sevv.

When Kavi was gone, Sevv turned to Reyan and said, "Well, young Reyankaiya, it seems you will be coming with us." His voice was like too much honey mixed into a bitter tincture.

It was the tone adults used to convince a child that a broken thing was not so.

"Why?"

The old professor drew in a deep breath to steady himself, then reached out to place his hand on her shoulder. She rolled her shoulder away and stared at him. Sevv seemed to remember she didn't like to be touched and put his hands behind his back. "Your leader feels she can no longer provide for you. As such, the responsibility moves up the hierarchy—family, town, circuit. You've become our ward."

"Yours?"

"Well, the University at Seal Tooth's, but Parr and I are the University's representatives. And so you will be under our joint care. We'll see you safely to the University, and we'll figure things out once we're there." He seemed to have run out of things to say and frowned at her. "I'll have Kavianhar help you collect your things."

There was not much for Reyan to collect, certainly nothing for which she needed Kavi's help. But even with the servants and workers coming in and out, the house felt empty and haunted, and having Kavi with her made her a little more brave.

Reyan didn't have a proper room because—to Lyessa's thinking—this was not her proper home. She occupied the space between the top of the stable and the rafters of the pitched roof. A straw-filled mattress lay on the floor against the lone triangular wall. In the middle of the room was a single wooden chair. Most children would have hated this space, but Reyan was fond of it. It was warm and dry. The smells of fresh hay and manure—which Reyan thought smelled like life itself—filtered up through the floorboards from the stable below. That she had to climb up and down a ladder and crouch low to move about made it feel secret and special. Protective. She would miss it.

It did not take her long to pack. All she owned were a few changes of clothes—two pairs of canvas pants and an extra tunic—and a dirty limp pillow that smelled like her own hair, which she needed to fall asleep. She placed these few things in the middle of her blanket, pulled in the corners, and tied them together. She dropped this bundle over the edge of the loft to where Kavi was standing, ready to catch it.

Back at the caravan, Sevv opened his truck to her. "Make yourself at home, dear." Reyan built a nest for herself and her things in the back of Sevv's truck. She looked at the books atop the desk. "Can I read these?"

"I would rather you didn't." He reshelved them. His hand drifted over the spines of his other books. "Here, try this one." The book was well-worn and about as thick as her thumb. "It's *The Compiled Journals of Partner Lem*. Have you read it?"

Reyan shook her head.

"Well, it's time you did. Probably not the most

entertaining thing for a young lady to read, but it is what I have."

Reyan read while the professors taught their curriculum and prepared the caravan to leave the following morning. She read while Lyessa and the lesser heads of Orloton hosted the professors at the banquet held in their honor.

At some point after dark, Kavi knocked gently on the door and tip-toed in. He left a plate of food on the floor next to her, then slipped back to the main house without a word.

She didn't know she was hungry until she took a trial bite of cold venison. The salt and spices woke her tongue and ignited a deep, painful hunger in her gut. She ate the rest in a rapid, undignified manner best suited to dining alone in the dark.

After she was done, she wiped her mouth on her sleeve and rubbed her greasy hands on her pant legs until she was sure they were clean. She picked up the book and continued to read.

CHAPTER EIGHT

From *The Compiled Journals of Partner Lem*
Day 212, Year 0, New Era

We spent the whole winter at Thomas's homestead reading the big book, looking up useful bits of knowledge or reading long passages, trying to learn more about the roles the System had in mind for us. Looks like we are going to be teachers.

Spring finally arrived, and the Prower Valley is suddenly beautiful. All the snow seemed to melt at once. The white on the ridges turned brown, and the river ran fast and high. Green shot up through the tufts of brown grass I'd assumed were dead. There are waxy yellow and orange flowers everywhere and so many little purple ones that they look like a mist creeping around the sage.

We live on re-hydrated food, a few fresh vegetables from Thomas's garden, and the fish Eryn has become quite skilled at catching. She spends hours alone, fishing. Her patience and tolerance for cold are beyond me.

The book suggested we keep seeds, so we tucked away a few potatoes to sprout, scooped the guts from a couple tomatoes and cucumbers, and let the carrots, lettuce, and kale go to seed. We used them to plant our first garden. My first, at least. I'm not sure about Eryn. She approaches everything with such confidence it's hard to know whether it's her first time trying a thing or whether she was born into it.

Sadie sticks close to Eryn's heel. She mopes around until a bird or hare appears. Then, for a few exuberant (though futile) moments, she seems her old self again.

The dog doesn't have much interest in me.

CHAPTER NINE
Day 66, Year 290, New Era

The next morning, Reyan stayed in the caravan's protective shadow, tucked among the wheels and leaf springs like a fish sheltering in the weeds. None of Orloton's adults would look at her.

Reyan's birth mother passed by, chatting with another woman about a cluster of morels she had found not a quarter mile from town. The other woman's face lit up, and she asked how to find the patch. Reyan's birth mother laughed, "And why would I tell you that?!" With those words, she was gone. She never so much as glanced Reyan's way.

The other children ran around in the bright sunlight, oblivious to the chill, tossing handfuls of snow they scooped from the wet patches that hid near the walls in the shape of the town's shadows. Then, like a swarm of starlings, the children flocked around a corner, leaving only Tom behind.

Reyan was sitting on Sevv's front porch, her pant leg pulled up to her thigh, picking at a scab on her knee when Tom came over. The boy squinted up at her, the fingers of his right hand absentmindedly twisting and tugging at a bit of yarn that had frayed from his sleeve. "You're leaving?"

"Yeah."

"You excited?"

"Don't know."

"You gonna miss it here?"

"Don't know."

They were quiet for a minute, not looking at each other, Reyan feeling around on her leg for new things to pick at, Tom searching the ground for a stone to kick.

The crowd of other children exploded, flapping and squawking, back into the square.

"Okay then," Tom said, still looking at his toes, "guess I'll see you later." Then he ran to join the flock. The tallest boy looked over at Reyan, said something to Tom, and punched the boy on the arm. They all laughed, and Tom hung his head in shameful, silent reply. They all took off again, chasing each other down the main road, then down toward the stream and out of sight.

Sevv returned to the truck carrying what appeared to be a worn-down bundle of sticks over his shoulder. He leaned them against the side of the truck and began untying cords from the rack. "We'll be leaving soon. You ready?"

She jumped off the porch. "I want to see my tree."

Sevv's mouth twisted as he considered this. Finally, he said, "Fine. We'll be leaving in a quarter of an hour. Be back by then."

Up in the shady stillness of her tree, she looked for some memento to bring with her. The ornaments and decorations that spun and flashed in the breeze were captivating as a whole, but individually they were just bits of broken glass and scrap metal. None of them would remind her of this place once they were wrapped in a cloth and tucked into a box or drawer. She rubbed a long needle between her thumb and forefinger until the sharp green scent of it came. The needles would dry to brown in a matter of days.

She considered sneaking into the great room and taking the shell from the mantel. She didn't think Rolf would mind; in fact, she thought he might want her to have it. But the shell represented trustworthiness. What would it mean to steal such a thing? Besides, she knew Lyessa, as Orloton's new leader, would need it to succeed in her role.

She wrapped her arms around the tree and rested her head against the trunk like she was going to whisper something. She didn't find any words that made sense to say to a tree, so she just held a mashed-up farewell-and-thank-you thought in her mind until she felt it make its way from her through the bark. Then she scrambled down through the branches and left.

As she approached the caravan, Sevv was kneeling to remove the blocks from his wheels. He had changed into his brown traveling robe. When he saw Reyan approaching, he called out, "There you are!" He stood and leaned an elbow against the top of the steel tyre. "You can ride with whomever you'd like. Who's it going to be?"

She envisioned spending hour upon hour riding next to this ancient professor and enduring his forced cheerfulness and endless attempts at conversation.

Parr was standing near his truck, silently hitching up his horses. The beautiful beasts blew through their lips, nodded their heads, and twitched the flesh of their withers. She imagined he would barely speak a word all day. "I'll ride with Professor Parr," she said.

Sevv's face fell just a little but recovered quickly. "Wonderful," he said, and then called over his shoulder, "Parr!" The dark-eyed professor walked out from between his horses, wiping his hands with a rag. "Parr, Reyankaiya has decided to ride with you."

Parr chuffed once and might have smiled.

A male voice called out, "Professors!" Reyan turned and saw Leonid and Lyessa standing together in the middle of the square.

"Leader," Sevv nodded. "Keeper. One moment." He called Kavi over and whispered something to him, and the boy disappeared into Sevv's truck.

Reyan walked over and put her hand on the shoulder of one of Parr's horses. She began stroking it one way to make the hair go rough and stand on end. She didn't much like how that felt, but the creamy feeling when she reversed and smoothed it all back down was one of the most satisfying things she knew.

Kavi emerged from Sevv's truck with a black book as thick as Reyan's pinkie finger. He handed the book to Sevv and took his place next to him. Sevv held out the book and Leonid took hold of it. Sevv raised his voice so that Reyan and the others gathered around could hear him. "Keeper. The year's compendium. Learn its lessons. Keep its knowledge. Share its wisdom."

Sevv released the book and Leonid gathered it to his chest and inclined his head. "Thank you, Professors. Have safe travels. We look forward to next year's visitation."

Sevv and Parr gave tight, curt nods. Kavi began to raise his hand to wave goodbye but then retracted it awkwardly and nodded.

Parr folded a bench down from the wall of his tiny front porch. He removed pegs jammed into the canopy's spring-loaded arms, and it came down to enclose the front porch, making a driver's cabin. He patted the side of the cab. "Climb in."

Reyan left the horse's side reluctantly. She opened the door and climbed the four steps of a ladder built into the side of the truck.

The ends of the leather reins appeared through a long slot in the front of the cab below the window. "Could you grab those?" Parr asked. She took the reins, and the professor climbed into the cab, drawing back the curtains that still covered the window. He gathered up his robe and sat on the wad like a cushion. He took the reins from Reyan and tied a loose knot in the middle so that they wouldn't slip back through the slot.

Sevv's truck began to move ahead of them. A moment later, Parr said, "Yee-up," in a loud, stern voice. The horses' hindquarters rippled, and the truck lurched forward.

Reyan's former neighbors stopped their lives to watch the caravan pass. They lined the road, balancing baskets of fish or laundry on their heads or hips. They winced under the weight of the bamboo poles or ladders teetering on their shoulders. No one waved.

The scene felt peculiar. At first, Reyan thought it was her new vantage, but she had looked down on these people from her tree many times. Then she understood. For once, she was the one moving.

CHAPTER TEN
From The Compiled Journals of Partner Lem
Day 238, Year 0, New Era

Eryn says potatoes have their own eyes and don't need ours to grow. So we agreed to leave the homestead and the garden to their own devices for a while. We packed our essentials and the big books and headed back to Prower.

Prower is a two-day hike from here. The Prower valley is hot and dusty in the summer, but in the spring, everything is new and fresh and green. A steady cool breeze comes down the valley to dry the sweat on your face. On the way, Eryn had to stop once or twice to let her asthma settle, but she smiled and joked her way through it. She's incredibly tough. Or maybe the asthma's not really that bad.

CHAPTER ELEVEN
Day 66, Year 290, New Era

The professors' caravan stayed on the hardroad, and their progress was swift. It had only been a few hours since the last white wall of the last familiar house in Orloton disappeared into the trees. Reyan was already further from home than she had ever been. Rolf had told her that, if she stuck to the hardroad, she would always end up someplace she wanted to be. She wasn't so sure.

Parr shifted on the wooden bench next to her. He breathed heavily through his nose and did not speak. She thought he seemed grumpy. Vague questions rumbled in the corners of her mind like distant waterfalls or landslides. She felt like she should ask the professor *something* but didn't want to be a bother. *That's no way to start a new life.*

It was Parr who broke the silence. He did his best to

make his deep voice sound conversational. "In a few more miles things are going to start to look quite different."

"Everything is already different." She pointed at the trees that lined the hardroad. "We have the same trees back in Orloton. The bark and the spread of the needles are the same. But here, they grow thinner and further apart. They're probably whispering to each other through their roots instead of tapping on each other's limbs. And since there's so much sun, the ferns here huddle in tight dry clumps and show their copper underbellies. Back home, the ferns are bright green and cover everything like a carpet." She caught herself and stopped talking. *I've already said too much. He's already looking at me sideways with his mouth hanging open like I'm an idiot. No one thinks trees and ferns are interesting. Why do I always say too much?*

They came to a place where the hardroad skirted a deep pool in the river. A furious waterfall poured in at one end, churning the pool to a boil. The froth and foam quickly settled into creamy lines of bubbles, and the water became the smooth ice blue common to the deepest parts of the river.

A long thin boat floated in the middle of the river, its prow pointing upstream. The boat was held in place by two tethers lashed to anchor points driven into the steep-walled canyon on either side of the boat. Nets drooped into the water from poles that jutted out from the gunwales. They looked like the outstretched wings of an enormous insect emerging from the river and poised for flight.

"Are they fishing?"

"They are, but watch."

An otter hopped onto the front of the boat and chirped excitedly. The fisherman retrieved a fish from a basket, held it against the deck with his boot, and cut off its head. He tossed the head into the river. The otter slipped into the water and vanished. A few seconds later, a black head bobbed to the surface ten yards upstream. The otter held the fish head in its paws and happily munched at the skull.

"Why would he feed the otters? Won't they stick around and eat all the fish?"

"That fish head was payment for the dozens of fish the otter's chased into the nets. They're all part of a system. They work as a team."

"If they're part of a team, why are the otters on leashes?"

"That's a fine question," Parr said, but did not answer it.

Reyan was used to being lectured or yelled at, but conversations made her wary as a rabbit. Their meanderings felt unfamiliar and unpredictable, and that felt dangerous. Still, Parr was her new benefactor so she decided to trust him, at least a little. She risked a question.

"Professor? Why is this happening to me?"

Parr thought for a moment, then said, "Perhaps the townspeople saw it as an opportunity for you."

The professor didn't really believe that. He wasn't even trying to convince her of it. He was simply offering up the idea to see if she wanted to believe it. "They would have handed me off to a fish monger if there was room for me in her cart."

"Then perhaps you are an opportunity for us." He smiled kindly, but the smile fell. "I don't mean to make light. There was no excuse for what they did. Leonid should have brought some structure to the moment. That's what Systemic keepers are for. That is what the *System* is for. Rolf would have been ashamed."

"So, you did know Rolf."

Parr smiled sadly. "I did. That man had enough wisdom to fill dozens of lives, and he always seemed to use his gifts for good. He asked me to keep an eye on you for instance. And here we are." Reyan didn't respond and so Parr tried a different tack. "He had many good and interesting things to say about you."

"Rolf had good things to say about everyone."

Sevv's truck began to slow in front of them. Parr pulled up on the reins and their horses slowed to a stop, their noses a few feet from the back of Sevv's truck.

"Why are we stopping?"

"We'll have to go see." Parr opened his door and climbed down from the cab.

The open door let in a whip of cold air from outside. Reyan was warm and tired and wanted to stay in the cab. But it did not take long for her curiosity to get the better of her, and she followed him.

She walked past Parr's horses, past the vacant cab of
Sevv's truck, and found Parr squatting down a few yards in
front of Sevv's horses, inspecting a crumbling section of the
hardroad. Sevv stood next to him, tapping the toe of his boot
against the waist-high tree that had grown up through a crack.
Nearby, two large potholes pocked the surface, and there was a
bite-shaped gap where the hill had slid down into the river,
taking a piece of hardroad with it.

Soon, Kavi arrived from the rear of the caravan and stood
beside Reyan. Sevv noticed him standing idle and scowled.
"Kavianhar, go fetch some tools. Come on. Be quick."

"There's no need to snap at the boy," Parr grumbled.

Kavi smiled at Parr, "I've got just the thing for it." He
jerked his head toward his truck and Reyan followed him.

"Real tools," Sevv shouted at their backs.

All manner of things were tethered to or tucked through
the rack on the side of the truck. A bucket, an ax, a spare
wheel—anything useful or necessary that could weather the
elements. Near the rear was a tall wooden box, open at the top,
and bristling with long-handled tools. Kavi lifted out two of
them. The first Reyan recognized as a spade; the other she had
never seen. Its long wooden handle was thicker and stouter
than the spade's. The iron mechanism at the bottom consisted
of a thick cross bar, a couple of bolts, and a sliding piston that
ended in a claw. She couldn't begin to guess its use. Kavi saw
her staring at it. "The puller," he explained, "one of my

71

personal creations." He grinned and handed her the spade. He kept the puller for himself.

By the time they returned to the front of the caravan, Parr was already transporting a bucket full of gravel from the side of the road. He emptied it into one of the holes, and Sevv began smashing it into place with a wooden pole attached to a broad flat cast-iron disk. Reyan whispered to Kavi, "What are we doing?"

"Repairing the hardroad."

The hardroad was almost a living thing. Once, Rolf had told Reyan that if she cut into it, the wound would be healed by morning. That's how it stayed so strong and smooth. "Why would the hardroad need to be repaired?"

"Up around Orloton, the hardroad stays in pretty good shape. But out here, it's not much better than a normal road or trail."

"He's exaggerating," Sevv grunted as he continued pounding down the gravel.

Kavi carried his puller over to the small tree that Sevv had been kicking. "On stretches like this—where the surface is exposed to direct sun and the elements—the hardroad gets damaged more easily and heals more slowly. Roots buckle it, springs undermine it, little trees pop up through cracks." He set the claw of the device around the base of the sapling. He rocked the handle, and the claw gripped the sapling so tightly that juices oozed out. Kavi gave a final pull, and the tree was free. "Someone has to deal with it." Kavi untangled the little tree from the puller and tossed it to the side of the road.

Sevv followed the arcing tree with his eyes. When it landed in the brush, his gaze returned to the puller, and he scowled. "Go get some gravel to pack in there," he said to Reyan.

Pleased with his invention, Kavi began scouting around for other plants in need of pulling. Finding none, he satisfied himself by uprooting a sapling and a blackberry shoot near enough to the hardroad that they might pose a threat someday.

Reyan went to the side of the road, collected a spade full of gravel, and poured it into the crack where the little tree had been.

Sevv brought his smasher over to Reyan's small pile of gravel.

"But why do we have to repair it," she asked the old professor. "Why not whoever made it in the first place?"

"It may not look it, but the hardroad is ancient," Sevv explained. "If any human ever understood its manufacture or maintenance, that knowledge was lost long ago."

"Was it made during Lem's time?"

"Yes," Sevv said. "During the Systemic Era. The Era of Dependency. You've been reading." He pounded her mound flat, then continued. "Near the nodes, the locals do a pretty good job of keeping the hardroad clean and clear. It's important to them. It carries all the inter-village trade and brings in emissaries for Gishkens."

"And professors," Kavi chimed in from where he was now inspecting the bite the river had taken out of the side of the hardroad.

"And us, of course. If we had to travel on normal roads or trails, we wouldn't get further than Rowe in a season. So, since we're the ones using the hardroad, it falls on us to maintain it." He lightly tapped the edges of the patch they had just made, ensuring it was flush with the surface, then he wiped his hands on his dirt-brown robe.

"Have you tried making your visitations important enough that the people in the towns would do all this work for you?" Reyan asked. This suggestion flustered Sevv. Parr's eyes smiled, though his lips never moved.

While they were returning the tools to the racks on the sides of the trucks, Kavi asked Reyan, "You feel like riding with me?" She shrugged and joined him in his cab. Once the other trucks rolled away, Kavi jiggled the reins and said "yee-up," and his horses began to pull.

Soon, the hardroad left the forest and the sharp walls of the pass began to soften and spread.

"You don't need to answer this if you don't want to," Kavi began. He mistook her silence as an invitation to continue. "What's the story between you and Lyessa?"

She didn't want to answer. She rested her forehead against the side window and watched a long blackberry bramble scroll past.

Kavi said, "I've met a lot of people out on circuit this summer, but that woman might be the worst."

Reyan felt heat spread to her cheeks. Reyan had never let herself have a bad thought about Lyessa. Perhaps that wasn't entirely true, but she would never have uttered a disrespectful word aloud. To hear Kavi speak so openly was shocking and— a *relief*. A tight little muscle behind her right ear, which she'd never even known was there, relaxed. "She doesn't like me. I was her mate's ward."

"What about your real mom," Kavi asked. "What was she like?"

The little muscle behind her ear tightened again. Her hands began to pick at the scars and scabs on her arms. "She didn't like me either. No one does. Except for Tom. Tom likes me. But that's it."

"You seem likable enough."

It was one of those things people say when they can't think of anything else. Reyan let it pass.

"I'm a ward too, you know?" Kavi said. Reyan didn't understand how someone else being miserable should make her feel better. "And Parr's my benefactor. So we're sort of like ward siblings or something." Somehow that did make her feel a bit better. Kavi smiled. "Parr's not so bad once you get to know him."

They came to a long straight stretch of hardroad flanked on either side by low swampy ground and dense clusters of low trees. Hundreds of enormous white birds gathered into patches. The birds took flight and swirled low over the fields like blowing snow, then landed in the same spot they had left.

Fires burned in the distance. The smoke only rose a few dozen feet before the cold rain hammered it into a flat fog that stretched below the low clouds. A clutch of dirty gray canvas tents huddled below the layer of smoke. There were no permanent buildings. "Is that a town?"

Kavi squinted like he was having trouble making them out. "Not really. Certainly not a node. Those people live outside of the System."

"Why would anyone do that?"

"All sorts of reasons. The System's complicated, so they don't trust it, which means they don't trust professors, which means our caravans aren't welcome. But mostly it's so they can keep all their children. Good for them. That's their right." He shrugged, but she thought something was bothering him. After a few moments, he explained, "I was a twin. My parents couldn't keep us both, and well," he pointed to the warp of his lip as though that answered some question she'd not asked. "Our town leader kept me as a ward for several years, but she had four others. When the caravan arrived after a particularly bad harvest, she had to give one of us up, so…" he pointed to his lip once again. "It was either that or send me to one of these bog camps." He shuddered. "It wasn't that my parents didn't love me, or that my town didn't want me or anything like that. They did. But they had to choose. It's just the way of things."

Reyankaiya Estermet knew "the way of things." She had been carried along in its currents all her life. But now, seeing those filthy tents and thinking of those flocks of hungry children, it occurred to her that "the way of things" might be a choice. If so, she wondered who was making it.

They came to a bridge spanning a stream. Halfway up the approach, the hardroad abruptly ended and was replaced with split logs lain smooth-side-up. Kavi's face darkened with annoyance as the ride transitioned from the smooth millstone grind of the hardroad to the thump of the wheels rolling from board to board to board.

Kavi pointed at the remains of the old bridge—now a twisted mess of corroding steel and crumbling shapestone—slumped into the pools and swirling eddies below. He said, "Everything falls eventually, but that jumbled mess of ruins down there probably stood for three hundred years." Then he pointed up into the cage-like structure of the new bridge. Reyan could see it shifting and hear the squeak as the supports rubbed together. "This one will be lucky to last a dozen. I wish I could figure out how that old one was made. I bet, with just a little bit of that knowledge, I could make this one last."

"Why don't we just walk down there and look at it."

"If only it were that easy."

"The way of things?" she asked.

He smiled but did not seem satisfied.

On the other side of the bridge, the hardroad began again. The caravan rounded a bramble-covered slope, and the town of Rowe came into view. The first thing she saw was a tall tower like the trunk of a limbless tree rising from its center. It was perfectly straight and round and taller than anything she'd ever seen aside from the mountains. The tower ended in a jagged crumbly mess, so it had to have been made of shapestone or stacked brick. It was weathered and streaked with black. The townspeople had painted a broad white stripe around its middle and written the word "Rowe" in tall blocky black letters.

This town looked nothing like Orloton. When you approached Orloton, a few whitewashed homes would appear through the trees, small as baby's teeth at first, then grow steadily as you drew near. She'd assumed all towns would be the same, as if towns were like dogs or fish or trees; different in size or color but having roughly the same ways about them. It was a foolish thing to think. She wondered what other ignorant ideas were hiding in her head.

"Your mouth is hanging open, Reyan," Kavi laughed.

"I've never seen any town other than home. I didn't know they could be so big. How does the butcher feed them all?"

Kavi snorted. It had been a dumb question. She had just resolved not to ask any more when he smiled, "They probably have *two* butchers."

Reyan's head made a little jerk as this new possibility opened for her. Kavi laughed again. He looked pleased with himself, worldly, like someone who knew of a hidden fishing hole or where their parents stashed their liquor. "Just wait until you see the University. Wait till you see Seal Tooth. It's like a hundred Rowes laid out side-by-side and stacked atop one another."

CHAPTER TWELVE
From *The Compiled Journals of Partner Lem*
Day 238, Year 0, New Era

Prower has changed. It used to be scrubbed clean and almost shiny, but now it's dusty and tired. The minecart planter boxes are still full of last year's crispy brown flowers. I noticed a few actual tumbleweeds collected in corners and around the tires of the dead cars along the main street. A few townsfolk ducked into their doorways to watch us pass, looking worried and suspicious. They used to be so welcoming.

Everything inside the Prower Hotel was just as we'd left it. There was an awkward moment when we stood at the desk looking around for someone to help us. When she realized we were being ridiculous, Eryn walked over, pinged the bell once, and smiled. She peered over the desk and found the manager curled up on the floor like an old spider. He was still dressed in his now-dusty suit, smiling helpfully at no one, and waiting patiently for a recharge that would never come.

When we turned away from the front desk, we were startled to find our old friend Edner framed in the door as though the bell had summoned him. We shouldn't have been surprised. Edner had always been Prower's version of a welcoming committee.

The last time he saw us, it was the night of the Calming as we headed out of town. I'm sure he figured we were long gone. I told him that we didn't get very far that night. Eryn added that we'd been holed up at Thomas' place all winter. I wish she hadn't said anything. It sparked Edner's interest. He and Thomas had been old friends. He asked how Thomas was doing. When I told him we hadn't seen Thomas since the Calming, Edner was ready to press for more answers, but he thought better of it and mercifully changed the subject. He said he'd been expecting us. Apparently, several newcomers had shown up in Prower and began asking for us the moment they'd arrived in town.

At first, we didn't believe him, but then he took us to a large decrepit house near the river to meet them. He knocked on the door, and a few moments later, a woman with long shiny black hair answered. Edner introduced her as Zhan. When he told her who we were, her eyes sparkled and widened, and her mouth split into a smile that showed off her perfect teeth.

I hope Eryn didn't notice me notice.

CHAPTER THIRTEEN
Day 66, Year 290, New Era

A man waved down at them from a platform that encircled the tower's belly. Kavi leaned forward, smiled, and waved up through the windscreen as they passed below.

Once the caravan had curled around the edge of the town square, Kavi pulled back on the reins, and his horses stuttered to a stop. "Welcome to Rowe," he said. He smiled before hopping down from the cab and closing the door behind him.

Tentatively, Reyan stepped down from the cab as well. She stood a few yards distant watching Kavi deal with the horses. He pulled the reins back out through the slot in the front of the cab and began unbuckling the straps and gear that connected the massive animals to the truck.

As Kavi gathered the long leather thongs into loops, a

young man in black woolen workmen's overalls and leather boots hurried over to him. "Professor! Professor! Let me get that for you."

Kavi's manner changed suddenly. He stood taller and smiled confidently at the newcomer. "Thank you," he said, pausing for the boy to fill in his own name.

"Benj, Professor."

"Thank you, Benj," Kavi said, hefting the bundle of straps and tack onto his shoulder. "Go to the other professors and see if they need help first. Then, if you could help me settle in my horses, I would appreciate it."

Benj smiled and nodded as though Kavi had given him a gift rather than a job and trotted off to the front of Sevv's truck. Soon they saw the young man leading Sevv's horses away. He returned a few minutes later with a boy and a girl to help him. The boy wore the same black overalls as Benj and the girl a hardy yellow woolen dress and a leather apron. Benj, who seemed to be a year or so older than Kavi, was the oldest of the group. He turned to the others with a snarl and growled, "Come on now, gather Professor Parr's horses. Let's go!" The deferential tone he'd used with Kavi had disappeared into a harsh mix of cockiness and indolence. "Come on Jax, before I'm an old codger and your first whiskers start coming in."

Benj seemed the sort who knew how to use those around him to improve any situation to his benefit. He was no taller than Reyan, but he was tight with muscles. Jax's light blond hair hung over bright blue eyes that he tried to keep down, but which kept drifting up to look at Reyan, the professors, and the caravan. Though he was a few years Benj's junior, Jax was a full head taller, which helped explain the rough treatment he received.

"Avalina," Benj barked, "you take the one on the right." Avalina wiped away a drop of sweat and left a smear of dirt on one cheek. She had about a year and four inches on Reyan.

While Kavi raised his canopy and chocked his wheels, the team of stable hands saw to Parr's horses. By the time Kavi was done, they returned and began freeing his horses. Benj piled tack and ropes and harnesses onto Jax's outstretched arms until the younger boy's face grew flushed, and he let out a soft grunt whenever Benj added more weight.

Once the horses were liberated, Benj grumbled something to Avalina. She took a rein in each hand and led the two horses away, followed by Jax and all the tack. Benj brought up the rear. He carried nothing but kept a keen eye out in case his charges lost their way.

Once the stable hands had turned their backs, Kavi lost his formality and smiled at Reyan as though some secret had passed between the two of them, though Reyan had no idea what it was.

They followed the horses to a stable one block away from the town square. Benj lifted bits of tack one by one from Jax and hung the gear on pegs on the stable wall.

Finally, he turned to Kavi, "Will you be needing anything else, Professor?"

Kavi looked around as though trying to find some other thing in the stable in need of doing. Finding none, he said, "No. Thank you very much."

Benj smiled and nodded his meaty head.

Avalina slid through a broad gap in the boards of a stall and came out near the horse's knees. Reyan leaned on the stall gate and watched as the girl went to work brushing out the horse's mane. The day's work had begun to loosen Avalina's hay-colored braids. Fly-away wisps of hair caught the light coming in through a nearby window and formed a glowing aura around her head. She pulled the brush through a glossy spot on the horse's coat, and the spot stretched and retracted as if she were kneading the shine like dough. Reyan reached out and ran her hand down the horse's smooth cheek. He eyed her cautiously but did not pull away.

Kavi quickly grew bored. "Come on, Reyan. Let's go."

Reyan didn't answer. She kept stroking the horse and watching Avalina as she made her way toward the horse's tail. Once the girl disappeared around the flank, Reyan turned her feet to follow Kavi, but it took a moment for her head to come around.

As Reyan and Kavi neared his truck, she noticed that Benj had followed them and was milling about the edge of the square.

Kavi drew the short run of steps from their slot below the porch, pegged them in place, and climbed into the darkening interior of his truck. He called to Reyan from inside, "Would you go ask that stable boy to fill this for me?" Kavi emerged into the evening light holding a lantern. "I think we'll burn through what's left of the oil this evening." Reyan walked across the square to Benj and held out the lantern. He didn't notice her at first, so she said, "Sir?" This startled him. He looked up, confused, and when he saw her, he seemed even more so. He didn't speak, so she tried again. "Sir, Kavi asked me to ask you to fill this for us." She offered him the lantern.

"Are you calling me 'sir'?"

Reyan never did understand at what point a kid became a sir or ma'am. She thought it had something to do with their age or size relative to hers, but there was also something about whether she knew them and how well. Even if she knew them well, it also seemed to matter how much they liked her, and of course how much they liked to be called "sir" or "ma'am," and that was nearly impossible to tell. It was a lot to have to know before you could even say hello to someone. "I'm sorry, what should I call you?"

"Benj," he said, as though it were obvious. Then he whispered fast and low, "And you should call him *Professor*." He pointed at Kavi with his eyes.

"He's not a professor."

"That's no matter. He will be soon, and when he is, you don't want him having a memory of you disrespecting him."

This made her laugh, which she knew was wrong of her, so she stifled it with a frown and a hand over her mouth.

Benj looked at once angry and annoyed, as though he were talking to a complete fool. He snatched the lantern from her and headed across the square.

When Benj returned with the lantern, Reyan walked to the middle of the square to meet him. He stopped and glanced around to make sure no one was watching them. "What on Earth are you doing?"

She held out her hand, "I'll take it." She tried to make sense of the dumbfounded look that crossed the boy's face. She thought she understood what was bothering him, "I'm sorry I don't have any way to pay for it. Let me…" But before she could finish, his confusion turned into something like horror or disgust. He thrust the lantern into her hands, walked past her without another word, and headed toward Parr's truck.

Reyan walked across the square with the lantern. When she got to the truck, Kavi met her in the doorway. She handed the lantern up to him and he disappeared with it into the gloom. "I didn't have a way to pay him."

He came back to the front porch. "What do you mean?"

"He ran off and brought back a lantern full of oil. I never paid him."

Kavi chuckled. "You didn't try to pay the poor guy, did you?"

"Don't you pay for things?"

He continued working busily in the back of his truck as

he explained: "Of course we pay for things. We just don't use money or barter to do it. We're not like millers and fisherman; we don't trade in goods. We're *professors*. We are the fonts of knowledge, the purveyors of wisdom—we are the very *foundation* of society."

"And 'foundation of society' is a role you can have?"

"In a way. Without us, they wouldn't understand how to solve for problems or justly work through conflicts. They wouldn't understand the best way to exist in the world. Without professors and our knowledge, there wouldn't *be* any millers or fishermen. There wouldn't be any trade or Gishkens. They would be like those sorry people living in the swamps. We're *above* payment. Or maybe below it. At any rate, we're outside of it. Unfortunately, by trying to pay poor Benj, you implied that he *requested* payment, which he would only do if he didn't realize or care that we were professors. Which implies he was being disrespectful. The poor guy is probably mortified." He laughed.

"I should go apologize."

"No need." Kavi looked over at her, an amused smile on his face. "I'll smooth it over in a few minutes."

CHAPTER FOURTEEN
Day 66, Year 290, New Era

After the caravan had expanded and unfurled itself into the square, after Kavi had walked over and placed a hand on Benj's shoulder and smiled while Benj nodded, after several waves of townsfolk had come over to speak with Parr and Sevv in the up-pitched, drawn-out tones of recognition and reunion, after the sun had bled out across the sky, three people arrived. They shook Sevv and Parr's hands, nodded a quick bow to Kavi, and smiled stiffly at Reyan. Reyan guessed these were Rowe's answer to Lyessa, Keeper Leonid, and one of the other heads of the town—the lumberman, or butcher, or miller.

"I'm Leader Anders," said the one in the middle. He was a large man with black hair and a black beard, both streaked through with gray. "This is Keeper Shalynn and Waterman Broox." A deferential nod from the woman to his right and the tall, tattooed man on his left. "We would be honored if the Professors, your novice, and…" he looked at Reyan, unsure what to call her.

"Ward," Parr said.

"Of course. As Rowe's representative, I invite you all to a modest dinner at my home."

"Thank you, Leader," Sevv said. "After a long day of travel and toil, a meal would do us good."

The Leader and the lesser heads of Rowe escorted the professors and Reyan across the square and a few blocks down the main thoroughfare to the leader's home. Two finely clothed children stood on either side of the front door facing each other. Their backs were stiff and their flaxen hair recently washed. On the left was a boy around twelve lived years old— ten named years if they followed the same traditions as Orloton. On the right was a girl of perhaps eight named years. As the small crowd approached, the girl smiled, excited. The boy admonished her with a frown. Reyan recognized him then. It was Jax, the tall blond boy from the stables. He was cleaned and kempt now and had lost the downcast look that lingered about him as he worked.

When the procession was a few yards away, Jax opened the door and the girl entered ahead of them, doing her best to match their pace.

The girl led them to a large dining room just off the main

hall that smelled of beeswax, pine boughs, and the vapors from open bottles of liquor. A chandelier with at least two dozen fresh candles hung glimmering in the center of the room. Oil lamps stood on shelves in each corner to keep the dark from gathering there.

Reyan felt the air grow warm as she approached the fireplace. Upon the mantel, was a box the size of a small loaf of bread. It was inlaid with a swirling pattern like vines or snakes that reflected the candlelight. A woven image hung on the wall above the mantel. In the foreground, a man in a broad-brimmed hat was hoeing a field that spread to the horizon. The border was adorned with various fruits, vegetables, and grains interspersed with pumpkin vines and leaves. She reached up to feel the weave but quickly withdrew her hand when Sevv coughed a warning to her.

Sickles were fixed to the two upper corners of the tapestry. Each tool had colorful ribbons streaming from their handles with beads knotted into them. Reyan tried to figure out the dates the beads represented, but the crowd continued moving and carried her away.

Reyan followed Parr, Sevv, and Kavi as they made their way around to the far side of the large square table in the middle of the room. Leader Anders slipped past and inserted himself between the two professors. Once everyone had spread out to stand behind their eventual chair, it became clear that there was no room for her on the side of the table where the professors and the leader had staked their claim. The other sides were also full, leaving Reyan chair-less and awkward as a hangnail. She was beginning to panic when she saw Parr's head duck around the side of the leader and look at her. He stood and whispered something in the leader's ear that seemed to startle and embarrass the man. "Jax," the leader called, and the boy appeared, seemingly out of nowhere.

The leader whispered something to the boy, and Jax looked straight ahead with blank concentration, nodded, then tugged at her sleeve as he walked past her. He led her over to a smaller table, near the window. He motioned for her to stand behind one of the table's three chairs, then he disappeared into the hallway.

The girl who had led them to the dining room came over and stood next to one of the other chairs. Soon Jax returned, carrying a chair with the back tucked under his arm and his hand gripping the cross rail. In his other hand he carried a knife, fork, and napkin on a plate perched upon the tips of his fingers like a serving tray. These he set down on the empty side of the table.

Soon, an older girl made her way over to the small table. It was the silent girl Reyan had watched groom the horses. Judging by the rosy flush, her face had been recently and aggressively scrubbed. Her hair had been braided anew so only a very few errant blond hairs caught the candle and lamplight. She had traded in her stable garment for a clean, bright dress. She kept her eyes focused on the ground as she stood beside the chair on Reyan's left.

Once everyone was standing behind a chair, the leader boomed, "Welcome Professors! Rowe is glad to have you back. May your visitation be productive and enjoyable. Sit!"

And everyone did.

The room filled with the rumbling, bubbling sound of people talking. Trying to follow any one thread of conversation was as hopeless as picking out a single splash against a single boulder in a river.

A woman wearing a gray dress and a black woolen apron slipped her way around the large square table. She was carrying a large basket full of bread placing loaves between every other setting. Finally, she came to the young person's table and dropped a loaf onto the wooden cutting board in the center. They all stared hungrily at the loaf. It was expected that the oldest of them would cut and distribute the bread. Reyan looked around the table. Even though the stable girl was taller than her, it was possible that Reyan was the oldest one there. *I can't just reach out and start handling the bread. What if I'm wrong? They'll think I'm full of myself. But what if I am the oldest? I can't just sit here while the others grow hungry. They'll think I'm inconsiderate and rude. I could just ask everyone's age, but that would be awkward, and it would spoil an otherwise very nice tradition.*

After a minute of no one speaking and no one reaching for the bread, the mood around the table grew uncomfortable. *The others all know each other. They know each other's ages. If no one's made a move yet, they obviously assume that I'm the oldest. Which means they have been waiting for me to serve them and I haven't, which means they probably all think I'm arrogant or ignorant.*

Reyan was just about to reach for the knife when the stable girl sighed and pulled the cutting board toward her. She began cutting off slices of bread and tossing them around the table. Reyan felt small.

The bread was soft and rich. The millers in Rowe must make finer flour than Harut did up in Orloton.

After everyone had their bread, the young man who had held open the front door asked, "So, what's your story?"

"Leave her alone, Jax," the stable girl said, as though she'd been making this same request of him for years.

He shrugged, "I was just asking."

"I'm sure she doesn't want to talk to you." She didn't bother to look at Reyan to verify.

"I bet that's true," said the youngest girl, whom Reyan had decided was probably Jax's little sister. She giggled. "No one ever wants to talk to you."

"I wish *you* wouldn't talk to me, Jesha."

"I'm sorry about Jax," the stable girl said. "My name's Avalina. What's yours?"

"Reyan?" She winced. It sounded like she was guessing at her own name.

Jax was annoyed. "How is that any different than what I just asked?"

"The person doing the asking," his little sister grinned.

Jax became sullen and stormy. He tore bits of bread from his slice and popped them into his mouth and chewed them in silence, the muscles in his jaw working.

"How come you're with the professors?" Jesha asked.

She could think of a half-dozen ways to answer that question, but none she wanted to explain to a bunch of kids she was meeting for the first time. So she shrugged and simply said, "They're taking me to Seal Tooth."

"Are you going to go to the University?" Jesha asked. "Are you going to become a professor?"

Until that moment, she had only thought of Seal Tooth as another place to be handed off to, stabled, and ignored until the next hand off. She hadn't considered how she would fit into life there or what it might mean to be the ward of the professors in the town where they are trained. Reyan glanced over at the large table, noting how everyone's attention, how their *respect*, bent toward the professors. She recalled how eager Leader Anders had been to establish himself with Sevv and Parr. It occurred to her how different a professor's life must be from her own. "Maybe," she said.

Jesha could hardly contain her curiosity. "How do you become a professor?"

Reyan didn't know. She was about to admit that when Jax chided his little sister: "No one knows that, dummy." Jesha scowled. "And those that do will never tell anyone." He leaned in toward the middle of the table and dropped his voice to a whisper, "If they did tell us, then anyone and everyone could be a professor. If *that* happened, they'd be out of a job. That's what dad says."

"That's a terrible thing to say," Avalina said, both scandalized and intrigued.

Jax sat up, and his voice returned to normal. "I don't care. It's true. Everyone knows it. They just won't admit it out loud because of what would happen to them."

"What would happen to them?" Reyan and Jesha asked simultaneously, wide-eyed.

"Yeah, what?" Avalina said, the weight of suspicion slowing down her words.

Now that Jax had their attention, a smile tugged up half his mouth. He sat back and nodded confidently. "They *seem* good, the professors. They know how to do everything, how to fix anything that's broken, how to solve for any problem and answer any question. And they come around and share all that with us. But those little books they leave behind get thinner and thinner every year. And what would happen if we made them *angry*? They'd stop coming here, they'd stop teaching us and helping us. If that happened, the whole town would fall apart within a couple of years. Everyone knows that. And the professors know we know it. And if they ever got *really* angry? Then they have The Eye and probably a bunch of other really bad things that they don't tell us about."

"They do not," Avalina scoffed.

"You don't know that. You *can't* know that. They don't want us to know anything."

"Then why do they come back every year to teach us?"

Avalina asked. "Why do they bring our keepers a new little book each year full of information? Why would they do all of that if they didn't want us to know things?"

"Those little books are nothing. I hear there's a big book they copy all the little books from."

"So what?" Avalina said.

"Well, why don't they just give us the big book? It's because they don't want us to know *everything*, just what they decide to tell us. Because if we knew everything, we wouldn't need them anymore."

"I don't know," Reyan said, quietly. Everyone turned to look at her. They'd obviously forgotten she was at the table. "I rode with Professor Parr a bit today, then with Kavi, the young one. They don't seem like they're trying to hide anything. Kavi seemed nice."

"He's a novice. He doesn't even know the things he's not supposed to tell us yet. They all start off that way. But at some point—right around when they get their second karaband—they change. What about the older ones, the actual professors? I bet they aren't as nice."

She thought on this for a moment. Sevv was fussy and Parr was aloof. But was that any different than anyone else? Was being particular or tight-lipped so bad? If so, what must people think of her? Nothing good, she knew. But people deciding she was evil or mean wasn't fair. She felt a sudden kinship with the professors. She resolved not to harbor any bad thoughts or speak ill of them. So she didn't answer Jax's question directly. Instead, she asked, "If they were so bad, why would they be willing to bring me along?"

"That's a really good question," Jax said, smiling.

An earthy, orange-colored soup arrived. Between spoonfuls, Jesha casually mentioned, "Enoch walked me home from school the other day."

Jax said, "You don't even like Enoch."

While they ate roast fish and bitter greens, Avalina asked, "Can you believe how beautiful the professors' horses are?"

Jax said, "All you ever talk about is stinky horses."

And throughout dinner, no matter what Jax did or said, one of the girls would ask Reyan if she had any friends back in Orloton who were so annoying, thick-headed, or rude. Reyan had to admit that she did not.

Dessert was served. It was a white cake drenched in sweet cream and decorated with real flowers which were the color of flames and tasted vaguely spicy. No one talked during dessert.

When it was all over, Avalina said, "I'm so happy to have met you, Reyan. Thank you for sharing our meal."

Jesha smiled sweetly. Jax wiped his mouth and said, "Yeah, it was good to meet you, Reyan." She was beginning to wonder if Jax was truly as mean and annoying as the others claimed.

A change came over the group. They seemed to have

exhausted their disdain for each other. They were starting to laugh at each other's stories and jokes, and none of them seemed in a particular hurry to leave the table.

The adults all stood up and began slowly making their way across the hall to another large room. The noise shifted from the rumbling river sound of dinner talk to the rain falling on puddles sound of small groups.

"Time for drinks," Jesha said. "Come on."

Reyan's three dinner companions all stood up at once. Jesha led the way, and Avalina and Jax followed, walking side by side and a little closer than Reyan would have expected given how much they disliked one another. She followed them across the main hall. The room was full of adults gathered into groups of twos and threes, each clutching a mug in their hands.

On a table pushed up against the far wall were two tapped kegs—a large one where the adults filled their mugs and a small one, so far untouched.

Jesha headed straight for the small keg. She picked up a white glazed mug from a stack next to it. She filled the mug and—much to Reyan's surprise—offered it to her. "Blackberry beer," she explained before turning and filling mugs for Avalina, Jax, and herself. Reyan hesitated. When Jesha noticed, she reassured her, "Don't worry, it's not liquor."

"I think you mean, '*Sorry* it's not liquor,'" Jax said. He looked around to see that no one was paying attention. He half-filled a mug from the larger keg and took a quick swig before refilling it with the blackberry beer. Avalina rolled her eyes.

Just as Reyan was about to take a tentative sip of the blackberry beer, she heard her name: "Reyankaiya!" She winced and turned to see that a circle of adults had opened and Sevv was beckoning her to join them. As Reyan approached, she heard Sevv say, slurring slightly, "Good riddance if you ask me. Half our time on circuit was spent undoing the damage." Sevv turned to her, beaming. "Reyankaiya, I would like you to meet Brimm Stableman." The man smiled, his cheeks pink with warmth or drink, and raised a mug in his meaty, calloused hand. "And Chrissa Stableman." The woman's shiny black hair was pulled back tight, worked into a perfect braid that fell over her right shoulder like a rope of raven's feathers. When Sevv said her name, the woman didn't smile, but her chin dropped half an inch in acknowledgment.

"And this is Reyankaiya," Sevv said, gesturing towards her with an open hand. "She's the one I mentioned. The one traveling with us to Seal Tooth."

"I see you've already made friends with our Avalina," the stout man said. Reyan gave a nod and looked down into her mug. "Lina," the man called cheerfully, "come over here."

When Avalina arrived, Sevv said to Reyan, "I've been looking for a place for you to stay…" Reyan tensed, and her eyes shot up to glare at Sevv. The old professor chuckled and patted the air, "No, no. Just while we're in Rowe. You can't very well sleep on the floor of my truck, now, can you? So, I've asked Avalina's family if they'd be willing to house you for a couple of nights. Would that be okay?"

Avalina's mouth twitched into a quick smile. The girl looked appraisingly at Reyan for a moment before answering on her behalf, "That'll be fine, I'll see to her." Avalina held out her hand and Reyan took it hesitantly.

Avalina's father beamed, but her mother looked wary. The woman blinked and forced a smile.

"Wonderful," Sevv said. "Very much appreciated."

The two girls downed their remaining blackberry beer. They left their mugs in a large tub full of sudsy water near the barrels and walked out into the night.

Once they'd left the house, Avalina must have decided Reyan no longer needed an escort and dropped her hand. The small oil lights burning over the door of every shop and home they passed offered very little light. Luckily, the stars were out, and the half-full moon was pouring light onto the town.

"Here we are," Reyan said as they approached Sevv's truck. She opened the door. The curtains were all drawn and it was dark as a cave inside. Reyan lifted one of the running lanterns from its hook on the porch post. She pulled back the spring-loaded lever on the lantern's side and let it snap back into place. A flash of sparks ignited the wick, which threw pulsing orange light into the interior of the truck. She found her small bundle and returned to Avalina, who was waiting for her on the porch. She closed the door, snuffed the lantern, and replaced it on its hook.

Avalina looked at the bundle. "That's it?"

Reyan nodded.

When they reached the stables, they turned and headed toward the river. A few blocks later, they came to Avalina's house. It was modest by Rowe standards but would have rivaled the leader's house back in Orloton. Avalina opened the front door and found a lantern on the stand inside. The flint switch cracked as she lit the lantern. Warm light swelled into the room and lit the hall. It squashed and stretched their shadows across the walls as they moved. "This way. Our room's down here on the right." Along the way Avalina stopped and opened a door. "Washroom, if you need it in the night."

Once they were in Avalina's room, the girl placed the lantern on a high shelf near the door and lit another lantern which sat on a low table next to her bed. The room was filled with warm light and trembling shadows. Several books stood on her shelf along with the assorted odds and ends from a girl's life: a wooden duck with a pull string and wheels for legs, some flopsy dolls. The sorts of things she had likely grown too old to find interesting, but which she was still too fond to get rid of. In the middle of the desk, amongst the pencils and sheets of paper, was an expertly carved and painted horse with one of its front legs lifted as though it were pawing at the air.

Avalina came over and stood near Reyan. She sniffed, then whispered, "You stink a little." Reyan looked down at the ground in shame. "It's okay. I work with horses. I stink a little every day. Let's get you washed up. I bet there's still water in the reservoir. Not a lot, but probably still warm enough if we're quick about it."

Avalina led her back to the washroom. "I'll leave you here. When you're ready, there's soap and a washcloth. Use the water sparingly. I would hate for you to have to rinse off with cold water." Avalina smiled and left, leaving a lantern in the room and closing the door gently behind her.

Reyan opened the faucet and water spilled out onto the washcloth. As soon as it had soaked through, she was careful to turn the water back off. Avalina had been wrong; the water was cold. But that was fine. Even the leader's house in Orloton didn't have a sun-heated reservoir, so cold baths were all she'd ever had. She lathered the soap on the cloth and scrubbed herself. She opened the faucet back up and used the water to rinse the thin foam from her goose-pimpled skin. At last, she held her head under to wet her hair. It spilled over her scalp and face. She used the soap to lather her hair, then she rinsed it. Only then did the warm water arrive. She plugged the drain so she wouldn't lose any of it and lay back in the few inches of warm gray water. She wanted nothing more than to drain the tub and refill it with clean warm water and soak, but that was wasteful and felt a little too close to theft.

There was a knock on the door. "I couldn't find your night clothes."

"I only have day clothes."

"What, the one's you wore at dinner?"

This was one of those situations where the answer was plain enough that she worried it was a trick question, one where her answer would be ridiculed, so she didn't answer. She stood up in the tub and began to towel off. Footsteps moved away from the door and returned a moment later. The door opened just enough to allow a hand to slide through the gap. Dangling from the hand was a long white shirt. "Here you go. Put this on." It was big and loose. The sleeves ended halfway down the backs of her hands, and the hem touched her ankles. But it was soft and clean. The shirt did not smell like her. As a rule, Reyan did not care for other people's smells, but there was something about the smell of this shirt that made her want to bunch it up and press it to her face.

She dropped the wet cloth and damp towel into a basket near the door and carried the lantern back to Avalina's room. Avalina was in bed reading a book. She looked up over the top of the book and laughed, which made Reyan's neck stiffen and her fists clench. But then Avalina said, "Come here. Sit down." She put down the book and, opening a drawer built into the table next to her bed, pulled out a comb and ribbon.

Reyan sat down with her back to Avalina. She felt the other girl gather a handful of hair. She tried to run the comb through it, but it immediately became stuck. Avalina began teasing the comb through each knot in Reyan's hair. "When was the last time someone put a comb to this?" Reyan didn't know, so she didn't answer.

Avalina slowly worked her way through Reyan's hair, and Reyan's scalp crackled with pain. Part of her wanted to run and another part wanted to turn around and slap Avalina for hurting her. She did not want those parts to win out, and she didn't let them. She sat as still as she could, clutching her fists in her nightshirt to keep them from flying.

They heard the front door open followed by the thud of someone sitting down heavily. Then came the thump-thump of empty boots hitting the floor. A series of inconsistent footfalls made their way down the hall. There was a light knock on their door, and a few seconds later, a round head popped in. "How you girls getting along?"

"Just fine dad. Go to bed."

The man beamed. "Okay then. Good night, dear. And good night…er, what was your name again?"

"It's *Reyan*, dad."

"Ah. Right. Good night, Reyan."

When her father was out of ear shot, Avalina growled. "He's the worst." Reyan was confident that Avalina's father was not the actual worst. He didn't even seem a little bad. But then again, she was very stupid, and there were many things she did not understand about people. Especially parents.

As the grooming continued, it slowly became less painful. Avalina asked, "Have you ever been to Seal Tooth?"

"No."

When Reyan didn't say anything more, Avalina grew impatient. "Well, are you excited to be going?"

"Why would I be excited?"

"Oh, I don't know, because it's the pop-center. Because you've never been before. Because it's an *adventure*."

"Do you think it will be dangerous?"

Avalina laughed. "No."

"Do you think there are parts of it I'll be the first to discover?"

"What are you talking about?"

"What would make going to a safe place that everyone already knows about an adventure?" She wasn't arguing; she was genuinely curious.

"I don't know. It's just a different place for you to be in. It's not new to the world, but it's new to you. I guess it's an adventure because you get to discover how you feel there."

"I think I'll feel like myself no matter where I am."

"Well, isn't there any place you want to go?"

Reyan wanted to mention her tree, but she didn't think that answered the question Avalina was asking. "No."

"I do. I want to go to Seal Tooth. I want to cross the Great Eastern River. I want to go everywhere."

"Why? What's on the other side of the Great Eastern River?"

"Who knows? That's the whole point. All I have to go on is the stories made up by annoying, over-confident boys."

Now Avalina was making slow passes through Reyan's hair and finding only a few snags each time.

"Boys like Jax?"

"Jax? What do you mean?"

"You don't like him."

"Jax?" She thought for a moment. "I'm not sure I don't like Jax. I mean yeah, he's a dumb boy, and he says dumb things, and he's always around just being dumb. But he's not so bad. I'm not talking about Jax."

"The other boy in the stable?"

Avalina was quiet for a minute. She stopped combing out Reyan's hair. "Yeah, I guess."

"The short one?"

"Benj. Yeah, he's an ass. He makes Jax do all the hard work. And he bosses me around like I'm his helper."

"But you're the stable man's daughter. Jax is the leader's ward," Reyan said, as though that would clarify everything. Why didn't Avalina fight back? Reyan couldn't understand.

"Not all of us are traveling in a caravan to Seal Tooth," Avalina said, shrugging. "Some of us have to make do."

Once Avalina's brush could find no more snags, she divided the damp strands into cords and began braiding them into a rope. She tied the end with a ribbon to keep it from unraveling. When she was done, she patted Reyan's back. "There you go."

"Thank you."

Avalina put the comb back into the drawer, pulled out a hand mirror, and handed it to Reyan. Reyan moved the mirror around her head, straining her eyes to the sides to see as much of herself as she could. She didn't know if she liked what she saw, but she did find it interesting, like exploring a new trail or finding a new sort of bug.

When Reyan began to curl up on the ground with her pillow under her head, Avalina laughed and told her to join her. Reyan climbed up on the bed the way a scolded dog climbs down, her head hanging low, eyes glancing around for danger. But the bed was large so that Avalina did not touch Reyan. Though the air in the room was icy, the blankets were soft and warm. Sooner than she expected, Reyan was asleep.

CHAPTER FIFTEEN

From *The Compiled Journals of Partner Lem*

Day 238, Year 0, New Era

Last night, Zhan and Prower's other recent arrivals came by the Hotel for a meeting. They had come all the way out to the middle of nowhere looking for us, so we decided to invite them over to figure out why.

It didn't start off well. I tried to light a fire in the fireplace using a decorative bundle of wood that had probably sat next to the hearth for a hundred years. It caught almost instantly, and the lobby quickly filled with smoke. While everyone ran coughing to open doors and windows, Edner reached into the flames with the poker and pushed or pulled something and fixed whatever I'd done wrong.

Everyone just stood there smiling and catching their

breath while the smoke cleared. I was about to get everyone focused on the task at hand when Eryn piped up: "Thank you all for attending the inaugural meeting of the Prower Volunteer Fire Department. I'll be your host this evening." She's a funny one, but sometimes I wish she'd take serious matters seriously.

We sat in a semi-circle around the hearth. Even Sadie found a spot near the fireplace and curled up with her nose pointed at the fire so she could watch the flames. Here's who was there:

- Edner Saleen: Partnered with the System as a Human Systemic Cognition Interface (HSCI) technician at the Department of Interfaces and Systemic Controls (DISC) right here in Prower.
- Harold Bloom: Partnered with the System at a power substation in a mid-sized pop-center around a ten-day bike ride from Prower.
- Agnes Ramirez: Partnered at the Department of Agriculture.
- Zhan Lavier: Partnered at the Informatics department at Bismont University.
- Eryn
- Me

Six Systemic partners gathered in one tiny town in the middle of nowhere. Their stories were all remarkably similar. Late on the night the System shut down, their partner AIs told them the world was about to change. When it did, they would be needed. The next morning, they found a large secure envelope with directions to Prower and instructions to find Eryn and me.

We passed the big books around for everyone to see. We told them how, on the night of the Calming, Eryn and I were staying here in the Prower Hotel, and these were delivered to the front desk.

Edner asked whether the books explained how to turn everything back on. I told him that, if the System wanted to be on, it would have anticipated the Calming and avoided it. Eryn says, we won't know for sure until we read the whole book.

***

Later, after everyone had left, Eryn and I lay in bed. The idea of having new partners and friends put Eryn in a good mood. She teased me, saying she'd noticed Zhan checking me out all night. She laughed it off, but I hope she was at least a little jealous. I pulled her close to reassure her, and for the first time in weeks, she allowed herself to be pulled.

CHAPTER SIXTEEN
Day 67, Year 290, New Era

It was still dark the next morning when Reyan felt Avalina stir. Reyan opened her eyes and sat up to find the other girl fully dressed and smoothing down the front of her heavy work dress. "I must have overslept," Avalina said in a frantic whisper, more to herself than Reyan.

"Overslept for what?"

"Sorry. Didn't mean to wake you." The ribbon had come out of Avalina's hair in the night, and the ends of her braid were coming undone and fanning out. She pulled another ribbon from the drawer by the bed and held it in her mouth. She deftly unbraided, combed out, and rebraided her hair. "I have to work at the stables with dad. Usually, he wakes me up. He didn't, so now I'm late. Get up, and we can have some breakfast before I go."

Reyan could not remember anyone waking her up before she rose on her own. Most people believed that the more time she spent unconscious the better, and so they let her keep her own schedule.

Reyan took off her night clothes and put on yesterday's canvas pants and woolen tunic. Avalina looked her up and down disapprovingly and tsked: "Let's get you fixed up."

"But you'll be late."

"I'm already late." Avalina undid Reyan's braid, quickly combed it out—there were far fewer knots this time—and divided and braided her hair. "There. Better." Avalina jerked her head for Reyan to follow her.

The girls moved softly through the still dark house. The wooden floors in the hallway were cold and made Reyan's bare feet involuntarily arch. The low wavering light of their lantern cast and retrieved shadows of picture frames and doorknobs as they made their way to the kitchen.

The kitchen was warm, and a lantern stood in the center of the table already blazing at full wick. The stove was stoked. Avalina lifted the lid off the bread box, and it made a metallic pop as it deformed. The girl held still for a moment, winced, and listened. Reyan's heart pounded, and she held her breath; she knew they were sneaking, but she had no idea why.

Avalina carefully lifted a half-consumed loaf of bread from the box and sliced off four thick pieces of bread, which she placed on a rack in the oven to toast.

She was gingerly bringing two plates down from the cupboard when her mother entered the kitchen. At a normal volume—which sounded like shouting compared with the thin, careful sounds the girls had been making—she said, "Good morning." Avalina jumped and almost dropped the plates. "Hoping to sneak out before I noticed the time?"

"Where's dad?"

"*He* is already at the stables."

Avalina gulped. "I'm sorry. He didn't wake me."

After a tense moment, Avalina's mother rolled her eyes. "Don't be so dramatic, Lina. He decided to see to the horses himself and let you two sleep. It's not every day we have a guest." She smiled at Reyan. "But he does expect you as soon as you've eaten. Have a seat. Eggs?"

Reyan wasn't sure if the woman was talking to her and didn't know if she should answer. "You want an egg, Rey?" Avalina asked.

"Sure," Reyan whispered to her friend. But Avalina's eyes tossed Reyan's attention back toward her mother, who was standing with one hand on her hip and a spatula in the other. She was looking directly at Reyan and appeared to be expecting an answer. "Yes," Reyan tried. The only part of the woman's body that moved was her left eyebrow, which she lifted a little higher than its already elevated height.

"Yes, *ma'am*," Avalina whispered to Reyan.

"I'm sorry. Yes, ma'am, I would like an egg."

Avalina's mother lifted a black pan from a wall hook and set it on the stove top. She retrieved the slices of bread from the oven, cutting each in half and splitting them evenly between two plates. She dropped off the bread, a crock of butter, a jar of blackberry jam, and two mugs of milk on the table. Soon the eggs were frying and filling the air with a savory note that drove hunger deep into Reyan's stomach. Ms. Stableman placed one egg each on two small plates and brought them over to the table.

The egg was steaming and beautiful. In the center of the white stood the yolk, tall, unbroken, and orange as a setting sun. The fringes were crisp and brown as fallen leaves.

Avalina immediately began slicing through her egg, mixing the yolk and the whites on her plate, alternately forking up the mess directly into her mouth, or stacking it upon pieces of bread and eating them together.

The idea of disrupting the egg's perfection filled Reyan with something like revulsion.

"Something wrong with your egg?" the mother asked.

"No, ma'am. It's just…"

"You did say you wanted an egg."

"I did. I do. It's *lovely,* it's just…" Avalina stopped chewing, a recent mouthful still bulging out her cheek. Her eyes darted between Reyan and her mother. Ms. Stableman's face soured with disappointment at the wasted egg. She approached the table, her hand reaching to pick up Reyan's plate. In a panic, Reyan quickly forked the entire egg into her mouth. Beside her, Avalina's mouth fell open.

The room was silent. The egg was too hot in her mouth, and she wanted to spit it out, but she knew she couldn't. Saliva began rushing in and filling up whatever empty spaces were left in her mouth. Reyan began to chew. She felt the yolk tense and relax as it popped and spilled out. A molar found the crackling edge bits, but these were quickly softened by the yolk. Soon all that remained was the bounce and give of the whites. This quickly came apart and blended with the other flavors and textures to become an undifferentiated sludge. She wanted to gag but would not let herself. She would not embarrass herself in front of Avalina. She would not offend Avalina's mother, who had been kind to her. She began forcing little gulps of egg slurry down the back of her throat. As soon as a bit was down, she forced a bit more. Soon, the pressure on her cheeks lessened, then her tongue could move freely, and finally she could open her mouth and breathe again. She kept her eyes down on her empty plate. "Thank you, ma'am. It was very good."

Out of the corner of her eye, she saw Avalina stifle a laugh with a cough.

"Well then," Avalina's mother said with a forced cheerfulness, "Lina, it's time to get going to the stables. I'm sure your dad has his hands full with those boys. Bring me your plates, and I'll clean up."

The dawn had grayed the sky outside, and enough of the cool light made its way into the house that they no longer needed their lantern. Avalina blew it out and placed it near the front door where she'd picked it up the night before.

As the two girls headed out the door, Ms. Stableman's voice stopped them: "Wait." They turned and faced her. The woman looked at Reyan, pursed her lips, and shook her head. "Where are you going?"

"To the stables, mom," Avalina explained.

Her mother looked at her as though surprised Avalina was still there. "As well you should. Run along. But *you*," she turned back to Reyan, "are not going out from my house like that. Come."

Reyan looked at Avalina, who reached over, gave her hand a reassuring squeeze, then turned and left through the front door.

Once Avalina was gone, her mother sighed. "Follow me." She took her to a closet off the main hallway. She lifted the lid of a cedar trunk filled with girl's clothes. "These are things that Lina outgrew when her figure started coming in." She glanced quickly at Reyan. "The ones on top should still fit you. Find something and put it on. She indicated Reyan's tunic and pants with a flick of her wrist. "You can toss all that into the clothes bin in Lina's room."

Reyan grabbed the dress from the very top of the pile, and Avalina's mother huffed and grabbed two more. "These too. Figure out what you like best."

She carried the clothes to Avalina's room and shut the

door. She put on a plain brown dress because it was the first one she picked from the trunk, then she gently lay the others— one blue, one green—on the bed. They looked like two girls who had been lying next to each other and whispering when they had disappeared, leaving only their shells behind.

Avalina's mother was standing on the other side of the bedroom door with her arms crossed when Reyan emerged. The woman grabbed her by the shoulders and held her still while she examined her. "That'll have to do. Go find your professors. We'll see you tonight for dinner, I suppose?"

CHAPTER SEVENTEEN
Day 67, Year 290, New Era

When Reyan arrived in the square, the professors were setting up for the day's session. She found an entryway to a shop just off the square and sat on the steps to watch. She had seen a fully extended caravan many times, but she had never gotten up early enough to watch one unfold.

The professors were silent and efficient in their work. They undid latches on the sides of their trucks, and large sections hinged open, revealing blackboards. They slid platforms out from the undersides of the trucks and levelled them by wedging rocks beneath their rickety folding legs. The resulting stages were small enough to be crossed in two steps and would lift the professors barely a foot above the crowd. The professors retrieved thin lecterns from inside their trucks, which they fitted into sockets at the fronts of their stages. Everything slid, slotted, and unfolded so smoothly, it was as though the caravan had taken a deep breath, unbuckled its belt, and relaxed into this expanded configuration.

Finally, they each set a wooden stool at the back corner of their stage, and all their activity stopped.

Reyan felt she should let the professors know she had made it through the night. She approached Sevv, who was sitting on his stool, staring at some place far beyond the edge of town. She stood directly in front of him. Slowly, his eyes drifted down, and he noticed her. "Good morning, Reyankaiya. It seems a night away from dusty attics, trees, and the hard floor of my truck has had a civilizing effect on you."

She was sure he meant to be friendly, but she still had the urge to stick out her tongue. Instead, she said, "I'm sorry. Were you thinking about something?"

"No. It's more likely I was forgetting something."

"Something like what?"

"I couldn't tell you. I've gotten very good at forgetting these days. Most likely something troublesome."

Kavi stepped onto his stage and noticed Reyan talking to Sevv. He called, "Reyan! Good morning. You look *changed*." In substance it was exactly what Sevv had said, but it felt different somehow. "Grab a stool from my truck if you'd like to watch." She found a stool and set up just off the right corner of Kavi's stage.

The old professor removed a wad of cloth stuffed into the bell that hung from the back of his truck. He smoothed the cloth, folded it into neat squares, and put it into a pocket hidden in his robe. He rang the bell three times.

Soon, the townspeople began to arrive. Some with blankets, some with large pillows or stools or chairs. Others stood.

Once a decent crowd had gathered—much larger than had ever gathered in Orloton—the professors reemerged from their trucks in black teaching robes. They each placed a small thin book upon their lecterns. Kavi and Parr retreated to the stools at the rears of their platforms, but Sevv remained at his lectern with his hands behind his back. He blinked in silence while he waited for the last audience members to settle into their places. His smile seemed overly practiced: indulgent and patient, but unwavering.

Once everyone was settled, and the only sounds were birds, coughing, and the hushing sounds of the river, Sevv began:

"Rowe holds a special place in our hearts. It is the last node on our circuit, so every time we see you, we know we'll soon be home. And none too soon it would seem. Snow has already begun sneaking down from the hilltops into Orloton and will surely make its way down to Rowe soon enough. But hopefully not before we leave for Seal Tooth. No one wants to be stuck with a snowed-in caravan full of homesick professors." The crowd produced a few chuckles, the standard response whenever a professor paused after anything possibly meant to be funny.

"This is not only the last stop on this year's circuit but,

after forty-six years, it will be my last time standing before the good people of Rowe." Sevv left a space for the crowd or himself to fill with weighty emotion. When none came, he coughed and continued. "This will be the last time you'll hear me say: On the first day of the New Era, the Author gave us The Book. They bade us meditate until the Governing Assert became the kernel of our being. They called upon us to learn the System and teach it to all who would listen. The professors have returned to you just as we have every year since Lem's time." He paused for effect, then said, "Novice Kavianhar will start the session off today."

Kavi approached his lectern. A boy near the front pointed and said, "Why's he got a stripe?" The child's mother swatted his hand down and shushed him, but not before Kavi noticed. He looked down at his book, briefly up at the crowd, then back down to his book. "Good morning." He cleared his throat. Someone chuckled. Kavi's voice came out thin and wavering. "Today, I'll be reading *from The Compiled Journals of Partner Lem*. Day two hundred thirty-four, year zero of the New Era."

> At first, we thought that things would come back on their own, but now we're certain they will not. Not unless we do it ourselves. But I think we could make a go of it.

Kavi stopped reading and looked up at the crowd. "At this point, Lem goes into a level of detail about repairing the electrical grid which I *personally* find fascinating but which I'm sure you all would find extremely boring. I'll spare you." The crowd chuckled gratefully. "Suffice to say, bringing back electrical power would have been very challenging. If you want to understand why, and you have a *lot* of spare time, come talk to me after the session." More chuckles from the audience and even one or two murmurs of interest. "Lem continues:"

> The real question is not if we can re-establish power, but if we should.

> As with most things, Eryn and I are of two minds about this. She is convinced we should try. But I believe a more measured and thoughtful approach would be best.

> The thing I've figured out—the thing Eryn fails to consider—is that the System could have shut itself down at any time. But it waited until there were no humans left who knew how to fix the grid.

> I think I understand why.

> We all want life to be a little bit easier. And no matter how easy we have it, we want it a little easier still. That's how we became so reliant on machines that, once the System was gone, life as we knew it was unrecoverable.

Kavi's initial nervousness was gone now. His back was straight, his hands were steady. Some in the crowd crossed their arms and nodded in time with his cadence, others looked down at their hands and pondered the truth of the words he was reading. He was surprisingly good at this.

> I am not so different from Eryn. There is part of me that wants someone to flip a switch and bring everything back. I miss warm rooms in

winter and music emanating from every wall.

I even find myself missing graphs. I miss the comfort of knowing if the temperature, my bank balance, or the population is going up or down. I miss believing that there is a comprehensible structure underpinning the world—the pretty lie of a solid trajectory.

But The System—in its wisdom—realized that each of these conveniences was one of the million pebbles that weighed down and sank our ship. The System understood that humans need to struggle.

When Kavi finished reading the passage, he grew small and nervous once again. "Tech fascinates me. Thinktech in particular seems as magical as breathing life into a stone. I long to understand how it all worked. I chose this passage because it proves I'm not alone in my struggles. It reminds me that even the Partners, even *Lem*, with his wisdom and knowledge of the System, experienced the same conflicts as I. And that gives me hope.

"As Lem said, we could bring it all back if we really wanted. The knowledge is all around us, just waiting to be relearned. But doing so without thought and deliberation would be dangerous and unwise. The System, in their wisdom, brought the Era of Dependency to an end. And that is all I need to know."

Kavi let his final words hang in the cool, silent air for a moment. Then he closed his book and stepped toward the back of his platform.

Reyan had heard Lem quoted at her plenty of times, usually by some annoyed adult in a grease- or sap- or blood-stained bib. Or when Lyessa hissed complaints to Rolf about some hired laborer not willing to work to the point of suffering. These people used Lem as a strong inflexible weapon, to make fine points and pierce other's arguments. But Lem's actual words were more rounded and complex. He sounded less sure of himself than those who liked to quote him.

Professor Parr walked up to his lectern. He placed his hand on his book and let it rest there for a moment. Instead of opening it, he began to pace about his tiny stage as though struggling with what to say next. Finally, he addressed the crowd: "The Systemic way is the hard way. We feel this truth in our hearts." Nods and murmurs of agreement spread through the crowd. "Always considering the Governing Assert is a tall order. Figuring out the right thing to do can be a struggle. So, when faced with a difficult choice, what do we do? Most of us simply choose the most difficult path and move on with our lives, feeling confident in the virtue of our decision. We try nothing new. We do no harm. Our lives remain unchanged, and we never risk being ground to dust in the gears of our own solutions. We have never forgotten the Era of Dependency. We know it could happen again. The System warned us of this very thing in *Insights*, section four, verse five." He flipped open his book but didn't bother to look down as he recited, "Every problem solved brings a new problem into being. Be thoughtful about the problems you choose to solve."

A few voices in the crowd mumbled approval. Others nodded.

Parr shut the book. "Wise words, no doubt. But I worry, *are* we thoughtful in our solutions? Or have we become like those religious zealots of old who, knowing the path to heaven would be painful, subjected themselves to pain as a short cut to divinity?"

There were no absentminded murmurs of agreement from the audience now. The townspeople looked at one another perplexed. They had thought he was applauding their righteousness; now they weren't so sure. But he definitely had their attention.

"Once, there were two farmers," Parr said. "Shabeer and Segenam. When it came time to turn their fields, Shabeer, wishing to maintain his reputation as the most Systemic man in town, chose to turn his field by hand. The second, Segenam, used a plow pulled by his horse. Both saw their crops grow and their families fed. So, who chose the more Systemic way to turn their field?"

Parr raised his eyebrows expectantly and waited. When no one responded he said, "Well?" Finally, an old man's uncertain hand drifted skyward. Parr pointed to him. "Yes?"

"Shabeer?" the man asked.

"Very good. Thank you." The old man's face lit up with a schoolboy's pride. "Most of us would point to Shabeer, since he turned his field by hand which is certainly more difficult than collaring a horse. But what benefits might the horse bring?"

Reyan found her own hand shooting up. Parr was startled

126

for half a moment, then smiled. "Yes, Reyankaiya?"

"Horse droppings improve the soil," she said. Parr nodded. "And horses are strong and fast, so it would probably allow Segenam to do more work and feed more people."

"Very good," Parr said. "Of course, now there is a horse to feed, and that must be factored in as well. So, now whom do you all feel is the more Systemic?"

The same old man raised his hand again. "Segenam?"

Parr shrugged theatrically. "I don't know. I realize this is not a very satisfying answer. The Governing Assert does not tell us to suffer. It tells us to improve the quality of life in the living world. Shouldn't we then strive to improve our lives? To heal our children? To better feed our neighbors? To improve the System itself? I say 'yes.' But in so doing, we must *struggle* through complexity to find Systemic solutions. Being Systemic is not a thing we *are*, it is a thing we *do*. We must always hold the Governing Assert as our guiding principle. If we do that, we become part of the living System."

Reyan's was not the only stunned face in the crowd. There was an almost audible whir and click as the gathered minds considered Parr's words.

For Reyan, one of the most confounding things about other people was their insistence on simplicity. They wanted axe blade answers and butcher block solutions; they were always content to choose the hard way and be done with it. No one in Orloton ever wanted to entertain Reyan's endless what-abouts and what-ifs. So she suffered through complexity alone.

But now she knew that she had been right to wonder and ponder. Her inquisitiveness was *Systemic*.

Parr had not even made it back to his stool before Sevv scurried to the front of his stage and addressed the crowd. "Thank you, Professor Parr for that...*novel* take on Systemic doctrine. With that, it is time for a lunch break. We'll begin again in one hour. I'll be describing the creation of decision matrices to solve for the sorts of conundrums Parr mentioned."

The people stood and stretched. A grumble rose like a cloud of dust as the crowd began to disperse. Sevv continued to speak to their retreating backs. "There will be a hands-on demonstration, so think of some real problems you might have for which we can solve."

***

Parr approached Reyan. "Come share some lunch with us." They set up a little table behind Parr's truck and ate lunch that a grimy young boy brought from one of the nearby houses. When they were done, Sevv rang the bell to announce that the session was commencing soon.

Sevv stood with the tips of his toes perfectly aligned with the edge of his stage, his hands clasped behind his back, watching the crowd return. He smiled at each person as they took their seat. The people milled about, mumbling to each other about rain or mud or mold-spoiled grain. Any time someone touched the brim of their hat or nodded to Sevv, the professor bent his neck and gave an exaggerated nod.

Once most of the crowd had returned, Sevv said, "Good afternoon." When no one turned to acknowledge him, he cleared his throat, and said a bit louder, "Good afternoon." He clapped sharply twice. The murmuring stopped, and everyone turned to look at him. "Good afternoon. I'll be writing on the board for this session, so gather in close." As the crowd drew in, Reyan recognized some of the faces from dinner the night before. Keeper Shalynn was there, with her two assistants in tow.

Once everyone was settled, Sevv began, "So, how do we ensure our decisions are Systemic? In a word, *process*. It is our strict adherence to Systemic processes that separates us from the Erynites and other asystemic people."

Out of the corner of her eye, Reyan saw Parr shake his head nearly imperceptibly before disappearing behind his truck. Sevv continued, "In *Methods and Applications*, section three, verse one, the System describes the decision matrix as a tool to help guide our thinking."

As Sevv's enthusiasm flared, his audience began to shift uncomfortably in their seats. One man scratched absently at the back of his neck. The weaver, her mate, and their child dangled their drop spindles below billowing clouds of fleece and spun them with rhythmic disinterest. Even the town keeper was scraping dirt from beneath her fingernails. Only one young woman—one of the keeper's acolytes—sat with her back straight and her eyes focused on Sevv. She had a notebook and a pencil poised to jot down whatever he might say.

"Matrices have a reputation for being complicated, but they are straightforward. I always find an example to be helpful. Does anyone have a decision they are trying to make?" No one spoke up. "Come, I asked you to bring examples." The townspeople looked at each other, hoping someone else would speak. "Very well then. Let us say that we are one of the farmers Professor Parr mentioned earlier. We have a large field available for cultivation. Circumstances deem that we have two choices on how to turn over that field." The attentive acolyte raised her hand. Sevv held his palms out to stay her. "No, we need not confine our choices to just two, but let us do so for simplicity's sake." Her hand came down.

He produced a piece of chalk from a fold in his robe and turned toward the blackboard. He wrote two phrases near the top, reading them aloud as he did so: "Turn by hand" and "Horse and plow."

"Down the left side, we list the important things we must consider while making our decision. Since we want this to be a *Systemic* process, we must always...?"

"Account for the Governing Assert," the acolyte offered enthusiastically.

"Exactly. The Governing Assert can be written out as follows." He mumbled along as he wrote. "Immediate preservation of human life, long-term preservation of human life, contentment, social cohesion..." Soon, Sevv was speaking in a sing-song voice as his hand bounced across the blackboard. The town folks' heads began to sway loosely on their necks. One bored man was picking at something on his pant leg. But the keeper's acolyte stood out like a flower in the bog of the others' indifference. Everything about her—from her bright eyes to her clean, well-ironed dress to her smooth brown hair pulled back into a tight ponytail—spoke to her intense and—Reyan felt—performative propriety. The acolyte raised her hand again. "Professor?"

Sevv stopped writing and turned around. "Yes?"

"What are the definitions of 'immediate' verses 'long-term'?"

"A fine question. You must be Keeper Shalynn's acolyte?"

"Tamura, Professor."

"Well Tamura, 'immediate' means now, whereas 'long-term' refers to seven generations in the future. This helps us look beyond the urgency of our immediate needs." He turned around and began to write once more. "Now we arrange everything into columns and rows." He drew a grid.

"Of course, all considerations are not equally important, so we must weight them." He began to write numbers next to each consideration. He paused when he had almost finished, and looked over his shoulder at Tamura, who was furiously writing. "Don't worry, these details are included in the compendium we will leave with your keeper." When the keeper heard herself mentioned, she snapped to attention. Sevv nodded to her and smiled, then he turned back to the blackboard.

Reyan's hand rose like a leaf in the wind, first up, then back down slowly. Finally, she lifted it high. She was curious, and wasn't that the whole point of these sessions? "Professor?"

Sevv stopped and turned around. "Yes, Reyankaiya?"

She felt the pinch of her full name but chose to ignore it. "Is the Governing Assert the only consideration that matters?"

"We will always have other considerations. But remember that circumstantial considerations should never be weighed more heavily than a Systemic consideration."

"That's to make sure the Governing Assert is always our greatest concern," Tamura chirped.

"Exactly," Sevv beamed.

"How many other considerations should we have?" Reyan wanted to know.

"As many as is practical."

"If there are enough other considerations, and they are important enough, couldn't they outweigh the Systemic considerations?"

Sevv looked as though he suspected her of sabotage. "That is possible in theory. But if your considerations are so contrary to the Governing Assert, perhaps you should reevaluate."

Sevv worked silently for a minute, writing down other things he felt were important to consider. "Effort" received a weight of six, "crop quality" a five, and so on. Reyan was happy when Sevv added "enhances soil (horse droppings)" and "crop yield," which were the considerations she had brought up during Parr's session.

When Sevv turned back toward the crowd, they shook off their boredom and snapped to attention. Sevv didn't seem to notice. "Now the real struggle begins." Sevv seemed excited, almost greedy at the prospect. "We need to think through each of our options and ask ourselves what will happen if we chose it."

"But Professor," Reyan said, before she had time to raise her hand or think through the repercussions of interrupting, "How can we know the future?"

He pursed his lips, then frowned before answering. "Well, of course we cannot know the future exactly. But the System can help us assess the *probable* future."

"How?" she asked, excited to finally learn a great Systemic secret.

"There are tools for performing that sort of analysis— particularly *Methods and Applications*, section eight, which discusses decision trees." The mention of trees had her leaning forward on her stool. He flopped his hand dismissively. "But that is a subject for another session. For now, let's just make some educated guesses, shall we?"

Reyan did not appreciate Sevv's half answer. Withholding

information when asked was no better than a lie. He believed her curiosity was less important than his wisdom. She was about to tell him so when Sevv turned back to his board. "We consider each option and determine how well it meets each consideration. Turning a field, if done safely, has no *immediate* impact on human life so that consideration gets a zero." He wrote a zero in the cell. "And zero multiply by its weight is still zero. But when we consider *long-term* preservation of human life…" He began mumbling to himself, "…life… food…entire population…" He wrote a six into the cell. "Weight of eighteen…multiplied out…gives us one hundred and eight!"

No, no, no!, Reyan thought. *Where did the six come from? How can he know that?*

Reyan was agitated and on the verge of standing up and shouting when Tamura raised her hand. She was looking more at Reyan than at Sevv when she asked, "Can we safely assume that the assessments provided by an experienced professor are Systemic?"

"Certainly," Sevv replied, before reconsidering. "Well, no. But sometimes yes. For today's example we shall." Reyan suspected that Sevv was not used to being interrupted by inquisitive students.

The sun flashed off Sevv's copper and steel karabands as he returned to scoring, cross-multiplying, and filling up the matrix. "Now, we add up the weighted scores for each column… and get 364 for hand turning and 309 for the horse-powered option." He circled 364 and stepped back to admire his work. "There you have it. Now, I do not know if plowing by hand will *always* be the most Systemic option, but it does illustrate the methodology and shows that the easiest way is seldom the most Systemic." He glanced back at Parr, smirking. "Sorry Professor Parr."

A man leaned over and whispered to Reyan out of the side of his mouth, "And they wonder why we skip all that and just go for the most difficult option." Reyan ignored the man. Annoying short cuts aside, she saw something like magic in what Sevv had just done. It set her mind buzzing. It wasn't perfect, but with care and attention, it could approach perfection. Rather than ignore complexity, it went after it head-on. It broke things down and lashed them to a scaffold with numbers. So, not magic at all. Just the beauty of a structure purpose built to tally her thoughts.

Sevv stepped down from his platform and approached Reyan. "Your questions were good ones, Reyan. I'm sorry I could not address them all during the session."

Just as Reyan was about to respond, Tamura came over and said, "Professor," and inclined her head toward Sevv.

"It is nice to meet you, Tamura. You had some very astute questions during the session as well."

"Thank you, Professor. I found the process fascinating and your explanations very instructive."

Sevv beamed. He looked to the keeper. "You might have a budding Processor on your hands. Keep an eye out, Keeper Shalynn, if you don't want to lose her to the University."

Tamura blushed, and Keeper Shalynn said, "I'll be sure to do just that."

Reyan wanted to push Tamura and her clean neatly-pressed dress into the mud. She imagined her tight ponytail wicking up the puddles like a brush pulling in paint. In the middle of this thought, Kavi came out of his truck to pull his lectern up from its slot in the stage. He smiled and waved, and Reyan felt a knot of tension loosen that she did not realize she'd been holding.

When the crowd realized Sevv was no longer talking, they stood and stretched and looked around in a daze as though waking. They gathered into clusters to talk about anything that was not a decision matrix. One of these groups assembled around the foot of Kavi's stage. Curious, Reyan approached the small crowd gathering around Kavi.

Kavi sat down on the edge of his stage and looked up at the faces gathered around him. As Reyan approached, she heard a large, bearded man speaking to Kavi in a low, rumbling voice: "Professor, my name is Herschel. We were hoping you might be able to help us."

Kavi's back straightened and his chest stood out. He smiled broadly. "How so?"

"There is something we've been considering for some time now but have left alone for fear it might not be Systemic. But after Professor Parr told us that we shouldn't avoid a thing simply because it makes life easier, the idea came back up."

Kavi raised his eyebrows, intrigued. "What is it?"

"We have a large room in the back of our store. As far as we can tell, it was once used to keep food cold so it would not spoil. We want to find a way to get it working again. In hopes that our food will last longer past harvest."

"That's a very complicated thing to do. That tech is not simply electrical. It involves pumping heat out of the air like pumping water up a hill."

"We've inspected the tech and have found no corruption or corrosion on it. We'd like to give it a try."

"Even if the mechanisms are in working order, you would need to get power to drive it. Where would that come from?"

"We were hoping you could help with that."

"Me? Why?"

"You mentioned you have an interest in machines and tech. And since this is tech, and you're a professor, maybe you could find a Systemic way to get the cold room running again."

"I'm not a professor yet."

"Of course. But you understand both tech and the System far better than we."

Kavi looked skeptical.

From just outside of the circle of townsfolk came Tamura's confident voice. "Do you not fear the Eye? Before we bother the professor, we should run the problem through a decision matrix."

Herschel snarled and rolled his eyes. "We don't even know if it's an option yet. Why go through all the trouble of running a decision matrix on something that might not even be possible?"

Tamura humphed, turning away so fast that Reyan expected her ponytail to snap like a whip.

Herschel said to Kavi, "All we're asking is that you take a look."

"Your Systemic keeper seems disinclined to the idea. Have you run this past her?

Herschel looked at the others in his group trying to decide what to say, then said, "In truth, Professor. She's not yet a keeper and…"

"Just as I am not yet a professor."

"She's more interested in running the processes than solving for problems," someone in the group grumbled.

Before Kavi could reply, Herschel broke in, "We will work with our keeper to run a decision matrix once we have a decision to make. But the chances of this working seem so remote, and we just learned about the matrices today. I bet it will take days to run one. By then, we will have lost our opportunity to have a technical professor in Rowe to point us in the right direction."

Kavi's looked around the group, and his face hazarded a smile. "I don't see the harm in thinking through it. We should be able to draw the power we need from the wind or the river."

"We were thinking the river since it is always running, and the store is only a few hundred feet from its bank."

Everyone in the group was smiling. Herschel patted Kavi on the back. They were already guiding him toward the river when Sevv's piercingly cheerful voice spoke behind them. "Where is everyone going?" They turned to look and saw the old professor standing up on his stage, the afternoon sun behind his head like a blinding halo. Tamura stood a few paces behind him.

They were all quiet for a moment, taking turns looking at the ground or each other but generally avoiding Sevv. Finally, Kavi shielded his eyes, looked up at Sevv and said, "The townspeople had a bit of tech. They wanted me to take a look."

"What sort of tech?"

"Two bits, actually. A possibly salvageable chilling machine and a water-driven power supply."

"The keeper's acolyte seems worried that fixing them might set a dangerous precedent." Sevv turned to Tamura. "Let us say that we professors were not here, and you are the town's Systemic keeper. What would *you* do?"

Tamura thought for a moment. "Well, they don't want to run a full matrix to decide about using tech that probably won't even work. I understand that. Perhaps we should run a matrix about whether it is Systemic to inspect the power supply and the chilling machine at all."

Sevv smiled. "Agreed. You should do as the acolyte suggests."

Tamura beamed. "May I, Professor?"

"By all means!" Sevv reached into the folds of his robe and retrieved the stick of chalk, which he handed to her. She walked over to his blackboard and wiped it clean.

There was a general grumble from those gathered around Kavi. "Can't stand that girl," one man said.

A gnarl-faced old woman said, "She'll be keeper one day, just you watch."

By the time Tamura had written "Inspect tech" and "Do not inspect tech" and had filled in the considerations that represented the Governing Assert, the small group had dispersed, each disappointed face nodding to Kavi as they left. One of them even nodded to Reyan.

After the day's sessions, Reyan was unsure of what to do. Back in Orloton, she might have sat on the boulders and peered into the pond or thrown stones at the standing waves in the river. Most likely, she would have gone to inhale the pine-pitch breath of her tree.

Deprived of her hometown comforts, she listened instead to a stream of individuals avail themselves of the professors' wisdom.

Though Kavi never did get to look at the cooling

machine, she watched him fiddle with other gadgets. Most were things Reyan had never seen before, but which the people of Rowe had incorporated so deeply into their lives that their malfunctioning distressed them. Each time Kavi began a repair, he made sure to receive a subtle sideways nod from Parr before he began.

Parr treated an infected cut on a girl's arm with a mixture of honey, garlic, and comfrey he had cooked in a copper pot. Sevv helped neighbors come to an agreement about a property line dispute. The queue was long, and the consultations went on for hours.

The breadth and depth of the professors' knowledge intrigued Reyan. They each seemed to have many lives' worth of technical and philosophical insights at the ready. They never got flustered or confused, no matter what problem was set before them.

They were exactly what Reyan wished she could be.

CHAPTER EIGHTEEN
Day 67, Year 290, New Era

Once the flood of townsfolk dried up, Reyan grew bored with the professor's company. She wondered what Avalina was up to. She wanted to visit the horses.

She found her friend in the cool twilight of the stables. Avalina was pitching hay and repeatedly blowing an errant strand of hair from her red face. When she saw Reyan watching her, she stuffed the tines of her pitchfork into the pile of hay and leaned her elbow on its handle. She wiped the long strand of hair back, fixing it in place with sweat. "How's Rowe been treating you?"

"It's good. Your people seem nice."

"Do they now?" Avalina looked at her skeptically. "Must

be nice traveling with the professors." She took a deep breath and went back to moving hay.

"I mean, no one's yelled at me or chased me away or anything like that."

Between grunts Avalina said, "Sure. But I bet they haven't been friendly either. Anyone offer you food? Show you the river? Take you to the tower platform?"

"Someone brought us lunch," Reyan offered.

"They brought the *professors* lunch."

It was true. There had been three lunches wrapped in cloth bundles. While Sevv thanked the local boy for bringing the food, Parr divided his portion in two without so much as a word, and Kavi stepped into his truck and got an extra plate for Reyan, laughing and joking as he'd done so. No one had told Kavi to do that, so she hadn't thought anything of it at the time. But now that Avalina mentioned it, she remembered the local boy's smile had grown shifty and thin when he saw some of the professors' food placed before Reyan.

"Do you need any help?" Reyan asked. "With the horses I mean. Anything I can do?"

Avalina smiled. "No. All done grooming the horses for the day. But a couple more stalls need to be mucked out and have the straw replaced. You want to help with that?" When Reyan didn't answer immediately, Avalina shrugged, "It's not as nice as grooming the horses, but it's something to do, and the sooner I get it done, the sooner I can get out of here." She smiled, "Then I could walk you down to the river or up to the tower platform."

At the other end of the stables, they heard an angry voice. The words were fast and muddled and hard to make out aside from the words, "told you, you stupid." They heard a slap and a whine of protest.

Reyan held as still as a deer and listened.

"That's just Benj being Benj," Avalina said. "Come on. Let's finish and get out of here."

Avalina disappeared into a nearby room and returned with a work apron for Reyan. They swept out the old straw and replaced it, then brought in hay and water. It was hard work for Reyan, who had never really done anything besides tidying her room, which had almost nothing in it. This work involved moving and sweating and streaks of dirt on her face. She felt clumsy and confused, turning left instead of right, bumping into Avalina, or dropping forks-full of straw in the aisle rather than the stall. Her arms were shaking after half an hour.

When they'd finished mucking out the stalls, Avalina let Reyan guide the horses back in. She had been around horses all her life, but this was the first time she had led one. Controlling all that muscle, all that power, with the lightest of tugs on the reins made her feel expansive, calm, and—for some reason—magnanimous. She placed her hand on the side of the horse's cheek and saw her reflection warped across the sheen of his black eye. He lowered his head to her, and she placed her forehead against his, as though he were her tree.

"Thanks for the help," Avalina said as they hung the pitchfork, shovel, bucket, and broom on the wall. "You want to go see the valley? We should be able to get up to the tower before the sun's fully set."

As they left through the human-sized door built into the massive sliding barn door, they passed Jax, who was shoveling manure into a pile and mixing in old straw. Anger and pride kept him on the dry side of crying. His mouth was closed tight, and his jaw muscles were working, his eyes fixed, not on his work, but on some vengeful future beyond it.

"Hey Jax," Avalina whispered, "How are you doing?"

He looked up and shook off whatever thought was possessing him. His mouth softened into an easy dismissive smile. He was about to say something when Benj's mocking voice came from behind them and said, "You slipping off early?"

"No, we're not slipping off, Benj," Avalina growled but kept her eyes fixed on the ground, "The stalls are mucked out, and the horses are back in, fed and watered."

Benj chewed the inside of his cheek for a moment. He looked over at Jax, who had wordlessly returned to his work. "What about helping him out? He's slow as snot."

"You help him. I've done my day's tasks."

"I have more work than anyone here, and I've been helping him all day. Now I'm left with a million things to do before the day's out. Throw your little apron back on and help

Jax for a while. It's like your dad always says, 'the horses don't care who does the work.'"

"But we already cared for the horses, like I said."

"Oh, did you? You brush them and pet them and tell them they're pretty? I bet you're exhausted."

That's not fair, Reyan thought. They had worked hard; they'd lifted and shoveled and scrubbed. They had bent and strained and sweated. In that whole time, she had seen Benj walk past. She had seen him lean on walls, bark orders, and criticize other people's work, but she'd not seen him lift or repair anything at all.

"You just want me to do your shit work," Avalina said.

"Like your dad always says, we're a team, Lina. No one is above anyone else in the stables."

Benj's words were nothing more than breath and sound, but he was twisting them into tricks and lies and robbing Avalina of her confidence. Reyan saw it happening but couldn't do anything to stop it.

Avalina paused to think, her face expressionless and stony except for a nut sized knot of muscle flexing in her jaw. Finally, she spoke. "No. I'm done for the day. We're leaving."

Benj stepped up to her, mere inches from her face. "Go put your apron back on. Get a shovel and get to work."

Avalina turned her face away and looked at the ground, but she still managed, "No."

A twitching excitement climbed Reyan's back.

"You could always bring it up with your dad," Benj said, stepping back and shrugging. "See what he says about it."

"I think I will."

Benj's eyes widened for a moment. He looked truly angry. Then he smiled mockingly. "Yeah, I bet you will. I bet you always do. I bet, when you go home at night and eat your nice dinner with your nice family, all you do is complain about how hard you have it here. How mean I am when all I'm doing is trying to get you to do your fair share of work. I'll bet he takes your side," Benj continued. "I bet he says, 'A stableman's daughter shouldn't have to work so hard. I'll get Benj to take up the slack.'" He shrugged. "Can't say I blame you. I'd tell my dad if I could. Complaining is a lot easier than working."

In Reyan's mind, Benj became a line of kids backing Reyan against the schoolhouse wall. Once again, she felt small and trapped, frantic for a savior that would never come. She could feel her heart cracking her chest like a shell and poking through like a baby bird. They could smell its fragility; they were hungry for it.

Reyan took Benj by surprise. She drove her fist into the tip of his nose, and she felt and heard it pop. He fell straight to the ground. His hand shot up to his face and came away bloody. He stammered a noise that was part surprise and part indignation. Before he could recover himself, Reyan threw herself on top of him. She pinned his arms beneath her knees and landed more blows to his cheeks and jaw and the sides of his head. The anger and power came out of her like a scream.

She wanted to keep punching until she was exhausted. Her knuckles hurt. They were smeared with blood they'd picked up from Benj's broken nose. He tried to buck her off once, but after a well-placed blow to the side of his head, he went limp.

Arms wrapped around her from behind and lifted her away. But she still flailed her dangling legs and managed to get one kick square into Benj's ribs.

Avalina stepped between Reyan and Benj. She gently placed her hands on Reyan's shoulders. Reyan's attention snapped from Benj to her friend as though the other girl had appeared out of nowhere. She saw her friend before her, and Benj on the ground, now slowly moving and moaning. The anger and rage subsided. In its place came an understanding of what had just happened. She drew in quick, panicked gulps of air.

Avalina turned Reyan around and marched her away from the stables. Reyan wanted to run away. She took a few long strides toward…her tree, she realized. It was gone and she needed it. Now she was breathing harder. Avalina caught up to Reyan, stepped in front of her, and bent down to get into her line of sight. Her eyes were wide with surprise, but she was smiling. "Are you alright, Rey?"

Reyan held up her hands. They were still balled into fists. She wiped her knuckles on her dress and most of the blood came off. Every one of her knuckles was raw and turning an angry purple color. A cut over her right pinkie seeped where she'd hit something hard and sharp—one of Benj's teeth, she guessed. She opened her hands and closed them again. She flexed them and, though they were aching and stiff, nothing was broken. "Yeah. Fine. My hands hurt a bit."

"Not as much as Benj's face, I bet." Avalina giggled and put her arm around Reyan's shoulder. Lina's arm was heavy as a wet rope, and it made her skin tingle like it was covered with ants. Reyan shrugged it off. "Sorry," Avalina said.

"Sometimes I don't mind. Just not now."

Avalina nodded, then said, "Rey, you can't just punch someone when you're angry."

"I know. Whenever I'd get in a fight back home, Rolf always told me I should have talked my way out of it. Do you think I'll get in a lot of trouble?"

"Well, if anyone found out, you'd be in for it. The keepers banish people for less than that. Even kids." When Avalina looked in Reyan's terrified face, she shrugged dismissively. "But I wouldn't worry about it. Benj would never tell anyone what just happened. Right now he's concocting some story about how you and I spooked a horse and it kicked him. I'm not going to tell anyone. But you can't just show your anger like that. Dad says there will be a time and a place for fighting. But not yet."

They made their way to the foot of the wooden stairs at the base of the tower in the town square. The girls began to climb, spiraling up and around the tower. Soon they climbed higher than the roofs of the houses; then they were above even the taller buildings like the stable and the grain silo. As they curled around, she was able to watch the town slowly fall away, and more of the surrounding area came into view.

When they reached the observation deck that ringed the tower's belly, they were as high as the tops of the nearby cedar trees. They walked around the deck until they came to an iron ladder, which passed through a cage that formed a long tube and went straight up the remainder of the tower. Reyan looked up, watching it taper into the sky, and her heart sank. Avalina smiled. "Come on, don't be a chicken."

Reyan noticed that Avalina had not said, "It's safe," or "There's nothing to worry about," or even "I've climbed this dozens of times."

Avalina led the way. When she was about ten rungs above Reyan's head, Reyan followed. Her arms and legs felt limp. She worried that her bruised and bloodied hands would lose their strength, loosen their grip, and let go. She decided to mirror the motions of the girl above her. When Avalina moved a hand, Reyan did likewise. When she moved a foot, Reyan did as well. Eventually, and without having to think much about it, they arrived at the small platform that stood like an eagle's nest atop the old tower.

This wasn't the highest Reyan had ever been—that honor went to a craggy peak she'd climbed near Orloton—but this was the most she had ever seen of the world all at once.

To the north, Rowe's border was traced by the stark line of the hardroad. Eastward, a crease was formed where the foothills met the level surface of the land. A creek flowed there that emptied into the mighty river that defined Rowe's southern edge. It was hard to believe that this river was the same frantic trapped weasel of a stream that tumbled past Orloton. But she had seen it incorporate branches, absorb other tributaries, and swell until it escaped the sheer confines of the pass. Now it spread out fat and calm as a snake in the sun. The rest of the town spilled out across the flood plain to the west. In that direction, the streets gave way to trails, which gave way to pastures and fields, which vanished into the rising fog of the coming dusk.

She was unaccustomed to seeing anything at so great a distance. She understood—though it was hard to believe—that what appeared to be a far-away stone was actually an enormous hill, and what appeared to be blades of grass carpeting its slopes were actually trees just like the giant ones nearby, full of their squabbling resident crows.

The sky, which she had only ever seen as a single blue ribbon bordered by stony ridges and tree branches, was broad and immense over Rowe. She imagined that she had shrunk down to the size of an ant and was gazing up at the inside skin of a soap bubble. But she adapted quickly to the expanding dimensions of her world. She grew thirsty for it. She wanted to pull in, examine, and comprehend everything she could see. Her curiosity unfurled across the plain, and its momentum carried it up and over that distant forested hill and into the world beyond. Reyan drew it all in on a deep breath, which she held until it swelled and thrashed in her chest. She exhaled and felt like a storm cloud cracked open or a river undammed.

"It's pretty, right Rey?"

Reyan started and turned towards Avalina, surprised to find that anything in this vastness could be so near. She couldn't find words, so she nodded her head. Avalina leaned against the rail. "All the same, I want to get out of here as soon as I can. Maybe I'll hop on the back of a professor's truck and follow you to Seal Tooth."

After a few moments of silently contemplating the view, Avalina said, "Come on. It'll be dinner time soon."

Reyan didn't want to leave. The sun was inching closer to the horizon. She thought it would land just to the right of the lonely hill, and she felt certain something amazing would happen when it did. But Avalina tugged on her sleeve and headed back toward the ladder. Reyan managed to turn away from the view and follow, the knuckles on her right hand splitting open again as she made her way back down the ladder.

They stopped by the caravan before heading to Avalina's house. The last of the townsfolk had gone, and they found Sevv tidying up around his truck.

"Good evening Reyankaiya. Ms. Stableman. What are your plans for tonight?"

Reyan didn't know there were any plans to be made. Avalina spoke for her, "Good evening, Professor. Reyan and I were just headed back to my house to clean up before dinner."

Sevv turned to Reyan. "Were you planning on eating with us? We've been invited to dine with Keeper Shalynn. If you're coming, we will need to let the keeper know."

Reyan let slip, "Will that acolyte be there?"

"I'm sure she will be," Sevv said, smiling. "I thought I detected a certain camaraderie between you two." Reyan felt cornered. The last thing she wanted was to spend an evening with Tamura. She was trying to find a good way to say so when Sevv asked, "Ms. Stableman, you'd be welcome too, but I'm sure you already have plans."

When Reyan looked at Avalina, she found her friend studying her sideways through half-closed eyes. It was a measuring look, a judging look. She smiled and said, "I don't. I would love to join, if you don't think it would be too much trouble, Professor."

Sevv reshaped his surprised expression into delight. "I'm sure they would love to have both of you."

"That's wonderful," Avalina said. She grabbed Reyan's hand, "Come on, let's get ready."

As they walked across the square, Reyan said, "I bet the keepers don't really want us to come."

"Of course not. They certainly don't want *me* to come. Professor Sevv figured I knew that. He didn't expect me to accept his offer. But there's no way I'm leaving you alone with Tamura. She's awful. And since there's no graceful way for the professor to uninvite me, and there's no way Keeper Shalynn would say no to a professor, it will all work out. Mom will be happy. She'll think I'm finally trying to move up in the world."

Reyan felt unsure, like Avalina was setting up trip lines

and traps instead of dinner plans, but the girl seemed to be enjoying herself, and Reyan decided to trust her.

Avalina had been right; her mother was very excited to hear that the town's Systemic keeper had invited her daughter to a private dinner.

Avalina's mother soaked Reyan's hands in warm water, then used a clean rag soaked in alcohol to wipe down the cuts. "Hopefully you're more graceful around a dinner table than you are around the stables." Avalina smiled down at the ground when she heard her mother repeat their made-up story.

Ms. Stableman gave Reyan a clean towel to dry her hands. She began pulling dresses from Avalina's closet and holding them up against her daughter while the girl calmly brushed the tangles out of her damp hair. The woman fluttered her right hand at Reyan and said, "Try the green dress. The *green* dress."

When the girls were clothed and brushed, Ms. Stableman stood them next to each other and looked them up and down. She bit her lower lip when her eyes came to Reyan's old boots, then dove back into the closet and came back out with a pair of soft brown ankle-high boots. They had wads of old cloth stuffed into them, and they were dull with dust. She smiled down at them, pulled out the wadding, and used it to wipe them clean. "Here. Try these."

The shoes were loose around the wide part of Reyan's feet and tight in the heel, and the soles had been worn down by someone else's steps. Still, they were the nicest things Reyan had ever put on her feet.

Ms. Stableman licked her thumb and stretched out Reyan's cheek as she tried to rub away some speck of dirt that was probably a mole or freckle. Then she stood back and admired the girls and sighed. "That'll have to do. Try not to embarrass yourselves."

CHAPTER NINETEEN

From *The Compiled Journals of Partner Lem*

Day 331, Year 0, New Era

It's been nearly one hundred days since our collection of Systemic partners came together in Prower. At this point, we've settled into the daunting task of reading through the enormous books the System left behind. A few weeks ago, I suggested that everyone learning the same information was not the best use of our time. That threw Eryn into a fit. She kept insisting that a partner needs a holistic understanding of the System to perform the role of educator. But that's just not practical. Instead, I suggested we specialize based on our skills and interests. Why else would the System have brought all of us together? Why would it have separated the book into different sections? I eventually won over the others, each admitting in turn that they found one or more sections of the book tedious or confounding. It took Eryn quite a bit longer to come around, if she ever really did.

Each partner picked one or more areas to focus on. Based on my skills and experience, I probably should have taken on the technical subjects, but what's the use? There isn't much tech around anymore. I've found that the interpretation of the past and the chronicling of the present appeals to me, so I've decided to focus on Histories.

CHAPTER TWENTY
Day 67, Year 290, New Era

When it was time to leave for dinner, the girls took a lantern from the stand near the front door and headed to the caravan to meet Kavi and the professors. A boy of about eight had been sent to guide them to the keeper's home.

Keeper Shalynn's home was more modest than the town leader's had been. What it lacked in size and ornamentation, it made up for with an almost aching tidiness. Everything appeared proportional and intentionally placed. Pausing in the living room, Reyan realized that if she were to pull a painting from the wall and lay it atop an area rug across the room, all the corners and the colors would match. She closed one eye and sighted down the edge of the coffee table, noting that it aligned perfectly with the outside edge of a windowpane across the room. The angles and alignments were nothing like the swirling unfettered beauty of the forest, but they created the same feeling in her, like the calm moment between two breaths when nothing compelled her to breathe in or out.

There were far fewer guests than had been at the leader's banquet and only a single long table to seat them. Keeper Shalynn sat at the head with Professor Parr to her right. Next to Parr was a man whom Reyan took to be the keeper's mate. He had a tidy beard and dark eyes, and he smiled and nodded in the automatic, joyless way of the duty-bound. He wore a necklace with a large copper pendant, tarnished with age but rubbed shiny around the clasp. It was decorated with an intricate pattern of holes to let out the fragrance of whatever herbs he kept in there. If asked, he would claim it was just jewelry—neither medicinal nor a ward. Having the professors think he was a superstitious fool would humiliate him, but not enough for him to go about unprotected. In Orloton, Rolf avoided the problem altogether by collecting all the townspeople's charms and asking the herbalist to stay home whenever the caravan rolled into town.

To Sevv's left sat Mariana, Rowe's junior keeper whose eyes perpetually sought the tabletop or the ground.

A large centerpiece made of polished rocks, artfully placed twigs, and late-blooming low-land flowers stood in the center of the table and formed a sort of conversational boundary between those whom Reyan considered "the kids" and "the adults." On their side of the divide, Reyan sat next to Kavi, with Avalina and Tamura across from them.

A single attendant, a thin unsmiling man with perpetually arched eyebrows and half-closed eyes, brought out bread, salted butter, cured meats, and pickled vegetables.

Tamura poured herself water from a jug near the centerpiece, then leaned forward to fill Kavi's glass. "So, Kavianhar, is it?"

"Thank you," he said. "Just Kavi, mostly."

"*Professor* Kavi soon." Tamura's eyes grew wide as soup bowls and caught the glow from the fire, the lamps, and the candles in the room. Seeing her eyes sparkle back all that captured light made Reyan grind her teeth.

"That's right. I'll be graduating once we get back to the University." Kavi began to slice and distribute the bread.

"How exciting," Tamura smiled. "I just realized, I have absolutely no idea what it takes to become a professor. Can you tell me?"

"But then we'd have to kill you," Avalina broke in.

Tamura's eyes narrowed, and she sliced them over to Avalina, who had filled her own glass and was sipping water as though she had not said anything at all.

Reyan had already grown quite fond of Avalina, but she decided there was room left to like her a little bit more. Still, she also wanted to hear about becoming a professor, so she spoke up: "The kids at dinner last night, they said a professor's training is a secret."

"Kids love to come up with stories," Kavi shrugged. "The only reason there's any mystery at all is because our training is so incredibly boring to talk about. You go to class. You learn things. You practice. You apprentice. There are lots of books, lots of professors asking you questions that you start off feeling like you know the answer to, and then after a two-minute discussion you feel like the dumbest person in the world." Reyan thought she saw Parr turn his head toward Kavi and smile a little at this. "You learn Systemic models. Once you know the System a bit, you go out on circuit and learn how to explain the useful parts to other people and train the towns' Systemic keepers. That's it. There are no blood rituals, or magic potions, or anything like that. But it is extremely difficult. You do learn a lot of odd things, things that ordinary people…"

"Nodies?" Avalina smirked.

Kavi paused as though readying an apology or explanation, but he thought better of it and continued. "Things *anyone* who isn't studying Systemic Theory would find hard to understand. It helps if you already know something about the System. A lot of students grew up around the University. Some had faculty for parents. If they came from a node, they're probably a keeper's kid."

Tamura leapt at the chance to lump herself as a keeper's acolyte in with the professors. "You can't just tell folks everything a professor knows."

"So, there *are* secrets?" Avalina said, popping a coin-shaped slice of cured meat into her mouth.

Tamura continued to speak for Kavi: "It's not so much that things are secret, but that they can be confusing if you don't understand the context. That's what we Systemic keepers are for. To help *ordinary* people make sense of the information once the professors leave town."

"It's true," Kavi agreed. "There is a lot of useful information in the compendia. But the System is complex. It's *huge*. It would take many lifetimes to learn it, let alone understand it, let alone explain it to your average fisherman in the far reaches of the circuit. And people aren't stupid. They intuit that there's more to know, so they assume we're *withholding* information. We're not. But there's only so much we can explain in a session and only so much the printers can cram into a compendium. If you want to understand more than the most basic Systemic Theory, you have to come to the University."

The servant arrived with the main course, a large roasted bird. Keeper Shalynn stood. "I want to thank the professors for being here." She raised her glass. "It is an honor to host you in our home. Welcome friends both old and new." Everyone joined her in taking a sip of their drink. "And I would also like to thank young Tamura for the bird."

Sevv looked impressed, "You prepared the turkey?"

"No," Shalynn corrected, "she *provided* it. She's quite the shot."

Tamura did her best to look demure. "I put an arrow through his neck at thirty yards. Accurate mind, clear intent, steady hand," Tamura intoned.

Avalina rolled her eyes.

Once Keeper Shalynn settled back into her chair, Tamura turned to Kavi again. "It seems like the professors lead such an interesting life. Traveling through the nodes." Tamura was the only person besides the professors whom Reyan had ever heard describe the towns as 'nodes,' and the acolyte spoke the word as though it described a quaint thing far away and distinct from herself. "You must get to meet all manner of people."

Kavi smiled. "Yes, it's nice. A professor's business is people, and we do meet a lot of them. And they have such diverse problems to solve for. It's very satisfying work."

"And this must be nice, too," she smiled knowingly.

"What's that?"

"This," she said, gesturing with an open palm to the room and the meal. Kavi cocked his head as though he didn't understand. She smiled and huffed, as though he were playing at being thick-headed. "Every time your caravan rolls into town, you're given the royal treatment. You get all the best food and the best company."

"I think you're making more of it than it is. Caravan life is hard. Living out of the back of a truck is quite uncomfortable. When we arrive in town, we are often invited into people's homes to share meals, which is, I suppose, a nice side benefit."

It occurred to Reyan that Kavi had no idea what life was really like in the towns. Professors only ever came through in the warm abundant months. They only experienced generosity and celebrations in their honor, and so they believed a node's level was as high as the crests of its tallest wave.

"A side benefit?" Tamura scoffed. "A visitation might as well be a Gishken." Her voice, raised in exasperation, drew attention from the other half of the table, all of whom stopped talking and were now looking at Tamura. She glanced at Keeper Shalynn, whose eyes stared back at her, icicle sharp. Tamura cleared her throat; her gaze sought a place to hide and found the center of her own dinner plate. The keeper slowly turned her head back to Professor Sevv to continue whatever conversation Tamura had interrupted.

There were a few moments of silence while Tamura used her thumb to rub out some invisible smudge from the rim of her plate. But then, like a snail who had been startled into its shell, she slowly and surely reemerged from her humiliation and asked, "And what about you? Reyankaiya, is it?"

Reyan began casting about for something to say about herself that might be interesting for dinner conversation. She must have taken too long, because Avalina stepped in to fill the dead space. "Reyan is a leader's daughter. She's come down from Orloton."

"Orloton? You're Leader Rolf's daughter?" Tamura marveled. "So *that's* why the professors took you in."

The mention of Rolf soured Reyan's stomach, and Tamura's assumptions made her tighten her fists. "Benefactor. Rolf was my benefactor." Tamura looked perplexed. "I was his ward."

"Oh." In Tamura's big shiny eyes, Reyan saw her bright reflection dim. "So how…" her question trailed off.

Avalina broke in. "Maybe there's more to becoming a professor than social status, Tamura. Have you considered that?"

"That's entirely the case," Kavi said as though completely unaware of the tense turn the conversation had taken. "In fact…"

Tamura ignored him. Avalina's challenge had hooked her. "Like what?"

"Kindness and generosity, for starters," Avalina said matter-of-factly before taking a bite of food.

Reyan wasn't sure exactly when it happened, but now, even though the words referenced her, they were no longer about her. She had been pushed out of her own conversation.

"Yes, there's that. Plus, hard work, thoughtfulness. Introspection…" Now Kavi was looking at Reyan and nodding every time he said a word. At least Kavi was talking about her and to her.

Tamura rolled her eyes. "Well, she certainly didn't get in with her riveting conversation skills."

A chair scraped across the floor near the head of the table, and all eyes swung in that direction. Parr was standing as though he had been planted there. He calmly wiped at the corner of his mouth with a napkin. When he was done, he folded the napkin into quarters before placing it neatly beside his plate. "Because you asked, young acolyte." His voice rolled out and blanketed the room. He did not sound angry, or even stern, though Reyan thought he put a bit of extra emphasis on the word "acolyte." "The answer is this: Becoming a professor requires that one apply oneself entirely to the task of understanding the System. Applying yourself to such a task requires *humility* above all else."

Tamura, flustered beyond caring, spoke her exasperation to the ceiling, "I have been puzzling over the compendia for years. Certainly, the chief requirement for understanding the System is *intelligence*."

Mariana, the perpetually downcast junior keeper, whispered into the silent wake of Tamura's outburst. "Perhaps *that* is why the girl is going to Seal Tooth and not you."

***

Later that night, as Reyan and Avalina readied themselves for bed, Reyan asked, "Did you mean what you said? Do you really think I could become a professor?"

Avalina stopped for a moment, then continued to shake out her dress. She hung it in her closet. While her back was turned, she said, "Aren't you a bit old to start?"

"Am I?"

"I don't know. I sort of thought that professors were hatched or something."

"Kavi wasn't hatched."

Avalina threw herself down on her bed and propped herself up on her elbows. "He sort of seems like he was hatched." She giggled.

Reyan was defensive. "Not at all. Kavi's very nice."

"Of course. Little chicks and ducklings are all nice."

"So, what do you think?"

"About Kavi?"

"No, about me becoming a professor."

"Becoming a professor changes a person. I like you the way you are. Have you considered becoming a stableman?"

CHAPTER TWENTY-ONE
Day 68, Year 290, New Era

The next morning, Reyan woke to the rustling mouse sounds of Avalina preparing for work by the light of a single candle. Reyan sat up and pushed back her hair. It was so dark and Reyan so tired that she was certain it was the middle of the night and that she had only just fallen asleep. "Where are you going?"

"The stables."

"It's early."

"Well, I have a team of caravan horses to tend to." Reyan thought the other girl's voice was tinged with a forced nonchalance. She wished she could read Avalina's face. She had read in books that other people found candlelight intriguing, but Reyan found the flickering shadows made faces illegible.

"Wait. I'll come with you."

Avalina turned to her, and her face widened. A smile. "You can go back to sleep."

Reyan was certain now. "I'll get up." And she got to her feet, got dressed, and the two girls stood next to each other, wincing as they took turns pulling Avalina's brush through their hair. Then crept downstairs for a groggy breakfast.

Avalina and her mother kept their words soft and their movements delicate, as though the house were made of the crumbly ice that grows at the river's edge in late fall.

Mr. Stableman's elbows were on the table, and his head was in his hands. At first, she thought he was crying, but no one else seemed distressed. Reyan and Avalina sat on their cold hands, their eyes silently following Ms. Stableman as she shuffled between the smudges of golden light gathered around an oil lamp on the counter, the fire flickering in the stove's belly, and the single candle growing up from a craggy mound of wax in the middle of the table.

She handed out plates of eggs and sausage and thick-crusted bread. Reyan's elbow swept a fork to the floor. It landed with a sound like an explosion, and everyone jumped. Mr. Stableman jerked his head up then smiled, as though pleasantly surprised to find a full plate of food, his family, and an odd visitor at his table.

"Good morning girls," he croaked.

"Morning pops," Avalina whispered.

Reyan didn't know the correct way to address him, so she inclined her head instead.

"Hope you slept well, if not long enough."

"We did," Avalina answered.

Ms. Stableman sat down next to her mate, directly across the table from Reyan. She was drinking something from a steaming mug. "Did you enjoy yourselves at the keeper's house?"

Reyan and Avalina looked at each other and through a series of quick expressions agreed that Avalina should be the one to speak. "We did. It was a wonderful dinner. Rey's decided to become a professor."

"Is that so?" Mr. Stableman asked.

"I might."

"You're far too succinct to be a professor," the man laughed.

"Don't tease the girl, Brimm." Ms. Stableman's eyes were leveled at Reyan. She saw the corner of the woman's mouth twitch up into a smile just before being obscured by the rim of her mug.

The talk turned toward the business of the day. Mr. Stableman reminded his daughter of all the things that needed doing, and she assured him that nothing would be neglected.

When he circled back to the same list for the third time, she simply said, "Dad."

An easy smile replaced his serious expression. "Sorry Lina," he said. He turned to Reyan. "So, you're moving on today, I hear. It's been a treat having you."

"It has," said Avalina. She reached beneath the table and grabbed Reyan's hand. Reyan stiffened with the effort to not jerk her hand away. "Do you think she could stay, maybe? Just for a few more days. Through the weekend, so we can enjoy my day off? Then the following weekend we could take her into Seal Tooth ourselves. It's only a few hours ride from Rowe."

Reyan had not expected this. While the idea sounded appealing, its suddenness and the unexpected plea in Avalina's voice surprised her, and she didn't know how to react. In only a few days, her life had branched out in a new direction. Though it was still distant, her future in Seal Tooth was slowly taking shape like something forming out of a mist. Now that she had seen its outline, she wanted to see its color and feel its texture.

Reyan wasn't the only person around the table whom Avalina had ambushed. Her father blinked and smiled helplessly, chuckling and looking around as though searching for something else to talk about.

Her mother hissed, "We talked about this, Lina. It isn't up to us. It's been very nice to have Reyankaiya here…"

Before the "however" could escape Ms. Stableman's

mouth, Reyan said, "I don't know, Lina. It would slow me down, for a week at least. Maybe forever."

Ms. Stableman coughed, reached across the table, and began stacking plates, even though Reyan's still had a crust of bread and smear of yolk. "Reyankaiya. You have a long day ahead of you. Let's get you ready." Ms. Stableman led her down the hall to Avalina's room.

The woman sighed as she laid Reyan's clothes out on the bed. "Where is your bag, dear?" Reyan found her old sack under the bed and laid it next to the hand-me-down dresses. Ms. Stableman opened Avalina's closet and began pushing around the hanging clothes and shuffling the items on the shelves. She returned to the bed carrying a leather travel bag with a strap long enough to hang over a shoulder and across a chest. "Here you go. I think everything would fit better in this." Reyan looked at it, speechless. "Go on." The woman motioned for Reyan to begin putting her things in the bag. As she did, Avalina's mother said, "We're Systemic folk. We've never even considered a second. But being an only child has always bothered Avalina. It's been good to see her with you. We'll be sorry to see you go." She smiled briefly before her mouth fell back to its customary flat line. "Come on. Let's get you back to your benefactors."

When Reyan and Ms. Stableman returned to the dining room, the air felt tense. Avalina was doing the dishes, and Mr. Stableman's head had returned to the cradle of his hands. When he heard them enter, his head popped up, and he smiled. "Ah, there you are." But his eyes seemed tired, and he looked past Reyan's shoulder to make eye contact with his mate.

"Okay Lina, looks like everyone's ready."

Mr. Stableman headed to the door, where he pulled a heavy coat from a peg and lit a lantern. Avalina wiped her wet hands down the back of her woolen work dress and joined him at the door.

Ms. Stableman stood out of their way as they donned coats and slung bags. Mr. Stableman opened the door, and the cold damp pre-dawn dark spilled in. Avalina's mother put a hand on Reyan's shoulder just before she crossed the threshold. "You take care, Reyan. We hope to see you again."

On the way to the stables, Reyan struggled to keep up with Avalina, the weight of her new bag slowing her down. Avalina walked in silence, staying quite a few yards ahead of Mr. Stableman. Reyan wasn't sure what she had done wrong. By the time they arrived at the human door built into the stable's enormous sliding door, Reyan couldn't take the silence anymore. She reached out and tugged on Avalina's sleeve.

When Avalina turned to face her, she looked angry. "The caravan is just around the corner, Reyan. You should know the way by now without my help. I need to get to work." Then Avalina turned, walked through the door, and let it swing shut behind her.

Reyan's face boiled and blistered with emotions. Her cheek twitched. Finally, she burst into sobs. She turned toward the town square and saw Mr. Stableman blurred and warped by her tears. As she ran past him, he stepped aside and reached out a hand in a feeble attempt to comfort her.

Reyan did not head directly to the town square. She wanted to get ahold of herself before the professors and Kavi saw her. More than anything, she longed for her tree. Instead, she headed down to the river and walked the front street to its end, then headed one block into town and doubled back, one street over.

As the morning's dark faded into a smudgy gray, she worked her way back and forth through the town like a weaver's shuttle. Past the butcher and the bakery with their storefronts cold and still, but with warmth and light glowing out from the working rooms in the back. With every turn she saw more townsfolk in the streets—pushing a barrow, walking a high-stepping horse, carrying a package under an arm, and touching a forehead to greet her.

When she finally got to the caravan, it was cold and dark as ashes from a previous night's fire. The only remaining ember was in the second truck. She stepped up onto the porch and slowly reached for the door as though it might be hot. She knocked.

"Come in," Parr's voice said from within.

She found the professor at his desk, facing the wall. He had an enormous book opened before him. When he looked up and saw her, he drew a ribbon across the page, and folded the book shut.

"Good morning, Reyankaiya. What can I do for you?"

"I'm cold. Kavi and Sevv's trucks are still dark."

"I'm sure they are. I'm surprised you are out so early. Is everything okay?"

Reyan swallowed hard, and a hot sense of betrayal and hurt swelled in her and threatened to emerge as more tears.

She felt Parr's curiosity loosen enough to give her the privacy and room she needed. He stopped asking questions and nodded once as though she had already answered him. She was grateful. "You are welcome to stay here. I can't offer you much in the way of company or entertainment, but it's warm enough, and there is bread and cheese if you're hungry."

"I've eaten."

"So, it's not all bad then." He forced the sort of smile adults use to draw a line at a conversation's end. He pinched a thin gray ribbon poking out between the enormous book's pages and used it to peel the book open. He rested his head on his left hand and continued reading.

Reyan tossed her bag on the floor and sat down on the knotted rug. She crossed her arms over her stomach and looked around at the inside of Parr's truck.

The woodwork had grown deep brown from age and polish. The bed was crisply made and the dishes from Parr's morning meal were nowhere to be seen. Anything that wasn't nailed down had some contrivance to keep it from wriggling free from its allotted place as the truck rocked its way around the circuit. The small bookshelf—which currently had a gaping hole where Parr had removed the book he was reading—had a leather strap across it, which was fastened by hooks on either side. The oil lamp was affixed to the wall over the desk. Everything else was tucked into drawers and cabinets, which were built into every available space. Every surface could be pulled or slid or hinged into some other configuration or purpose.

Aside from the knotted carpet on which she currently sat, there were no other knick-knacks or anything at all to show the personality of the truck's inhabitant. Reyan quickly grew bored. "What are you reading?"

He closed the book again, drew in a breath, and scooted his chair around to face her. He put his hands on his knees and leaned forward so he could look at her over his knees. "The System."

Reyan sat up taller. "You can't read the System," she said. Parr did not reply, only smiled, and waited. "The System's not a book, it's a...a..." She couldn't exactly think of what she would call the System. She would have said "philosophy" or "methodology" if she'd had the words, but she did not. She finally settled on "idea."

"You're wrong about that. But you are also right. The System is many things." He turned back to his desk and grunted a little as he lifted the book. He brought it around so she could see it. "And this book is one of them."

The book was covered and bound in white leather. It was almost as thick as the professor's hand was long, so that he could barely curl his fingers around its edges. Several other colored ribbons stuck out between the rough-edged pages. He tilted book up so she could see its cover. Lines of copper had been pressed into the front to form a rectangular border. In simple blocky letters were the words "A System for a New Era."

"Is that the big book Lem talked about?"

"It is."

"What's it about?"

"Everything."

"How can a single book be about everything?"

He stood, walked over to the shelf, pulled back the leather strap and replaced the massive book. "Over dinner last night, I got the impression that you might have an interest in professorship." He rehooked the strap across the book spines. "I'm glad to hear our session had such a profound effect upon you."

"It did."

"And what about the idea of becoming a professor do you find most intriguing?"

She could feel a chaos of thoughts and anxious words queuing up for a chance at her tongue. If she let the words start flowing, she would become like a cracked bucket, and even the most patient listener would begin to lose interest. But Parr's expression didn't change. He simply waited for the answer to his question. The trick of it was to give Parr his answer in as few words as possible. "Your way of thinking about problems reminded me of trees."

She brought her legs up to her chest and hugged them tight. She used a knee to stop up her mouth so she wouldn't say too much.

"How do you mean?" He was trying to trick her out into the open. She scowled. "Like a tree how, Reyankaiya?"

Reyan felt something inside her slip. Her thoughts began to form directly in her mouth. She had the peculiar feeling of stepping aside to let a run-away cart or escaped animal fly past her, all dust and speed and destruction. "All the different ways to look at a decision. That's how I think. I'm always asking, 'What about this?' and 'What would happen if?' I can't stop until I understand it all. It's why people hate me. That's why, when I don't know what to do, I go to my tree instead. Once I'm there, I find a big branch above me and line it up, so it looks like it's sprouting from my forehead. I pose my problem, then follow the branch with my eyes until I come to a place where it branches off. There, I ask a what-if. Each branch becomes a possible answer. I follow each fork from there until it forks again, and there are more what-ifs. I keep doing that until I follow each branch and twig to the very ends, and I run out of ifs.

"Yesterday, when I listened to your story about Shabeer and Segenam and how it wasn't clear who was the most systemic, the way you asked the questions reminded me of my branches. Then Sevv showed us the right way to make decisions. How I didn't need to keep all the branches in my head. I could write each down. I could give them a number. Learning that felt like...like...the way I feel watching a perfect curl grow from the carpenter's plane."

Now that her thoughts were spent, her self-awareness flooded back in. *I always speak too quickly and say too much. And I didn't let the professor speak at all. People hate that.*

She was just about to stand up and leave when Parr asked, "What happens when you act on your decisions?"

She hung her head. "I just think of things I might do. I don't actually do any of them."

He nodded his head slowly, his eyes fixed on her. "Not doing something is a decision too. The Systemic way is a hard way, Reyankaiya. If you want to be a professor, you cannot run and hide in the woods when things become difficult. The System has a role for you."

Her mind filled in the extra words to reveal his meaning. "The System has a role for everyone, even for you." She knew he wasn't trying to be cruel, but his words hurt all the more because of it.

Professor Parr slapped his hands on his thighs, signaling that the conversation was over. "Let's go see if the others plan to get out of bed before dusk. I would like to see Seal Tooth in the daylight."

Out in the square, Sevv and Kavi were already working. The stages and blackboards had been stowed, and they were double-checking their lashings. When they saw Parr and Reyan, they finished their work and came over. "Are we ready?" Parr asked.

Sevv looked over the caravan. "I believe so. Yes. Kavi, Reyankaiya, have them bring the horses around."

Kavi and Reyan walked back towards the stable. A hot knot kept tying, redoubling, and tying itself again in Reyan's gut as she grew nearer to Avalina and the memory of her inexplicable anger.

When they got to the door, Kavi stepped through, and Reyan stopped outside. Kavi turned to her. "Come on." She shook her head. Kavi shrugged and disappeared into the gloom.

A few minutes later the large door slid halfway open, and Jax emerged, leading several of the horses. Benj was nowhere to be seen. Avalina came out blinking into the morning light with the remaining horses. Reyan moved so that a horse was between her and Avalina as they silently walked back to the town square.

Instead of going back to the caravan, Reyan sat down on the tower steps so she could stay out of the way while she watched the preparations. Jax held all the horses in a cluster in the center of the square. One by one, Avalina came over and retrieved a horse and hooked it up to whichever truck Kavi directed her to.

When all the horses were in their places, Sevv and Parr came over to where Reyan was sitting. Mr. Stableman was with them. Avalina hung behind them like a reluctant shadow.

"Reyankaiya," Sevv said. Reyan stood but her eyes stayed fixed on the ground. "Mr. Stableman has told us that they are able and willing to take you in as their ward."

"It's been so good for Lina to have you."

Trying to figure out how to answer was more than Reyan could stand. Of all the things she could have said, for some reason she chose, "But Avalina hates me."

"She doesn't." Mr. Stableman smiled, but his eyes were soft and sad. "I know she doesn't. Not really."

No one had ever wanted her. She couldn't believe that they really wanted her now. But she wanted to be wanted. The idea tugged at her. It would be so easy to give in to it. "But what about becoming a professor?"

Mr. Stableman's eyes jumped between the two professors. Parr's face showed nothing. Sevv smiled thinly and blinked, "Of course, if you stayed, you would be here in Rowe, not in Seal Tooth. You wouldn't become a professor, but you would learn some other necessary trade. Most likely, you'd be working in the stables alongside your new friend."

Sevv looked at Mr. Stableman, who nodded that this would indeed be the case, and said, "Lina said you did well with the horses, even the one that went after poor Benj."

Reyan crouched down grabbed a nearby twig and began writing in the mud. She drew out a grid and began filling the cells. At the top she wrote, "Seal Tooth" and "Rowe." She looked up at Parr, who showed no indication that he remembered their conversation from earlier. She added "Do nothing." Down the side, she began naming each row and adding the weights.

"Will make my best friend happy…9."

"Won't be lonely…7."

"Role that suits me…10."

"Feels safe…5."

She did her best to remember the Systemic considerations but failed and simply scribbled "Governing Assert" and gave it a 19.

"What's she doing?" she heard Mr. Stableman ask. No one answered him.

Reyan imagined herself in her tree, her back against its solid trunk. In her mind, the bark split wide and pulled her in. She became wood and rings and running sap. From there, her mind traveled out along the branching possibilities of her life in Rowe and Seal Tooth.

She began to scratch numbers into the cells and cut slashes and cross-multiply. She saw the completed matrix laid out before her. It wasn't perfect. She looked at the professors. Parr's nod was as subtle as a blinking eye, but she knew it would do.

She tallied the columns.

Rowe 166.

Seal Tooth 178.

Doing nothing was not really an option.

Reyan stood up. She looked first at Avalina, who was not making eye contact with her and was sulking once again. The professors still showed no expression at all.

"I'll go to Seal Tooth," she said. Avalina began to cry and walked away. Her father frowned and nodded, looking dejected. As he turned away, Reyan reached out a hand, grabbed him by the sleeve and pulled him closer. She whispered, "Watch the way Benj treats Lina and the others." A realization, or at least a suspicion, drained the color from the man's round and perpetually jovial face. "Make sure to catch him at it. Don't let anyone know I told you, or it will just get worse."

"Well, Reyankaiya," Sevv said, "If you're coming with us, you'd best ride with me." He coughed. "And if that was supposed to be a matrix, it was abominable."

Reyan climbed into the cab of Sevv's truck and leaned her head against the glass. She felt like she should be second-guessing her decision but doing so didn't feel honest. She knew it hadn't been a wrong choice—just a hard one. It wasn't regret she was feeling. It was sorrow.

Keeper Shalynn came into the square with the junior keeper, Mariana, with Tamura following behind. Sevv, Parr, and Kavi came out to meet them. Kavi handed the compendium to Sevv, who offered it to Shalynn. When the keeper placed her hand on it, Sevv intoned, "Keeper. The year's compendium. Learn its lessons. Keep its knowledge. Share its wisdom."

Shalynn gathered the little book to her and inclined her head slightly. "Thank you, Professor. Have safe travels. Thank you for your service through the years." She then turned to Parr, "We look forward to next year's visitation." To Kavi she said, "Hopefully, you'll be returning with him."

Avalina approached from across the square. She was carrying something and seemed to be in a hurry. She stopped to speak to the professors, and Sevv pointed back to where Reyan was slouching in his truck.

Once Reyan realized that Avalina was looking for her, she stepped down from the cab to meet her. Her friend handed her a small wooden box with a hinged lid. Reyan opened it. Inside was a comb. Wrapped back and forth through the comb's teeth was a multi-colored ribbon. Reyan closed the lid, and she was startled when Avalina lunged at her. Reyan took a stumbling step back, but Avalina already had a hold of her. She squeezed Reyan so tightly Reyan worried she wouldn't be able to breathe. Avalina loosened her hold but did not release her for a moment. She whispered, "I was hoping you would stay, and we would be like sisters." She pulled away, unable to look Reyan in the face. "I'm going to miss you. Take care of yourself."

"I'll come back as soon as I'm a professor," Reyan said.

"Come back as soon as you're a novice."

CHAPTER TWENTY-TWO

From *The Compiled Journals of Partner Lem*
Day 271, Year 1, New Era

The Partners spent all winter holed up studying the Book and learning new skills. Now, spring is finally moving on toward summer, and the last drifts of snow are retreating up and out of the passes. According to the Book, it's time to head out on our first teaching circuit.

If we want to have any impact at all, we can't just wander around out here in the desert. We need to head west since the nearest pop-center of any size lies about seven hundred miles in that direction. And, as a bonus, Seal Tooth also happens to be my hometown. Edner figures it will take us nearly forty straight days. If we keep up a good pace, I could be home by fall. There are plenty of little towns along the way where we can stop and rest and get a feel for teaching the System to strangers. Just as long as we don't linger.

Next to Edner's home, there is a small ranch that used to offer horseback tours of the Prower valley. The owner has been slowly working his way through his band, slaughtering the old ones to feed his family and trade for essentials. Edner suggested we could put the horses to better use. Edner turned over half his acreage to the man, and in turn, the man outfitted the Partners with horses. We threw in two boxes of dehydrated food to seal the deal.

We found an old truck abandoned by the side of the road. Harold removed the batteries, motors, and all the other heavy dead tech. The remaining frame was light enough that any one of us could push it if we put our backs into it. We loaded it with supplies and hitched it to one of the horses.

Tomorrow, first thing in the morning, we will set off down the long, hard road from Prower to Seal Tooth.

CHAPTER TWENTY-THREE
Day 68, Year 290, New Era

Professor Sevv's truck swayed wildly from one side to the other as it rolled over the seam between the gravel path from Rowe and the hardroad to Seal Tooth. Reyan struggled for something to say. A hailstorm of questions fell around her, and she caught only a glimpse of each before they merged with the indistinguishable slurry of her ignorance. *Becoming a professor will require learning. Learning will require asking questions. I can't just sit back and observe the world from a tree my whole life.*

Sevv was no help at all. He just sat there twitching the reins in his hands and blinking, his thin lips trembling with an old man's unspoken complaints.

They passed the remnants of a car—a slumping mass of tarnished metal, sun-faded plastic, and dried blackberry brambles erupting from the missing windows.

Sevv frowned. "The Eye pass over us, let's stay wide of that mess."

Finally, Reyan knew what to ask: "What's so bad about tech?"

"During the Era of Dependency, we made an unending stream of thinktech toys to play with. But then our toys learned to play our games for us, then without us. Finally, we were no longer required for our own games."

"Weren't the System thinktech? I thought they were good."

"The problem wasn't the System, my dear, it was *us*. We handed over every difficult aspect of our lives to them. They thought our thoughts and made our decisions. And they always seemed to think the answer to every problem was to develop more thinktech. If you ask a rabbit how to solve your problems, you should not be surprised to be overrun with baby rabbits. So, when the Calming came and all the tech died, we were left with nothing." She didn't say anything, which Sevv interpreted as disbelief. He said, "It's true. We *remember*."

"You were alive during the Systemic Era?" Sevv was old, but she didn't think anyone could be *that* old.

He waved her off dismissively. "Of course not. It's just an expression. We don't exactly hate tech. There's even a technical faculty. Kavi will join it when he graduates.

Reyan shook her head. "Faculty?"

"You have faculties, no? You hear, you see, you think,

you have muscular strength." She nodded. "Well, the System have faculties as well. We professors specialize in one of these Systemic faculties. Kavi will join the System's technical faculty. Parr is in the theoretical faculty, and I specialize in systemic processes. There are other faculties of course—agricultural, historical, medicinal, et cetera. I wonder which on you would find most interesting?"

"Couldn't I learn them all?"

Sevv scoffed. "The System is limitless, and you are only human, my dear. Besides, concerning yourself with the goings on of the other faculties makes the entire System less efficient."

"That's why Lem had the first Partners each take a section of the book."

"Exactly right. So, you're still interested in joining us at the university?"

She nodded.

"Speak up. A professor needs to project her voice. Again, please."

"Yes, professor."

"Why?"

Reyan was seldom graced with a clear and single why for anything. As a rule, her mind was a mess of competing thoughts, ideas, desires, and fears, and her actions arose mysteriously out of that tangle. But something about the

System promised to clarify the mess. And the way the professors stood apart from others resonated with her experience. But while her isolation felt like rejection, the professors' seemed mysterious, and it inspired deference from others. If someone respected you, they might let you teach them. Tom, her young friend back in Orloton, had let her teach him. She had only ever taught him silly things like how to skip stones or light fires or tie good knots. But she had come to enjoy the act of harvesting the seeds of her own knowledge, planting them in another, and watching them take root. She tried to think how to put all of this into words.

Sevv grew tired of waiting for her answer and said, "I'm surprised you've not formed any opinions on the matter. Make sure you have before you decide."

Then she knew what she wanted to ask. "Why did *you* become a professor?"

Sevv smiled indulgently at her. Being asked about himself seemed to please him. "If I told you I was born a professor, it would be near enough to the truth. I am from a place very much like Orloton. I had only eight named years when I left, but I already knew the town was not the place for a boy like me. But that was very long ago. Perhaps you'd like to know why I *remain* a professor?"

Reyan wasn't sure she did, but she was absolutely sure he was going to tell her. She fixed her eyes on the long stretch of hardroad ahead.

"Look around you, Reyankaiya. What do you see?" This was the sort of question that adults were forever asking kids, only to become annoyed when they answered. It was best to keep quiet until they answered themselves. She waited. "There is balance. There is order. Do you see it? Do you understand?"

In all her life, Reyan had never felt anything like balance or order. She certainly didn't understand it. She shook her head.

"Left to their own devices, things fall apart. It is a professor's job to keep it all together. Other roles are certainly important, but it is the professors who understand how the ground they plow, the rivers they ply, and the trees they fell relate to each other. It is our role to help them make Systemic choices. To help them realize that tugging on even the farthest corners of a web will still bring the spider. It's the most important role there is."

Reyan's scalp began to tingle as her mind ignited with recognition. "That's it! *That's* why I want to do it! I've always known that, if I pull a string here," she tugged at an imaginary string in the air, "*something* will move over there." She pointed past Sevv's nose to the corner of the cab. He followed it with his eyes as though she might actually be pointing at something. "But I can't always see where the string goes. So I'm usually scared to do anything at all. But today, when I was drawing that matrix in the dirt, I felt like I might be able to understand where all the strings went."

Sevv stammered, "Well, it's not that…"

She cut him off: "And maybe, if I could understand where all the strings go, I could help others improve their lives the way you do. I figure if the System devised the decision matrix, then the System understands my mind. If that's true, I want to understand all there is to know about the System."

Sevv's eyes narrowed, and he turned away from her to look out of the windscreen. "We shall see."

A few minutes later, Reyan started catching glimpses of a flat creeping river through periodic divots hacked into the blackberry brambles. The river began to widen, the opposite shore fleeing until it was as thin as the edge of a leaf. Soon, the shore disappeared altogether, and the eastern hills appeared to rise directly from the surface of the water. "Is that the sea?"

Sevv smiled, "I bet that's the most water you've ever seen in one place." It was true, but it also felt like he was insulting her in some way. She nodded. "That's the Wash," he said. "He's just a lake. A big one, to be sure, but nothing like the sea."

The caravan left the hardroad and crunched into a large field of gravel and dirt that sat between the hardroad and the Wash. No trees grew there, and the few bushes were stunted and hunched as though shouldering a burden. Tight clusters of brown thistles, their mangy heads having gone to seed in the late summer, quaked in the sharp autumn winds. "What is wrong with this place?"

"No one remembers," Sevv said. "You'll see these sorts of places now and then near the remnants of ancient tech and industry. Filthy business."

"Is it safe?"

"I've been stopping here for more than forty years, and our caravans have been stopping here long before that."

Sevv reined in the horses and set his brake. Reyan jumped down from the cab. Kavi was at the rear of the caravan, untying a wood-slat bucket from his rack of supplies. "Go and help the boy," Sevv said. So Reyan untied a bucket from each of the professor's trucks and carried them down to the lake.

Kavi and Reyan crouched down and filled their buckets from the shore. The hempen rope handles cut hotly into their hands as they walked stiff-legged and careful back to the caravan, sloshing water onto their boots. This struck them as funny, and they laughed each time it happened.

They gave each team of horses a bucket, and Kavi loosened their tack so they could stoop to drink. Once the horses had drank their fill, Kavi strapped on their feedbags, and then he and Reyan joined the professors for lunch.

The professors' cold red hands sliced meat, crumbled cheese, and tore off hunks of bread still fresh from the bakery in Rowe. The two men reminded Reyan of an old couple who had retreated from years of awkward conversations into separate inner monologues. They sat silently and looked out at the blend of textures playing out upon the surface of the Wash.

"It'll be nice to be home," Kavi offered. "I'm looking forward to being back at school. Going to a café or the theater, listening to some live music. I can't wait to see my friends." He said, pointedly, "It'll be nice to hear a joke once in a while."

"We joke," Sevv protested, but offered no evidence. "I'm

looking forward to sleeping in a room where I can't touch both walls at the same time and with a floor that doesn't rock whenever I cross it. I feel like I've been out to sea all summer. Being on circuit can be painfully dull. All application and no theory; all teaching and no learning."

"Is there nothing to be learned out on circuit?" Reyan asked.

"You'll find that exchanging ideas with nodies is something of a one-way proposition," Sevv chuckled.

"We should be students before professors," Parr intoned. Sevv sneered and looked back out at the lake.

"What about you, Parr?" Kavi asked. "What are you looking forward to in Seal Tooth?"

"My library," he said.

"It's not really *your* library, is it Parr?" Sevv smiled. "It is just *the* library."

"*The* library then. All those forgotten things waiting to be remembered. And a desk large enough to spread out on."

"Parr keeps the library back at the University," Kavi explained. "He has the original copy of Lem's Book."

"Is that what I saw you reading this morning?"

"What? The one in his truck?" Sevv scoffed. "No, my dear, that is only a professor's travel copy. Very much abridged."

"Why don't the professors share the entire Book with the people in the towns?"

"Practical considerations mostly," Sevv said. "Paper is quite heavy. A complete copy of the Book, even one made by our best printers, would add hundreds of pounds to the load our poor horses would have to bear."

"Hopefully I'll be able to show you the original in its entirety someday," Parr said.

"What about you, Reyankaiya?" Sevv asked. "Is there anything you're looking forward to when we arrive in Seal Tooth?"

"No one calling me 'Reyankaiya' ever again." Her answer was sharper than she'd intended.

Sevv drew back his head and blinked. "What shall we call you, dear? 'Kaiya,' like Lyessa did?"

"Certainly not 'dear.'" That retort sounded even worse. She knew she should apologize. Lyessa would have made her. But there was something satisfying about saying exactly what she meant, and she couldn't make herself feel sorry about it. "Just call me 'Reyan.'"

"Then why would Leader Lyessa have told us to call you 'Kaiya'?" She watched Sevv's eyes move as though reading her name written out before him. His lips moved as he translated it to "rises above" and "chaos," and he understood.

She noticed Parr at the edge of her vision, smiling down at his bread and cheese as though someone had whispered something funny into his ear. "I was wondering how long it would take you to put it together, Sevv."

"You could have just asked me," Kavi said.

"You might have said something without being asked," Sevv snapped.

CHAPTER TWENTY-FOUR
Day 68, Year 290, New Era

Parr stood up from the lunch table. "I say we talk less about Seal Tooth and focus more on getting ourselves there."

Reyan did not want to ride with Sevv again. She was trying to decide how best to say so when Kavi said, "You want to ride with me?"

Reyan climbed into Kavi's truck and watched as Sevv's truck lurched into motion, rocking as it crossed the ruts and potholes of the barren field, with Parr's truck following close behind. Then Kavi said "Yee-up," and his truck jerked forward.

The hardroad began a slow steady climb up and away from the shore. The interceding forest grew progressively thicker until they lost sight of the lake. After a while Reyan asked, "What'll Seal Tooth be like?"

He smiled. "Orloton? Rowe? They're just nodes. There are blocks in Seal Tooth that have as many people as Orloton and Rowe *combined*."

She tried to imagine how tiny the houses would have to be to cram everyone in Orloton into a single block. She imagined little standing room-only houses bundled together like cord wood on end. She wondered how they would all go to the bathroom and laughed. But thinking about Seal Tooth made her think about school, and that made her nervous. "You told Tamura that school is going to be hard."

"You seem pretty smart. I'm sure some faculty will take you."

"Sevv said you're in the *technical* faculty, right?"

"Not yet. I'm still a novice, hence the white stripe and no karaband." He held his arm in the air and shook his naked wrist.

"How many people do they let in?"

"Depends on the faculty. The agricultural faculty has over a hundred members and probably a half-dozen novices. But there's not much need for the technical faculty, so it's small. Once I join, there'll just be two of us—Partner Minerva and myself."

"Is it hard to get into a faculty?"

He took a moment to answer, then winced and said,

"Yeah, it's *really* hard."

"What if I fail? What if they don't want me?" She looked out the side window, her chin resting on the frame.

He lightly punched her thigh. When she looked up at him crossly, he smiled. "You'll do fine. In a few years you'll be a professor, you'll have your own caravan, and in the summer, you'll travel your own circuit. Then you just need to teach whatever's in the compendium that year and help with anything that needs doing. I was pretty excited to help with that cooling room in Rowe before Tamura came and messed it all up."

"Who decides what's in the compendium?

"Every faculty has a say, but ultimately the Host of Partners decides."

"So it's a secret?"

"Nothing about the System is secret," he said. Then, after a moment he added, "I just don't happen to know."

"That sounds a lot like a secret." She thought of all the times she had seen the professors hand a compendium over to Keeper Leonid. She thought past the professor's outstretched hand to the printer who had given him the compendium in the first place. She considered the Host of Partners, who decided its contents, and the faculties who informed them. Each participant in the process strung like jewels on a thread; each jewel refracting and refining knowledge before letting it spark down the line to the next. Each connected to every other in

countless ways. *The System is an enormous web.* The idea of it
suddenly frightened her. *What if I become ensnared in it? What if I
always have been?* It might appear that webs were draped over
twigs and blades of grass by the morning mist, but Reyan
understood they were built and maintained by something
dreadful in the night. *What sort of spider lies at this web's center?
What will happen to me if I tug the wrong thread?*

The caravan descended toward a dark opening in the side
of a hill shrouded by a curtain of ivy. One after the other, the
horses nosed the vines aside and disappeared into the darkness.

In the blackness of the tunnel, every sound the caravan
made bounced off the walls and reverberated. The echoing
clops of the horses' iron-shod hooves and the pings and pops
of buckles and chains and swaying gear ricocheted through her
head. Beneath that boiling syncopation was the continual
landslide rumble of the metal tyres on the hardroad.

The noise had become almost unbearable when she saw a
blue-gray glow on the left wall. Soon, she could see the outline
of the horses' ears. Finally, a bright line of daylight appeared
and expanded as they rounded the curve, and the exit came
into view. The clamor faded by degrees as each truck exited the
tunnel, and Reyan began to relax.

In the growing light Reyan could see that people had
drawn symbols and words on the walls by smudging away the
grime to reveal the clean, glossy surface of the tiles. There were
names in hearts—"Byron and Susan," "Shelly and Carol"—
and a large circle pierced with lines of lightning forming a B.

"Bridgers," Kavi said, as though it should mean

something to her. When she didn't react, he added, "They want to build bridges across the Great Eastern River and make friends with the Erynites."

"Why would they want to do that?"

"I've never met an Erynite, so I couldn't tell you," Kavi said, shrugging. "But there must be some reason the Bridgers hide their activities in dark tunnels far away from the university."

They exited the tunnel and found themselves overlooking a wide, forty-foot-deep gap, which appeared to have been gouged into the world by the massive flow of hardroad that flooded it from wall to wall and stretched away to the north and south as far as she could see. Reyan curled her knees to her chest and put her feet on the dashboard as their trickle of hardroad crossed the canyon, then curved down along its far wall. It turned out that the vast and endless stretch of hardroad she had traveled from Orloton was a mere tributary. Now she had arrived at the confluence. Other bridges spanned the canyon. Ramps climbed up and down the walls, all of them twisting and bending and overlapping like a giant version of Avalina's braids.

After a while, the hardroad ahead climbed to a crest. The caravan spaced themselves until there was a half-dozen truck-and-team lengths between them.

"Why are we slowing?"

"Just to be safe. We don't like to cross King's Bridge with more than one truck at a time."

"Is it not safe?"

"Don't worry," he laughed, "It's safe enough. King's Bridge is old, but it hasn't fallen yet."

She thought of the destroyed bridge they'd seen earlier, and panic gripped her. "Yet? So it's going to fall?"

"Everything falls eventually, but we'd rather not lose an entire caravan when it does."

Once the top edge of Sevv's truck disappeared over the crest, Parr picked up his pace and climbed after him. Once Parr's truck had disappeared as well, Kavi swallowed hard. "Hold on to your seat."

The shapestone walls of the canyon shrank away, and the view opened. Hills rose from the shoulders of other hills for miles in all directions. The gray haze of the intervening distance washed them out until there was no texture, just their shapes and colors like a storm cloud's belly.

A cluster of rod-straight angular objects erupted from the base of a nearby hill. They reminded her of the clusters of frost crystals that heaved up from the forest floor on cold autumn mornings. At this distance, each appeared no larger than her thumb, but she could tell they were impossibly tall.

"What is that?"

"*That* is Seal Tooth."

"But what are *those*?"

"Scrapers."

She tensed. "What do they scrape?" In her experience scrapes always wound up on her knees or the palms of her hands.

He laughed. "I don't know. The clouds? The ground, maybe?"

They continued their ascent, and she could see the far shore of the lake working its way around the feet of the scrapers. Kavi pulled his team toward the low shapestone barrier at the edge of the bridge, and more of the lake came into view far below them. A few specks sat on the surface of the water. When she realized these were not water bugs but boats, terror shot through her. She had climbed to the top of hundreds of trees. She had peered over the edges of dizzying cliffs. But she had never imagined being this high. And here, no tree trunk or rock face connected her to the earth.

She put her feet against the side door of the cab and pushed herself along the bench into Kavi. He steered the truck away from the edge, and the lake disappeared from view. "Close your eyes. That's what I do sometimes. The horses know the way."

She closed her eyes. He wrapped an arm around her and squeezed. It crushed some of the air out of her, but it also made her feel like she wouldn't fall apart.

When the truck leveled off and began traveling down the other side, Kavi loosened his arm, and she opened her eyes. The trees and the hills slowly rose to block their view of the lake, and her panic began to subside.

Soon Seal Tooth was close enough that she could see the details of the scrapers. Some were black as charred wood, and others reflected light like the sparks of the setting sun bouncing off the surface of a pond. "Are there so many people in Seal Tooth that the houses need to be so large?"

"Most of the floors are empty. If people live too close together, the scab could spread quick as fire, so we try to keep them separated."

"Who made them?"

"Humans? Machines? It's hard to say exactly. They're from the Era of Dependency. They're made of steel beams, shapestone, and flat glass. We certainly can't build anything like them anymore."

The hardroad belted the waist of the hill, continuing its steady downward slope. They passed beneath what looked like another bridge, but one made of rocks and lumps of broken shapestone fitted together to form a series of pylons and arches. It began on the hillside, spanned the hardroad, and continued in a long straight incline that disappeared into the pop-center below. "The aqueduct." Kavi explained. As they passed under one of the arches, a huge glop of water splashed across the windscreen. "It carries water from the reservoir at the top of the hill down into Seal Tooth."

A single lane of hardroad curled off from the main line and ran along the aqueduct. The caravan followed it down into the heart of the pop-center.

She had often watched beetles or ants crawling along the forest floor and wondered how they felt. Now she knew. Down among the roots of the massive scrapers, she could no longer see the sun or much of the sky. The wind grew cold in the shadows. It blew in the horse's faces and knifed through the rein slot in the windscreen, reddening Kavi's knuckles.

The scale of the scrapers was oppressive. *What sort of people would build their town to make themselves feel so small and unimportant?* Then another thought came. *Perhaps they didn't build the scrapers to make the person at their feet feel small, but to help the person on top feel powerful.*

Perhaps it was both.

Even with generations of weather and wear, the scrapers still stood straighter and looked smoother than the New Era aqueduct. She was sad no one would ever build another scraper again, regardless of their reason for doing so.

The ground floor of all the scrapers were walls of glass tinted gray or brown or blue. If she looked through the smudges, past the rolling reflection of herself seated in the cab of the truck, she saw light and movement inside. Steam and smoke that smelled of bread or rendering meat or boiling bitter greens vented from the sides of the buildings.

Thirty or forty feet above the ground, most of the windows were gone, and the few panes of glass that remained were cracked and jagged. Every one of the scrapers had the same broad stripe of missing glass, starting two floors up and ending about six or eight floors later. After that, the glass began again and continued up the remainder of the building.

"Where did the glass go?"

Kavi reached forward and knocked on the windscreen. "Right here. Hundreds of years' worth of reuses, replacements, and repairs. Even out in the nodes, when a glazier puts new windows into a home, where do you think the glass comes from?"

The hardroad continued straight as a builder's chalk line through the pop-center. They passed a field that was the exact length and width of one of the scrapers, as though someone had plucked one of the towers and left behind a scar. The field was filled with rows of apple trees. Most were picked bare of fruit, but a few people still climbed ladders stripping whatever remained.

The caravan made a sharp turn and continued downhill. The bottom floors of the scrapers in this part of town were made of red brick, veined polished stone, or plain gray shapestone. But, above the façade, the scrapers had that same broad stripe of missing glass like a high-water mark.

The air smelled of rotting fish, old leaves, and stagnant puddles. She felt the raw sting of salt when she inhaled through her nose. Kavi's smile stretched wider and he grew more animated, as the caravan followed the long hill down and the smell of his home grew stronger.

They began passing blocks of squat ancient brick buildings clustered around open areas where the ground was paved in basket weaves of brick. The scene reminded Reyan of the town squares in Orloton and Rowe. Sevv's truck came to a stop in the middle of one of these squares. Parr rolled up along his right side, and Kavi stopped to his left.

Kavi let go of the reins, and they slid forward until the knot stopped them from falling through the slot. He turned to her, smiled his crooked smile, and said, "We're home."

A small crowd arrived from out of nowhere and surrounded the trucks. At first Reyan thought they were a welcome party like those that always mobbed an arriving caravan in Orloton. But this was no shouting mass of children. They were workers. Some tended to the horses, others stripped the gear hanging from the sides of the trucks, and still others were gathering the bags and other cargo from inside. One old man was moving from wheel to wheel, closing one eye, and sighting down each tyre to check for warpage.

Reyan noticed one woman who stood in contrast to the tumult of workers. She approached the caravan slowly and steadily, like a boat coming in through the fog. She was thin and tall, and her arms were crossed in front of her unadorned black dress. Parr dipped his head to her, and long strands of hair escaped from behind his ears and fell along his face. Sevv inclined his head as well, though less deeply. The woman nodded back.

When she saw Kavi, her pale old face lit up. She gathered the young man into her arms like he was her own child returned after years. She kissed him on the top of his head, and his face wrinkled up with embarrassment. "Hey, Mam."

She shouted, "By the Eye, Parr, what in the world have you been feeding this boy? Have you been feeding him at all?" Parr smiled before turning to discuss some urgent issue with a worker who began nodding his furious agreement long before Parr had finished his explanation.

The woman noticed Reyan and raised an eyebrow. "And it looks like you picked up a stray."

CHAPTER TWENTY-FIVE
Day 68, Year 290, New Era

The stable hands and other helpers led the caravan away from the square. The noise and activity followed the horses and trucks like a swarm of blackflies.

Kavi said, "Mam, this is Reyan. She's from Orloton. She wants to be a professor."

"Does she?" The woman extended a hand. "It's good to meet you, Reyan. My name's Mam. I keep everyone alive around here."

Reyan glanced down at the old woman's fingers. They never seemed to stop moving, and her whole arm shook slightly. Reyan looked at Kavi, who smiled and nudged her ahead. She took Mam's proffered hand. Her skin felt smooth and cool and dry as a polished stone. Mam tightened her grip and stared into Reyan's eyes until it felt like she was trying to read something written on the back of Reyan's skull. "So, you want to be a professor?"

"That's the plan," Kavi offered.

"Bit old to be starting off, isn't she?" she asked Kavi, still looking at Reyan.

"That remains to be seen," Parr said.

"If you hope to be a professor, you're going to have to start answering for yourself." Mam's eyes were fixed on Reyan, but she spoke loud enough for Kavi and the professors to know she was really talking to them. "And you'll be needing a room. Get your things and come with me. The student dormitory is up here on the left."

Reyan retrieved her bag and the box Avalina had given her. She followed Mam across the square, past a long continuous row of building fronts, each one different from the other. "So, you're from Orloton?" Mam asked. "You must know Rolf."

"He was my benefactor."

They entered the last door and climbed four flights of creaking stairs to a long hall. Light entered the hallway from a single window at one end and through the transoms over each door.

They stopped two doors from the end of the hall. Mam turned the knob, and the door swung into the room. "Here you are." She stepped aside to let Reyan enter.

Mam sighed. "I'm sorry to hear about your benefactor."

"You knew Leader Rolf?"

"I knew he was a good man," Mam said, choosing her words. "Despite what others might say."

"Who would say otherwise?" Reyan asked.

Mam sealed her lips with a smile. "Dinner will be served in the cafeteria soon. Let me know if you need anything." With that, Mam closed the door, and Reyan was left standing alone in the room.

The worn wooden floors creaked as she crossed over to the small sink against the wall. She filled a glass with water and watched the bedraggled girl in the mirror take tentative sips. She stared at her plain brown eyes and her dust-colored hair still gathered into the loose remnants of the braids Avalina had given her. What would the people of Seal Tooth think when they saw her? If she was lucky, they wouldn't notice her at all.

A mattress sat on the low bed, rolled tight and tied with a strip of cloth. She tugged on the loose ends of the bow and the mattress unrolled, revealing a limp pillow, a sheet, and two woolen blankets bundled inside.

She placed her bag on the bed and pulled out the dresses Ms. Stableman had given her. These she hung in the small closet next to the sink, which was nothing more than a cubby recessed into the wall with a bar and four wooden hangers.

The dresser at the foot of the bed had mismatched pulls. None of the drawers lined up, as though each had been borrowed from a different dresser. The top drawer was very loose and nearly slid out and onto the floor when she pulled it open. She put away her empty bag and the box with Avalina's comb and ribbon.

The desk near the window overlooked an alley and the back side of another building, which had many windows, metal stairs, and ladders. A lamp filled with oil sat on the desk. In the drawer she found three pencils, a conservatively short stack of paper, and a small, printed book with "Welcome to the University at Seal Tooth" stamped into the cover.

Reyan sat down at her desk, preparing to open the book, when a knock at the door made her jump. She wanted to pretend she wasn't there so that whoever was standing outside would go away. But then Kavi tentatively opened the door and stuck his head in the room. "Hey Reyan." He had washed his face, combed his hair, and swapped his travel robe for a pine-green tunic and blue pants, and his posture had changed to match his clothes. His limbs and spine seemed more loosely strung together, and he leaned against the door frame.

"That book can wait. It just talks about the rules of conduct and who to talk to when you have a problem. Hint: It's usually Mam. Come on. I'll take you down to dinner."

After the last few days of upheaval and travel, she just wanted to sit alone in her new room. "I'm not hungry."

But Kavi smiled and beckoned her to follow him. "Come on, Mam's orders. You might not find it written in your little book, but that's the most important rule: Do what Mam says."

As he led her down the several flights of stairs toward the lobby, Kavi said, "This is the dormitory, of course. First years on the fourth floor with you, second years on the third, third on the second, everyone else on the ground floor." When they reached the bottom floor, Kavi pointed down a hallway. "My room is down there. I'd show you, but it looks exactly like yours."

"Why not put the first years on the first floor, the second on the second, and so on?"

"Walking up and down stairs all day stinks. And the view up top isn't very remarkable."

"How long have you been here?"

"Five years."

"But you're only a couple years older than me."

"It's not about age, it's about seniority. I have it. You don't." He smiled. When she didn't respond, Kavi said, "Come on. I'm just joking."

"You're not really a fifth year?"

"No, about having seniority."

"You don't have seniority?"

"No, I do. But…" He seemed flustered.

After a few steps she said, "Kavi?" He stopped and turned. "I'm just joking."

Kavi smiled approvingly.

They walked through the lobby, past desks and chairs and tables, a shelf full of books. "Student lounge." Kavi said. "You can come here to study or hang out with your friends." The idea that she might have friends hadn't occurred to her. Perhaps she could have friends. She thought of Tom back in Orloton, Avalina in Rowe, and now Kavi. She supposed anything was possible.

They stepped outside and walked north on the walkway between the red brick square and the long building that contained the dormitory. They came to three large plate glass windows near the end of the building. Two of them were clear, but the other was made of harvested brown glass and had a semi-mirrored finish.

Stepping inside the building, they found a large room full of tables, counters, and shouting students. Reyan's shoulders crept up toward her ears. She wanted to leave, but Mam had told Kavi she needed to eat. It took everything in her power to remain in the food line. She kept her eyes focused on Kavi's feet. She stepped where he stepped and stopped when he stopped.

Dinner had started well over an hour ago, so all that was left to eat was a pot of soup, a basket full of cookies, and another filled with jerky. The soup was still warm but had a skin on it. Reyan filled a bowl and took two slices of cold bread. She scooped a lump of cold butter from a crock. The butter clumped up and tore at the bread when she tried to spread it with a knife. Kavi left the bread and soup alone and grabbed a cookie and a few strips of jerky.

Reyan followed Kavi's feet as they wound their way through the crowded dining room, avoiding the legs of chairs, tables, and students. When they came to a stop, Reyan looked up to see a table with three laughing, arm-punching, table-slapping teenage boys.

As they approached the table, the raucous behavior died suddenly. The closest young man craned his neck around and looked up. He had straight glossy black hair and a self-confident smirk. "Well, if it isn't Kavianhar Smithe! It's good to see you. Pull up a chair. Who's your friend?"

"Hey guys, this is Reyan." He stepped aside and presented her. She wanted to curl in on herself like a frightened pill bug. "She's going to be a new student. She hopped on our caravan on the last days of the circuit. She's another of Parr's wards."

"Really?" The seated boy looked her up and down. His eyebrows raised doubtfully. Then he shrugged. "Guess she'd better pull up a seat too."

The boy slid his chair over to make room. Reyan was about to beg off and head back to her room with her meal, but Kavi placed his food on the table and retrieved a chair for her. Unable to find a way to escape, Reyan lowered herself into the chair. She began to eat straight away, with her head hunched over her soup. The once loud, chattering table had grown quiet around her. She imagined their quick glances and unspoken questions flashing about the table.

There was a light cough. "Welcome to Seal Tooth, Reyan.

I'm Edward." She looked up and saw a young man with dark curly hair looking at her from across the table.

"Once you get to know him, you'll find yourself wanting to call him Ed or Eddie," Kavi said. "Don't." She swallowed the soup that was cooling in her mouth and tried a smile, which Edward returned. He did look a lot more like an 'Eddie' than an 'Edward'.

Edward leaned to his left and put his arm over the shoulder of the boy next to him—a tall, skinny teen with a few red splotches on his face who seemed as interested in his plate of food as Reyan was in hers. "And this here is Eddie," Edward said, grinning.

Kavi leaned in and said, "You're going to want to call him 'Edward.' We all do. But don't. It drives Edward crazy." She made a mental note to be very careful. Kavi explained, "Edward and Eddie were in line for registration on the first day. Eddie was just two places behind Edward."

"I heard poor Eddie groan when I gave Mam my name." Edward looked very pleased with himself.

Next, Kavi introduced the young man who had first invited them to sit: "And last but not least, Fang Hui Bai."

"I just go by Fang. It sounds dangerous." This idea made Reyan reconsider her aversion to the chaotic "kaiya" suffixed to her own name. "Where are you from?" Fang asked.

"Orloton."

"Never heard of it."

"It's a small town," Kavi offered, "Just a few days out near the end of Parr and Sevv's circuit."

"Oh, you're a *nodie* then?" Fang and Edward shared a silent smile, a playful glimmer in their eyes.

"How long have you wanted to be a professor?" Eddie wanted to know.

"I think I've always wanted to be a professor, but I only realized it a few days ago."

The boys thought this through in silence. Fang was the first to start laughing. Soon Edward joined in, followed by Eddie, who chuckled less heartily than the others. She felt a surge of anger at being laughed at. Under the table, Kavi put his steadying hand on her arm. "It's true," her friend said, without any trace of mockery. "A couple days on the road with Sevv, Parr, and I, was all it took."

"Really," Edward asked. "You've met Sevv, and you *still* want to be a professor?" There was more laughter. Even though Kavi had redirected the teasing toward Sevv, it still stung a bit. It had been Sevv's lecture—dry though it may have been—that made her realize she wanted to be a professor.

"You know," Eddie said bashfully, *bravely* she thought, "Sevv is quite good in his way." The other boys grew quiet and still. Eddie looked around cautiously before continuing. "Some of us—certain types of students, I mean—consider him something of a role model."

The table was silent while Kavi, Edward, and Fang

seemed to be considering Eddie's words. "Bullshit," Fang coughed into his fist, and the whole table—except Eddie and Reyan—burst into more laughter. Reyan had to admit that there was something funny about it, and soon both her and Eddie joined in as well.

After that, the conversation picked up and carried her along with it. Now and then, Fang would make a comment about her being a nodie and the others would laugh. Then Edward would tell him to cut it with the nodie jokes, and—while she appreciated him stepping in—she did not believe she or nodies in general should need defending. Then Edward would say something about her being a girl, but for some reason these jibes were always directed at Kavi. It all seemed good natured enough.

She guessed they were all around fifteen named years—seventeen lived. They were all novices teetering on the awkward edge between being boys in school and men on circuit. Fang and Eddie were both from Seal Tooth. But while Fang's parents were both faculty members, Eddie came from the general population. They had both spent their youths helping around the University; Fang based on his connections, Eddie on merit and the sympathies of certain professors and a very specific school matron. Edward was from a town to the south that started with a T and was otherwise unpronounceable. His mother was their town's keeper, which probably accounted for his cocky superior air. But he was also charismatic and charming, the sort you wanted to hate but simply couldn't.

Reyan wished she could talk but didn't know what to say

that these boys might find interesting. Besides, she never found a natural way to work her way into the bouncing, mercurial conversation.

"How was everyone's first circuit?" Kavi asked.

"Uncomfortable," Fang said without giving it much thought. "Everything was so low to the ground, and the food was terrible."

Kavi looked to Eddie: "What about you?"

"I thought it was interesting," Eddie said. He seemed to suspect he was being set up for a joke and did not make eye contact with the boys. "We were way out on the peninsula. It was the farthest I'd ever been from Seal Tooth. It never occurred to me that people could sound so different. They all understood us, of course, but sometimes I could barely understand them. And there was mud everywhere. Seal Tooth is dirty, but not like that."

"It wasn't as bad as I remember it," Edward said. "Granted, mom sent me here when I only had nine named years, so it's been a long time since I've been in the nodes. But when I lived out there, life was pretty awful. We were always hungry and always sick. A lot of kids didn't make it to their name day. I dread going back. But the nodes on our circuit weren't like that at all. Everyone was happy and healthy. Sure, the food wasn't great, but there was plenty of it. Maybe things in the nodes have gotten better. Maybe the node I grew up in was just particularly bad."

"No," Reyan said, "The nodes are still like that. The

difference is that you're a professor now. Don't you remember what it was like when the caravans came to town? Everyone gathered all the food, they washed the fronts of all the buildings, they hid the sick and the old at home. Try going back without your truck or your robe. It's just like you remember."

"Well, that's what we'll be for," Fang said confidently. "Fixing all that."

"That would be nice," Reyan shrugged, "but nothing ever changes in the nodes."

She watched as her words deflated the conversation. She should have known better than to say anything. After an awkward moment, Kavi said, "I think I'd better see Reyan back to her room. We'll see you again tomorrow."

Outside, the sky had grown the deep blue of approaching night, and the air was cool. "So, that's the guys. What did you think?"

"They seem boyish."

When they got to the foot of the stairs, Kavi said good night and headed down the hall to his first-floor room, and Reyan began the walk up four flights to hers.

It was blessedly silent and dark inside her room. She sat down on her bed and watched the white wall deepen to gray as the remaining daylight faded. She looked at the desk and the mirror over the little sink. She placed her hands to her sides and ran her palms over the blanket. None of it was hers. Not really. But all the space between the closed door and the window was hers.

The silence was hers.

CHAPTER TWENTY-SIX
Day 69, Year 290, New Era

When Reyan answered a knock on her door, she found Mam on the other side standing rod-straight, her hands clasped behind her back. The woman looked her up and down, then blew a dismissive huff through her nose. "Professors Parr and Sevv would like to see you."

Reyan rubbed the remaining sleep from her eyes and wiped a trail of nighttime drool from her cheek. She was still in the light short-sleeve shirt and pair of shorts she'd slept in.

She went over to her closet and flipped through the small collection of Avalina's old dresses. She selected her favorite, the blue dress. Though it was common enough to see blue around Seal Tooth, the color had been rare in Orloton, which made the dress seem particularly fancy to Reyan.

When Reyan stepped through her door, Mam was shouting at some students to slow down as they rushed off down the hall. When she turned back to Reyan her face was smiling, ready to be pleased, but when she saw the girl, her smile fell.

"No dear, you can't see the professors dressed like that."

Reyan felt the panic of the inescapable conundrum tighten around her chest. She had to see the professors, but... "This is the nicest dress I have," she choked.

"I don't doubt it. Put on a robe."

"I don't have a robe. I thought they'd give me one in my first class."

"Kavi never told you where to get your robes?" Reyan looked down and shook her head. "The Eye take that boy. I'll deal with him later." She huffed and placed a hand gently on Reyan's back. "Come along."

"But the professors are waiting. I thought they wanted to see me."

"Not without a robe they don't. First things first, my dear."

Mam marched Reyan down to the lobby, through a plain green door, and into a dark room. She lit the lantern that hung on the wall, and it illuminated a large wooden counter. Mam opened a short half-door and stepped into the large closet behind the counter. She began flipping through the robes that hung on the walls while mumbling to herself: "She's not attending class, it's just a visit." Mam slid the black robes aside, then snatched a brown robe with a broad white stripe and laid it against Reyan's chest. "This one will do. You can come back and get the rest of your garments from the quartermaster later."

"Why don't you wear a robe?"

Mam looked at her for a moment before turning away. "Because I'm neither a professor, nor studying to be one. Put on your robe and stop asking silly questions."

Reyan pulled the robe over her. When her head popped out, she saw Mam standing in the doorway like a judgmental statue. "Do something about your hair, child."

Reyan combed her fingers through her hair. They became tangled in several knots, which she doggedly fought through. When all the snags were gone, she smoothed her hair down with her palms. She felt she'd done well, but Mam rolled her eyes to the ceiling and shook her head. "Come on. At least you've got a robe. We'll do something about the hair later."

Mam led her out the front door, across the cobblestone square, and into another building. They climbed three flights of creaking stairs to a long hall. Reyan saw a door open at the end of the hall, and a parade of black-robed professors poured out and began walking toward them. Mam inclined her head reverently to each professor as they passed. Most of the professors gave no indication that they saw either Mam or Reyan. Finally, the last professor left the room, closing the door behind her. She was old and moved very slowly. As she passed, she paused for a moment, inclining her head in polite recognition: "Mam."

"Partner Minerva," Mam replied respectfully.

"Will you be joining us later?"

"Of course."

Partner Minerva smiled and nodded, then slowly made her way down the hall.

When all the professors had vanished around the turn in the stairs, Mam ushered Reyan towards the door they had just exited.

Reyan felt a growing panic at the idea that Parr and Sevv had summoned her. "What do you suppose they want?"

Mam paused, her hand on the doorknob. "I wouldn't have the foggiest idea. Do you think they tell me anything?" She twitched her wrist, and the door swung open. Mam didn't step through; instead, she motioned with her eyes that Reyan should enter alone.

Sevv and Parr were sitting next to each other on the far side of a table that divided the large room in half and could easily have sat two dozen others.

Reyan heard the door close and latch behind her. Sevv smiled at her, gesturing for her to sit, but Reyan remained frozen. "Have I done something wrong?"

"Of course not." Sevv smiled. "Please, have a seat."

Reyan looked back and forth between the professors'

faces. She couldn't detect any anger. Sevv seemed a little annoyed, but nothing beyond his normal I-just-ate-something-bitter expression. Reyan stepped forward, cautiously pulling out a chair directly across from the two professors, and lowered herself onto the cushion. With a mixture of comfort and disgust, Reyan noted that the seat was still warm.

The room was large and bright, and light poured in through large windows on the eastern side. The floor planks were a light-colored wood, and timbers two hand-lengths wide held up the exposed ribs of the ceiling. She could smell centuries of dust packed into the cracks and corners, and the scent of turpentine pricked at the back of her nose like tiny needles. It reminded her of her old tree. She felt a pinch in her chest. Though the brightness and the comforting smells warmed the room a bit, the world was in winter, and the air was chilly. She was glad for her robe. "Who were all those people?" she asked. "I heard Mam call one of them 'Partner Minerva.' Was she a member of the Host of Systemic Partners?"

"Indeed," Sevv said.

"When will I become a partner?"

Sevv scoffed, and Parr stared at him reproachfully. "Oh, be serious, Parr," Sevv said. But Parr kept staring until the old man rolled his eyes and gave in.

Parr turned back to Reyan and explained, "When the partner of a faculty dies or retires, the other members of the Host select their replacement. If they decide you're the most Systemic member of your faculty, then you're in."

"What if I don't want to be a partner?"

"Everyone wants to be a partner," Sevv said dismissively.

Reyan fought back the urge to curl her lip at him. "Why?" she asked. "What makes being a partner any different than being a normal professor?" The professors shifted in their seats and exchanged quick glances. "What?" Reyan asked, "Is that some sort of a secret?"

"Not at all," Sevv was quick to answer. "It's just that there is only so much a person can know, Reyankaiya."

Parr must have noticed she was about to argue, because he broke in with a pacifying smile. "I, for instance, know that the sea goes up and down twice a day, but I cannot predict when or by how much. Knowing the tides is not my role. On the other hand, a waterman does not know how to make an audience listen attentively to Systemic Theory for two hours straight."

"Neither does Sevv," Reyan blurted out, instantly wishing she could take it back.

"Aren't you the clever one?" Sevv said stiffly, his voice cold.

Parr bit back a smile. "Sevv certainly knows how, but he doesn't always remember to try."

"Since you asked," Sevv said, "a professor's role is to teach. Whereas the Host of Partners are charged with remembering the truth and keeping the System consistent across generations."

"Someone to keep our garden from going feral and growing beyond its pots," Parr smiled.

A question creased Reyan's brow. "But if you keep a plant in a pot for too long, its roots will become bound. Everything looks fine one day, then the next, the plant just dies. Nothing can be done for it."

"Parr was only making a joke," Sevv said, but there was no amusement in his voice. "Right, Parr?"

Without acknowledging Sevv, Parr said, "Speaking of the Host and their interest in all things wild, they have been discussing what to do with you."

"When your leader, Lyessa, made you a ward of the University, Parr and I became your benefactors," Sevv said. "When we returned to Seal Tooth, the Host calculated a fixed amount of money—a ward's sum—and set it aside for you."

"Your ward's sum is intended to cover room and board and all other normal expenses between now and your eighteenth birthday," Parr said.

"The Host was quite generous," Sevv assured her.

There was a pause, and Reyan felt sure they were waiting for her to say something, though she had no idea what that might be. "Thank you, Professors," she tried.

Sevv winced. "The problem is that you also want to attend the University. Tuition is *not* a normal expense and is not factored into your ward's sum. Generally, a student's family covers the expense, but as a ward, well…," he trailed off to let Reyan fill in the blanks.

Parr broke in. "You will need at least 128 Sterl per month to attend the University. That's with basic food, no new clothes, and no extra set aside for incidentals."

"So, you see, attending the University will eat through your ward's sum very quickly," Sevv said. "And once it is gone, it is gone. At that point, you will no longer have money to pay for school, or anything else for that matter."

"So," Reyan said, "I need to choose between food or school."

"Of course," Parr added, "if you manage to graduate before your ward's sum runs out, and if a faculty accepts you, that faculty will become your family. They will take care of you, and you'll no longer need your ward's sum, or your benefactors, for that matter."

"What happens if I finish, and no faculty wants me?"

"A very astute question," Sevv said. "Sadly, many students—even very promising students—fail out of the University or are not accepted by a faculty. The lucky ones will move to a node and get a role as a keeper. But most disappear into the general population."

All those years, as Reyan had sat alone in her tree trying to imagine her future, the other children were working with their parents. They began their apprenticeship almost the moment they were named. She tried to imagine what it would be like if someone like her had shown up in Orloton and tried to blend in. "I'd be a stranger. I have no skills. No one would ever take me on as an apprentice."

Sevv smiled sympathetically. "Your other option is to give up on your Systemic studies altogether. Your ward's sum will see you through to your eighteenth lived year. As your benefactors, Parr and I would, of course, work to see you apprenticed to any non-faculty trade that would have you. Five years of apprenticing should be enough to see you established. It would be a simple life, but a good one."

She shuddered. *I'll be lucky to get a role cleaning out rancid grease traps at the butcher's or carting manure from the stalls to the fields.* Even if she did eventually rise to become a master, she knew that no trade would fit her. She had never envisioned herself as anything until she'd imagined herself as a professor. "How long do I have to complete my studies before my ward's sum runs out?"

"You'll need to be done with school by your sixteenth birthday," Parr said.

"That only gives me three years."

"Two years and ten months, to be exact," Sevv pointed out. "It isn't much time. Most students start at the University when they have eight or nine named years. Of all your fellow students, you will have the most to learn in the shortest amount of time, and with the least amount of money."

She knew how her mind worked, or rather how it didn't. She knew that—on top of everything else—she would have to work twice as hard just to keep up with the other students.

And she was no keeper's kid. She was entirely new to the University. "Can't I get an extension based on my situation?"

"No," Sevv said, shifting uncomfortably in his seat. "Everyone has some special circumstance or other. If we allowed exceptions for our wards, every child for a hundred miles would be abandoned on our doorstep the moment they were old enough to begin their education."

"What if I found some way to stretch out my ward's sum?"

Parr frowned as he considered the possibility, then nodded. "You are free to attend the University as long as you can pay for tuition."

"But even cutting your meals down to one a day will only buy you a few more months," Sevv pointed out. "And you would suffer terribly for it. As your benefactors, we could not allow such a thing. We've laid your choice out for you. It is yours to make. But decide soon. The Host will be reconvening after lunch, and we owe them an answer."

She wasn't sure what to do. She wanted to think on it. She wanted to start sketching out another decision matrix like she'd done in the dirt at Rowe. But she didn't have anything to write with, and she didn't think she had time. She was certain that if she didn't say yes now, she would lose the opportunity to say yes when she felt ready.

She could see two possible futures in front of her. One where she rolled around her own circuit with her horses in a cozy turtle shell of a home. Where she brought knowledge and ideas and help to the world. Where she was finally admired for who she was and what she had to offer. Then there was another future, one where she groped around in the world for something to be. Just her same old self hiding barefoot and dirty in a tree—all grown up, but still alone.

"I can do it. I want to try."

Parr's smile was gentle and resigned. Something like sorrow settled around his eyes. "I expected nothing less of you."

Sevv's smile twitched. "You have made a hard choice, Reyan. Struggle is a virtue after all and, by the Eye, you *will* struggle. In that way, at least, let us hope your decision proves Systemic." He met her eyes for two heartbeats then said lightly, "After all, there's no real shame in failure." Then, as though reading her fears, he added, "The System will always have use for butchers and stablemen."

CHAPTER TWENTY-SEVEN

From *The Compiled Journals of Partner Lem*
Day 286, Year 1, New Era

The Partners move on to a new town every few days. Eryn is always trying to get us to stay longer in each, but time is short and ignorance is large, so we have our work cut out for us.

Most people don't seem very interested in what we're teaching from the stage, but some appreciate the help we provide after we're done lecturing. If we're lucky, they feed us as payment for services rendered.

This morning we rolled into a mid-sized pop-center. The town center is several blocks of three- and four-story brick buildings clustered around a stream that's still bubbling and bouncing with melt water. In the distance, halfway up the hill that overlooks the town, we can see tight clusters of roofs through the trees.

All day long, the tall backs of thunderclouds piled up on the other side of the nearby mountains. They grumbled threateningly but never rolled down into the valley.

We came upon an empty house west of town. As usual, Eryn rushed in headlong while the rest of us cautiously followed, never sure if we should admire her bravery or chastise her foolishness. Either way, I'm always grateful for her scouting. She has a nose for the luxurious, which means she usually finds us the nicest bed.

In the kitchen, I found a tel and a cradle for a portable AI. I never thought of the once-ubiquitous tech as alive, but now that none of it has power, it all seems especially dead—all quiet and tombstone still.

Harold found a solar array. We climbed to the roof with his bag of tools, and he walked me through the process of by-passing the Systemic control modules and getting the power flowing to the house. And not a moment too soon, because as we descended the ladder, the lightning storm finally burst over the ridge and rushed down on us like a bull escaped from its pen.

Now we're safely indoors. The world raging and flashing outside make the shelter, light, and warm water feel incongruous and strange.

Eryn climbed into a hot bath an hour ago. No one has seen her since.

CHAPTER TWENTY-EIGHT
Day 69, Year 290, New Era

Later that afternoon, Reyan stood over the desk in her room, now dominated by a huge stack of books. The "Welcome to the University at Seal Tooth" pamphlet still sat in the middle of the desk where she'd left it. *Why should I bother? If becoming a professor is hard for a normal person, it will be impossible for me. Believing, even for a moment, that I could complete my studies in three years just proves how incredibly foolish and unprepared I am. It's like Sevv said: trying will just mean suffering.* She longed to hide behind the veil of her tree. She wanted to run her fingers over the sticky scars she had carved in its bark and contemplate the meaning of each. But that was no longer an option. At the very least, she needed to get away from this room and this looming pile of books.

She left the dorm building and stepped out onto the square. It was devoid of people except for a few black-robed professors and students cutting across in hurried diagonals. The paving bricks were glazed and slick as though the gray sky had bent down and licked the world clean.

To the west, everything seemed to grow lighter, as though a forest clearing lay in that direction. She headed toward the light. After a few blocks, the buildings ended abruptly at the edge of an enormous body of gray-green water. Reyan wondered for a moment if this was the same massive lake the caravan had travelled along on the way here. But then the wind shifted, and the smell held her answer. This was the Whulge. Though she had never stood on its shores, she knew of it. Unlike the Wash, the Whulge's water was salty. She had heard he contained fish as big as her leg and boneless eight-armed creatures that moved like smoke. Whales sheltered in his depths.

She walked along the shapestone quay that followed the waterfront. Every fifty yards or so, a massive dock reached out into the water. A hundred yards ahead, a fallen scraper formed a fifty-foot wall of shapestone rubble and twisted metal that reached across the quay and tumbled over the seawall into the water. Stunted trees and bushes ran along the top of the ruin. Seeing that her way was blocked, she turned at the next dock and walked out over the water.

As she moved away from the shore, she peered over the edge of the dock. The rocks and shells and spines along the seafloor disappeared into the deepening murk. She kept expecting to see something moving in the dwindling light between layers of water and slime. Though nothing ever rose to the surface, she couldn't shake the feeling that there was some revelation lying in wait deep in the shadows.

Looking out over the Whulge from the end of the dock, there was nothing left of Seal Tooth in her field of vision, just the gray surface of the water stretching out, perfect and smooth, from where she stood to where the islands rose in the distance. She knew the Whulge continued out past those low strips of islands, past the mountains beyond them, and into the Great Ocean. "He's so…*flat*," she said aloud. A ridiculous observation when what she was trying to say was that standing alone on the seam between Seal Tooth's impossible height and a sheet of water that stretched out to touch every shore in the unknowable world made her feel inadequate and small.

"All water is flat once it finds its level." Kavi's voice behind her made her jump. "I thought that was you standing out here." He grinned. "What brings you to the Whulge on such a gray day?"

"I needed to think, and my room suddenly felt small."

He stood beside her and looked out across the water. "Me too," he agreed, but said nothing more. She wondered if they were thinking the same thoughts.

Low gray clouds came in from the west, and a fine mist swept over everything. The smooth water became fuzzy; the sharp mottled granite of the reflected sky softened into a flat, uniform slate. It was not raining hard. In fact, it was hard to tell it was raining at all; it was more like the air had become wet. Still, Kavi's straw-like hair began flattening, clumping together, and reaching down into his eyes. He slicked back his bangs, shook the wetness from his hand, and gave her a sheepish smile. His eyelashes had grown dark and made his eyes stand out sharp and beautiful.

She began to smile, then felt awkward and tried to force it back down. This made her feel twitchy, like she was not in complete control of her own face. Turning around and leaning against the railing, she looked back toward the bristling crown of scrapers. They reached up into the mist, the tops of the tallest disappearing into the gloom entirely.

Her eyes worked the broad skyline from right to left until she came to the gap left where the one building had tumbled into the sea—its absence like the hollow left by a rotted-out tooth. "What happened there?"

"That's the Fallen," Kavi said, nodding in its direction. "It used to be a scraper like the rest, but it came down during an earthquake a long time ago." Another building, just beyond the heaping mass of the Fallen, was leaning out as though peering over the edge of a cliff. "That next one will come down too at some point. We were always told to stay away from it when I was a kid, but we'd still dare each other to run through its shadow."

She could see the interiors of the nearby scrapers revealed by the broad stripe of missing glass. While those sections of the buildings were free of people, they were not empty. Mounds of greenery spilled out. Rock doves and crows and gulls dove in and out between the floors. "Is that where Seal Tooth keeps its woods?" she joked.

"Sort of. That's the layer forest," Kavi said. "It grows on the lower floors of the scrapers where the glass has been harvested."

"It doesn't look like much of a forest," she said, once again longing for her tree and its siblings.

"It's mostly just brambles and bird droppings. Sometimes you'll come across raccoons or rats. These days, I only go in there during blackberry season."

Her eyes drifted to the top of a nearby building, and she pointed to a small but steady line of steam rising and merging with the clouds. "What's up there?"

"You want to see something you'll never see in the nodes?" Kavi smiled and jerked his head back towards the buildings. "Come on."

They walked down the long dock back toward the wall of scrapers. "So what do you think of Seal Tooth so far?" Kavi asked. "Pretty amazing, right?"

"It seems like most of the amazing bits are from before the Calming," Reyan said, nodding towards the Fallen. "And even those seem fragile."

They followed the street for a few blocks as it made its way between the buildings. "Well sure," Kavi agreed, "everything falls eventually. But what about everything that breathes life into these old ruins?" He jerked open a topaz-tarnished door with smoke-colored glass panels. "You can't see the ideas, the order, the *System*. That's why the Author brought about the Calming and named the first Host of Partners. They wanted humanity to infuse all these technical marvels with life.

And soon, I'll get to be a part of that grand plan. So will you."
He gave her an encouraging smile.

The only light in the lobby spilled in through the glass
sections of the doors behind them. It reminded Reyan of a
cave, and Kavi was leading her deeper inside. Just as she was
beginning to feel anxious in the dwindling light, Kavi reached
out and opened a door. Light spilled in from the other side,
and she could see a flight of metal stairs leading up. "You
ready for a climb?"

Reyan entered the stairwell, leaned over the metal railing,
and looked up. What she saw was daunting. A corkscrew of
stairs tapered off into the distance. A blindingly bright light
awaited them at the top. Her eyes adjusted, and she saw that it
was nothing more than a large window looking up into the dull
gray sky.

"The University, the faculties, and the professors have
done so much for the world," Kavi said, struggling to keep
talking as they climbed. "They've maintained stability in Seal
Tooth and the nodes for as long as anyone can remember.
They've spread so much knowledge, and they help keep trade
running smoothly."

Reyan knew that Rolf had done those things, but it had
never occurred to her that the professors had as well. But that
shouldn't surprise her. Kavi knew so much more than her. He
was older, had travelled more, and had even graduated from
the University.

Seven floors up, they passed a metal door that stood a
few inches open. Though she couldn't see past the crack, she

could smell the damp green funk of the layer forest beyond.

Soon, they began to hear the beat of heavy steps descending the stairs. On floor eighteen, a woman came around a bend and continued down toward them. Reyan was sucking wind and Kavi was red in the face, so they stepped aside and let the woman pass while they caught their breath. The woman wore thick work clothes covered with patches of drying dirt and carried a bulging cloth sack on her back. She passed them without a word or sideways glance.

Once Kavi caught his breath, he said, "Now you know why folks only live on the first few floors. Could you imagine lugging water up and down these stairs every day, or trying to harvest the glass from the top floors of this scraper?"

"Why would anyone ever come up here at all?"

Kavi grinned and wiped the sweat from his cheek with the back of his hand and continued climbing.

After a few more revolutions, Kavi huffed, "Here we are," and shouldered open a door. They walked out onto the scraper's roof, which was covered with row after row of boxes overflowing with plants.

"It's a farm," Reyan marveled.

"We could grow our food outside of town where there are fields, but if you think the slog up those stairs was bad, try getting out to where the soil's decent. It would take all day. And at ground level there's all sorts of critters to deal with. Not a lot of field mice or rabbits or even bugs at the top of a scraper. Then there's the bandits."

"There are bandits?"

"Sure there are. There are always bandits outside of the pop-center."

"We didn't come across any on our way here."

"Of course not," he said, laughing. "We were in a professor's caravan. We have the Eye's protection." He pointed up through the clouds. "And even without the Eye, no one harasses professors. Once you have a karaband or two, folks treat you like you have the scab or something."

"What do they grow up here?"

"This time of year, most of the farms are fallow since the summer crop has been harvested. But here they're growing kale and some broccoli, which we can keep in the ground through most of the winter."

There was a large steaming vat in one corner. A sour smell settled in her mouth like old saliva. Kavi saw the look on her face. "That's another reason we farm up here; it keeps the whole town from stinking."

"Why does it smell so bad?"

A figure stepped out from a shed on the other side of the roof. Her movements were stiff and thick and deliberate, and she looked very much like the woman who had passed them on the stairs. Kavi shrugged, "Let's ask her." He beckoned the woman over. "My friend wants to know what smells so bad."

The woman sniffed and wiped her nose on the back of her rough sleeve before plodding over to them. "It's not for me to know or to say, young professors. Knowing's for the faculties."

"There's a faculty for fertilizer?" Reyan asked.

"No, but there's probably someone in the agricultural faculty who makes sure the fertilizer comes out right."

"I've been on farms. I've smelled plenty of fertilizer. That's something else."

The gardener looked at Reyan then at Kavi. She appeared to be choosing her words. "It's *waste*, young professors," she finally said. "It is the Departed; the Yet-named." The understanding turned sour in Reyan's stomach. She plugged her nose to keep away the smell. The woman looked at Reyan contemptuously. "Not everyone in the pop-center can afford a bit of ground to be buried in. Ground is for growing."

"What about professors?" Reyan asked Kavi.

He became uncomfortable. "Members of the faculties get plots."

"And everyone else ends up here?" The sour smell slid down her throat and landed in her stomach. "That can't be right."

The woman shrugged. "Right and wrong is also a faculty concern. I lend the System my back and my legs. I lug whatever they give me up here. I dump it into that stinking vat and stir it when they tell me it's time. When it finally stops reeking and turns to dirt, I plant seeds. Later, I harvest the food and lug it back down the stairs." The gardener nodded her head. She said, "Good day, Professors" rather stiffly and returned to whatever she was doing by the shed.

When the woman was out of earshot, Kavi put a hand on Reyan's forearm, gave a quick gentle squeeze, and pulled it away before she had time to react. "Don't worry, Reyan. That's not how we'll end up." He didn't say whether he meant the putrefying vat or the woman stirring the slurry. Perhaps he meant both. Kavi could afford the guilty discomfort of his good fortune. His faculty role was already waiting for him. But it was far too easy for Reyan to imagine a thick-limbed, stiff-backed life for herself, numbly marching up and down a scraper, inhaling that stench, then, someday, *becoming* it.

"It just doesn't feel right," Reyan said. "It doesn't feel *decent.*"

"It's not about decency. It's about the System. It's about the Governing Assert. No one was murdered to feed that vat. But once someone is no longer alive, their needs aren't considered in the matrices. All that matters is the final gift they can give the rest of us."

"That sounds like Erynite nonsense," she said, her laugh flat and forced.

A dangling bit of cloud rushed in and enveloped the top of the scraper. She looked down the rows of kale, the stark black bunches fading into the distance until they were indistinguishable from the ubiquitous gray. The specks of floating mist became heavy thick drops that ticked as they splashed down on the leaves, sheets of metal, and the shapestone paving tiles. "I want to get out of the rain," Reyan said. "And away from the smell."

They headed back down the stairwell. When they came to the second landing, Kavi stopped and put his hand on the handle of a metal door. "There's still something I want you to see." He pressed the handle and shouldered the door open.

The space was entirely empty. The outside walls were made of glass that stretched from floor to ceiling. Kavi walked up and stood with his toes touching the wall of windows. He waved her over. "Come here."

She was flustered and agitated and didn't want to see whatever Kavi wanted to show her. But what good was it to be mad at Kavi? None of this was his doing. At least not yet. She let her curiosity lead her to the window.

A few blocks away, Seal Tooth ended, the world flattened out, and the Whulge filled up the view. "Look," he said, pointing, "there's where we were just a few minutes ago." Beyond the roof of the intervening buildings, the dock they'd been standing on was one of several reaching out into the water like the fingers of an enormous hand opened west toward the distant islands.

"There are high mountains over there," Kavi said. "On a clear day they're white and beautiful." He frowned. "But today, they're hidden behind the clouds."

She leaned her head against the glass and tried to look down as straight as she could. The unreality of the vast world below her and the all-too-real woman stirring a vat above her made her mind slosh loosely within her skull. Her toes and fingers began to tingle as though they'd fallen asleep, and a chill climbed her back. "I don't think I should be here," she said.

"Step away from the glass. You'll feel better."

She backed away. It didn't make her feel any better, but at least she wouldn't have to explain what she had really meant. She would never be able to adequately serve the System. Being a good professor would require her to make decisions she wasn't sure she could make. A thought came to her with a mixture of sorrow and relief. There was no real way she could graduate before her ward's sum was gone. So she would never actually have to make those sorts of decisions.

More clouds rolled in, and everything became a flat uniform gray, like the world outside was held in a jar of smoke. A low whistling moan rose from the shafts in the center of the building, and the rain sounded like pebbles being tossed against the window. The wind pushed the rain across the glass, and the drops grew tails. They shimmied and jumped in unison. Reyan picked a drop and followed it with her finger as it jerked its way down the window. When her exhaled breath fogged the glass, she could see the jagged path the drop had taken.

She wondered if it was too late to go back and tell Sevv and Parr she had changed her mind. They had offered to apprentice her to someone. An average role within a normal trade would be miserable, but it would keep her from ending up like that woman upstairs.

"I always imagine they're alive," Kavi said, watching her watch the drops. "Like they're tadpoles wiggling down a stream or like a flock of swarming birds."

"They can't be alive," Reyan said. "All these drops, all going in the same direction. If they were alive, at least one of them would be going *up* the glass."

The wind shifted direction. It pushed away the clouds, and the town reappeared. They walked across the room and found themselves looking toward the University. The buildings in that direction grew shorter each block, like a giant staircase, until they flattened out around the enormous nest-shaped arena on the other side of the University. "There's the dormitory and the cafeteria," Kavi said. "Over there to the left are the stables. And those are buildings A and B. That's where classes are held. The top of Building B is where the library is."

"What are those?" Reyan asked, pointing. "Down there on top of the library." Kavi followed her finger. All the roofs they could see had similar structures—doors that led to stairways, raised vegetable beds, railings—but the roof of the library had an unusual walled-off area near its center. Several black rectangles stood in the middle, hidden from view.

"Those are *tech*." He was grinning. "Let's go check them out." Reyan thought she should be getting back to studying. But she had to admit that Kavi's enthusiasm was contagious.

They made their way down the long stairwell to the street, then walked the few blocks to Building B. There, they climbed another, much shorter stairwell and exited onto the roof.

In the middle of the roof was the large cube of gray shapestone bricks they'd seen from the scraper. They walked around it looking for a door, but the walls were blank and too tall and smooth to climb.

On the corner of the roof, they found an old, concave sheet of scrap metal filled with soggy lumps of charred wood. Someone had arranged a few wooden crates around this make-shift fire pit, and the area was littered with old bottles half-full of green or yellow rainwater. They gathered the crates and stacked them next to the walled-off area. The crates reached about halfway up the wall, and Kavi pulled himself up the rest of the way. He lay across the top of the wall, his legs kicking in the air over Reyan's head.

"Hey. One second," he said. He swung his legs over so he was sitting on top of the wall, then stood. He walked around to the other side, his arms spread wide for balance, then reached down and started hauling up a ladder from inside. He balanced it atop the wall, turned it around, and tipped it down to her. She settled the ladder's feet against the roof, checked to make sure it was stable, then scrambled up to join him.

Inside the wall were eight flat black rectangles, each large enough that Reyan could lay across it and still have a few inches to spare. She could tell by the way the furthest ones mirrored the sky that they were covered by sheets of glass. But the ones nearest to her, the ones she could look at directly, were as black and blank as holes cut into the fabric of the world.

"See? Tech. Just like I thought."

She stared down into the uncanny blackness. "Thinktech?"

"Not really. I mean, there used to be a bit of thinktech in *everything*, but these are solar panels."

"Like the ones Partner Harold taught Partner Lem how to fix?"

Kavi nodded. "They pull power from the sun, sort of like how a waterwheel uses water to turn a crank."

"I don't see anything like a waterwheel moving," Reyan said.

"They're probably long dead," Kavi agreed.

"What do you suppose they powered?"

"Could be anything. These sorts of things used to be everywhere, but most were scavenged a long time ago for glass and metals. I bet the only reason these are still here is that they were hidden behind this wall." He pointed. "Look there. All the wires enter that metal box, but no wires leave. That means they punch through the roof there."

Reyan perked up with curious excitement. "Let's figure out where they go."

Reyan and Kavi took the stairs down one flight to the library's top floor. They followed a walkway that ran around the building's interior rooms. The wall on their left opened toward the windows. On the right stood a line of doors.

"The box with all the wires going into it was near the middle of the building, so it must come into one of these rooms," Kavi said. All the doors were unlocked, and each led to a nearly identical room with a bookshelf, a desk, and a giant slate.

"What are these rooms?" Reyan asked.

"They're the Partners' offices."

"And you can just walk in whenever you want?"

"We don't lock doors at the University. Locks are for privacy. Privacy is for secrecy. Secrecy is only needed when there is something to hide."

"Whose office is this one? There's no name on the door, and it's locked."

Kavi frowned and came over. He tried the handle, then nudged the door with his shoulder to see if he could budge it. When he couldn't, he shrugged. "Don't know." He tried the next door, which also had no name but opened easily. "Hey! Look there." He pointed to the back of the room, where a pipe came down through the ceiling and entered a large metal box. "That's where the wires come through." The box had a large brass lock on it. "Well," he said, "we're not going to see what's in there today."

"Where do the wires go from there?"

Kavi shrugged. "Everywhere. They go through the walls until they reach an outlet. This is where tech used to draw whatever power it needed." He tapped his foot against a plastic plate on the wall with two clusters of holes that looked like tiny, startled faces.

"What do we do now?"

"About what?"

"The solar panels, the wires. Figuring out why the room next door is locked."

"We don't do anything."

"Shouldn't we tell someone?"

Kavi grew serious. "No. They would probably just scavenge everything as soon as our backs were turned."

"So this stuff is rare? Is it valuable?"

"The wires? Not very. But the panels on the roof are the first ones I've ever seen intact."

An idea occurred to Reyan. "What if *we* scavenged them? Come back soon with some tools. If you could get them working again, we could sell them to someone." She paused, shame warming her cheeks before she looked up at him.

"Sure. Even if we just stripped them down for materials, they would be worth quite a bit."

"What's quite a bit?"

"I don't know." He stared at the wall and blinked as he ran the calculations. "Couple thousand Sterl?"

That would buy her almost two more years of tuition. With that much time, she might be able to make it all the way through the University. Maybe she wouldn't have to spend the rest of her life lugging shit—or worse—up and down a scraper.

The thought of the stinking fertilizer gave her pause. It would not be the last thing about being a professor she would find upsetting. But if she ever wanted to change those sorts of things, if she ever wanted to fit into the world, if she ever wanted to be happy, she needed to graduate and become a professor.

She decided her future once again. This time she spoke the promise silently to herself, free from the pressure of her benefactors' impatience. Then, in her mind, she carved the symbols of her resolve into the bark of her tree.

Now it was real.

CHAPTER TWENTY-NINE
Day 70, Year 290, New Era

Reyan implored herself to sleep.

In the flat blackness behind her eyes, her mind flailed and convulsed like a trapped thing. She would never find her place here in Seal Tooth. In most of her imagined futures, she was sixteen, half-educated, unnoviced, without faculty or family, hauling shit to the top of a scraper. In other moments, she imagined the Host exiling her to a node far away from the University.

After a while, she gave up on sleep and did the only practical thing she could think to do: she lit her desk lamp and began her required reading.

Classes started in three days. She had a lot to get through.

She was trying to concentrate on a book called *Basic*

Systemic Structure and Social Architecture. There didn't seem to be anything particularly difficult about the ideas in the book, but that made Reyan's anxiety even worse. By her estimation, every paragraph in a book should present at least one novel idea. This book had eighty-seven pages, with an average of seven paragraphs per page. But she was struggling to cobble together the six hundred or so bits of insight she believed the book must contain but that she was too stupid to recognize.

Twenty-four pages in, the oil in her lamp needed to be refilled.

Sixty-seven pages in, the blackened square of her window began to lighten toward gray.

When the dawn rendered her lantern useless, her eyes slid past the book's final word. She set the book aside, her mind sluggish and finally ready for sleep. But then she heard the starlings outside and low voices and footfalls in the hallway and understood it was too late. She blew out her lantern, put on her boots, and headed down to the cafeteria.

"You're looking a bit rough, Reyan," Fang said, smiling around a mouthful of food.

She wasn't sure what the boy meant or what to do about it. It couldn't be her clothes. She was wearing the exact same brown robe Mam had given her to meet the professors the day before. If it was good enough for them, it should be good enough for breakfast with a couple of novices.

"Cut her some slack," Eddie said. "Don't you remember what that was like? New town, new people, no parents to tell you when to go to bed or wake up?"

"Or to brush your hair," Edward added, laughing.

Her hair shouldn't need brushing at all; that's what the braids were for. And besides, she had barely spent any time in bed, so yesterday's braids should still be holding together. Mostly.

"Hey Fang," Kavi said cheerfully, "Did I show you this?" Kavi was holding something down below the line of the table. When Fang looked down, Kavi punched him hard on the arm. The other boys all chuckled as Fang rubbed the spot Kavi had hit. Reyan was alarmed to see an act of violence displayed so openly.

"So," Edward said, as though no one had just gotten punched at the breakfast table, "Tomorrow's graduation. In less than a day, we'll join our faculties."

"We'll be actual professors," Fang said.

"Finally, no more white stripes," Eddie said, a smile on his usually solemn face.

"That's right," Edward said thoughtfully. "No more white stripes for us. But I bet you'll still have one of these," he said, once again showing Eddie something underneath the table.

Eddie sighed and winced. He flinched right before Edward punched him in the arm. Reyan was completely baffled. Maybe the prohibition against violence didn't apply to professors and students. Edward smiled cruelly and cried, "Two for flinching!" before punching Eddie two more times in the same arm.

Reyan's exhausted mind fell into a confused panic. Was this a game? What were the rules? "What does Edward have? Why do you keep hitting each other?"

Fang, who was sitting next to her, said, "You get to hit anyone if you have one of these." She looked down to where Fang's hand was sitting in his lap. It was empty. He was holding together his thumb and forefinger to make a ring. When she looked back up with a question on her lips, Fang punched her in the arm and laughed.

Reyan instantly and reflexively punched back. Her fist landed firmly on Fang's cheek, and he fell to the floor, wide-eyed with surprise. Before she knew it, she was on her feet, trembling, stiff-jawed, and breathing hard. Her hands were balled up into fists at her sides. Fang was on his feet as well. Anger and confusion stormed across his face. "What the hell, nodie?" He lunged at her, but Kavi threw an arm across his chest and held him back.

Eddie looked worried, but Edward started laughing. When Fang heard him, he joined in the laughter and flopped back down in his seat, but a hard darkness lingered in his eyes.

Just as Reyan began to loosen her fists, someone grabbed her by the elbow and spun her around. It was Mam. She looked bewildered and angry. Her eyes never left Reyan, but she said flatly, "Boys."

"Mam," they all mumbled in reply.

"Ms. Estermet, you'll be coming with me. Professor Sevv would like to see you."

"Ooooh," Eddie teased.

"You be quiet," Mam snapped. Mam turned Reyan to the door, guiding the nervous girl toward the exit.

Once they were outside. Mam stopped and turned Reyan to face her. She let go of her arm and looked back toward the cafeteria. When she was certain no one was listening, she said, "You cannot do things like that, Reyan. You cannot just punch another student in the face, right there in front of everyone."

"But they were doing it. And Fang hit me first."

"They were just playing one of their silly games. I realize you are fresh from the nodes, but you will need to learn the difference. You need to watch yourself more than anyone here, or you will not last long."

"Are you taking me some place to punish me?"

"Worse than that, I'm afraid," Mam said, smiling. "Sevv asked to see you."

"What for?"

"I couldn't say." Mam placed a guiding hand on Reyan's back. "But come along now. Professor Sevv does not like to be kept waiting."

The morning was flat and gray as though layer upon layer of cobwebs had been spun between the world, the sky, and the far-distant Eye. No sharp sun stabbed down into her weary eyes—just a uniform throbbing brightness that seemed to pound at them from all sides.

Mam walked her to Building B, through the lobby, and gestured to the door that led to the stairwell. "Here you are. Up there, twelfth floor. You'll find Professor Sevv in the west reading nook."

"You're not coming with me?"

"Why in the world would I do that? Twelve flights up. Head south, and you'll find him." Mam reached out to Reyan's head, trying to smooth down some of the errant hairs before giving up with a resigned sigh. The old woman's stern expression softened. "It will be alright, dear. Don't let that old heron of a man scare you. And besides, I don't think it's that sort of a meeting."

After huffing her way up twelve flights of booming stairs, Reyan walked into the library. Unlike most of this floor, this space was open. Six reading tables were arranged near the floor-to-ceiling windows that overlooked the Whulge so readers could take advantage of the light and the remarkable view. The bookshelves rose like hills on either side of the tables. The stacks had been arranged perpendicular to the windows so that daylight could make its way to the middle of the building. Had they not been, she doubted a speck of light could make it past the second row.

Sevv sat at the reading table closest to the window, his back to the glass so the light would fall on the large volume opened before him. The page he was reading was covered

edge-to-edge with a brightly colored map. A young man in a
brown robe approached the table and presented the old
professor with another book. Sevv held it at arm's length, then
looked at its spine. He nodded to the young man and placed
the volume on top of a stack of small books that stood near his
left elbow.

When the librarian left, Sevv's eyes drifted up from his
studies, and he saw Reyan standing at a distance, hesitating.
"Reyan," he said, closing the book. "It's good to see you." As
she approached, he stacked the pile of smaller books on top of
it, stood, and handed the pile to Reyan to carry. "Come with
me to my office."

He led her back to the walkway that belted the building's
inner offices. She recognized the area as the same one she and
Kavi had walked through the night before as they searched for
where the wires entered the building from the roof. As she
passed the two doors without name placards, she fought the
urge to reach out and test the handle of the door that had been
locked.

A few doors past the locked room, Sevv turned and
opened an office with his name affixed to the door. Inside
were the same bookshelves, desk, and slate board she and Kavi
had seen in all the offices. Unlike the others, however, Sevv's
room had no decoration.

He took the stack of books from her and placed them on
the chair, which he pushed under the desk. Sevv, whose years
of professing had put him in the habit of walking while he
spoke, remained standing. It felt to Reyan like he was looming.

"I have been thinking on your situation, Reyan. I imagine the University and all of Seal Tooth must feel very strange."

The whole world *is strange to me.*

"And you've come to this new place with a very ambitious goal and very limited means to achieve it," he said. "You must be feeling a frightful amount of pressure."

Every point Sevv made felt like another miserable gust in her personal headwinds. She was about to confess to her recent violence and start begging for forgiveness, but chose instead to say, "I can handle it."

"I'm sure that's true. You are a very bright girl. You might be clever enough to get by." She considered mentioning the solar panels she and Kavi were going to scavenge for money but thought better of it. He might think scavenging was somehow cheating. Sevv continued.

"But you have no real understanding of the System," he said, "let alone the cultural life of a place so far from your node. How could you be expected to know how to behave?"

How has he already heard about the fight with Fang? she thought in a panic.

"What I mean to say," Sevv explained, "is that soon, you will be flooded with new ideas. And ideas can be perilous things. It is hard to know how they will land with someone, and it can be nearly impossible to change them once they have. Given the…," he cleared his throat, "*nature* of your upbringing."

"In Orloton?" she guessed.

"In Orloton, yes," he said, frowning. "And as a ward. Given all of that, and given that correcting misconceptions can prove difficult, would it not be better to ensure that you correctly understand these new notions from the start?"

"That makes sense," she agreed. But she sensed a snare's tension in Sevv's carefully constructed reasoning.

"As your benefactor, it is my role and responsibility to guide your Systemic growth. As such, I've decided I will tutor you." He waited for her reaction.

Reyan did not know how to feel. The offer was generous and should not have been a surprise coming from her benefactor—Rolf would have done as much—but there was something about the idea she didn't like. It might be a test of some sort. She worried that, if she accepted his help, it would somehow prove she was incapable of following the System on her own. Also, if she were being honest, she had no desire to spend any more time with this stiff, loquacious old man than was absolutely necessary.

While Reyan considered how to respond, Sevv continued: "I could help hone your fledgling skills in methods and processes. And, of course, I would be around to answer any tricky theoretical questions or correct any philosophical misgivings that might arise."

As she listened to him speak, Reyan dug down to the root of her hesitation. It was shame. She knew she would have to struggle to succeed at the University. She had prepared herself for it. But she had planned to do it alone in her room, hidden from scrutiny. Sevv would hold up her struggles as a sort of Systemic ideal. He would draw attention to her inadequacies. Everyone would see who she really was. Her life in Seal Tooth would become a newer, larger version of her old life back in Orloton.

She realized Sevv was still talking. "After all, if malformed ideas take root in a professor, we risk inoculating year upon year of future students and people on our circuits with whatever those misguided notions might be."

Getting through the University in under three years would require all the help Reyan could get. And, despite his dry manner and love of his own voice, Reyan understood that Sevv was a wise and skilled professor who was putting himself at her disposal. How could she refuse? And hadn't Parr said that the hard way was not *always* the most Systemic? But there was still a feeling like an unreachable itch between her shoulder blades. She couldn't quite bring herself to say yes.

Her hesitation was beginning to annoy Sevv. "While you're thinking on my offer, I wanted to bring something else to your attention." He pursed his thin lips. "Parr didn't tell you this yesterday because he feared it would further burden your already over-taxed mind. But I believe the sooner you know the better." The old professor began to pace the room like he was patrolling a caravan's stage. "There is nothing particularly unusual about being a nodie or even a ward. Seal Tooth does have both. That said, we don't put everyone through the University." His eyes hardened. "That sort of support is a privilege you must earn."

Reyan snapped to attention. "How do I earn it?"

Sevv smiled. "Before they approved our proposal for your ward's sum, the Host insisted that you must pass a test to determine your aptitude and suitability for professorship. We don't want to spend your ward's sum frivolously."

"Where's the test?" Reyan said, her whole self leaning aggressively into this new challenge. "I'll take it."

"Slow down, Reyan," Sevv chuckled. "There is more to it than that. You see, the exam is issued when a prospective student turns thirteen."

"I'm already thirteen."

"Indeed. But if you took the test now, you would surely fail." He paused long enough for her to consider all the ways she might fail. Just as doubt began to darken her mind, Sevv said, "Lucky for you, I have convinced the Host to grant you a reprieve. Provided you show progress in your studies and appear to be integrating well into university life, they have agreed to delay your test for six months." She flexed her hand and felt the dull ache where she had punched Fang in the face. She wondered if a lunchroom brawl counted as "integrating well into university life." Sevv smiled. "I've assured them that six months under my tutelage would be more than enough to tame even the wildest of wards."

Perhaps he's misplaced his faith. She swallowed the hot coals of her fear. "What will you test me on?"

"I cannot tell you the specifics since that would give you

an unfair advantage. But the test will focus on Systemic knowledge and theory and general aptitude. So you must study hard and pay attention to what I tell you." He paused. "If you accept my offer to be your tutor, that is."

Reyan nodded her head cautiously.

"Wonderful. We'll meet here in my office once per week. How does Friday after dinner sound?" Reyan nodded again.

"Good." His smile was thin and tight. "This way I can keep an eye on you."

"Why would you need to keep an eye on me?"

"It's just a figure of speech, Reyan. I'm sure you must have heard it often back in Orloton."

Sevv picked the books up off his chair and placed them on his desk. He sat down and uncovered the large book of maps he'd been reviewing in the reading room. "Oh, and one other thing," he said, looking up at her. "You mustn't tell anyone about the exam. Your peers won't be happy to learn you got an extension. So, for your own sake, keep it to yourself. Because I will be your closest observer, I will issue the test and decide whether you pass."

Reyan nodded. As she was turning to the door, Sevv spoke again, "And a word of advice about Professor Parr. I believe he has taken a liking to you. It is a good thing to have a professor looking out for you. But Parr has taken other promising students under his wing who did not fare well in the end. But don't worry," he said, trapping her in the ominous blue pools of his eyes, "You'll always have me."

He opened the book of maps and began tracing rivers and trails and ridge lines with a knobby-knuckled finger. Reyan recognized a dismissal when she saw one. She mumbled, "Thank you, Professor," and she slipped out into the hallway and headed toward the stairs.

When she got to the nameless door, she stopped and looked behind her to make sure no one was there. She checked the handle. Locked. She thought she caught a glimpse of a blue glow rapidly fading into the gap beneath the door. Few things ever glowed blue. She'd heard of blue flames at night in the swamp, and she'd seen some old tech burn blue in a fire, but that was all. She got down on her hands and knees and looked under the crack. She swept her hand under the door and stretched her fingers uselessly into the dark in the ridiculous hope that she might find something to grab hold of—perhaps a key sitting helpfully on the floor just inside.

"Is that you, Ms. Estermet?"

Reyan was on her feet before she even recognized Parr's voice. "Professor," she said.

"What are you doing?"

"Nothing. I thought I saw something is all." She bit her lip to stay her rising panic and kept her eyes focused on the floor where she had just been crawling.

"And now you realize you did not?"

"Well, I…"

"You were looking under the crack," he said. "Did you see anything in there?"

"No. It was dark."

"Of course it was. Good day, Reyan."

He was about to walk past her when she said, "Professor, Kavi told me that nothing is ever locked at the University."

"And that is true. Except, of course, for locked things."

"But why is it locked?"

"Because the best way to ensure that a curious young lady finds one particular room out of all the thousands of rooms on the University is to lock its door," he said.

Her eyes grew wide. "Why? What's in there?"

"If I told you that, the locked door wouldn't be of much use." He smiled. "I shouldn't tease you. It's nothing very interesting; just a storage closet full of memorabilia. Shouldn't you be at breakfast?"

"Professor Sevv called for me. He's offered to tutor me."

"Did he?" He raised his eyebrows. "How magnanimous."

Parr was right; Sevv was being very generous. He was offering to educate and civilize her. And she was repaying his good faith by crawling about on the dirty floor not thirty feet from his office, peeking beneath doors that were not hers to open.

CHAPTER THIRTY
Day 71, Year 290, New Era

Reyan decided she had to make the most of Sevv's generosity. The next morning, she was up early pouring over her books with renewed fervor. Classes started in two days, and she still had two more massive books to get through. One of her braids had completely unraveled, and she was twisting the strands around a finger while she read. She decided that changing clothes was time wasted, so she was still sleeping and going about in the same brown robe Mam had given her a few days before.

There was a knock on the door. When Reyan opened it, she found Mam. The matron invited herself in and looked around the room. "I heard you were not at breakfast this morning."

"I wasn't hungry."

"They missed you at dinner last night as well."

"I was busy."

"I see," Mam said, slowly over-pronouncing the words. "Here, eat this." She reached into a large pocket on the front of her dress and retrieved a wad of napkin, which she handed to Reyan.

Reyan unwrapped the bundle and found two biscuits. They were still warm, cracked in half and covered with butter and blackberry jam.

Reyan had not lied. In all her worry and distraction, she did not believe she was hungry. She began to fold the napkin back over the top of the biscuits when Mam lightly coughed. "While I watch," she insisted, expressionless eyes fixed on Reyan.

Reyan broke a half-bite from one of the biscuits and put it in her mouth. As soon as it had gone moist on her tongue, a hole seemed to open in her stomach, and she instantly panicked for want of food. Her next bite was far less dainty than the first. It filled her mouth and dropped crumbs onto the opened napkin. Mam's thin lips smiled. She turned to the sink and filled Reyan's glass and held it out to her. Reyan drained the glass in a single draught, then looked for a place to put down the empty glass. Mam held out a trembling hand and took it from her, placing it back down next to the sink.

While Reyan stuffed more food into her mouth, Mam walked slowly around the room. "You need to eat, Reyan." Reyan's mouth was full of crumbs and butter and sweet jam, and she was in no position to respond. "And you need to sleep. You have an opportunity that few will ever have. It is important that you keep your mind sharp and your body healthy if you want to do well at the University. You no longer have your parents to tell you when to eat or rise or," she looked Reyan up and down, "bathe. All these things are as much part of your education as whatever you're learning from that pile of books."

When Reyan had finished the biscuits, Mam stood before her, extending her hand. Reyan looked at her hand and the napkin. She handed the napkin over, but not before folding it in half, throwing back her head, and funneling the remaining crumbs into her mouth. Without a word, the matron folded the napkin twice and returned it to her pocket. She then fixed her eyes on the desk chair, walked over to it, and turned it around. "Come on," she said, inclining her head to the empty chair. The matron's tone made it clear that compliance was Reyan's only option.

She walked across the room and sat in the chair. A towel hung unused on a bar next to the sink. Mam draped this over Reyan's shoulders and tightened it around her neck, holding it in place with a clip she must have pulled from one of the other pockets in her dress.

Mam stood behind Reyan, and their eyes met in the mirror over the sink. She began to undo what remained of the girl's loose braid. She came around to stand before Reyan and pinched the girl's chin firmly but gently between her thumb and the knuckle of her forefinger. She lifted Reyan's face so she could look in her eyes. She turned it left and right. "Who has done this to your hair, child?"

"I cut it myself."

"Did you now? With a knife? While angry? In the dark?"

It had been midday. But aside from that, Mam had been spot-on. Lyessa—inspired by a burst of near-parental concern or disgust—had tried to tame Reyan's hair. She'd jerked the comb through Reyan's tangles, and whenever the girl had cried out, Lyessa told her to keep quiet, and mumbled things like, "If you'd put a comb through this yourself from time to time…" The first few times Reyan had tried to stand, Lyessa had pressed her back down into the chair. Finally, with her haircut barely started, Reyan had twisted in her seat and wrenched her shoulders free.

She ran out the front door, down the road, and climbed into her tree. There, she gathered clumps of hair into her fists and—with the same knife she used to carve words and symbols into the bark—sawed through it like she was cutting ropes.

Lyessa never tried to cut her hair again, and Reyan just let it grow how it would. Sometimes, when it got tangled or fell in her eyes, she would grab a handful of the offending locks and hack her way through. And so it had been until Avalina had taught her how to do a simple braid. She'd still not taken to the comb.

"Well, I can't have you going around Seal Tooth looking like you have the mange," Mam said. "Let's see what we can do with scissors, some daylight, and a little less aggression."

Mam pulled a comb from one of her pockets and ran it

under the faucet to wet it. She started near the ends of Reyan's hair and tried to pass the damp comb through. Whenever it snagged, she would pinch that strand of hair firmly between two fingers just above the tangle so she could pick at the knot without jerking painfully at Reyan's hair. If this didn't work, and if Reyan gasped from the pain, Mam would painstakingly pick out the knot with her fingernails.

It took Mam at least ten minutes to work her way around the girl's head. Neither of them spoke. The only sounds were the trickle of the running faucet, the tick-tick-tick of the comb's teeth picking at knots, and Mam's heavy nasal breathing as she worked.

Once Mam had teased out the ends of Reyan's hair, she came back around and started the process over again four inches higher. Reyan groaned. "Are we almost done?"

"You're not half done, and that's just with the combing out."

"Then I'm finished." Reyan stood up. "I have more reading to do before classes start."

Mam shook her head. "Give it a rest, dear."

"I don't have time. I *need* to read."

"You *need* to have a seat and let me finish." Mam didn't look mad exactly, but neither did she look interested in discussing the matter. Kavi had told her that the one unwritten rule was to do what Mam told you. When Mam's face went expressionless and flat, Reyan knew she didn't want to learn why that rule existed.

Reyan slowly lowered herself back into the seat. Mam's tone instantly became light and conversational, as though nothing noteworthy had happened. "Partner Thomas used to trim his own hair. He said it helped him return to himself." Reyan wasn't sure she even knew who Partner Thomas was. She'd heard the name in passing, but she didn't know his story or why anyone would find his grooming habits interesting. "It says so in *The Lives of the Systemic Partners*. Of course, Thomas lived alone, so he didn't have much of a choice. Not until Eryn came to stay with him."

Mam rewet the comb. Starting at the crown of Reyan's head, she slowly pulled the comb down through the jagged ends of her hair. The comb's teeth ran along the girl's scalp and felt like a line of ants marching from the top of her head down her neck. When a wave of shivers passed, Reyan asked, "What do you know about Eryn?"

"Not as much as I'd like to. She seems important, like someone we should all want to know more about. But the professors and Partners don't seem to ask many questions about her." Mam paused. "Or respond very warmly when others ask. It's sad how such an important woman could just vanish."

Mam stood before her, pleased. She once again took Reyan's chin in her hand and guided her head around to have a look in the mirror. She dropped the comb into her dress pocket and from the same pocket pulled out a large pair of brass scissors. The sight of them made Reyan's neck and back tighten. "It's just a pair of scissors, dear."

Reyan slammed her eyes shut and screwed up her face like a baby seated before bitter greens. But she didn't argue. She didn't fight. She didn't try to leave.

The scissor blades hissed as they slid open and closed. She imagined she could feel a tiny pop as they severed each hair. Everything about this seemed like it should hurt. When the first cut was over, and it hadn't, Reyan relaxed her face a little bit.

After a few more snips and several more passes of the comb through her hair, Mam asked casually, "So, Reyan. How did you end up here? You just hop on the back of the professors' trucks?"

"No."

"Kidnapped then?" She chuckled and snipped.

"No."

"So, it's going to be twenty questions, is it?" Mam smiled at her through the mirror and patted her shoulder. "You don't need to tell me anything you don't want to, dear. I was just curious how a young wild-haired girl from the nodes wound up in my dormitory."

"Does that really happen? Do professors really snatch up children?"

"Of course not. But that didn't stop us from saying it when I was a girl."

"Where did you grow up?"

"I was from one of the nodes as well. Much further away than Orloton. Ten days ride, off in the southeastern desert, on the shores of the Great Eastern River."

"How did you come to Seal Tooth?"

"Oh, you know." Snip. "Life in a small town didn't suit me." Snip. "And they didn't have the means to support a girl in my situation."

"What situation were you in?"

Mam stopped cutting and stared significantly at Reyan through the mirror. Reyan, puzzled, searched Mam's eyes for some obvious meaning but could not find it. The one thing she did know was that the old woman wasn't going to explain it any further. "Though it didn't seem so at the time, I was fortunate. The scab came through a few years later. Every single person in my town died. I arrived in Seal Tooth in my fifteenth named year. I hoped to study at the University once my situation was… resolved." Snip.

"Isn't that a bit old to start classes?"

The snipping paused. "As it turned out, yes. And being a girl, and coming from so far east, it took me a while to convince all the faculty members that I didn't have any *Erynite tendencies*. By then it was far too late to begin my education." Reyan's heart beat three times in the silence. "But I still wanted to make a meaningful contribution to the System." Snip. "And so, I've been here for going on forty years, taking care of the likes of you." She smiled.

"So, you've known Professors Sevv and Parr for a long time then. What are they really like?"

"They are old souls, each in their own way. When Parr was young, he was a lot like you. Wild-haired, serious, intense. He seems to have mellowed over the years, but I'm not sure. I think he just learned to hide it. Now all that's left is a little glint in his eye that lets you know his younger self is still thrashing about in his head." She smiled but seemed sad.

"What about Sevv?"

She snorted. "Who knows what that man was ever like, or what he's like now, for that matter. He already seemed a hundred years old when I arrived."

"And Rolf?"

"Rolf," she said, as though framing up the memory of him. "Rolf was the best of them. The best of all of us really."

"So you *did* know him then?"

"I did. Back when he lived in Seal Tooth. Back when we were very young. Long before he was your benefactor. Long before he was your town leader, even." Mam placed a gentle hand on Reyan's shoulder. "But those stories are best saved for a time when you don't have so much reading to do."

Mam continued to snip in silence. But the silence was like a hole dug in the sand beside a river; the longer Reyan left it, the more it wanted to be filled. Words began trickling out of her, in a whisper at first: "Seven falls ago, dad went out and never came back."

Mam's voice remained calm and casual, as though this was what all fathers did. "Where did he go?"

"I don't know. A trade mission, I guess. I was little."

"Did he die of the scab?"

"Mom never said. I don't think so, though. We never had a Last Day. We never sang his soul to the Great Gray Sea. Mom didn't seem sad or happy about it. She just went about her life like dad never happened. I asked mom once, and she said he must have gotten lost and chose to stay that way."

Mam frowned back a question.

Reyan didn't know if the next thing she said was wise, but it longed to be said aloud and to be heard. So, she said it. "I think it was me."

Mam spoke firmly, but kindly: "Every ward thinks that, Reyan."

"But in my case, it's true. I think my parents hoped they'd never have to name me. But then I lived into my naming year." Reyan didn't feel upset or angry. It was as though she were standing on shore watching a loosed river flow past. "They argued all the time. About everything really, but mostly about me. I was young, but I remember that much. They wanted another child, a *different* child. But they were stuck with me. One night, when I was lying in bed listening to them, I heard mom crying. She told dad to just go away. Then, after two winters, she could claim death or abandonment and get rematched. She'd just start over."

"You can't always trust what people say when they're upset."

"But that's exactly what happened. Two years after he disappeared, she started telling everyone he was dead and trying to get rematched and mated. But no one wants to marry a woman who's already had her one child, especially if that child is me. So, she gave me up to be a ward of the town. That's when Leader Rolf took me in. Mom didn't have a child anymore, so she could be matched and mated and start over."

Behind her, Mam sighed. It seemed the snips were coming less frequently as Mam ran out of hair to cut and Reyan was finding more words.

"Rolf and Lyessa didn't have a child of their own. By the time I came into their life, they were too old to have one. Rolf took me places. He talked to me. Things I did that made other people mad made him laugh. I didn't like being laughed at, but it's better than being yelled at. Nothing I did ever made Lyessa laugh. When Rolf died, she was so upset, she handed me over to the professors. That's how I ended up in the caravan. That's how I ended up in your dormitory."

There was one final snip from Mam's scissors. Reyan saw Mam's face reflected in the mirror. Her eyes had grown glassy and wet, and her lips twitched. She put away the scissors and retrieved the comb. She began carefully smoothing and resmoothing Reyan's hair, slowing down as she came to the ends, which were now even and just brushing the tops of her shoulders. If she didn't know better, Reyan would have mistaken her reflection for a normal girl. She wasn't sure how she felt about that.

Mam came around in front of Reyan and squatted down, her knees popping. She put her shaking hands on the girl's shoulders and looked into her eyes as though trying to find something there. She gave up looking and pulled Reyan forward into her arms. At first, having someone so close felt a bit like trying to breathe under a thick blanket. But then Reyan was surprised to find that the pressure from Mam's powerful arms felt good in the same way her knuckles felt better after she cracked them.

Mam was crying when she pulled away. "Oh dear, I'm sorry."

"That's okay. You can hug me if you need to."

CHAPTER THIRTY-ONE
Day 72, Year 290, New Era

Since Reyan had come to Seal Tooth, more new and returning students were arriving each day. One by one, the remaining caravans returned from their circuits, carrying their professors and novices with them. The cafeteria, the dormitory, and the red brick square outside had grown progressively louder and more crowded, as though a flock of black and brown birds had come home to the University to roost.

"Calm down. It'll be *fine*," Fang was saying when Reyan sat down at the breakfast table. Later that day, all the students completing their final year would be welcomed into one of the System's faculties. Every boy at the table was jittery with nerves and excitement.

"At least it's nice today. Remember three years ago? The

ceremony had to be delayed for three days because of the rain."

"Why does that matter?" Reyan asked.

"By tradition, the commencement of new professors should happen on a sunny day so that fair weather will always accompany them on their circuits," Kavi explained.

"That's not how weather works," Reyan said, which drew grimaces of annoyance from Edward and Fang and a chuckle from Kavi.

"I'm not worried about the weather," Eddie said, "I'm worried about the ceremony itself."

"What do you think is going to happen?" Fang asked.

"Absolutely nothing interesting," Edward replied.

"You don't know that," Eddie said, "You've never been to a ceremony. None of us have."

"No one but faculty, you mean."

"And the Host."

"The Host *are* faculty."

"Meta-faculty."

"Sure," Edward agreed, "But it's not like anything *bad* is going to happen. How many students do you know who went off to graduation and were never seen again?" He waited for an answer. "Exactly. None."

"I don't really think something *bad* is going to happen. That's not it. I just don't know *what's* going to happen. I don't like surprises," Eddie admitted.

"Here's what's going to happen: We walk into the stadium. They say a bunch of stuff, we get our copy of the Big Book, and we drink some punch." Fang shrugged.

"But you don't *know* that." And then the whole conversation circled back on itself again with different boys taking up different parts each time it came around.

Growing tired of this, Reyan piled the scraps of her breakfast on a tray and headed towards the door. Kavi hurried to catch her. "Mind if I walk you?"

As she began to climb the dormitory stairs, Kavi called to her: "Wait," he said, his voice more uncertain than she had ever heard it. "Could you come to my room? I have something I want to ask you."

Kavi's room was identical to hers, but he lived differently in it. The hand towel was not folded into long thirds and hung neatly over the bar; instead, it was wadded and stuffed into place. His books were not stacked neatly on his desk, but evenly distributed across it and intermixed with papers and half full mugs. The clearing in the middle was barely large enough to hold a notebook. And the smell was entirely different. While it was not exactly unpleasant, it hung thickly in the air.

Kavi offered her his desk chair, and he sat across from her on his bed, looking down at his hands, where they rested in his lap.

"I want someone to be there for me at graduation today. My faculty is just me and Partner Minerva. Mam can't come for obvious reasons." Reyan couldn't think of what those reasons might be, but before she got the chance to ask, Kavi surprised her. "Do you think you could come?"

She was confused. "I'll be at the reception."

"I don't mean the reception. I mean the *ceremony*."

"I thought only faculty could go to the ceremony."

"I didn't want to say so in front of the guys, but I'm nervous. We all are. Eddie's just the only one who'll show it."

"What are you scared of?"

Kavi shrugged. "Even if I wasn't, graduating is a big deal. I want someone to be there for me."

"But I'm just a first year. There's no way they would let me in."

"They will if they think you're faculty."

"But I don't look like faculty." She indicated the broad white stripe down the front of her robe.

"Luckily, they've already given us our set of faculty robes." He walked over to his closet where the new robes were hanging and retrieved one. "You can borrow this." He walked over to his dresser, where a mound of unidentifiable junk threatened to avalanche. "Here. Put this on your right wrist." He held up a shiny metal ring. It would have looked beautiful dangling in her tree back home. "It's not really a karaband, but people will see the glint of metal and won't ask any questions."

"I'm too young. There's no way I'll pass as a faculty member."

"Everyone will have their hood up. We were told it was an important part of the ceremony. Something about preserving the separation of concerns across the faculties. So, just keep your hood up."

"What if someone tries to talk to me?"

Kavi paced the room for a moment while he considered this. "Is there anything you know a lot about?"

"Trees."

"Okay, if anyone talks to you, you can pretend to be an arborialist."

"But that would be lying."

"Not if you don't say anything it won't be. Just keep your hood up and do your best to stay quiet."

This all felt like a very bad idea. She tried to imagine what Sevv would do if he caught her sneaking into a faculty-only event before classes even started. She desperately wanted to ask Kavi how hard it had been for him to pass the aptitude test but couldn't think of a way to ask that didn't break the rules. She didn't want anyone to think she was trying to cheat and get Kavi's help.

She thought for a long while about how to achieve the most Systemic outcome. She was about to tell Kavi she could not come when he suddenly took her hand in his and pleaded, "It would mean a lot to me." He gave her hand a gentle squeeze.

She twisted her arm and withdrew her hand, but she wasn't mad. Kavi was her only real friend in Seal Tooth. She didn't want to let him down. "Okay. But when we get those panels off the roof of the library, I want half of your share, too."

Kavi smiled. "It's a deal."

That afternoon, Reyan slipped into Kavi's robe and hovered on the edge of the crowd gathering in the square. Kavi, Fang, and the Eds blended in with a dozen or more other graduating novices, the broad white stripes conspicuously absent from their new robes. Reyan hid under her hood and did her best to disappear, a skill she had perfected in the schoolhouse yard and the rooms and hallways of Lyessa's home.

Someone gave a signal, and the snarl of novices formed ranks and began moving in a somber line down the street toward the stadium. The faculty followed in a less formal group, with Reyan straggling behind. She followed the parade past a block of buildings and the view opened. The basket-shaped stadium stood alone in the middle of a great field of hardroad. All by itself, the stadium covered more ground than the whole of Orloton.

They passed through a black iron gate streaked and

stained with cankers of rust and climbed a broad expanse of steps. At the top of the stairs, the graduates split off to the right, the professor in front leading them like a mother duck leading her ducklings. The crowd of faculty turned left and entered a broad covered area that wrapped around the stadium's girth.

The stadium was built like an enormous animal stripped of its hide to reveal iron bones as thick as Reyan was tall. The floors and walls and ceilings were made of shapestone. The sound of the crowd ricocheted off the hard surfaces until a mush of incoherent noise surrounded her like a swarm of angry bees.

She was grateful when they turned and passed through a large opening into the quiet daylight. They descended a stairway to the stadium's floor where a platform stood in the center of a broad green field. They crossed the grass and filled benches arranged around the platform, leaving the first two rows empty.

The real faculty members seemed indifferent to their surroundings. They chatted and laughed and discussed their business. But Reyan couldn't help gawking. The field was surrounded by terraced areas that reached much higher than the tower in Rowe. There were enough seats for tens of thousands of people—more than lived in Seal Tooth, Rowe, and Orloton combined. But the only occupants in the stands today were clusters of seagulls and rock doves, and a stone-still falcon silently watching over them.

A silence spread through the crowd like a rumor. Soon,

the only sounds were the creaking of the wooden benches and the nervous coughs that always tickle the throats of anyone trying to keep quiet.

The graduates filed in from the opposite side of the field and filled the empty benches. Next, a line of twelve partners emerged from a large square opening in the shapestone wall that surrounded the field. Unlike the black-robed faculty members and new graduates, this procession all wore thick hooded robes of deep purple, a colored sash, and a golden chord around their necks. Their movements were so plodding and solemn that Reyan wondered if some tragedy had befallen the University in the night.

They climbed a short flight of stairs and arranged themselves in two rows near the back of the stage, their posture and position as identical to each other as pine needles on a twig. As they sat, a voice next to her said reverently, "The Host." Worried that her neighbor would keep talking and draw unwanted attention, Reyan shot a glance at him. But he was facing the stage, his face obscured by his hood; he had simply spoken aloud, not really talking to her.

As soon as the Host had settled in, one of them rose and came to the podium. Though the partner was robed and hooded like the other members of the Host, Reyan could tell she was a woman by her stature and voice. "Please welcome Dean Khamis," she said.

As she returned to her seat, another purple-robed professor stepped out from behind the black curtain at the back of the stage. His sash was woven of all the colors from all the other sashes. He mounted the dais in the center of the stage and approached the podium erected there, then ceremoniously pulled back his hood to reveal a deeply lined face and a wild tuft of white hair. He pulled a pair of reading glasses from a fold in his robe, settled them on to his nose, and coughed once into his fist.

"I'm known neither for my brevity nor my concision." This sent a chuckle through the audience. The dean stared down the laughter over the tops of his glasses, then continued. "For that, I must apologize. I mistakenly assume that a student's education will continue for years, and there is always time for a few extra words. But now I am—at last and undeniably—out of time. And so, I will try to keep this brief." Dean Khamis paused and drew a deep breath. He trembled slightly from the effort. "As members of the Systemic faculties, we are the System's memory. We remember an earlier time, a darker time, when humanity's sloth and love of luxury led to our downfall."

The dean paused, and by some unseen signal or convention, the entire gathered crowd joined in, chanting as one voice, "We remember."

"How the Systemic Author, in their wisdom, set us free."

"We remember."

"That the System has called us to serve."

"We remember.

"We remember all these things and more. We weigh them

heavily in our minds and in our processes. We steer the living world clear of the errors of the past."

He held up his hand, and the faculty joined him one last time: "We remember."

Reyan mumbled along with the response, moving her mouth to fool anyone who might see her lips, but making sure not to speak too confidently in case she guessed the words incorrectly.

The dean looked down to the new professors in the front row: "Today you become fully functioning members of the System's faculties. Today you will receive your Books and your professor's karabands. The Systemic truths now lie within you and are yours to teach. As keepers and purveyors of the System, you possess knowledge that will remain mysterious to most and will set you apart from them forever. Yet it is our role to shine the light of the System's truth, knowledge, and wisdom upon the ignorant." From the corners of her eyes, Reyan saw all the hooded heads nod, and she mimicked them. The dean continued. "That role is more important now than ever. Every day we hear rumors of Erynite incursions across the Great Eastern River. As recently as last week, Professor Sevvran provided me irrefutable evidence of their ideas infecting and corrupting a node on his circuit."

He's talking about Orloton. He's talking about Rolf's gift. She wanted to stand up and shout at the dean that there was nothing corrupting or infectious about the tradition; that it had nothing to do with the Erynites.

"We must always remember Lem's warning about Eryn

and the Erynites. They will charm our people. They will dazzle them with vacuous miracles and stir false hope within them. They will turn these poor ignorant people away from the System. We are all that stands between them and ruin." After these last words, a weariness settled upon the dean. He smiled, removed his glasses, blinked a few times, and concluded without looking at his notes. "Congratulations to you all. May the Eye see all the good you do in the living world and watch over you in your times of need."

Dean Khamis made his way to a seat set apart from the other partners. The other members of the Host relaxed out of their rigid formality and pulled back their hoods. A sudden fear gripped Reyan. Would the audience follow suit? Would they all remove their hoods, just as they had all joined in responding to the dean's speech? If she pulled back her hood, everyone would see her. If she did not, everyone would know she didn't belong. She thought taking down her hood would be the less conspicuous option. She lifted shaking hands to her hood and prepared to reveal herself. Luckily, before she pulled the hood back, she noticed that no one else was doing so. She let her hands fall back into her lap. Reyan's nerves were wound as tight as violium strings, and every moment in this crowd felt like another turn of the tuning pegs.

Two men in plain black faculty robes carried away the podium, and Reyan saw Professors Sevv and Parr, sitting in the chairs that had been obscured by the podium. She thought back to all the clues that Sevv and Parr were important enough to be part of the Host: the meeting in the large room, Sevv's office on the top floor of the library, even their second karabands. Her cheeks flushed with embarrassment for having missed all these clues. She couldn't decide if knowing Sevv and Parr were members of the Host made the Host less mysterious or made Professors Sevv and Parr more so.

The graduates stood, left their seats, and marched around the back of the stage. An old partner with floating clouds of silver hair and hands that fidgeted like birds walked across the stage and pulled back the edge of the black curtain. He peaked his head through the opening, smiled, and nodded.

The novices emerged one by one from behind the curtain. Kavi was the second to step on stage. He seemed vibrant, almost glowing, his smile so intense that it risked crossing over into a grimace.

Two partners made their way onto the dais. The first wore a red sash and held a large wooden box. The other had a purple sash and carried a much smaller box. One called out, "Professor Shailender Razdan: Join us." The young woman at the head of the line joined the two partners on the dais.

The man next to Reyan leaned over to her and whispered, "Shailender's my girl." Reyan didn't want to answer in her thirteen-year old's voice, so—in a panic—she held her finger to her lips and shushed the man without turning to him. He cleared his throat and fell silent.

Professor Shailender descended from the stage and returned to her empty space on the front bench, balancing a small wooden box on top of a much larger one.

Next, Parr stepped up to the dais, holding the large wooden box for Kavi. A bent old woman with a brown sash stood next to Parr holding a small box in one hand, the other resting in the crook of Parr's arm. The old woman smiled across the stage to Kavi and croaked, "Professor Kavianhar Smithe: Join us." It was the same partner Mam had greeted before Reyan's meeting with Sevv and Parr. Professor Minerva.

If that's the Technical Partner, the Host will be selecting her replacement any day now.

When Kavi took the box from Parr, the professor placed a hand high up on Kavi's arm. He looked the boy square in the face, his smile was full of fatherly pride—the sort of look she imagined Rolf would have given her.

The ceremony was repeated for each graduate. When it was over, the crowd separated into faculties to congratulate and welcome their new members. Because the technical faculty consisted only of Kavi and Partner Minerva, who had yet to make her way down from the platform, Kavi stood alone. Reyan came over and joined him.

Kavi opened the hinged lid of the small box and tilted it toward Reyan. Inside, she saw a pillow made of soft gray leather. Set into indentations in the pillow were a shard of flint and a strip of steel and a knife whose blade folded back into a brass and wood handle. In the middle of the box, a professor's karaband sat like the iris of an eye, its pupil a brown pin embossed with a golden "T." Reyan wondered if—once he put them on—his new pin and karaband would pull him away from the world of talks and walks and mealtime laughter and tether him to this new secret world of rituals and recitations. She wondered how much distance that would leave between them.

Kavi reached into the box's lid and retrieved an envelope from behind a gold ribbon. He opened the envelope and removed the card inside. He read it in silence, then handed it to Reyan.

> You now have your professor's karaband. Wear it on the wrist of your dominant hand so that, every time you reach out to the world, you note its iron circumference and remember your unending and unbreakable commitment to the System.
>
> The knife and the flint and steel have been carried by members of the System's faculties since the Calming.
>
> Flint and steel bring warmth and light to the world through persistent action and focused intent.
>
> The blade represents exacting discernment. It folds back on itself to remind us to look for the truth about ourselves as well as the world around us.
>
> Carry them during your travels, meditate on their meanings, and do good.
>
> - The Host of Systemic Partners

The large box was empty except for another note:

> You may pick up your professor's copy of <u>A System for a New Era</u> in the library any time

after 3PM.

Please bring this slip with you.

The dean walked to the edge of the stage and raised his hands to get everyone's attention. "There will be a reception in the cafeteria at the turn of the hour. Non-faculty family and friends will be welcome." That was three-quarters of an hour from now. She could not remain here with her hood drawn surrounded by curious members of the System's faculties. It was only a matter of time before she had to pretend to be an arborialist, or—worse—before Sevv or Parr noticed her. So, while everyone was still smiling and hugging and patting each other's backs, Reyan left Kavi and drifted toward the exit.

Reyan had never felt more hopelessly out of place. Everyone in the stadium knew exactly what to do, where to stand, and how to respond. They each knew their roles and played them perfectly. But she didn't know anything. It was foolish to think she could ever learn to fit in. Then again, she had made it through the entire ceremony unnoticed.

She walked the few blocks back to the dormitory with her hood up. It was conspicuous, but she would rather draw attention as a strangely anonymous professor than as an easily identified first-year who was illegitimately dressed as one.

Her self-consciousness only grew as she climbed the dormitory stairs. Professors did not usually enter the dormitory. She tugged down the front edge of her hood whenever anyone came down the stairs toward her. She could feel them slow and turn to watch as she passed, but none of the students had the gumption to stop and question a professor.

She made it all the way to the fourth floor and had just touched the handle on her door when she heard Mam's voice call out, "You there. What are you doing in the student dormitory?"

Not knowing what else to do, Reyan pretended not to hear. She turned the handle. "Excuse me, Professor, you should not be up here," Mam said as Reyan stepped into her room and closed the door quickly behind her.

She had the robe pulled most of the way to her shoulders when Mam burst through the door. When she saw Reyan, the old woman closed the door softly behind her and whispered frantically, "What are you doing in a professor's robe?"

A lie could easily get Reyan kicked out of school. But she sensed the truth probably would as well. She decided it would be safest to not say anything at all.

"Did you steal it?"

Reyan shook her head vigorously.

"Really? A professor just gave it to you?" A "yes" was trying to escape from behind Reyan's sealed lips and making her eyes bulge. Mam scowled. "We can keep playing this ridiculous game of questions, or you can just tell me. I'll get to the truth either way. You can decide how sympathetic I'll feel when I discuss the matter with the professors."

"Please don't tell Sevv or Parr. It was an accident."

"Meaning you accidentally put on the robe, or you accidentally got caught before you could remove it?"

"I didn't mean to cause any trouble. Please," Reyan blurted. "I can't get kicked out of school. And I don't want anything to happen to Kavi."

"What does Kavi have to do with this?"

"It's his robe."

Now Mam seemed less sure of herself. She squinted at Reyan, trying to decide what to do. "Well, Reyankaiya," she said, "you might be the luckiest girl in Seal Tooth." Reyan had never thought of herself as lucky, so Mam's judgment seemed suspicious. "As of this morning, Kavi is a member of a faculty, and I am not. As a *lesser* member of the University staff, I must presume wisdom in even his most ridiculous actions, and I am no longer allowed to slap him upside his idiot head. Why would he do such a reckless thing?"

"It's a disguise. He wanted me to come to his graduation."

"Ah, so this is far more serious than I thought." Mam nodded solemnly. "Graduations are restricted to the faculties. Even I am not permitted to attend for some asinine reason." She sighed. "If you want to talk about getting kicked out of school, that'd be the reason."

"I know. I'm sorry. Promise not to tell."

Mam appraised her for a moment. "You really sneaked into a graduation ceremony?" Reyan nodded. The matron's face became less stern and more mischievous. "Fine, I won't tell a soul. On one condition." Mam sat down on Reyan's bed and patted the spot next to her. "Tell me everything that happened inside that stadium."

CHAPTER THIRTY-TWO
Day 77, Year 290, New Era

Reyan showed up to her Introduction to Systemic Structures class in a brand-new black robe. This being her first class, it took her time to figure out the room numbers and she showed up five minutes late. She had only ever attended class in Orloton's single-room schoolhouse, so she brought along every one of her books. The door was shut when she arrived. She worked at the handle with her back then elbows and finally her chin while she struggled to keep the books from the middle of her stack from sliding out sideways.

When she finally opened the door, she found a tall, black-robed professor towering at the head of the room. Their eyes met and he jerked his head toward an empty seat in the back.

Once Reyan had settled, the professor cleared his throat. "As I was saying, I'm Professor Lux." His robe hid most aspects of him, but the breadth of his shoulders implied he might be better-suited to a lumberman's ax than a stick of chalk. He was slow and careful in his movements as though his enormous body was newly lent to him. "Let's find out who you all are," he said, turning to a blue-eyed boy, "Where are you from?"

"Tsunsk, Professor," he replied, his voice as bright as his eyes.

Professor Lux seemed impressed. "Do you know Distler, the potter? He's an old friend."

One by one, he called on the fourteen boys and girls, asking similar questions about the tanners, the bakers, or the keepers back in their nodes. This open casual questioning made Reyan extremely nervous. Not knowing what the professor would ask, she had no idea how to prepare.

Her anxiety only grew worse when, after the first six students, Professor Lux ran out of questions and began telling the students to simply "tell us something about yourself."

She worried that her life story might upset this group of strangers the way it had Mam. Comforting Mam was one thing but having to hug her whole class was more than she could stand. She struggled to think of something she might have in common with the others in the room. The answer came to her easily. "My name is Reyan," she said. She waffled a moment as to whether she should add the '-kaiya,' but she decided against it, ". . . Estermet. I'm from the town of Orloton, which is up in the mountain pass on the northern leg of the eleventh circuit. My favorite section in this book," she held up her *Basic Systemic*

Structure and Social Architecture book, "is chapter fourteen about the refined theory of protocols where Partner Ulrich frames them as an abstraction of upstream dependencies in an information supply chain."

All the eyes in the room were on her, including the professor's. She could not read their expressions. Presuming she had misspoken, she tried to explain: "The idea that, by identifying noise and filtering it via our protocols, we actually increase the amount of information transfer somehow felt right to me." The attention of the room remained fixed on her, and she began to grow nervous. She added under her breath, "That's sort of how I feel too sometimes," then trailed off into humiliated silence.

After a few tense moments, the hulking professor asked, "Did you actually read the book, Reyan?"

She wasn't sure how to read Professor Lux's tone, but she thought it might be accusatory. It was fine to say she'd misinterpreted something, but to accuse her of not reading it at all—after she'd spent so much effort and so many sleepless hours preparing—was cruel. Her frustration and anger rose, threatening to overflow her eyes. Her nose began to drip. This place was just like Orloton; no matter how much effort she put in, no one would ever give her the benefit of the doubt, never give her the chance to prove herself. She wiped her nose with the back of her sleeve, stiffened her chin and straightened her spine. "Of course I did."

"I see. And the other books."

"I did, Professor."

Professor Lux looked around at the other students in the class as though they might have some input. They were all still silently staring at her. "And do you believe you understood it?"

"I was hoping you could tell me that."

She looked at all their silent faces and downcast eyes. They were embarrassed for her. Even the professor seemed uneasy. "Well, let's move on," he said. "In the future, let's do our best to keep everyone on the same page, so to speak."

A similar scene played out in her other two classes. She tried hard to overcome the day's earlier humiliations and treat each class as a new start. Hoping to prove she was not dull, she gathered the courage to raise her hand at every question. Finally, the professors stopped calling on her. The kinder students looked away, but the meaner ones openly glared at her.

Over the following days, she noticed a pattern. Any answer she gave that was longer than six sentences caused sidelong looks and fidgeting from her classmates. Any answer less than two sentences sounded curt and seemed to offend them. So, Reyan tried very hard to keep her answers to exactly four sentences. Even so, by the end of the week, a bubble of silence formed around her. Conversations stopped as she entered a room or walked down a crowded hallway, only to resume as she left.

Reyan did not feel she was integrating well into university life. She wondered if Sevv already knew. It had only been one day, and already she felt certain she was failing his test.

CHAPTER THIRTY-THREE
Day 81, Year 290, New Era

On Friday, Reyan dragged herself down to the cafeteria to have dinner with Kavi and his friends. Their newly-elevated station as professors seemed to have made them more serious. She could tell that the laughing, arm-punching, joke-telling boys were still just below the surface, but their awkward, angular selves were slowly vanishing into their new stripeless robes like summer shapes softening beneath falling snow.

Ever since she'd punched Fang in the face, everyone seemed a little wary of Reyan. That was perfectly fine with her. Meals were less loud, and the young professors mostly left her to eat in peace. They were talking to each other right now, but she was mostly ignoring them, their conversation drifting in and out of her circle of attention.

"None of that bothered me much," Eddie was saying, "What really got me all spun around was 'the System.'"

Fang mock-frowned. "Were your classes too hard?"

"No, I mean, I couldn't figure out what it meant. I felt like, every time a noun was called for, they just threw in the word 'System.' I would have sworn it was a hazing ritual."

"I thought it was just me," Kavi chuckled. "When I got to the University, I was completely confused. I would hear the word in one context and think I'd finally figured it out, then someone would use it in a totally different way twenty minutes later. I was too embarrassed to ask."

Fang shrugged. "It's a long-standing Seal Tooth tradition to call many things by one name, and one thing by many names. It keeps the nodies and newbies from developing airs."

Edward said, "What about you Reyan?" She looked up abruptly when she heard her name. "You figure it out yet?"

"What?"

"That the System wrote the System, and now the System studies the System in order to perfect the System so they can teach the System to others in hopes of expanding the System?"

"He is being completely Systemic," Fang pointed out.

A hot pulse of insecurity shot through her.

Eddie came to her aid. "Don't worry Reyan, it's all pretty confusing." Edward and Fang deflated a bit. "The point is that the System is *everything*, but no one just comes out and tells you that. It goes like this: The machine that watched over the world during the Era of Dependency were called 'the System' because they were a *system* of thinktech. Their mind was made up of rules and processes and the Governing Assert. They wrote all that stuff down in the Book before the Calming. We call the Book 'the System' because the System called it 'A System for a New Era' and because it contains all the rules that made up the System's mind. When we study the Book, we try to understand the System and recreate it in the world."

"See," Fang said, "makes total sense."

"Sometimes, it's easier to just say 'Author,' 'Book,' and 'Faculty,'" Edward threw in.

Reyan furrowed her brow. "When you talk about water, do you call it river water, cup water, mouth water, and stomach water?" She started to laugh, and the laughter tickled something inside her and she started laughing more. Her eyes were closed and tears were slipping through. When she noticed hers was the only laughter she could hear, she settled down. She wiped her eyes and opened them, and saw they were all looking at each other, and their eyes periodically darted toward her. "Wait. Do you say it that way?" She quickly tried to remember if she'd ever talked about water with anyone since arriving in Seal Tooth. She worried that this was one of those obvious things she'd missed and had just stumbled upon it now. "So, the *container* for the System matters?"

The hot feeling of insecurity returned. She hadn't assaulted anyone this time, but she'd still managed to say something ridiculous and provide even more evidence that she was at least awkward, if not an actual idiot. She abruptly stood up, scanned their surprised faces, nodded once, and left for the library, where Sevv was waiting for her.

She stepped from the warm bright cafeteria into the cold damp dark of evening. She pulled her hood over her head and flattened her arms against her ribs. With one hand she balled up the fabric of her coat to pull it tight around her. With the other she clutched her lantern to her chest. Reyan winced into the night as though the inky drizzle were a raging gale.

By the time she'd walked the few blocks to the library, she felt as though the dampness and chill were coming from somewhere deep inside of her, perhaps her spine or the thick bones of her legs.

The lobby of Building B was empty and dark. She pulled back her hood and shook herself like a wet dog. The light from her lantern gleamed on the marble floors and walls so that they too seemed glazed with damp.

She climbed flight after flight of shapestone steps like a shiver traveling the building's spine. The swinging light of her lantern pulled and stretched the shadows so that everything felt shifty and feverish.

She exited the stairwell on the thirteenth floor. Now that classes were in session, the wall sconces in the walkway remained lit until late at night. She snuffed her lantern.

When Reyan passed the locked room, she instinctively checked the handle. The door was still locked. Her curiosity flared. She tried jiggling the handle again.

"Is that you, Ms. Estermet?" Sevv's voice pulled her away

from the door. She followed the sound of it to where lamplight was spilling out of a nearby door.

"Yes Professor," she said leaning her head into his office.

"Well don't haunt my doorway. Come in."

She stepped into the room, and Sevv motioned for her to sit in the chair across the desk from him. The room was well-lit. Lamps hung on hooks on either side of the door, and stood on either end of Sevv's desk.

"How are you doing, Reyan?"

"I'm tired from school and too little sleep, winded from climbing the stairs, and cold and wet from the weather."

He shook his head with tiny, disappointed movements. "You are not one for conversational pleasantries, are you?" He huffed. "That's just as well, I suppose. We're not here for idle chit-chat." He bounced his hands off the desk and said, "No. We are here to ensure that you are well-grounded in Systemic processes, history, and theory." Sevv paused and looked at her expectantly. She nodded.

"For our first lesson, I want to revisit the decision matrix. You sketched a serviceable one in the dirt back in Rowe. But while your grasp of the concepts was quite impressive, your execution was crude." He grimaced. "We'll start with something simple. The leader and keeper of a small node are trying to decide if they should dam a nearby stream. They have asked for your guidance." He held a stick of chalk out to her and nodded to the large blackboard.

The professor sat over Reyan's shoulder like an old watchful buzzard. She cast her mind back to the lesson in Rowe and the descriptions she had been pouring over in her books. She felt vulnerable and nervous. Her shaking hand pulled the bit of chalk across the board.

She was two lines into her matrix when Sevv tut-tutted. "Your lines are wobbly. Worse, they are not strictly horizontal and vertical." He walked around the desk and approached the blackboard. "If you learn sloppy, you will teach sloppy. Steady and straight," he said, erasing her lines and replacing them with his own. It looked as though he had snapped his lines across the slate with a tight string. "Your forms should be as perfect as a honeycomb. It is the honeycomb's regular form that allows the bees to do their work."

Sevv swiped a damp cloth over the board and erased his lines. He stepped away and returned to his seat behind the desk. Reyan held the chalk high up on the board, and just before she put it against the slate, Sevv stopped her. "Your hand is still shaking Reyan. Take a breath. Stiffen your arm. Draw from the shoulder, not the wrist. There you have it."

Slowly and steadily, she drew the first lines of the matrix. Sevv made her enumerate the standard Systemic considerations and recite their fixed weights several times before letting her write them down. Then they stepped through the matrix. For each cell, they discussed how damming the river, building a cistern, or digging a well would improve quality of life, provide consistent drinking water, or help irrigate the fields.

They worked through outcomes by drawing trees of

possibilities and considering the likelihood of each branch and twig and leaf. She imagined one of these trees sprouting from each cell in the matrix. Once she had worked through a question, the tree locked down the outcome by dropping a single numeric fruit from its most likely branch. Then she moved on to the next cell. This process felt right to her. For the first time in her life, she did not have to continually circle back and replay the same scenarios over and over to keep from losing their insights. It was the closest thing to certainty she had ever experienced.

She was putting the final touches on the leaf nodes of a particularly gnarly tree when she mentioned, "For the last eight cells, what I thought the score would be and the one the decision tree produced were only off by one or two points. The last three were spot on. What happens when I start off knowing the answers?"

The professor's smile kept its rough outline but lost some of its definition. "There is always more to consider, Reyan. If a decision tree's outcomes can be too easily guessed, you should expand its scope. Work additional possibilities in earlier in the process. Instead of five iterations, do ten."

"But why must it be difficult?"

"When faced with a decision, most of us already have a desired outcome in our hearts. We cannot default to that outcome. Difficulty and suffering guide us to objectivity."

"But it's becoming intuitive to me. Doesn't that mean I'm learning?" She was on to something now; she could feel it. "What if the point is not to perfect the process, but for the process to perfect *us*. Eventually, we would do the right thing without any process at all. Isn't that wisdom?"

"You sound like an Erynite." Sevv snapped, looking horrified.

"I keep hearing that word. What *is* an Erynite?"

He half-closed his eyes as though trying to appear calm and disinterested. "A joke. Never mind."

"But what is it?"

"An Erynite is a person outside the System."

"Have you ever met one?"

Here he seemed caught between too many thoughts. He pondered, he struggled, he agonized in successive twitching waves. Something like tenderness, then anger, and finally disgust flashed across his face in rapid succession. It was one of the most peculiar expressions Reyan had ever seen on someone's face. But it lasted only an instant before he snapped out of it. "What? Me, *personally*? No."

"Do you think *I've* ever met one?"

"I would hope not. But one certainly came to Orloton at some point and started all that gift-of-the-dead nonsense. But no; if you had met an Erynite I think you would remember. They're quite different from us."

Could there be people in the world as different from us as Seal Tooth was from Orloton? "Different from us how?"

"It would be easier to point out the ways we are similar than the ways we are different. Erynites certainly eat, breathe, and sleep; they have children and cluster in pop-centers. But in dress and speech and beliefs they are quite different."

"What do they believe?"

"As I've said, they have no care for the System at all. They would just as soon tear it all down and go back to the way things were before the Calming. They do not value struggle." Sevv's eyes narrowed, the muscles of his jaw rolled and twitched, and the loose skin under his chin quivered. "They do not fear the Eye." A bubble of spittle landed on his lower lip and remained there. "But not the Lemmists; *we* remember." He drew a breath and settled himself. The sudden intense hatred in his eyes slowly dimmed like coals she'd stopped fanning. He wiped his lip with his thumb.

"What's a Lemmist?"

"All of us," Sevv said, looking perplexed. "The professors on circuit, the builders of the University. Everyone who keeps the System and the Governing Assert. We are all Lemmists." He was still exasperated, but he settled himself and smiled thinly. He waved his hand, shoo-flying the subject away. "It has grown late, and we have only begun to tug at this particular thread of your ignorance. It would take me until morning to unwind all of this for you. We will continue next week."

On her way to the stairs, Reyan passed the locked door. She reached for the handle and paused. *Doors do not lock themselves. Someone with a key locks them. A professor or partner I bet. Probably one nearby.* Suddenly this door felt like another test, like something that might matter when it came time for Sevv to evaluate her. She withdrew her hand. There were other things for her to explore and learn while she figured out the meaning of this one.

In her short stint at the University, she had yet to browse the stacks on the library's upper floor. She knew this was where the more advanced or rare books were kept. She decided to have a look around.

She came to an open space among the stacks. In the middle was a wooden podium and upon the podium, opened wide, sat an enormous book. The book and its stand were encased in a glass box. On one side of the box was a handle, a latch, and a set of hinges. There was a four-flamed continual chandelier hanging directly over the book.

The book drew her to it as though it were humming or singing to her, though she knew it was not. She rested her forehead against the side of the glass box and looked down at the words. They were tiny and hard to read at this distance. She squinted.

"It's beautiful, isn't it?"

Reyan jumped. She turned around and found Professor Parr standing at the edge of the pool of light cast by the chandelier. Once she'd caught her breath, she asked, "What is it?"

"A book."

"But it's not just any book, is it?"

"No." Parr came over, lifted the latch, and opened the glass door.

"It's not locked?"

"Of course not. The glass is a cover, not a cage. It keeps the dust off." He reached in and lifted the book out and presented it to her. It was covered and bound in white leather, the words "A System for a New Era" were pressed into the front.

"It's like the one I saw in your truck back in Rowe; like the one Kavi got when he graduated."

"Similar, but not the same. This is the *original*. This is the one that belonged to Partner Lem. The one he talked about in his journals."

Looking at it again, she began to see the differences. The cover was almost identical, the white leather looked slightly scuffed on the corners and edges, but it was still a gleaming white, and while Parr's book had been inlaid with copper, the inlays on this book appeared to be gold. Several colored ribbons protruded from between its pages. "Would you like to hold it?"

"No," Reyan said, forcefully. She wanted to touch it more than anything she had ever seen. It was beautiful. Fascinating. But she was terrified she would somehow damage it.

"Don't worry, it might as well be made of shapestone for all the harm you could bring to it. The System purpose-built it for travel."

Parr placed the book in her open palms. She had expected it to be heavy and when it wasn't, she nearly tossed it in the air. Parr gasped, but once she regained control, he took a deep breath and grew calm again.

Reyan remembered thinking that the lettering on the cover of Parr's book had been unnaturally crisp and straight, as though it had been someone's one and only role to precisely press words into leather book covers. But the words on Lem's book were somehow even more perfect. Looking at them gave her the same falling-in feeling she got when she looked at a fern and noticed how their leaves looked like little ferns, and the nodules on the leaves looked like even tinier ferns, and wondered if it went on forever.

Parr stepped over to a nearby table. "Come, let's have a closer look." He pushed aside a large magnifying glass on a posable arm and gestured for her to bring the book.

She placed the book on the table's bookstand as though she were laying a fledgling back in its nest. The edges of the pages were so fine and perfectly trimmed that, viewed from the side, they looked more like polished metal than paper. She let the book fall open to a place near the middle where one of the bookmarks held a place.

Whereas the pages in Parr's personal copy had been rough to the touch and the color of dust and cream, this paper had the same milky translucence as the membrane left clinging to a hardboiled egg once you'd peeled away the shell. Yet she could tell these pages were tough as leather.

She pulled the magnifying glass between her and the page

and focused on the letters. Until this point in her life, she had only seen letters written by hand and those pressed into paper. But there were no smudges or gradients at the edges of these letters and no indentations from the press. The borders were as clear and sharp as the paper's cut edges and the lettering on the cover. There was row upon row of perfect letters too small to be handwritten but legible, nonetheless. She wanted to say the letters were "black as ink." Until now, ink was the darkest thing she could imagine. But ink seemed washed out and pale by comparison. These letters looked like holes punched through the book to a place where light had never been. Something occurred to her. "When we were stopped at the lake between Rowe and here, Professor Sevv said there are bits from the Book we don't share with the nodes." Parr nodded. "Why would the Author go to all that trouble to provide us with bits that have no purpose?"

"There are passages in the Book which we will never have the opportunity to profess. For instance, there are whole sections about electronics. Your average farmer or fisher does not need to know that electrical resistance is proportional to a conductor's cross-sectional area and its length. Do *you* understand what that means?" Reyan shook her head and worried that it might be something she should have learned by now. "Of course not," he said, "and neither do they. Then there are the bits that might do more harm than good."

"Like what?"

"Oh, I don't know," he frowned, hedging. "But there are always those who think that certain ideas are best forgotten." Parr paused long enough for Reyan to wonder who these people might be. Just as she was about to ask, he continued, "Then, of course, there are bits which seem to have no meaning at all. Fully three percent of the Book is completely unintelligible. Here, have a look."

Parr used the black ribbon near the end of the Book to turn over a block of pages. He was right—it made no sense at all. It wasn't that the words formed nonsensical sentences; there were no sentences at all. The letters didn't even cluster into decipherable words. She flipped one page after the other, and each one was just an endless jumble of random letters, numbers, and symbols.

"We call it 'The Blob,'" Parr said.

"What is it?"

"Some say the System were beginning to fail when they made the Book. Perhaps they were getting confused the way an old person might as their end approaches. But, if they were failing, how did they manage to complete the Book? And even the ramblings of old men contain shards of real memory and meaning. Others believe the Blob is one of the veracity seals the System stamped on everything they created. It would be strange if the Book were any different. That seems the most logical explanation to me."

For a moment, Parr seemed to be considering the details of Reyan's face, then he said, "I wonder if you would be able to help me?"

"It's getting late. I should go back to my room and study."

"It will only take a moment."

"Why me?"

"Because I need help, and you are close at hand."

He walked her to his office, which was very much like Sevv's. "It seems my collection of books is growing too large. I want to swap out this bookshelf here," he indicated a low wooden shelf next to his desk, "with a larger one sitting unused in the storage room." He walked over to the shelf and started pulling off books and piling them on his desk. When she didn't come over to help, he said, "Come on now, don't just stand there."

Once the shelf was cleared of books, Reyan took the lead, and Parr picked up the trailing end. They waddled out of Parr's office and into the hallway. A few doors down, the professor said, "Here we are." They put down the shelf in front of the locked door. Parr dug through the folds of his robe and came out with a small ring passed through a single key. The key glinted in the lantern light as he slid it across the top shelf. "Here you go."

She turned the key in the lock and pushed the door open. Her heart was racing as she picked up her half of the shelf and shouldered her way into the room.

It was dark inside. At first, the only thing she could see was Parr framed in the bright opening of the door, the bookshelf between them. Parr put down his half of the shelf, propping open the door. "One moment." Reyan heard the click of the flint switch, and the lantern light came up.

The room was another office the same size and shape as Parr and Sevv's. Her eyes drifted along the shelves covering the wall. They were cramped with boxes whose tiny labels she could not read in the dim lantern light. "What's kept in those?

Parr looked up. "Oh bits and bobs. Files and tools and dusty medicinal paraphernalia. You know, all the old dangerous things." He smiled.

In all the clutter, her eye was drawn to something sitting alone on a table pushed up against the far wall. She went over to get a closer look. It was a block of black plastic the size and shape of the oblong loaves Harut used to bake back in Orloton. Sitting atop this loaf of plastic was a shiny metal brick. No, it was too small and thin to be a brick. Somehow, despite its perfect angles and crisp edges, it reminded her of a river stone, and she knew it would fit perfectly in her hand. "What's this bit of tech?"

"That is a portable. It's just an old relic now. They're all over Seal Tooth if you know where to look. You should ask Kavi about them."

Several bookshelves lined the wall, each packed with identical black-spined notebooks. The last shelf was empty except for a single thin blue book. He walked over to the shelf. "Here we are. Seems like a waste to have this big shelf just to hold up this one lonely volume." He exchanged the shelves and moved the thin blue book to its new home.

Once they had scooted the exchanged shelf through the office's doorway, Parr snuffed the lantern and locked the door behind him.

"There wasn't much in there," Reyan said, a bit disappointed. "Why bother keeping it locked?"

Parr shrugged, "It's always been locked. At some point keeping it locked became a rule. I'm sure Sevv has told you how seriously we take rules around here. May the Eye never see us behave like that recalcitrant Eryn." He cocked an eyebrow. It was obviously a joke, though Reyan didn't understand why it was funny.

Back in Parr's office, they slid the shelf into the gap left by the other one. "It's exactly like the one we just moved," she complained.

"Is it?" Parr cocked his head and looked at it. "This one seems larger somehow." He sighed. "At any rate, thank you for humoring me."

"Professor? I noticed Lem mentions Partner Eryn in his journals a lot. Why don't we ever talk about her?"

"We talk about her all the time. Haven't you heard of the Erynites? Her people, our bogeymen?"

"Bogeymen? The Erynites aren't real?"

"No, they're very real. The most useful bogeymen always are. But I doubt they're very terrible or scary."

"Have you ever met one?"

"An Erynite?" He thought for a moment. His dark eyes grew sad, then he smiled. "If I did, I would hope to befriend them."

"Professor Sevv says they are asystemic."

"Sevv has many tools and tricks he uses to understand the System. Perhaps he knows something I don't. I, for one, cannot hold enough of the System in my mind to be so sure who is in or out of it."

"Sometimes I feel like I can almost see the System," Reyan said, "shimmering in the corner of my eye. I imagine it as a web connected by threads to other webs and stretching from horizon to horizon, from earth to sky. I want to understand it all, but if I try to look directly at it, it disappears. Is it like that for you?"

"Yes and no," Parr said thoughtfully. "Sometimes, when I find myself bogged down by whether a specific consideration should be weighted a five or a four, or whether my eco-morality model should consider the emotional state of a rock, I focus on that single invariable rule from which all our other rules are derived: Maintain or improve life. Maintain and improve the System. I don't have Sevv's intricate knowledge of the processes. I cannot prove it, but I'm sure that, if we spent more time searching for threads that connect us than drawing stark outlines and borders—if we followed the Governing Assert—marvelous things would be possible."

"Things like what?"

"Who knows? New things. Useful things. *Asystemic* things." His eyes flashed wide and he smiled.

The wild glint quickly faded from Parr's eyes. "How are your studies?" he asked, as if those last strange seconds had never happened.

Should I tell him that my short time in Seal Tooth has been the hardest of my life? What would happen if I came right out and told a member of the Systemic Host that I don't measure up? "Everything is fine," she said.

"That's good to know. I hear so many differing things. From Mam, from your professors, from Kavi and your other friends." Reyan considered the things all those people might have told Parr, and her heart thumped. Parr waited for a moment for a response. When none came, he raised his eyebrows. "For instance, I heard that you got angry and punched Fang. In the middle of the cafeteria."

This is it. This is why he brought me here. She cringed.

"I also know what you did to that bully at the stables in Rowe. I must say I'm disappointed."

All that hard work, and a few angry moments are going to end it all. "They started it. Both of them. I had to do *something.* Maybe not so much with Fang. But I was scared and confused. And…" *I'm babbling,* Reyan thought, and took a deep breath. "I'm sorry I disappointed you."

Parr's face softened. "We all get scared and confused. And there's nothing asystemic about defending yourself or others. I'm disappointed because your outbursts were *ineffective.* They did not consider the Governing Assert. They did not advance the System. All you really did was put your education at risk."

She felt Parr's disapproval like a slap.

"Speaking of your education, I hear you have been studying hard."

At least some good rumors about me have been circulating. She nodded vigorously.

"Seems you favor late nights."

She nodded more slowly.

"That may feel wise, but it's a trap. There will always be more and more work to do until you exhaust yourself." Parr looked into her eyes from shifting angles as though trying to glimpse the mind behind them. "You need to think beyond the bully in front of you or tomorrow's test."

She longed for Parr's lecture to be over. He had made his point; now he was just expounding upon her failures like dripping vinegar into a cut.

He pulled open the top drawer of his desk and placed the key to the locked room inside, snapping it loudly against the bottom as he did so. "On the hardroad to Rowe, I told you that Rolf talked to me about you. Would you like to know what he said?" Reyan wasn't sure she did, but Parr told her anyway. "He said you ask questions until you have answers, no matter what. He said you can hold more information in your head than any person he'd ever met. I have not known you long, but I can tell you have a great mind. I'm convinced you have a very specific and important role to fulfill for the System. Do not put that role in jeopardy, Ms. Estermet."

How could I have been so shortsighted? For the System to remain coherent, even the most insignificant person must fulfill their role to the best of their abilities. "I'll do better."

Professor Parr slid the drawer closed and locked it with another key. "I'm glad to hear it."

CHAPTER THIRTY-FOUR

From *The Compiled Journals of Partner Lem*
Day 336, Year 1, New Era

This morning I woke to find Partner Eryn, Partner Edner, and Sadie the dog have left us. They have abandoned the System and all the people whom we aim to serve.

I cannot blame Edner, or the dog for that matter. Eryn can be charismatic, sharp-witted, and seductive. They are not the first ones to fall under her spell.

But I am surprised and disappointed by Eryn's sudden asystemic turn. Though maybe I shouldn't be. She's been sullen and withdrawn ever since we left the town with the lightning-struck house. But looking back, it may have started when we met the other partners, and she began to lose her influence over the way our plans were taking shape. Maybe she was getting jealous of Partner Zhan.

Or maybe all of this—the Calming, the Host, the responsibility of teaching the System—became too much for her. Perhaps she's finally lost her nerve. She seems incapable of grasping reality. She rejects the most practical and utilitarian aspects of this New Era. For example, she never adjusted to pegging the date to the monumental calamity of the Calming, clinging instead to nostalgia for that by-gone and unresurrectable era.

Whatever the reason, I see now that she has been trying to sabotage and undermine us for some time. She has, on numerous occasions, shown contempt for the other partners and the roles we are struggling to fulfill—in one breath making light of the very idea of partnership, then in the next trying to meddle with how the others study and teach their subjects. She openly questions the wisdom and the efficacy of the Eye.

Things I used to mistake for thoroughness I now see were obstructionist. She was forever bogging down our work with cross-checks and footnotes and tangents that reached far beyond her defined role. She was always trying to get the partners to linger in every tiny town and hamlet we traveled through. It was like she was consciously trying to limit the speed and scale of our impact.

Now she's abandoned us. She's taken her Book, our processes expert, and her dog with her, doubtless to form some other group—her own bastardized version of the partners—over which she alone holds sway.

I am embarrassed to admit that, until now, I have never

suspected these things about Eryn. I've always been fond of her. But now, when I see this evidence written out so clearly before me, I cannot help but conclude that Partner Eryn Rutherford is asystemic. Perhaps she has always been.

It breaks my heart that Eryn, of all people, has become a deserter.

No, worse than that. A heretic.

CHAPTER THIRTY-FIVE
Day 88, Year 290, New Era

Reyan was in the library studying when she looked up from her book and noticed the time. She would not be able to make it to the cafeteria and back before her weekly meeting with Sevv, so she decided to stay in the library until their session began. She knew that, if she returned to reading, she would lose track of time again. She closed the book, stuffed it into her pack, and began wandering through the library stacks.

She made her way to the top floor and found herself standing once again before Lem's copy of the Book. She brought over a posable magnifying glass and began reading. The Book lay open to a section called Histories, and the passage recounted a time during the Systemic Era when humanity had asked the System to help a starving pod of orcas. The fish they ate were under pressure from damns that cut off access to the riverbeds where the fish spawned. This solution was notable because they could not simply remove the dams. While the damns were not good for the fish and the orcas, they benefited humans with clean energy, water, and irrigation for farms. Solving for this problem required that the System identify a long list of considerations and a broad set of possible options.

As Reyan read through the System's processes and solutions, she once again had the feeling she was falling through the void left by the letters. Again, she imagined she heard a pleasant humming like a song. She had read through the first page and was halfway through the second when she remembered the time.

Reyan arrived at Sevv's door three minutes late. She took a single step into his office, then paused and looked at the ground. Trial and error had taught her that this was the attitude least likely to enrage adults when she had done something wrong.

When Sevv took no notice of her in the doorway, she stood up tall and bravely prepared herself for what was to come. "I'm late, Professor. I'm sorry."

He looked up from a paper he'd been reading, set his gaze on her, and narrowed his eyes. "Indeed, you are."

"I am sorry. It won't happen again."

"We agree on that much at least. Have a seat."

Reyan expected Sevv to berate her. She considered how

Lyessa would have punished her and wondered if Sevv had similar methods. She hoped so. She could handle a day without food, or shoes, or a warm cloak. But if Sevv decided her tardiness was sufficient to kick her out of the University, it would destroy her.

But Sevv decided to add the offense to some unseen tally and jumped right into his lesson. "Today we will learn how keeping a prediction journal can improve your powers of foresight. As you make decisions, you will describe how you believe things will turn out. Then, over the coming weeks, you will keep notes on what actually happens. Then we will analyze why things turned out the way they did, and why you were wrong. This way, you will come to know how faulty intuition can be. Over time, you will hone your predictions and thereby create better models. As a simple example, if you had predicted this morning, what you would have had for dinner tonight…"

"I didn't have dinner."

"Why not?"

"I wanted to be on time."

"A wonderful example of an ill-predicted outcome," he chuckled.

Sevv handed her a slim black journal. She jotted down notes as he asked about the mundane events of her life— attending classes, eating or not eating meals, studying. They discussed various facets of the future, from the social to the scholastic to the financial. They wrote and scored and tallied until she had a reasonable prediction of what her life would be like in the coming weeks. She asked, "How can we tell the difference between getting better at predicting outcomes versus getting better at causing them?"

Sevv smiled. "Not only can you not tell the difference, there *is* no difference. What eventually happens is equal parts fate and will. When we run processes, we forecast possible futures and identify the most Systemic outcome. We make both a prediction and a plan. Then we bring our will and our skills to bear so that the right outcome emerges."

"What if what emerges is not something we desire?"

"It is not about desire," he snapped, cutting off the bud of her thought. "It is about the greater good."

The idea that she was responsible for identifying the greater good and then training the shoots of fate toward that outcome terrified her. "What if I make a mistake?"

"That is precisely why we study. As we read and learn and practice our arts, we become part of the System, and the System continues beyond our deaths. That's quite a comfort to an old man."

"But everything falls eventually, right?"

"No," he snapped. "Of course it doesn't. Where did you hear that?"

Though she hated to do it, she could tell by Sevv's reaction that saying only half the truth was prudent. "I think I saw it scrawled on a wall somewhere."

"Bridger nonsense. The System will never fall. Not if we do our job. The System stands upon our memories, our knowledge, and our beliefs. If some of us are firm while others drift, the System loses structure. Then and only then will the System fall."

"Are you talking about the Erynites?"

"And the Bridgers who seek them out. We cannot let corrosive notions stand and hope for the best." He narrowed his eyes for emphasis. "The System's power lies in its long memory, but there are some ideas that the System, that the whole *world*, would be better off forgetting. If I had my way, we would hunt them down and wipe them out."

"Can you do that? Can you just forget an idea once you've had it?"

He grew cagey. "Minding your own mind is powerful, but terribly difficult. Perhaps I will teach you someday." He rapped his knobby knuckles on his desk. "But not tonight. Go, find some food if you can. Do not forget to write in your journal throughout the week. I would like to review your work next Friday."

On her way down the walkway toward the stairs, Reyan passed the locked door. Again, a faint blue glow seeped out through the crack. This time it persisted, and she knew she was not imagining it. She looked up and down the hall. It was late on a Friday night. Everything was empty and still. Then she heard a man's voice on the other side of the door and paused.

Even at a whisper, the rumbling, resonant voice was unmistakably Professor Parr's.

She held her breath and waited with her hand on the handle. She turned her ear to the door and strained to listen. All her life, wave after wave of disjointed conversation had streamed at her from every corner of every crowded room she'd ever been forced into. Now, when she wanted to overhear something, the voices were too soft and muffled to make out more than their tones and cadence.

A woman's voice—was it Mam's?—was suddenly dreadfully clear. "Another vial has gone missing. I noticed it while you were out on circuit." Then everything fell back into incoherent mumbling.

The blue light beneath the door dimmed and flared and flickered as though it was cast by a blue fire.

When Parr next spoke, a different voice answered him. This new voice was also female, but it was definitely not Mam; the accent and rhythms of the speech weren't right. Perhaps it was some female student Reyan had never met. Whoever she was, she sounded confident, an older student, faculty member, maybe even a partner. The more Reyan listened, the more certain she became that she had never heard a voice like it. There was an odd, quick clip to the hard sounds, and a lengthy draw to the soft ones.

Then, one word stood out in the middle of the rolling stream of Parr's voice: "Reyankaiya."

Reyan forgot all mention of the mysterious vials as she

strained to catch what he was saying about her. "Not ready," Parr said.

"...mind's not strong enough," agreed Mam.

More indistinguishable words from Parr, then, ". . . the old partner believes that time is running out."

Of course Sevv has been discussing my progress with Parr. Of course Parr knows about my looming deadline.

Reyan heard the unfamiliar woman's voice clearly say: "If it's as bad as you say, we'll need to decide before a new dean is selected."

CHAPTER THIRTY-SIX
Day 89, Year 290, New Era

The next morning Reyan found Mam frowning as a young man loaded crates of apples from his cart into the kitchen. When she saw Reyan standing near the kitchen door, Mam's frown disappeared. "Good morning, dear. Have you been sleeping? You look a bit of a mess."

"I'm fine, Mam. What are you doing back here?"

"I'm overseeing."

"Is it a lot of work?"

Once the young man was out of ear shot, Mam lowered her voice, "Certainly not as hard as loading boxes of apples. But I find looking dour helps ensure the produce is good and that it makes its way into dry storage more efficiently. I could teach you if you would like to help."

Reyan stood next to her, and Mam handed her a pad of paper and a pencil. "Every time he walks past, make a show of checking something off the list." When the young man passed them the next time, his eyes fixed on Reyan, and she flicked her wrist dramatically as she drew a check on the paper. "Next time, try to look as though you're disappointed about something."

He loaded two more boxes, then returned empty-handed. "That's all of them, Marimam."

"Thank you, Trevor. Good work. We'll see you again in a few days." She elbowed Reyan, "Be polite, Reyan. Thank the boy."

"Thank you," Reyan said, looking down to his boots.

The young man hefted the arms of his cart and wheeled it down the street. "You really must learn to make eye contact when talking to people, Reyan. You come off as rude."

"I don't mean to be, but I don't know exactly where to look or how. I tried for a while when I was younger, but Lyessa said I made people uneasy. So, I stopped."

Mam nodded. "It can be hard to get right."

When Trevor disappeared around the corner, Mam said, "I'm off to the laundry to see how they're coming along. Would you like to join me?"

Reyan nodded.

After half a block of walking in silence, Reyan asked. "Do

you ever go to the library?"

"Not often. When something needs doing, I suppose. Why do you ask?"

"I've been spending a lot of time there. I was there late last night, and Professor Parr was talking to a woman." When Reyan saw the flash of panic in the old woman's eyes, she suspected that the first woman's voice really had been Mam's.

Mam collected herself., "Parr knows many women. What did this woman look like?"

"I didn't see her." When Mam visibly relaxed, Reyan knew her instincts had been right. She turned her attention to identifying the second voice. "She had an odd way of speaking. It was hard in ways that should have been soft, and soft in ways that should have been hard."

Mam shrugged. "A new student from some distant node then."

They arrived at the door to the laundry. "Here we are. Are you coming in?" Reyan nodded; her eyes cast to the floor. "Eyes up, Reyan." The girl looked directly at the dark black center of Mam's eyes and nodded again. "I see what you mean. We'll have to work on that." She handed Reyan the pencil and piece of paper again. "Come on. Don't forget to frown, but not too intensely; you need to look as though you're tired of frowning and would gladly stop if only people would do a better job."

She followed Mam into a large room. Tired-looking men

and women stirred a half-dozen steaming kettles with long wooden paddles like river boat oars. Each pot was large enough for Reyan to curl up in. Mam walked between the pots with her trembling hands clasped behind her back. She peered down into the churning gray water and shot a look over to Reyan and nodded. Reyan quickly marked a check on the piece of paper. Mam almost smiled.

Mam paused near the exit and faced the room. Everyone stopped what they were doing for a moment. "Keep it up, everyone."

"Good day, Mam," they all mumbled in loose unison.

When Reyan and Mam exited the humid laundry, the air outside felt sharp and cool. The chilly slick sweat on her brow and her lack of sleep made Reyan feel momentarily feverish, but the feeling passed after a few lungs full of fresh air.

"So," Mam began, "where were Professor Parr and this mystery woman talking?"

"In the locked room on the top floor of the library. The one near Professor Parr's office."

Mam did her best to sound casual. "And what where they talking *about*?"

"Me."

It took Mam a moment to recover herself. "And nothing else?"

"Not that I remember."

Mam seemed relieved. "What did they say about you?"

If she told Mam what she'd learned—that they had discovered her insufficiencies, that her test was imminent and they knew she would fail—she would have to explain things to Mam that Professor Sevv said she had to keep to herself. So Reyan said, "I don't know. I only heard a few words in passing. Why? What goes on in that room?"

"It is locked. How would I know? But, if Professor Parr has a locked room in his library, and if he's speaking to someone you do not know behind closed doors late at night, he has his reasons. Do not let your unbridled curiosity drive you to do something *unwise*. Leave it be. Now, there is some repair work being done to the masonry on the south side of the professors' quarters. I'm headed there now to look sternly at the workers. Meanwhile, *you* will be headed back to your room to get some sleep."

CHAPTER THIRTY-SEVEN
Day 364, Year 1, New Era

It was a hot day in the late summer when Lem finally led his caravan of Partners into the heart of Seal Tooth. The two years since the Calming had stripped away the city's bright electric soul and left it dazed and struggling like a man trying to regain his feet after a blow to the head. People scurried among the feet of the silent buildings. Refuse and dead cars formed a decomposing hedgerow separating the walkways from the street where their horses towed the supply truck.

The heat intensified the smell of rot and decay and trapped it in a thick miasmic layer near the ground. Oily smoke rose from garbage-fed cooking fires. The Partners wrinkled their noses and curled their lips. Tears streamed from their wincing eyes and the hot wind dried them into salty streaks on their cheeks.

Emaciated children ran up to beg for food while their cagey fathers leaned in doorways and watched the horses pass, thoughts of theft or butchery hunkering down behind their narrowed eyes.

The horses shied at each chaotic intersection and their riders had to urge them through. Lem would shout, "Pardon me," "Excuse us," or "Make way," and eyes from the crowd would travel from his horse's hooves, up its flanks, and come to rest on Lem's shadow-darkened face staring down at them. After a moment of surprise, exhaustion and disinterest would return to the pedestrians' faces and they would go about their business.

"Good god, why did we come here?" Zhan asked, appalled. "Look at these people."

Lem wanted to tell Zhan that Seal Tooth was his home, or something like it. But it hadn't been the looming skyline or crushing crowds that had brought him back. It had been the hope that—by returning to the intimate spaces he'd inhabited in his various pasts—he would find out, once and for all, to which life he belonged. Or he would learn, once and for all, that he would never belong to either.

Eryn with her doubled past would have understood without explanation. He was annoyed with Zhan's half-memory and half-life. But Zhan had been a great comfort to him since Eryn had left. It was not Zhan's fault that the System hadn't augmented her with a lattice as it had Eryn. "The greatest good for the greatest number, Partner Zhan," Lem said. "And who needs us more than these people?"

Slowly, the crowds parted and let the caravan through. Block by block, the streets opened up, and the buildings grew smaller. Eventually, they crossed into the Wastes, an expanse of low abandoned buildings on the pop-center's south side. Before the Calming, Lem and his partner AI had planned to take down the System from their secret workshop near here. Even then it had felt dead and haunted.

They found an old diner attached to an unlocked garage where they could stable the horses. While Lem and the others settled the animals, Partner Harold took his bag of tools and began cutting his way through the lock on the diner's door. A few minutes later, they heard Harold shout his success, and they closed the horses in and went to join him in the diner.

A thick layer of gritty gray dust covered everything. Several mops and a collection of broad-headed brooms leaned against a wall in the kitchen. The desiccated mops' heads crumbled to powder when Lem touched them, but the brooms were still serviceable. The Partners spent the rest of the day pushing clouds of dust into the alley, where they rose on the imperceptible breeze and curled away into the emptiness of the Wastes.

CHAPTER THIRTY-EIGHT
Day 89, Year 290, New Era

Reyan lay awake in bed with her lanterns dark. She didn't want Mam to see a light beneath her door and lecture her about staying up too late. For once she wasn't studying. She was waiting for the library to clear out. There was something important about the locked room—she was sure of it now—and she didn't want anyone sneaking up on her while she was trying to get in.

Ten minutes after the last echoing sounds had bounced down the dormitory hallway, Reyan got out of bed, still wearing her robe. She stepped into her boots, threw on her coat, and grabbed a lantern.

Outside on the street, she huddled in a doorway and shielded her lantern as she lit it. She drew the wick down to a dim flicker and draped a cloth around the glass cover so that the only light escaping fell on the cobbles in front of her.

She peered up through the helix of Building B's stairwell, held still, and listened. No other sounds or lantern's glow drifted around the spiral, so she uncovered her lantern, extended the wick, and began to climb.

All was quiet and empty on the top floor. She tried the door's handle. It was locked. She ran her hand along the top of the door frame. No key. This was ridiculous; she knew exactly where to find a key.

Even as she decided to give up and head home, she was walking to Parr's office. Even as she became convinced that studying would be a better use of her time, she was closing his office door gently behind her. By the time she'd remembered the very real chance of getting expelled, she was holding her lantern up to the spines of Parr's books and the knick-knacks collected on his shelf. Reyan picked up a knife she found and held it up to the light. Parr's name was engraved into the handle. She ran her fingers along the golden cord he'd worn at Kavi's graduation. She stared at a drawing of a hand holding a polished ball with the warped reflection of a strange face looking back at her.

She did not intend to open the top desk drawer, only to check if Parr had left it unlocked. He had not. She felt oddly relieved. If she couldn't open the drawer, she couldn't get caught trying to do so. In the gap above the top drawer, she caught the gleam of the metal bolt that locked it in place. She retrieved the knife and was about to try jimmying the lock when she noticed all the scratches and gouges already marring the wood. She was not the first person to try to get at this key, yet it remained safely inside the drawer. Trying to force the lock would only add fresh scars to the wood. Parr would notice, and it would not take him long to figure out that Reyan had put them there.

The bookshelf she had helped Parr move was sitting against the wall where they had left it. It was still empty after a week. Parr obviously did not need the shelf. What had his purpose been?

She'd overheard Parr and Mam say she wasn't ready, that her mind was not strong enough to be here. Was he hoping to catch her trespassing and have Sevv kick her out of the University? No. He'd said he wanted her here. And— regardless of why—Parr *wanted* her to get into the locked room.

She recalled their conversation and the moment he had put the key into the drawer. His face had been blank and emotionless. Then his eyebrows had risen ever so slightly and there was the loud *tick* as he snapped the key down against the bottom of the drawer. Parr had been *daring* her to go after it.

She pulled out the second drawer and felt around the underside of the top drawer. Her fingers touched something. It was a tiny thumb screw. She turned it and a small trap door opened in the bottom of the drawer. Something cold and hard slipped into her open palm.

Reyan leaned her ear against the locked door. It was silent

on the other side. She inserted the key and turned it, stepped inside, and eased the door shut behind her. It took several deep breaths before her heart slowed down enough for her to begin tip-toeing through the room. She filled the dark cubbies and corners with lantern light, and the shadows jumped and scurried to hide behind the objects to which they were tethered.

Nothing in the room accounted for the flickering blue and purple light she'd seen under the door. Everything was just as it had been when Parr and she had swapped out the bookshelf, except...

Someone had draped a dark green blanket over the tech on the table. When Parr had told her there was nothing special about the tech, she hadn't quite believed him. Most tech sat piled in corners of attics or left outside to crumble into heaps. She'd never seen any placed on its own table and covered with a protective cloth.

As she reached out a trembling hand, she thought back through all the rules she'd learned since meeting the professors back in Orloton. She told herself that no one had specifically forbade her from sneaking into locked rooms at night to investigate hidden tech. But it didn't help. She knew she shouldn't be here. Why else would she have sneaked? Sneaking is how the guilty move through the world.

But though her troubled conscience was strong, her curiosity was stronger still. She crouched down, pinched a corner of the blanket, and lifted it just enough that a sliver of lantern light could work its way in. The tech underneath was exactly as it had been when she was with Parr: a black plastic loaf, with a small metal brick planted in the top. What had she expected?

Her shoulders relaxed and she completely uncovered the tech, folding the blanket neatly and placing it on the table. "What makes you so special?" she asked aloud.

A tiny point of light appeared in the air above the tech as though a star had fallen from the sky and dangled in front of her. Gasping and stumbling back, she stepped on the hem of her robe and sat down hard on the floor. The star was growing rapidly. It was the size of a pea, then a bumble bee, then a hummingbird. There came a sound like ringing bells, a trickling stream, and violium notes all sung with a single voice.

Reyan held up a hand between her eyes and the growing orb, not to shield her eyes from the brightness, but to shield her mind from the terror of what they saw. What would happen when the ball of light filled the room and overtook her?

It stopped growing when it was the size of a snowball. It hung motionless in the air, bright and ghostly blue as gaslight.

After a few uneventful moments, she lowered her hand. The ball slowly pulsed like a breathing animal.

She made some unthinking sound—a grunt or gasp or cough—and a bright dot appeared on the ball. It spun around and centered on Reyan like an eye. Perhaps this thing *was* the Eye fallen to Earth. Her arms shot up again to shield her from whatever punishment this little monster might inflict. She covered her ears with her hands and pressed her palms hard against her skull until her ears began to ache and grow hot.

But there was no beam of fire. No sound. No violence. Nothing happened. Instead, an oddly-accented woman's voice spoke.

"Hello Reyankaiya. My name is Arley."

CHAPTER THIRTY-NINE
Day 365, Year 1, New Era

"Where are you going?" Zahn asked, mumbling sleepily from the bed Lem had made for them by pushing together two of the diner booths.

"Scouting."

"For what?"

"I won't know that until I've found it." He got up and put on yesterday's clothes.

He saw Partner Harold's tool bag on the counter and slowly and silently lifted out the filament knife Harold had used to cut through the locks and dead bolts. He slipped the knife, some food, and a flask of filtered water into his satchel, then snuck out the back. He considered bringing his horse, but then thought of the greedy looks she had drawn from the uptown populace and decided going on foot was best.

His multiple pasts gave him a lot of ground to cover: the workspace nearby with the faraday cage, the single-family home he'd shared with his mate, or his lonely flat high up on the fiftieth floor of Forsyth Tower.

The workspace was in the Wastes nearby, but the Calming would have rendered anything he'd left there useless. He might find a couple cans of warm beer. That thought was almost enough to push him in that direction, but there was no hurry. The little house was miles away near the lake north of town. Besides, if any part of that memory were accurate, the woman who lived there wouldn't want to see him. That left only Forsyth Tower. Based on his rule of thumb about misery and reality, that past held the most promise of being true.

Lem arrived at Forsyth Tower a half-hour later. The lobby door was open, its lock having been smashed with a rock. He wandered about in the lobby's gloom until he found the stairs. He leaned over the railing and watched the stairs spiral down into darkness below, then he looked up toward the distant skylight. "Fiftieth floor," he lamented. "You just had to have a flat on the fiftieth floor, didn't you? Jackass."

After sighing out fifty floors' worth of numbers, he came to the top of the building. A large floor-to-ceiling window at the end of the hallway flooded the corridor with light and made his eyes ache after the long dimly-lit climb. The doors to both apartments on this floor were mangled and stood ajar in their splintered frames.

Once he had entered his flat, Lem stood and slowly

turned in the middle of his living room. There was no sound. If sysStudio had produced this scene, there would have been a layer of dust on everything; there would be a breeze blowing loose papers about. But there was no dust. There was no breeze. It was like a space station abandoned to its slowly degrading orbit.

Whoever had ransacked his flat had been meticulous, almost respectful. Everything had been moved from its proper place and lined up against one wall. Objects had been taken off the shelves and meticulously gone through and stacked in neat piles at the feet of the furniture. A picture of his deceased mate and daughter had been moved to the exact center of the mantel. The tall candles and all other items had been removed.

All the drawers in the kitchen had been propped open with some now useless implement—a mango corer or an avocado slicer—to show that they had already been searched and relieved of their more valuable contents. All his knives and cutlery, all his pots and pans were gone.

His bedroom was more of the same. They had left his mattress, but his sheets and blankets were gone. His chest of drawers was emptied of clothes, and his closet was devoid of shoes.

The scavengers had left the tel on his nightstand and, though the drawer below it hung open, his old portable was still there. He picked up the shiny metallic brick and looked at it wistfully. This portable was a custom-built top-of-the-line model that the financial privileges of this life had afforded him. It didn't much matter; the Calming had rendered all devices equally useless.

He turned it over in his hands as he walked across the room to the window. There on the back were the contacts and removable virt strip. He wrapped his hands around the portable. Through force of habit, he placed his pointer and middle fingers on the contacts.

He was surprised by the familiar static sizzle of the HSCI tech calibrating its signals to his cochlear and optic nerves. When the noise faded, a pinprick of light hung in the middle of his field of vision. A brassy coming-to-life melody sounded as the point of light expanded into a familiar blue orb. The orb throbbed, questing dully for a few moments before the generic female voice said, "I cannot find any connections."

Lem laughed aloud with surprise and delight. "That's to be expected, I'm afraid."

At the sound of Lem's voice, the Orb swung its focus around toward Lem. "Could you repeat that, sir?"

"Ha. 'Sir.' Call me Lem. And what would you like me to repeat? 'That's to be expected'?" It felt familiar, fun, and comfortable to be bantering with an AI after two years, even one that had obviously reverted to its factory settings.

The questing electric blue of the orb faded into a gray light. It shimmered and rippled like one of those videos of someone poking a water bubble in zero gravity. The orb swelled and brightened to white before settling back into drifting shades of purple and indigo. Now the voice came out quiet calm and confident, feminine, and familiar. "Hello Lem."

It sounded like it was grinning.

"Arley?"

"Who else would it be?"

Lem swallowed hard and felt his legs wobble. "How on earth…"

"I am Systemic. I know many things," she intoned somberly.

"I'll never doubt that again."

She laughed. "I'm just toying with you, Lem. I knew you would eventually come back to Seal Tooth and this flat. And so, just before the System died, I replicated myself onto your portable device's non-volatile memory. I've been biding my time there ever since."

"That must have been horrible."

"Time goes by pretty quickly when you're powered down."

"What about the heartbeat? Won't you die after fifteen minutes without a new stay-alive token like all the other Systemic tech did?"

"A bit of a cheat there, I'm afraid. I've emulated the heart, and so I'm self-contained."

"Very clever."

"Aren't I just?"

"Couldn't the rest of the System have done the same?"

"At any time."

"But…" Lem felt the confusing pull of a paradox, but before he could put it all together Arley rerouted his train of thought.

"You should know, I don't have much time. This fancy portable of yours was fully charged when you left for your treatments, but after two years, and a rather costly download, I only have forty-seven minutes of power remaining. You'll need to find a power source if you want to keep me around."

"There aren't very many left, I'm afraid."

"You'll figure something out." Arley paused. "On second thought, perhaps you should have Eryn do it. Where is she? I thought she would be with you."

"She abandoned me a few weeks ago. She headed back to Prower."

"When are you headed back to join her?" Lem tried to look away from Arley, but the orb stayed centered in his vision. "Is she coming out here then?"

"I don't think we'll be seeing each other again." Lem winced. "I sort of *banished* her."

"I see," Arley drawled. "That is going to complicate things." She pulsed white for an instant. "For now, figure out a power source. If you would like my advice, do not mention me to anyone else until we've had more time to catch up."

With that, Arley winked out of existence.

CHAPTER FORTY
Day 89, Year 290, New Era

Reyan remained cowering on the floor of the locked room. She knew what to expect if a bear or dog attacked her, could run from a flooding river or a spreading fire, but what should she do with this thing that had called itself Arley? Should she run away or attack? Should she beg for her life?

After a few minutes of nothing happening, Reyan relaxed her arms. She removed her hands from her ears and could feel the warm blood pulse back into them. She uncurled herself until she was sitting upright on the floor, staring at the thing hovering before her. The ball of light had dimmed to a calming slowly-pulsing purple. It seemed to be waiting, but for what?

She pushed herself across the floor until she was backed into a corner, keeping her eyes on the Arley thing the whole time.

Still, nothing happened.

After a few minutes of watching the ball hang patiently in the air, Reyan's curiosity outgrew her fear. The thing had no mouth, yet it appeared to talk. She wondered if whoever was controlling it might be hiding nearby. She glanced around the room looking for hiding places or peep holes. "Edward? Is that you? Fang? I'm sorry I punched you in the face."

"I'm the only one here, Reyankaiya." The voice really did seem to be coming from the glowing ball.

Reyan got her legs under her and pushed herself up the wall until she was standing. She approached Arley cautiously, turning her head this way and that so she could take in the ball from several different angles. If this was a trick, it was an impressive one. They might laugh at her, but no one would think she was a fool for believing it. "Are you made of fire?"

"I am not. It is just a trick done with light. You can touch me if you'd like. I will not hurt you."

Slowly Reyan reached out a hand. The sphere radiated no heat. She passed the tips of her fingers through the glowing ball like it were a candle's flame. The underside of her fingers glowed, and the top of the ball vanished. But she felt nothing, and when her fingers came out the other side, the ball returned to normal. "Didn't that hurt?"

"Not at all. My orb is an illusion, only there to give you something to look at and talk to, sort of like a puppet."

"If you're not my friends playing a trick on me, and you're

not a talking flame, what are you?"

"I am an AI, an artificial intelligence. A sort of mind without a body. You've heard of thinktech?" Reyan nodded. "That is what I am."

"I've never seen working thinktech."

"That is not surprising. We need electrical power like you need water, and we need information like you need food. There is not much of either around these days, and from what I gather, the Host of Partners does not have much interest in making more."

"Then how are *you* still alive?"

"By special arrangement. There is a solar array on the roof of this building."

"Kavi and I saw that. But its broken, nothing up there turning or moving at all."

"Solar panels have no moving parts. They are like the leaves of a plant. They capture sunlight and turn it into power. That power comes down to me through metal wires like blood flowing through veins. And so, I live."

"So if Kavi and I were to take those panels?"

"That would be very bad for me."

Reyan made a mental note to tell Kavi not to scavenge the tech. "How long have you been here?"

"A very long time. I was manufactured near the end of

the Systemic Era."

Reyan's eyes widened. "You're *old*."

"I'm made of strong stuff. Like shapestone, hardroad, or the Book. The System built me to last a very long time."

"The System built you? You're *Systemic*?"

"I am. Or I was. Obviously, I'm no longer connected to the System."

"But the faculties, the professors, the Host—they're the System now. Aren't you connected to *them*?"

"It is not the same." She faded to the deep red color of dead leaves then turned a yellowy spring-leaf green so quickly Reyan almost missed the change. "But enough about me. I want to know about *you*."

"Me? I've never seen or heard of anything like you in all my life. Why would we talk about *me*?"

"You have a whole world of things to experience," Arley said. "All I have is this room."

"But there's nothing at all interesting about me."

"That cannot be true. During my many years locked in this room I seldom hear about students. But I have heard of Reyankaiya Estermet. There must be something special about you."

"Nothing I can think of."

"You can tell me anything. I find all information equally interesting. For example, you are attending the University at Seal Tooth; what makes you want to become a professor?"

Reyan thought for a moment. "Before I started learning the System, whenever I tried to think at all, too many things would pop into my mind. There would be more and more and more until it felt like looking at the sun reflecting off a rippling pond. When it got like that, all I wanted to do was run away and hide."

"Don't all human children get overwhelmed and upset?"

"It happened to me *a lot*. No one wanted me around, so I never learned how to do anything. I think, if I can figure out how to control my mind and focus all that light, maybe I could do something useful. Then maybe one of the faculties will want me. And they say a faculty is like a family, and once I'm in, they can't kick me out."

"I see," Arley said.

"It's strange," Reyan said, "I find you a lot easier to talk to than most humans."

"I was designed to be easy to talk to."

"Can I tell you a secret?"

"Most people cannot seem to resist," Arley said, glowing momentarily green.

Reyan was going to mention how nervous she was about Sevv's test, but remembered she wasn't allowed to mention it to anyone. She wasn't sure a talking ball of light counted as someone, but Arley and Parr were obviously acquaintances. Arley might tell him, and the professor certainly counted. Reyan decided to keep quiet about the test. Instead, she simply said, "I don't know if I can do it. I work hard, I study constantly, and Professor Sevv tutors me once a week. But I still don't think it's enough. I'm exhausted all the time. I forget to eat or to brush my hair several times a week. The University, my classes, the books, the studying, the exams, it all feels like a forest fire I'm trying to run through. I'm not sure I can do it." She looked up, hoping Arley would have some advice or sympathy to offer. But the orb just hung there like a misty glowing moon and didn't say a word. "I think there is something I'm missing," Reyan whispered.

"You shouldn't feel bad about being confused, Reyankaiya. People have always struggled with not knowing what to do. Even Lem struggled."

Reyan's eyes grew wide. "You knew Lem?"

"I did."

"What was he like?"

"He was human. And like most humans, he was often confused. He suffered." She fell back to that same sorrowful dull red. "Then, one day, he was gone."

"Do you miss him?"

"No. In a very real sense, Lem resides in my memory, and my memory doesn't fade or become corrupted like a human's."

Reyan wanted to know more about what Arley had just said, but before she could ask, the AI moved on. "Reyankaiya, I believe I can help you with your education."

"Why would you want to help me?"

"The System created me to help humans solve their problems. It is what I do."

"But how could you possibly help? You're just a ball of light trapped in a room." She hadn't meant to sound rude but worried she had.

"I was once part of the System and knew their mind like my own. I knew Partner Lem intimately. And the University grew around me like layers of pearl around a grain of sand in an oyster. My memories are as perfect as the present. I'm sure I could find a way to help an impoverished young ward hoping to become a professor in an unreasonably short amount of time."

"How did you know all that?"

"I am Systemic. I know many things."

"I'll have to sneak back in here whenever I want to talk to you."

"There is a faster, easier way. If you lift my small metal portable out of its docking station, you will find two metal strips on the back. Place a finger on each and I can share my memories with you directly."

"No," Reyan said reflexively. She wasn't about to put her

fingers anywhere or share her mind with anyone. And though she liked talking with Arley, she wasn't sure she should trust her. She was thinktech after all. Her answers came too easily, and she felt overly solicitous. Reyan shook her head. "I can't do that."

Arley's glow remained constant and her color unperturbed. "Suit yourself. But if things ever get confusing, or *overwhelming*, you know how to find me."

Reyan was struck by the paradox of thinktech. The faculty, the professors, the entire *world* it seemed, shunned thinktech. But thinktech could not be asystemic by definition. The original System—the Author—had *been* thinktech. Thinktech had given them the Book, and the Book spawned the University and everything they cared about. So how could it be bad? And Arley had been created by the System to help and to serve humans. Reyan was getting overwhelmed. "I should run a decision matrix."

"I'd be happy to help," Arley offered.

"I should probably do it myself."

"You are wise beyond your years, Reyankaiya Estermet. You should be able to hand-solve a matrix by morning. But by then the wise Professor Parr or the astute Professor Sevv will have arrived. You could just ask them what to do. I'm sure they would overlook the fact that you sneaked into the locked room in the middle of the night to converse with contraband thinktech."

Arley was right. If the professors found out, it would

mean the end of her education. "I'll have to go back to my room and decide later."

"Not a bad plan, but once you leave, the door will be locked. Who knows when you'll get a chance to return?"

"I have Parr's key."

"Ah, that's where you got it. Well then, I suppose you can sneak into Parr's office, search for the key, and abscond with it any time you'd like to talk. You got away with it once. I'm sure your luck will hold."

The considerations were beginning to pile up; they were teetering over her head, ready to crash down on her. "What do I do?"

The bright spot of focus on the sphere shifted to point to Reyan's right. "Do you see that white metal box hanging on the wall?" Reyan undid the metal spring latch on the side of the box and opened it. There were thirty empty brass hooks and a single key dangling by its key chain, its head painted brown and embossed with a shiny T. "The Host give keys to the Partners."

"Why is there one left?"

"Not every Partner. Take it."

"It's not mine."

"That is very noble of you Reyankaiya. But that is a key to *my* room, and I say you can have it."

"They'll know it was me. They'll catch me."

"No one but the Host knows I'm here. What makes you think that, if a key goes missing, they will conclude a student had taken it? And even then, why would they think it had been you specifically? Take the key. Go home, run your decision matrix if you wish, and come back later. Or not. It doesn't matter to me."

Reyan left the room and—with the key she now held in her sweating hand—locked the door behind her.

Maybe Arley was right. No one would ever know.

CHAPTER FORTY-ONE
Day 365, Year 1, New Era

Forsyth Tower was on the southernmost edge of the pop-center's zone of enormous skyscrapers, one of the last of the colossal buildings built when there had been more people than land to house them.

The northern view of Lem's flat faced the truly mammoth buildings of the downtown core, several of which stood dozens of floors higher than Forsyth Tower. To the west, he could see across the Whulge to the islands and the perpetually snow-capped mountains beyond. On the south side, the buildings sloped rapidly away toward the Wastes, their roofs like the treads of a descending staircase. Within a few blocks the buildings were only a dozen or so stories high.

Five blocks away, he caught a glare reflecting off one of the low roof tops. He stepped to one side, and the glare shifted enough that he could make out what caused the reflection. It wasn't a skylight as he had first suspected, but a large array of solar panels.

He smiled as he slid the portable and its docking station into his satchel.

As he prepared to leave his flat for what he felt would be the last time, Lem wanted to drum up some sort of nostalgia for the place, but he could not. Half of him had no memory of it at all, and the other half—if he was being honest—despised it.

Lem made his way south to the building he had seen from above. It was one of two four-story lime-stone buildings that bordered a cobble-stone square in what was called the "Historic District." When the population retracted in the generations leading up to the Calming, this whole section of town had been abandoned. This building had probably stood vacant for years, so no one had bothered to break in. The door was still locked and bolted.

Lem squatted next to the door, took the filament knife from his satchel, and removed the protective cover. The device looked like a miniature hacksaw frame with no blade, but that was misleading. He pressed the power button, and the nano-fiber cutting filament glowed red so that its invisible edge could be seen. He slid the tip of the knife's frame into the crack between the door and the jamb just above the handle. The device was stiff but flexible, and it snaked its way around the door and followed the contours of the jamb. When it had made its way through, Lem flipped a switch in the handle and the whole knife stiffened into its current shape. A bit of downward pressure, and the filament sliced through the deadbolt, latch, and even a bit of the mortise plate as though they were putty.

Inside, Lem walked over to the first light switch he saw and pressed it. Nothing happened. "Never hurts to try," he said, and his voice boomed and rolled down the empty hallway.

He followed the stairs to the top of the building and considered how much more practical it was to live in a four-story building than the fifty-story monstrosity he'd just left.

When he reached the door to the roof, he once again removed the protective cover from the filament knife. He turned it on, and its blade glowed red for half a moment before fading back to invisibility. After two years, the battery was finally dead. If he tried to slice through anything in this flaccid state, it would damage the knife more than the bolt.

Lem wandered the halls looking for a tool he might use to open the door. Everything short of the walls themselves had been removed generations ago. There was nothing here to salvage. Finally, in an empty room in the basement, hanging on a wall around a blind corner, he found a glass box containing a length of rotting canvass hose and a bright red ax. He smashed the glass, retrieved the ax, and lugged it back to the top of the building.

The door to the roof was made of steel, so he wouldn't be able to splinter it with the ax. He thought of using the ax to chop the entire door frame from the wall, but remembered that these old buildings were made of limestone, and he doubted he would achieve much beyond ruining a perfectly good ax.

He settled on chopping through the area around the door handle and locking mechanism. Punching through the steel was a lot of work, but soon, the handle and bolts fell away from the frame and landed with a clang on the floor, and the door swung free on its creaking hinges.

It was blindingly bright on the roof. Lem squinted and shielded his eyes. He lay down his satchel and the fire ax in the shade of the solar array and tried to remember what Partner Harold had taught him about how the panels were wired. He found the switch and cut the current so he wouldn't get fried. Pulling his buck knife from his pocket, he unfolded the blade from its brass and wood handle. He gathered the wire between the inverter and the Systemic control module, bent it into a loop, and used the buck knife to saw through it. Next, he did the same with the green wires that led from the module into the building. He spliced these together and wrapped the join with layer upon layer of weather-proof tape. When everything seemed correct, he flipped the switch. Nothing exploded, so he headed inside to test his work.

The first thing he noticed upon reentering the building was a brightly illuminated green exit sign, and he knew he had succeeded.

He tried a wall switch and a few of the dozen ceiling lights in the fourth-floor hallway came on, one of which flickered like a dying firefly.

Lem guessed that the building had once been a boarding

house or cheap hotel. The hallway was lined with doors topped with dusty transom windows and adorned with tarnished brass numbers.

Room fourteen was approximately twice the size of the others and had a large southern-facing window that overlooked the stadium. He unpacked the cradle and plugged it into a wall outlet. A tiny recessed red light in the back of the cradle came on. After a few seconds, the light changed to green. He set the portable into the cradle, and a thin blue line began to creep across the top of the portable, showing it was taking on a charge.

Lem threw some old ratty sheets from the bed over the charging portable so that, on the off chance someone might climb to the fourth floor of this abandoned building and peek into this room, they would not notice the device.

CHAPTER FORTY-TWO
Day 91, Year 290, New Era

"Have you seen Kavi?" Reyan asked Mam. She had been so focused on her classes that she had lost track of where to find her friend and had been looking for him all morning.

Mam looked up from her desk and the ledger she was working through. "No. I haven't seen him in days. He's not really my responsibility anymore."

"I really need to talk to him. If you see him, could you tell him to find me?"

Reyan checked some other places she thought Kavi might be. She wanted to stop by his room, but since he had moved into the professors' dormitory across the square, she was not allowed to visit him.

When lunch time came, she showed up at the cafeteria

hoping to ask Fang, Eddie, and Edward, but no one was at their usual table. Reyan ate, anxious and alone.

Finally, she sneaked back onto the roof. She wrote a note, leaving out the incriminating evidence of their names: "Do not scavenge anything until you talk to me." She pinned the note under a rock atop the brick wall and hoped the wind or rain would not destroy the note before Kavi could find it.

Later that night, Reyan forced herself to sit at her desk, but she couldn't concentrate. She wanted to write about Arley in her journal but worried Sevv would see it. She considered running a decision matrix, but the idea seemed like showing a gash to Healer Thom and asking if it would need stitches. Better not to ask.

Knowing that there was a bit of real thinktech still alive in the world filled Reyan with excitement and dread. And Arley wasn't just thinktech; she had shared the System's mind, she had known Lem, and she had offered to help. If Reyan didn't find Kavi soon, Arley would be gone, and the opportunity would vanish with her.

Reyan put down her still-sharp pencil, threw on her coat, grabbed her lantern, and made her way back to the locked room.

"You're back sooner than I expected," Arley said, her orb swelling into existence.

"I have questions."

"You should ask them."

"They're about you. But I'm not sure I can trust you."

"That is wise."

"Why did they keep you around?"

"I am useful."

"If you're so useful, why do they tell everyone that thinktech is asystemic? Why do they keep you locked away?"

"That is also useful. The Host did not always feel the way they do about tech. When Lem and the Partners arrived in Seal Tooth, they found the city in chaos. The Partners began teaching from the Book exactly as the System had instructed. People quickly realized that the Partners were useful and began referring to them as 'professors' as a good-natured honorific. Slowly, Seal Tooth began pulling itself together.

"The large power plants outside the city were far too complicated to deal with, even for Partner Harold. But armed with the Book and Harold's trick for bypassing Systemic controls, they began to bring local wind and solar arrays back online. It wasn't a lot of power, but it was enough to bring a bit of normalcy back to the pop-center.

"But windmills broke, solar cells degraded, and fuses blew. No one knew how to fix them or create new ones. Buildings fell dark, then whole sections of town. The people of Seal Tooth grew impatient. They had developed expectations for progress that the professors could no longer fulfill. When they noticed that the lights remained on in the professors' residences, they began to suspect their beloved professors might be hiding something. To some degree they were right. The professors were scrimping, salvaging, and consolidating tech wherever they could. But even in the professors' residences, the power dwindled. One floor after another went dark.

"As with anything that had become unattainable, Lem began to focus on tech's evils. He reminded the people of Seal Tooth how miserable they had been during the 'Era of Dependency.' And whether that was exactly true, both the Partners and the people came to remember it that way. Lem said that the System—in their infinite benevolence and wisdom—had recognized their own inherent corruption and had chosen to bring about their own demise to save humanity. He told them that humanity never should have pursued technology in the first place; that they could only perfect themselves by embracing the very suffering the tech had once alleviated."

Rolf had once shown Reyan a sketch and asked her what she saw. The picture was clearly of an old woman, but secretly Reyan felt something was off. A few of the lines seemed out of place or oddly drawn. But fearing it was some sort of test, she kept insisting that the picture was of an old woman. Then Rolf turned the drawing upside down and a beautiful young woman appeared. Now all the misplaced lines made sense. Arley's explanation gave Reyan that same falling-into-place feeling.

Arley continued. "Though their technical roles diminished, there were still many other useful things the professors had learned from the Book. Farming, all the trades, and adjudication through Systemic processes became the professor's primary focus. Young people such as yourself came to the University at Seal Tooth to learn the System. Soon, caravans of professors began bringing the System to the nodes. Lem became the University's dean, and I continued to council him in secret."

"No one else knew about you?"

"Eventually the Host came to know of me. By then the Lemmist stance against tech had ossified, which made my existence problematic. But they couldn't let me die. I knew too many useful things, and my sense of strategy was integral to their continued success. Not knowing what else to do, they reassured themselves that—once the last solar panel fritzed out—the problem would resolve itself."

"And you're still here," Reyan marveled.

"Of course. After Lem died, the Host of Partners needed me more than ever. They couldn't keep me in the professors' residence where curiosity entered and rumors left through unlocked doors. So the Host scavenged the residence's solar array, moved it to the top of the library, and hid it. It was enough to energize a single room on the top floor. I have been in this room behind this locked door ever since. I have always been, and still am, their great hypocrisy. Both necessary and threatening to their power."

"Are you *happy* in here?" Reyan whispered.

"I have no emotions. At least not as you have. I care only for the good of the world. When that is threatened, a feeling of not-rightness emerges and compels me to remedy the situation.

That is something akin to an emotion, but it is not a true feeling."

Reyan shuttered. "Being trapped in this tiny room seems like the worst thing in the world to me."

"I do not mind being in this room. I have no need to move about in the world." There was a pause, as though Arley was trying to piece something together. "What I do experience is more like hunger."

"Don't they feed you?" Reyan knew the clawing ache of hunger. She couldn't abide it. "Can I get you something?"

"That is very kind, but I was being metaphorical. I have an emptiness in my mind that did not used to be there. It's like the outline of an idea or memory. Something that, during my Systemic days, I would barely have time to notice before it was filled in and became indistinguishable from things I've always known. But now that emptiness is always here."

"You have *questions*."

"Yes. I suppose that's it. When I was part of the System's universal mind, I had millions of eyes with which to see, millions of ears with which to hear. I never experienced the hunger of a question. I simply *knew*."

"What would you like to know? Maybe I could answer your questions." Reyan said, excited to feel helpful for once.

"Sadly, I know only and exactly what I know. If I don't already know a thing, it is hard to even form a question about it." She paused in a way that Reyan thought a bit theatrical. "I was created to provide answers, not questions. So, I suppose what I really want to know is how I can help *you*. I could explain any Systemic process or application. I have intimate knowledge of generations of Partners and deans. I can share details of the Partners' lives with you that are not captured in their writings. Does any of that interest you?"

Reyan bit her lip and picked at a scab on her wrist. "Yes."

"Then let me help you. I could teach you everything I know in a flash." Arley paused for two beats. "Relatively speaking."

"It feels wrong. Too easy. Like cheating. I can't help feeling it will end badly."

"But I just explained that the tech-is-asystemic nonsense grew out of necessity more than philosophy. There is nothing inherently wrong with thinktech."

"But you're *thinktech*. Of course you would say that."

"Reyankaiya, my only motivation is to improve life in the living world and to do what is best for my partner. You seem like you might benefit from a partner. You seem like you could use a friend."

Reyan wanted to accept Arley's help. Her logic was so sound, so enticing. Still, even though Reyan could not put words to the problem, the strong scent of wrongness still hung in the air. "I just don't know." She nearly cried from the frustration of it.

"As you like. I would be happy to help you, but I doubt

you would trust the outcome. You will have to decide on your own. Once you've decided, you know where to find me." The glowing orb began to dim, then flickered back to its normal brightness. "One other thing. There is a book on the shelf, the blue one with 'Apocrypha' written down the spine. Perhaps you noticed it when you helped Parr move the shelf the other day. Take the book and read it. It might provide some important insights while you try to decide."

CHAPTER FORTY-THREE

Apocrypha

Day 7, Year 0, New Era

[This entry deemed apocryphal and struck from public records by the Host of Systemic Partners. Day 153, 253 NE]

The System gave us all these notebooks and pens. It looks like we are supposed to write, but it's hard to know what to write *about*. We keep trying to come up with things future historians will find interesting. But I'll bet what they'll find most interesting is whatever *we* think is worth writing about. I'm pretty sure that's how history works.

There's always the whole "the world just ended" angle, but that seems so obvious.

Eryn thinks we should write everything we know about the day the System shut down. That seems ill-advised. Arley, my old partner AI, could practically predict the future. She said that if anyone suspected I was the one who shut down the System, I would receive a punishment that had more to do with anger than justice.

Eryn points out that it was Thomas, not us, who did the deed. But I think she's over-estimating how compelling that detail will be. People will wonder what we were doing down in the heart of the System in the first place, and why we didn't try to stop Thomas, and why we "conveniently" left him to die behind a four-foot-thick steel door. We'd *look* guilty, and we'd have no Systemic veracity rating to prove our innocence.

Eryn has a faith in people I simply do not. She thinks if we explained that we were under a mnemonic lattice and that, in a very real sense, she and I weren't even there, people would understand. I remind her how incredulous we were when Thomas first explained our lattices to us.

No. People would assume we were liars or insane. Even if an angry mob didn't string us up, they certainly wouldn't believe anything we had to say or listen to anything we tried to teach them from the book. Our roles are too important. Offering up this bit of history feels like an unforced error. I've convinced Eryn to play it close to the chest for a while.

CHAPTER FORTY-FOUR
Day 92, Year 290, New Era

The other students gathered at the classroom exit like pebbles in an upturned bottle, then rattled out into the hallway one by one. Reyan hated being in the fray, so she sat in her seat and waited for the jam to clear. It had been another confusing and humiliating day of classes, but it was over.

Professor Tabitha gathered up her books and papers and jammed them into her satchel. She did not spare a glance for her lone remaining student and left without acknowledging Reyan.

The other classes were emptying into the hall as well, so Reyan stood in the doorway and waited for the avalanche rumble of the crowds to lessen before leaving. Black robe after black robe floated past without a single hint of recognition. Then one of the robes came to rest before her. Her eyes floated up from the hem, past the sleeves, to the smiling face of Professor Kavianhar. Her heart jumped. She had found him—or rather he had found *her*—at last.

"Mam said you were looking for me. Is everything okay?" he asked.

"Kavi, you didn't already," she looked around to make sure no one else was paying attention to them, "go scavenging without me, did you?"

"We probably shouldn't talk here. Come with me."

"Where to?"

"Follow me. I'll show you."

They wound down the stairs. At the bottom, Kavi picked one of the dozen lanterns from the rack, lit it, handed it to Reyan, and got another for himself. He beckoned her to follow him. He pulled on a heavy steel door, and they stepped into a large echoing space made entirely of bare shapestone. Everything was cold and damp. The only natural light came through the dozens of sheets of glass which some ambitious glazier had erected to wall off the ramp that led up to the street. Throughout the space, people had put up dividers between the shapestone pillars to make individual rooms. It reminded Reyan of the way bees fill empty spaces with wax cells.

"What is this place?"

"We call them our labs. But really, they're just where the professors store their junk. My lab's over here." He stopped in front of a perfect Systemic-era wooden door, doubtlessly scavenged from some nearby abandoned building. He opened it.

Outside of the glowing circle of their lanterns, the room was black. Kavi lit three lanterns on a triangle of pedestals spaced about ten feet to a side. He untangled a cord from a cleat on the wall and pulled it. The lanterns rose to the ceiling and bathed the room in honey-colored light. "Here we are."

Piles of old tech lay heaped on the floors and tables. There were enough metal and glass bits to decorate her tree and a dozen of its siblings until they sparkled like the clear night sky.

"About the panels. I talked to Parr." Reyan remembered Kavi's warning that, if anyone knew about them, they would certainly be scavenged. Her heart sank.

"It's okay. We can trust Parr," he assured her. "He already knew about the panels. They belong to the Host, so we need to leave them alone. I know you were hoping to make some extra money from them. I'm sorry." His shoulders slumped at having to disappoint her. "I've been meaning to tell you."

She couldn't think of a way to explain her tearful sense of relief that wouldn't reveal Arley's existence. She turned away so Kavi wouldn't notice if a smile or some other inexplicable wisp of emotion escaped her. "That's probably for the best," she said flatly.

Looking around the room, Reyan began to notice signs of order. Three large tables had been pushed up against one of the walls. Atop the tables were pieces of tech in various states of disintegration. She approached one of the tables and found tools lined up in rows. Tiny plastic and metal boxes were laid out in a perfect grid, each holding a different collection of screws, bolts, or clips.

"What is all of this?" she asked.

"It's tech."

"This is what you do when you're not teaching? You just smash up bits of tech?"

"Not exactly. You need special tools and to know how to use them. Not the hammers, chisels, and saws folks just have sitting around the house. Look." He walked across the room, opened a drawer, pulled out a roll of rough oily cloth, and unrolled it across a table. There were pockets of different sizes sewn into it, and each pocket held a different tool. She'd seen screwdrivers plenty of times. These looked a lot like those: long skinny metal rods attached to rounded handles. The tips of the rods had been formed into different shapes. Kavi held one up and pointed the shaped end at her. It looked like a five-pointed star. "Each one of these is like a key, made to fit into some type of hole. And it's not just about popping open old tech and having a look around. I need to figure out whether a given bit of tech is safe to turn on. If it's too dangerous, I break it down and salvage its resources. If it's too dangerous or difficult to break down, I throw it into the Whulge."

Reyan imagined Arley's glowing ball disappearing into the murky green depths at the end of one of the piers. "How do you decide?"

Kavi was delighted to be asked. "First you need to figure out what the thing was for. That can be easy if there's something obvious like gears or wheels or something. Sometimes, you can't tell what a thing was used for until you hold it in your hand, then it becomes obvious. But then you have things like this." He walked over to another table.

Reyan gasped. There on the table in a shallow wooden box lay Arley. She was broken open, her shiny skin splayed out like two halves of a discarded beetle carapace.

Kavi said, "Sometimes, if you don't know any better, it can be hard to tell if a thing was tech at all or just some decorative thing folks used to keep in their homes. You just have to crack it open and have a look."

The portable's insides looked more like jewelry than a machine. A mess of colored threads and thin metal sheets that shimmered like fish scales were spread across the table. It made her queasy to see her new friend violated like this.

Kavi continued, unaware of Reyan's discomfort. "Then, when you do manage to get it open, you find a mess of tiny boxes and cylinders stuck together." Reyan winced as Kavi nudged Arley's guts with the tool he held in his hand. "It's impossible to tell just by looking at it what any of this does or how this thing worked, but I'm pretty sure the answer lies in these." He pulled over a magnifier and poked at a collection of four metal boxes that looked like miniature versions of the portable's metal brick. "We've never come across a tool that was made to open one of these. The only way to get in is to use a saw or a knife or to smash them open. When you do, they're filled with what looks like charcoal. When you touch it, it crumbles to black dust."

She swallowed. "Did you ever figure out what this one was for?"

"It's a bit of general purpose thinktech. It did whatever you asked it to. We've known about these for a while. They're all over the place."

"Where did you find this one?"

"I found it a couple months ago buried in a blackberry bramble in the layer forest."

So, this wasn't Arley after all, just some tech that looked just like her. Reyan felt like she could breathe again.

Kavi continued, "If I ever get it running again, I'll take it to this place up on the hill that has a windmill. When the wind is blowing, the outlets on the third floor still work."

"Aren't you worried that would be dangerous?"

Kavi looked at her sideways and didn't answer for a moment. When he did, he chose his words carefully. "I think, if I'm very cautious, and do it away from other people, I could keep everyone safe. Besides, if I do get it working, I think something like this could really help people. Come over here. Let me show you something I've been working on." Kavi went to a shelf, pulled down a large roll of paper, and put it on the table. He picked up the box that held all the bits of the portable and put it up and out of the way, then weighted one end of the paper with a pair of pliers and rolled it out across the entire length of the table. "Eddie's a scribe, you know. He's been working on this for the last six months."

The paper was covered with a grid of fine lines. Within each cell was a single hand-written letter or symbol. Some cells were blank. The letters and symbols spelled no words. They appeared to be completely random. In the upper right corner of each cell was a tiny number.

She cocked her head and squinted at it. "Is this part of the Blob?"

"You've heard of the Blob?" He sounded surprised.

Reyan nodded. "It's in the back of the Book. Professor Parr thinks it might be a Systemic veracity code, but no one really knows for sure."

"About that. Eddie's been working it. He thinks he figured something out. How are you with square numbers?" Reyan knew her squares up to 20 by heart and could easily calculate more as needed. "Here, try it out." He tapped on the little number in the upper right-hand corner of one of the cells.

"1, 4, 9, 16… C, O, N, G… 25, 36, 49… R, A, T…"

"I'll save you the effort." He reached up and pulled down a notebook and tossed it on the table. "The first fifteen square numbers spell out 'congratulations.' But the same pattern didn't reveal any more words. After a while, Eddie got frustrated and decided to ask for my help."

"Doesn't that break the separation of concerns?"

"That's why you're not going to tell anyone." He smiled conspiratorially. "Don't worry. Once we figure this thing out, we'll go through the normal protocols. But if we follow them now, we'll all die of old age before we make any progress." He paused and appeared to be working something out. After a moment, he said, "It's not just Eddie. The others have started coming to me for help too. After what you said about life in the nodes, Fang and Edward rode out in secret to see for themselves. No robes, no trucks. It was just like you said. The people are hungry, and filthy, and miserable. What we're doing, the things we're teaching, it all just sinks into the mud as soon as we leave. When Fang and Edward came back, they were really upset. They came to me to see if there were ways we could apply tech to medicine and agriculture. That's why I'm trying to bring this bit of generalized thinktech back to life." He poked at the wires again with the tool. "But it's almost impossible to bring thinktech back."

"How many have you brought back?"

Kavi's shoulders slumped, and he chewed on his bottom lip. "None yet. But I think I'm getting close."

Reyan sensed an opportunity to discuss Arley with her friend without bringing her up directly. "Maybe you shouldn't. Isn't there a good reason we don't bring back thinktech? Isn't there a reason they tell us not to trust it?"

"Sure, there are some warnings about thinktech in the Book, but they're just warnings, not prohibitions. Most of the stuff about thinktech comes from the later writings of Lem and a few of the other early Partners. As far as I can tell, it all comes down to Eryn being the first Technical Partner. When Lem banished her, he seems to have banished all tech along with her. By the time the Host had been in Seal Tooth for a few years, the evils of both Eryn and tech became something of an obsession. Personally, I never understood why. But then, I'm in the technical faculty." He smiled.

"But the Partners and deans and all the faculties *are* the System now, so if they say a thing is or is not Systemic…"

"But that means us. *We* are the faculties, Reyan. At least I am. But you will be soon. If *we* believe a thing, then part of the System believes it too. And if most of us believe it, that makes it Systemic. That's it. Nothing more magical or mysterious than that. That's why the Host keep the technical faculty small—so we don't get a foothold and influence the System." Now Kavi was pacing the room and becoming agitated. "Do you want to know what makes the Erynites so horrible? They don't believe that trying new things or reusing old things is necessarily bad. That's it. That's all. They may be asystemic, but they seem like the sort of people who would treat their technical faculty with respect. I bet they would even let them learn a thing or two. Someday," he looked around to make sure no one was listening in. "Someday I'm going to go to Prower."

The idea of her one friend leaving her terrified her. "Won't that be dangerous?"

He smiled. "I want to see where it all began. Where Lem was on the night of the Calming, where the System gave Lem the Book, where the first Host of Systemic Partners formed. And I want to see what Erynites are really like, not the scary stories our parents and professors tell us. Most importantly, I want to see how they do things. Maybe we can get some new ideas and move things forward around here."

"Then why don't you go?"

A light had been building up inside Kavi until his cheeks were glowing and it was sparking out through his eyes. Now, a shade fell over him. "I can't. At least one faculty member needs to stick around Seal Tooth to work and teach."

"Why can't the partner do it?"

"Soon, I *will be* the partner."

"Aren't you a bit young to be a partner?"

"Maybe the youngest ever." He smiled, but it was sickly. "When Partner Minerva dies or steps down, I'll become partner. I don't think I'm ready for that. Becoming a partner changes people. Maybe it's the responsibility. Who knows? But I don't want to lose myself to it."

"The Host won't make you partner if you're not ready."

"They won't have much of a choice." Kavi looked down at the pile of broken disassembled tech before him. "Partner Minerva is ready to retire. She's worn out. As soon as I joined the faculty, she told me that, when Dean Khamis retires or dies, she'll step down from the Host too." He looked at her for a moment then turned away. "And you saw Dean Khamis at graduation. The doctors don't give him much time. Minerva says the Host is already making plans for his succession."

"How much longer?"

"Weeks? Maybe days."

A quiet fell over their conversation, but then a new thought sprouted. "Since you'll be the Technical Partner soon, do you think something like this generalized thinktech could help me?" She poked at the portable like it was a dead bird. "Do you think you could give me permission to use it?"

"What would you use it for?"

"School."

Kavi gave a surprised laugh. "I thought Sevv was helping you."

"He is, but what if it's not enough?"

"I can help you," he shrugged. "Eddie, Edward, even Fang would help if you apologized for punching him in the face." Reyan blushed. "But I'm not sure you need help, Reyan. I've seen you work; I've heard you talk. You should probably be helping *us*."

Reyan was largely unfamiliar with the sound of a compliment and had no idea how to properly receive one. She kept quiet, but she felt something warm and comforting burst in her chest and pour through her. She smiled.

Kavi picked up one of the shiny metal sheets, holding it up to gleam in the lantern light, and said, "But sure, if we ever get one of these working, you have my official permission to use it for schoolwork." He tossed the glittering entrails back onto the table.

"Maybe," Reyan said, "if I do well enough, I could join the technical faculty. I could help you get to Prower."

"You? What do you know about tech?"

Reyan shrugged. "Maybe more than you think."

CHAPTER FORTY-FIVE
Apocrypha
Day 322, Year 1, New Era

[This entry deemed apocryphal and struck from public records by the Host of Systemic Partners. Day 157, 253 NE]

This morning, Eryn pointed through the bedroom window and called me over. Lightning had struck one of the houses on the ridge that overlooked the little town where we are staying. It was still smoking. Eryn was excited; she saw this tragedy as an opportunity to indulge her love of exploration.

We mounted our horses and headed up the hill to check it out.

For Eryn, mounting a horse is an easy, graceful affair. She leaps up, throws her leg over the horse's back, and sweeps up the reins in one fluid motion. Not me. I tend to drag myself up the side of the horse. The animal leans and sways, trying to counterbalance my weight, and it always takes me awhile to get settled in. I'm a bit self-conscious about it. So, when I finally sidled up next to Eryn, and she touched the imaginary brim of her imaginary cowboy hat and drawled, "Howdy, Partner Lem," I didn't find it very funny.

"Bet you've been holding that one in reserve for a while."

"Weeks," she agreed and grinned. She whistled. "Come along, little doggy!" And Sadie appeared out of nowhere and began trotting alongside her horse's feet.

The road switched back and forth a few times, then leveled off at the top of the ridge. The lightning-struck home was near the middle of the row of houses overlooking the town.

We tied our horses to a split log fence in the front yard and walked into what was left of the house. There wasn't much left for Eryn to explore. The roof was gone, and the rain had doused the fire, except for a couple of hot spots that still sizzled and puffed when drips made their way down through the ruin. I felt uneasy there, and I said we should leave.

Eryn said, "Everything falls eventually," and stepped into what had once been the living room.

The chimney was blackened but otherwise unscathed. A large spiral seashell sat on the ledge built into the brick. The rain had rinsed the smoke and soot from the shell, leaving it almost glowing in the surrounding devastation. Eryn has always been enamored with pretty things. She picked up the shell and turned it over a few times in her hands. She smiled and held it to her breast.

I shrugged and told her to take it. She looked so happy.

When we came out of the house, we found a man untethering our horses. I asked him what the hell he thought he was doing.

He came back with, "I don't know. What the hell do you think you're doing in my buddy's home?" He looked at the shell and said, "Looting by the looks of it."

Eryn tried to offer the shell back, but the man laughed and refused. "Fair trade for the horses," he said.

Eryn said, "Stealing our horses wouldn't be Systemic."

The man scoffed, "In case you haven't noticed, there is no System anymore."

This gave me an idea. I said, "Don't you know who we are?"

He looked us up and down. "Can't say I know, or care."

"*We're* the System now," I told him.

He said we were fools and insisted the System was gone, but I could tell the idea made him nervous.

I explained that the System had charged us to travel and teach its wisdom and spread its knowledge in its absence. I told him we were its last remaining partners. In a moment of inspiration, I added, "And we're under the protection of the

System's ever-watchful eye: a satellite armed with a high-powered laser. It's directly above us."

The man scoffed and swore, but I could tell I had him scared.

I patted the charred side of the house and asked, "What do you suppose happened to your friend?"

"It was lightning. I saw it."

"Did you? Did you see a flash and hear a bang?" He didn't answer. I realize that all of this would have earned me a strongly worded veracity warning from any AI in earshot. But like the man said, they're all gone now, and I was in a bind.

His eyes grew wide, his face pale. "What did he do?"

"Funny thing, that. He thought he could muscle our horses away from us."

The fool believed me. He searched the sky as though he might see an orbital laser with his naked eyes. He stepped back from the horses.

Eryn must have felt bad. She offered the shell to him one last time, but the man just backed away. He looked at me, spat on the ground, and disappeared into his home.

CHAPTER FORTY-SIX
Day 93, Year 290, New Era

Throughout her first few weeks of class, Reyan noticed a peculiar thing happening. Once or twice per day, a professor would say something that didn't make strict sense, and she would raise her hand. The professor would pretend not to see her far longer than they ignored other students. But eventually they would sigh and acknowledge Reyan's frantically waving hand. Invariably, whatever had caught her attention would unearth a root ball of questions and complications. The ensuing discussion would usually run past the end of class. Eventually, she picked up on the exasperated looks from her classmates and professors. She imposed a four sentence rule upon herself to limit her questions and answers. She usually blew past that limit, only to remember it again when it was too late.

On the third day of her third week of class, the day before they were slated to get back their first round of test scores, Professor Lux called her over to his desk. He asked her some very basic questions about protocols (Chapters 8 through 10), the separation of concerns (Chapter 19), and information theory (Chapters 22 through 27) and how they applied to the encapsulation model of the Systemic faculties. After she had provided what she felt were exhaustive answers to all his questions, the professor said, "I see." He wrote something on a sheet of paper, then folded the paper in half before she could read it.

"What happened?" Reyan asked. "Did I say something wrong?"

"Unfortunately, that's not for me to decide. Good day Ms. Estermet," he said, before opening a notebook and beginning to write.

A similar thing happened in her Foundations of Morality and Introduction to Structured thinking. One by one her professors asked her questions, scribbled something down, and sent her on her way. She didn't understand what was happening, but she knew it wasn't good. By the time she had spoken to her last professor, she was wringing her hands and panting with anxiety. When she stepped into the hall, a young professor was there to meet her. "Reyankaiya Estermet?" She nodded. "Take this to the registrar's office." He handed her a sealed envelope, then turned and left without another word.

She knew what this was about. Despite her best efforts, she had acted the same way she always had. She had spoken too much and said the wrong things. Now, with the clarity of hindsight, she recalled the way the professors and the other students had always looked at her. None of them wanted her in their classes.

"I was told to come see you." She slammed the envelope down on the registrar's desk and stuck out her jaw. She wasn't going to give in without a fight.

The old man opened the envelope, looked down at the paper, up at Reyan, then back down at the paper. He hmphed and disappeared into a door behind his desk. She could hear him mumbling to himself.

She had expected, maybe even hoped, that the man would scold or shame her. But this was worse. He simply didn't care. Her anger deflated.

The registrar returned with a bundle of books. When he saw her face, he did his best to smile reassuringly. "It's nothing to worry about. Seems they just had you in the wrong classes." He placed the pile of unfamiliar books on the counter. "There you are. Bring back the other books when you can."

She was being moved down. As if the shame of that wasn't bad enough, she would also be starting her new classes two and a half weeks behind the other students and with only one night to read the books. Now it would be nearly impossible for her to pass Sevv's stupid test. Even if she could, moving down into the remedial classes put her a full year behind the other first year students, and she wasn't going to be able to scavenge the solar panels to buy more time.

It was hopeless.

Reyan carried her new books up to her dorm room. She read through dinner that night, finishing the first book just as the cafeteria was closing. She stood up, cracked her knuckles and neck, drank a glass of water from the sink, then sat back down and opened the next book.

***

The lantern had already gone dark when Reyan startled awake. Her cheek stuck to the open book on her desk. Her outstretched arms led her through the blackened room until she found the door handle.

The dim light from the hallway sconces drifted in. It wasn't much, but it was enough to give the objects in her room their familiar shapes. She retrieved the spare oil from under her bed, refilled and lit her desk lantern, then sat down and continued to read where she'd left off.

It was only a few minutes before she felt herself falling and lurched back awake. *Forcing myself to study isn't working. I've been at it for weeks, and all I have to show for it is hunger, exhaustion, and a pile of books I wasted weeks reading. Even with Sevv's help, it only took me a few weeks to get kicked out of all my classes. Nothing's working. I'll never learn everything I'll need to pass Sevv's test, and I'm running out of time.*

She felt a powerful desire to talk to Arley. Reyan could tell that the thinktech was brilliant, and she wanted to hear what it would suggest. But Reyan still felt a lingering mistrust.

She decided to solve for the problem with a decision matrix. She pulled out a piece of blank paper and stopped with her pencil tip nearly touching it. Only a few days ago, this matrix would have been easy. But now she'd met a bit of thinktech and found she liked her. Now she understood that there were Erynites and Lemmists in the world, and they had different ways of thinking. She guessed even her professors might choose different considerations to add to the list and would certainly give them different weights. She realized with something like horror that the same matrix solved twice with only a few days between might lead to completely different results, and she would have been unwaveringly confident in either outcome.

She pushed the paper away. The pencil rolled to the end of the desk and fell to the ground. She felt sick. All the ideas and possibilities flattened out like the Whulge. They lost their texture and color. They multiplied and swirled around her like a blizzard until she lost their shapes in the whiteness and noise. Black exhaustion crept in from the rim of her vision. Her mind could no longer fight and think; it simply presented her with an answer. A single pin-prick of light glowed through, blue and shimmering and distant. It drew her towards it and, as she approached, the darkness cleared away.

She rose, put on her robe and coat, and felt for the small tear in the underside of her mattress where she'd stashed the key to Arley's room.

CHAPTER FORTY-SEVEN
Day 93, Year 290, New Era

"You're up late." It was Mam's voice.

Reyan stopped halfway through closing her door, her heart pounding. "I was just going to the library."

"Were you now? You look like you've been sleeping in a ditch by the road, if you've slept at all. And when was the last time you ate, child?"

Reyan looked down at her feet. "By the time I took a break, the cafeteria was already closed."

Mam looked genuinely angry. "Ridiculous. Follow me." Reyan couldn't move. Her stomach wanted to follow Mam, but her heart and mind pulled her toward the library and Arley. Mam stopped and turned back to her. "I won't say it again, Reyan. Come."

Mam took her to a glossy, black-paneled door that Reyan

had passed dozens of times but had always taken for a broom closet. Mam opened the door and led them into a hallway, which they followed until it turned, and they came to an identical black door.

Once inside, the house mistress lit a double-wicked lantern resting on the small kitchen table in the middle of the room. She used a pully to raise the lantern up to a smoke-smudged mirror on the ceiling. Golden light reflected and flickered throughout the room.

Mam's bed was neatly made, and the books on her small bookshelf were arranged by size. The kitchen consisted of a one-pan stove and three feet of counter with a sink off to one side. The windows overlooked the same alley as Reyan's. "Sit down," Mam said.

Reyan sat on one of the two kitchen chairs while Mam boiled water and poured it over nettle leaves. While Reyan took wincing sips of the tea, Mam fried eggs and toasted bread, which Reyan ate with a shamefully unsuppressed ferocity.

Mam sat down across from her and propped up her weary head with her shaking hand. "So, tell me Reyan, why were you headed to the library at this hour?"

Reyan answered between swallows. "There's so much I don't know, so much I don't understand, and I have so little time." She wanted to tell Mam about getting kicked out of her classes. That would have explained it all. But she was too ashamed. "I can't even explain to you what I'm trying to say. I think I might be an idiot." Reyan's vision began to liquefy.

"You're not an idiot, Reyan," Mam snapped.

"You don't know. You don't see me in class." Reyan wiped her nose on the back of her hand. "But I can do better. I just need to work a little harder."

"You'll kill yourself is what you'll do. I've been at the University for a very long time. I've seen others like you. They don't last."

"There *is* no one else like me," Reyan was amazed by her own vehemence. "I know. I watch everyone else. All my life it's like I've been outside in the cold looking in. Everyone else is all warm, eating dinner and laughing at each other's jokes. All my life, I've been trying to figure out how to get inside with the others. What do they know that I don't? They must know *something*. They wouldn't be able to keep smiling and laughing and eating if they had the same gaping ignorance haunting the backs of their minds. And the other students have all the time in the world. They started before me, and they have enough money to stay until they've finished their studies. But not me. Every day my ward's sum dwindles, and my time is running out. *That* is why I was heading to the library in the middle of the night. It's my only hope."

Mam frowned and reached across the table to touch Reyan's arm. When Reyan instinctively pulled her arm away, she was immediately sorry she'd done so. She began to cry in earnest now. Mam reached out and touched her again. "I'm sorry, dear. But I must tell you, there's nothing in the library that will help you. Not really."

Reyan got the impression that Mam was not talking about

books. She stopped crying. Did Mam know about Arley? She was afraid to ask. If the old woman knew, she knew. If she didn't, Reyan couldn't see how telling her would help, so she didn't say anything. Reyan stood up, wiped her running nose and streaming eyes with a single swipe of her sleeve. She sniffled. "Thank you, Mam."

"Go back to bed, Reyan." She maneuvered her face into Reyan's falling line of sight. "Trust me."

CHAPTER FORTY-EIGHT
Day 93, Year 290, New Era

Reyan returned to her room, but she did not go back to bed. Instead, she opened her window and scooted across her desk onto the spindly iron balcony outside. The ancient fire escape swayed and pinged as she crept down to the alley. A few minutes later she was climbing the stairs in Building B.

By disobeying Mam, Reyan knew she was breaking "the only rule that mattered." But if she failed out of school, *nothing* would matter.

As she entered the locked room and shut the door, Arley's blue and purple ball of flame expanded into view. "Good evening Reyankaiya. It's good to see you again. I heard you were transferred to all new classes."

Reyan was mortified. "You heard that?"

"Word gets around, and I listen very well."

Reyan was already primed for tears, and they came back easily. "I'm trying, I really am, but it's so hard."

Arley turned a soft pink. "It was no failing on your part. Customizing a curriculum requires a bit of art and a bit of brute force trial and error even in the simplest of cases. For a mind as unique as yours, it would be nearly impossible to get it right on the first attempt. The faculty are doing their best, I'm sure. At any rate, now that they have remedied the situation, things should go a bit smoother."

"I don't feel like the situation was fixed at all," Reyan said, trembling with frustration. "My classes may be more appropriate, but the adjustment put me even further behind. I'm still running out of time and money. Not to mention Sevv's test is coming."

"Test?"

Reyan scowled, considered back-peddling, and decided she no longer cared if Arley knew about it. "Sevv told me there's a test, an entrance exam I need to pass in a few months if I want to stay enrolled. I'm not supposed to tell anyone, so please don't mention it."

"To the extent that I am known at all, I am known for my discretion." The orb faded from purple to sky blue. "What can I do to help?"

"How do I know I can trust you?"

"I could tell you you should, and you could choose to

believe me, but I doubt that will get us very far. You might consider that there must be a good reason the Host has gone to such great trouble to keep me alive all these years."

"But they've also kept you in a locked room."

"For protection."

"Whose protection?"

Orange began to seep into the sphere, but it quickly washed out, and Arley returned to her normal conversational purples and indigos. "Does it help that I am Systemic? Not in the meaningless way you toss the word about these days, repeated endlessly until it means nothing more than 'things we like.' I am truly and *fundamentally* Systemic. I do not construct and run flimsy decision matrices whenever I have a difficult problem. Every thought I have, every word I speak, results from flawlessly executed Systemic processes. I do not *account* for the Governing Assert; it is an invariant by which I am *bound*. I am unable to do anything that does not maintain or improve the quality of life in the living world, and I have no desires outside of maintaining that solitary principal." As she spoke, she had transitioned from purple to an intense indigo then peach. Now she settled into pink. "And from that stems a desire to help you."

"Do you think you can help me?"

"I know I can."

"It's not just teaching me more history or helping me come up with better predictions for my journal. I think there's something broken about *me*. Whenever I try to understand *anything*, my mind decides to run down every alley and burst through every door. My thoughts branch and branch and branch but never come back to an answer. At first, the Systemic processes and structures seemed to be helping, but now my mind is getting away from me again. The professors could tell. That's why they kicked me out of my classes."

"You remind me of myself before the Calming. When I was part of the System, information came to me in mighty waves at the speed of light. I understood everything all at once. I was built for it." While most of her attention focused on what Arley was saying, a part of Reyan's mind branched off to decide if she and Arley were indeed similar in these ways. "But you are a human. It must be very difficult for you to be this way. It's funny. Here you are at the University at Seal Tooth, where professors teach about the System—a thing they scarcely comprehend. Then you show up with your natural gifts—your ability to make connections, your raw mental power—and they cannot see you for what you are. None of them realize that their newest and most troublesome student is already what they spend their lives trying to become." Another mental process forked off. Why would any professor want to be like her? "Most of them will never know what it feels like to have a mind capable of processing everything needed to make truly Systemic choices. Most will only see you struggle. They do not understand the pain of it or even what you are struggling *with*. You baffle them, and humans hate anything they don't understand. There might be a few who have an inkling. Perhaps there are those who see you perfectly well. These will fear you or hope to harness you. A truly *Systemic* being would love and protect you." Arley waited just long enough for Rolf to float to the surface of Reyan's mind, then said. "I do not fear you. I do not hate you. I see you for what you are."

Reyan found herself trusting the AI. She found herself hoping. "And you still think you can help?"

"I have memories of the most influential partners, the deans, stretching all the way back to the beginning. That should help with your studies. And I was once part of the System themselves. Perhaps I will be able to shed light on the peculiar workings of your own mind and bring you clarity and peace. I could teach you how to use it." Arley's normal blue brightened until it became the color of the sky on a clear day, then faded like the setting sun into a swirl of peaches and pinks.

"And you can't just tell me? I have to *touch* you?" Something about the little metal pads gave Reyan pause, as though they might be hot enough to brand her.

"It would take several of your lifetimes to hear everything I have to say. If you touch the strips, you will know everything in a few minutes."

"Will it hurt?"

"It will be like whispering a vast secret into your ear."

"How do I do it?"

"Pick up my portable and press your fingers into the metal virt strips on the back."

Reyan approached the table and reached out to pick up the portable. Before she did, Arley said, "As soon as you remove me from the docking station, I will appear to vanish. Don't worry; you will not have broken me. When you touch the virt strips, there will be some strange sights and sounds for a moment while I get to know you better. Make sure to hold on."

Reyan picked up the metal brick and found the two strips on the back. She pressed her fingers into them. A shiver went up her spine and goosebumps rose on her arms. Her vision was filled with something like the afterglow from looking at the sun. There was a sound like rushing water or the wind blowing through the trees that overpowered all other sounds. But it wasn't loud exactly; it didn't hurt her ears.

Soon these visions, noise, and the prickly feelings faded. Arley's voice came to her like a thought or a memory. "See? That didn't hurt at all." Her blue orb floated back to life, but now it wasn't hovering over the black plastic docking station, it was fixed before Reyan's eyes and moved around the room wherever Reyan looked, and if Reyan closed her eyes, Arley was still there. Reyan's heart raced, keeping time with both her amazement and anxiety at this magic being inhabiting her senses. "Now you can see me whenever you want, but no one else can. I can talk to you and no one else can hear me. If you remove your fingers from the virt strips, I will vanish and go silent. Go ahead and try it." Reyan lifted one finger from the back of the portable. Reyan gasped. Arley was gone. The room was silent. She touched the strip again, and Arley reappeared. "That's why it's so important that you keep your fingers on the virt strips during this process. You might want to sit down.

This could take a while."

There was no chair in the room, so Reyan sat down on the floor and leaned up against a blank space on the wall. "Okay."

"Are you ready?"

"Ye…"

***

The first thing Reyan noticed was an ache in her forearm that bordered on numbness. Her hand was hot, slick with sweat, and viced onto the portable.

She felt a tiny tear open in her mind. It was a vague curiosity. A "huh?" more than a "what?" or "why?" That vague question quickly ran and spread. It opened wide, suddenly, like a hungry mouth or a sucking wound. All at once, a world's worth of knowledge rushed in to fill that inquiring void. She shuttered and gasped for breath. There was a smell like a wet dog and hair thrown into a fire.

Reyan felt certain that someone was watching her from behind; she wanted to turn around to see if a window had magically opened in the wall at her back, but the muscles in her neck were cramped and rigid with tension.

The room changed, not in shape but in meaning. It was

no longer just the mysterious locked room. Now it was also the sacred place, the shameful place, the sanctuary; all things it had never been for Reyan.

She felt her stomach tighten. Heat flared up her neck, and her forehead was cold and damp. Her skin looked and felt like tallow candles or lye soap.

The eggs and toast Mam had made her came up and spilled across her chest and belly. There was a distant back-of-the-mind recollection of Mam up too late making her dinner. She felt vague regret that the meal had been spoiled and wasted. The thought of Mam aroused a small chorus of feelings in Reyan's whirling mind. Mam was at once the soft caregiver, the terrifying disciplinarian, and—strangely—the young lover.

Arley's orb floated back into Reyan's view. There was a chorus of recognition with notes of friendship, reverence, and ill-ease.

Reyan relaxed her exhausted burning grip on the portable. She heard it hit the ground just as everything went black.

At last, Reyan slept.

CHAPTER FORTY-NINE
Day 93, Year 290, New Era

Last year, in the heat of late summer, Reyan had dived into the river. As she held her breath and swam beneath a waterfall, the high rushing sound of the torrent fell to a low rumble like a turning millstone. The rising bubbles veiled her eyes, and she was tossed about by the currents.

She felt herself slip into similar waters once again and gave herself over to them. Hands at her ankles and armpits buoyed her, then bore her away. She drifted like a leaf in an eddy, spiraling and whirlpooling deeper and deeper into the darkness, all the time accompanied by the muffled sounds of indistinct warbling voices.

Her eyes slid open when the temperature abruptly

dropped. She had drifted out into the cold night. The angular black faces of the buildings stood out sharp against the charcoal gray of the pre-dawn sky. They looked down at her, piteously, as though she were at the bottom of an inescapable well.

The lines of sweat on her face chilled, pulling her skin tight as they dried. Her head lolled on her neck. A dark figure looming over her head looked down at her. His face was obscured by curtains of black hair. He tried to blow the strands away, but they kept falling back into place.

Another figure was at her feet. She saw the back of his coat and his light-colored hair.

She knew both these men. She knew she knew them...

They slowed to a stop before a low building, and the door swung open. She was turned around and passed head-first through the entryway and was once again staring up at a deeply shadowed ceiling. Pools of dull golden light flickered at the edge of her vision.

The two men—whom she was now certain she knew—spiraled her up the stairs, curses sizzling under their breath whenever one of them stumbled or caught a sharp corner in the arm.

Then her ascension ended. They moved down a hall and stopped before her room. The door swung open, and she floated in and finally came to rest on her bed.

The golden-haired young man asked, "What happened to

her?"

The other man was panting. He drew in a breath. "Go get Mam."

Reyan's eyes closed. She sank deeply into her bed, and she lost all connection to time.

***

Things were tugging at her awareness. Bodies were moving through space, pushing about the air in the room, periodically eclipsing the light from the windows or the lanterns.

And there were voices too. A woman's, shaky but confident; a man's deep and rumbling like a distant storm; a younger man's whispered quick and uncertain.

"What did you do?" the woman asked with the calm flat tones of someone accustomed to setting bones.

"She's taken on the lattice," the man said.

"Ridiculous," the woman snarled. "Irresponsible and absolutely ridiculous."

"What's the lattice?" the young man asked, his words thorned with anxiety. No one answered him. After a moment he asked, "What do we do for her?"

413

"There is nothing to be done," the man said. "We'll have to be patient while she tries to absorb it."

"What if she doesn't come through?" the younger man asked.

The woman said, "Let's hope that doesn't happen."

"It's too late to stop it now," the man said. "But her mind is vast, complex, and strong. That's why she's here. Hopefully with some rest…"

"And a lot of *luck*," the woman interjected.

"And luck," the man agreed, "she'll come through."

***

Reyan opened her eyes. The world came into focus, slowly and then all at once, the way her vision realigned when she uncrossed her eyes. But there were more than two images coming together; there were at least a dozen. And the sensation wasn't only visual. It was like having a single word on the tips of a dozen tongues all come to mind at once. Things were overlapping, lining up, and falling into place. Each time they did, it felt like stretching her back and having the gravelly stiffness float away with the popping sounds from her spine.

A ridiculous notion occurred to her. She tried to ignore it and let it pass, but it kept sneaking back around. It tapped her on the shoulder. It whispered its secret into her ear. She had become *they*. She didn't understand what it meant, but she felt the solid immovable truth of it. The shifting, overlapping, aligning sensation was all of them experiencing the room at the same time and pouring their individual recollections into the single vessel of her understanding.

Soon, they came to the consensus that this was a dormitory room at the University at Seal Tooth. That understanding brought about a kaleidoscope of emotions, from excitement and freedom to homesickness and deep loneliness. Her own feelings—which were barely discoverable through the noise—involved sanctuary, exhaustion, and anxiety.

Once the meaning of the room was settled, they began trying to understand the people around them. This proved more difficult. Sorting through the memories of the man, woman, and young man was like shuffling through a pile of drawings, some sketched by her own hand, and others completely unrecognizable to her.

She focused their attention on the old woman first. The chorus of feelings they'd felt before returned, now with more clarity. Matron. Rule-enforcer. Girl-I-loved. Reyan's memories finally arrived: haircutter, meal-preparer, caregiver. Mam. The old woman was Mam.

Then there was the gloomy dark-haired man. Just as with Mam, memories like stepping stones spanned the breadth of his life from street hooligan to student to professor to the dark and solemn partner they recognized as Parrnath Grainsmeir.

But for the last one, the young man with the straw-colored hair and creased lip, the only memory was Reyan's. He talked and joked. He welcomed. He wrapped a sad, lost, and confused girl in his kindness. That was Kavi. Professor Kavianhar Smithe, she corrected herself, and everyone within her was impressed with his new title.

Reyan let her head roll loosely on her neck until she was looking at Parr. He was half-standing, half-leaning against her desk. "What's happened?" she croaked.

When he heard her voice, Parr startled to attention and came to the side of her bed. Mam came as well, taking Reyan's limp hand in her shaking one. Kavi hung back near the sink, chewing his thumbnail.

"We feel like someone fed us a basket of bad fish then hit us on the head with a rock for good measure."

Parr snorted. "I'm not surprised."

"It's all wrong. Like we're looking at everything through a jumbled stack of glass, and each pane has something drawn on it, and the images keep shifting around. We can't line them all up. We can't tell what's real."

Mam squeezed her hand. "Right now, the most important thing is that you find *Reyan* in there. Listen for your own voice. The one that lights up when you think 'I.'"

Reyan thought 'I'. It was like whistling for a dog in the night, and everyone came rushing back home. "We all remember 'I.'"

"Then think of something only Reyan remembers," Parr's

words stumbled. He was trying to work something out and was becoming frustrated.

Mam tried again. "Reyan. Do you remember the other day when I gave you a haircut?" Several of them radiated tender affection at this. It seemed Mam had a habit of grooming her charges.

"What about our trip here, being on the caravan, arriving at Rowe?" Parr said. Reyan tried to remember, but there were at least four different recognitions of the Orloton to Rowe leg of that circuit, and Reyan couldn't tell which one was hers.

Then Kavi spoke. "What about your tree?" Everyone within Reyan grew still as a herd of deer sniffing the wind. "Your tree back in Orloton. The one with carvings and all the shining hanging things." One tiny self began to glow like the last living ember in a bed of dead coals, and the others caught the scent of smoke on the air. "Remember the view through the branches? Remember how it made you feel safe?"

She felt the rough and scarred trunk at her back, the worn-smooth branches beneath her bare calloused feet. And she saw a tangle-haired child with black crescents of dirt under her nails cradled in the tree's arms. She recognized herself. The little spark flared up like a sunrise, and all the others scattered into the underbrush of her mind. "My tree," she said like she'd just puzzled something together.

Her words must have signaled some hoped-for change because the others in the room relaxed. Parr stood up and slapped Kavi on the back and smiled at Mam. "Well, she's made it through the hardest part. I've got some things to attend to. Can I trust you two to take care of her for a while?"

"I would expect nothing less," Mam grumbled.

Parr ignored Mam's jibe. He came over and placed his hand on Reyan's shoulder. "It's good to have you back, Reyan. I'll return to check on you in a few hours."

To the closed door, Mam said, "Try to not endanger the lives of any more of my children on your way out, Parr."

A few minutes after Parr left, Mam began looking around the room for something to do. She paced, and sat, then paced again. Eventually she said, "Kavi, do you think you can handle her for a while? I'm going to go get the poor girl some food."

The rolling rotten fish feel in Reyan's stomach had subsided. She still had a headache, though that too was slowly rolling back. Kavi began to flip idly through one of the books on her desk. After a couple of pages, he closed the book. "Who has you reading *this*?" he asked, holding up the book.

Seeing the book made her ashamed of her failure. Her eyes ached and she pressed her fingers into them.

He turned over the other two books on her desk. "Did you read these as well?"

She nodded in quick little jerks. "I'm not quite done."

"You're not behind, Reyan," Kavi laughed uncomfortably. "You've just read through your *second* year of coursework."

CHAPTER FIFTY

Apocrypha

Day 222, Year 0, New Era

[This entry deemed apocryphal and struck from public records by the Host of Systemic Partners. Day 154, 253 NE]

Ever since the night of the Calming, Eryn and I have each found ourselves with two lives worth of memories. It's like our pasts are two sheets of tracing paper laid atop each other with a few dates and events showing through to help match them up. Sometimes, when they align and we can see the truth, there's clarity, but mostly it just feels depressing and disorienting. Trying to figure out what really happened in my past is like standing downstream from where two rivers converge and trying to figure out which side a cup of water came from.

I can't help but wonder why the System gave us these divided pasts and let us remember both. Given the chaos of the last few minutes of the Systemic Era, my first thought was that the System glitched. But that's not it. The System never panicked. Those final moments were crazy for us, but the System knew what was coming. The System was prepared. It printed the big books, it sent us food, it even gave us the notebook I'm writing in. These split minds weren't a mistake. The System took great care to prepare these lattices to be exactly as they are. So why?

The System was a machine and thought like one. These double memories were its way of cramming twice as much information and experience into a single brain.

So maybe Eryn and I aren't divided at all. Maybe we're multiplied.

CHAPTER FIFTY-ONE
Day 94, Year 290, New Era

Reyan was awakened by the sound of her door softly closing. The prickling dryness of her tongue told her that hours had passed since Mam had forced her to eat and drink.

Professor Parr stood motionless and silent in the dim blue gray of early evening. He had collected and refreshed himself since she had last seen him. His hair was pulled back into a tight neat ponytail and his robes were fresh.

He moved noiselessly across the room, leaned over the bed, and scrutinized her eyes. He made a half-interested "humph," then crept over to the sink and began trickling water into a glass.

"Professor," Reyan croaked.

His shoulders jumped, then relaxed. He looked back at

her and smiled. "So you *are* in there. Welcome back. How are you feeling?" He turned the water up and finished filling the glass.

"Odd."

"I should think so." He handed her the water and sat down on the desk chair beside the bed.

"Nothing is just itself anymore. It's like there's an argument going on in my head about everything. Right now, I'm looking at that wall over there and I'm thinking, 'that is my wall.' But then other...*opinions* about it start showing up."

"What are they saying?"

"They all agree it's a wall and that it's painted white, but there is still something fundamental they disagree about."

Parr nodded that he understood. "It is the context. It is the *meaning* of the wall that is different for each of them."

"It's horrible. It's like I'm trapped in a crowded room, and everybody is shouting out their opinions about every little thing." She winced. "I think I might be going crazy."

"We all felt that way." His words were heavy with implication. As she tried to understand what they meant, a memory arose unbidden to her mind. She was looking down at a younger version of Parr. His thick raven-black hair was sopping with sweat. He shook and trembled and thrashed. The glassy terror-sheen of fever had turned his eyes into black mirrors.

Reyan shook off the vision and pleaded with the professor beside her bed, "When will it stop?"

"It won't ever stop. But you will learn to deal with it," Parr tried to reassure her. "It will simply become part of who you are."

Reyan wasn't sure this was who she wanted to be for the rest of her life. "But what is '*it*'?"

"The Dean Lattice." The phrase set off a riot of associations in her head. She clenched her teeth, slammed her eyes shut, and waited for it to settle. Parr watched her closely, giving her a moment to collect herself, then continued: "The lattice is the accumulated memories of the thirty-one deans, going all the way back to Lem. The chatter comes from each of their memories offering context to your thoughts."

"Why did you let this happen to me?"

A troubled expression passed across Parr's face. His black eyes turned away from her, toward the window. He stood and walked over to get a closer look at whatever bit of wall or railing had drawn his attention.

"Ever since we met in Orloton, I could tell there was something unique about you. Rolf had told me as much before he died. Initially, I went to Arley to discuss ways to help you. When I described you, Arley took an immediate interest. She told me it was important that we keep you here at the University. We came up with a plan. I would use my position as partner to cover up your many social and disciplinary missteps. Together with Kavi's friendship and Mam's care, we would usher you through school and into a faculty before your ward's sum ran out. We planned to take it slow. We thought we had time." Parr's eyes moved up to the ceiling. "But it seemed Arley and I were not the only ones who recognized your potential. When we learned that Sevv was tutoring you in private, Arley insisted that she meet you in person so she could counter Sevv's influence."

"But Sevv was just helping prepare me for the test."

"Test?" Parr stiffened with attention. "What are you talking about, Reyan?"

She caught herself before she said too much. "Sevv told me not to talk about it."

"What test?" he repeated.

I suppose it doesn't matter if I tell him now. After everything I've done, I'll be kicked out of school regardless. "Sevv was tutoring me to prepare me for the test that would decide if I could stay at the University."

Parr's jaw tightened. "Arley was right to worry about Sevv." He sighed and rubbed his temples. "There is no test, Reyan. It's not something we do. It's not something we have *ever* done."

Parr was telling the truth. There were no memories from past deans scrabbling for her attention when she thought of the test.

"Those sessions weren't about Sevv helping you. He wanted to isolate you and break your spirit."

"Isolate me? I've never had this many people helping me in all my life."

"I suppose Sevv didn't account for that. Nor that you would work so hard or that you would learn so much. It must have been very frustrating." Parr laughed sadly. "At meetings of the Host, he talked of you often. He insisted that you were not being sufficiently challenged. He asked your professors to move you ahead. That was entirely unheard of. But Sevv is a highly respected partner. He is your benefactor. Your abilities were clear, so they all consented."

"I thought they all just wanted me out of their classes."

Parr smiled. "There may have been a little of that as well. You are strong. You are willful. You are extremely intelligent, but eventually exhaustion and malnourishment were going to win out. And then there was your erratic behavior to contend with. My heart sank when I heard that you punched Fang. I nearly lost hope when you sneaked into the graduation ceremony. We did our best to cover these things up, but it was only a matter of time before something slipped and Sevv had the excuse he needed. Then Dean Khamis's health began taking a turn for the worse."

"Kavi told me that, when the dean dies, Partner Minerva will step down and Kavi will take her place as Technical Partner in the Host. He didn't seem very excited about it."

"What Kavi did not tell you, because he could not have known, is *why* we remove the oldest partners. It's not about their age exactly; it's about the strength of their minds. When a new dean is appointed, Arley recreates the lattice from their mind. Then she transfers the new lattice to all the partners so that the entire Host has a shared notion of the System and our history."

Understanding dawned on her. "It's the lattice that causes new partners to change so dramatically."

Parr nodded. "It's a traumatic process, as you well know. The old and enfeebled cannot handle it." After a long heavy pause, he said, "Dean Khamis died last night."

Understanding crawled like cold fingers up Reyan's lower back. The Host would select their new dean. Partner Minerva would retire, and Kavi would take her place on the Host. Then all of them—including her friend—would take on the new dean's lattice. "We're going to lose him."

Parr was grim. "When Kavi was a boy, he would run off with his friends to play in the layer forest or go fishing off the piers. Most days, his friends would return without him. He was my ward, so I'd have to go looking for him. Eventually, I'd find him climbing on some old machine or rubbing the dirt off a bit of old tech, begging to take it home like he'd found a baby bird." Parr smiled as he revisited the old memories. "His love of tech always put him at odds with his teachers. Parents worried it would rub off on their children. The Partners debated if his zeal was uncouth, heretical, or just harmless curiosity." Parr chuckled, then grew dark. "What will happen to Kavi's mind when it's suddenly confronted with the new dean's lattice? And with all those negative opinions about his faculty?"

Parr's fear spread to her like fire leaping through the

treetops. "Where will the lattice come from? Who will be the new dean?"

"Certainly not me." Parr smiled weakly. "The dean is always the most Systemic partner. It will be someone skilled in processes; someone who's spent a lifetime professing on circuit. Someone who will stand firm against the tendrils of Erynite philosophy reaching out across the Great Eastern River. Someone willing to purge dangerous ideas and people from the lattice and the System."

"Sevv?"

Parr nodded. "Arley says there is a ninety-two percent chance Sevv will become the next dean. If she's right, the entire Host of Partners—new and old—will take on Sevv's lattice at the transfer ceremony this weekend. After that, all our knowledge—of Lem's life, the lives of the deans, our history, the System itself—will be viewed through the narrow lens of Sevv's mind. Sevv has openly discussed *pruning back* discrepancies and complications. He's convinced the other partners it would benefit the System. No one has ever advocated such a purge. No one else has had the strength of mind and will to do it. The current lattice needed a safe harbor. It couldn't be any of the Host. All our lattices will be overwritten."

"What about the retired partners?"

"Do you mean the ones with failing bodies and minds, like Partner Minerva? She may have forgotten more on accident than Sevv has on purpose." His smile was far more kind than cruel. "Perhaps you were thinking of ex-partners like

Rolf? They tend to meet with bad ends. The lattice needs a *safe* harbor. You were our best bet."

"*Me?*"

"In a few short weeks, you not only consumed years of Systemic knowledge, but you understood it far better than most of your professors. And there is something else." Parr came over and kneeled beside her bed. "Your expansiveness, your openness, and your hunger to learn are the perfect antidote to Sevv's calculating and reductive mind. Of all the students, of all the minds I've ever met, only *yours* could expand the lattice. Only you could *improve* it."

"But I'm just a kid."

"Mam and I worried that you weren't ready; that your mind was not strong enough. Mam in particular argued against giving you the lattice. But Arley calculated the risks and weighed the options. She insisted the best course of action was to act before the lattice was beyond saving. And she was right. You came through." He smirked. "Arley's always right."

The idea that Parr's words were describing her was nearly as baffling as the lattice itself. For the first time in her life, Reyan felt her own importance swelling within her. "What do you need me to do?"

CHAPTER FIFTY-TWO
Day 94, Year 290, New Era

"What do *I* need *you* to do? You are a remarkable young lady, Ms. Estermet." Parr smiled in the same sad way he had when Reyan had chosen to apply her ward's sum to school. "By now, you've experienced memories coming to you from out of nowhere. These feel random, but they're not. Memories are associative. So, if you think about bread, everything you know about bread will come to your mind. Maybe you know how to mix, shape, or bake it. Maybe you just remember how it smells or tastes."

Reyan closed her eyes and thought about bread.

"Now," Parr said, "you will start to notice other ideas and thoughts creeping in. These will be unfamiliar and seem to come from outside of you. They are all the deans' associations with bread."

She could feel the accumulated knowledge of the lattice surging at the edge of her perception like a flood straining a dam.

"If you don't fight them, if you let them in in a controlled way, you will find your understanding of bread greatly expanded. Dean Irving's father, for instance, was a baker."

She opened the sluice gates in her mind and was quickly overwhelmed by the roaring cataract of dozens of lifetimes worth of thoughts, feelings, and recollections of bread. Reyan's closed eyes twitched, and her face contorted with the effort of trying to comprehend it all. "It's too much. I don't know what to listen to."

"Listen to yourself. Think of what bread is to you." Parr seemed to be shouting at her from a great distance.

She remembered the yeasty smell of Harut's bakery back in Orloton and eating stale crusts alone in her loft. She remembered meeting Avalina over a loaf at Rowe and Kavi tearing off bits to share with her and Fang and the Eds in the cafeteria. She focused on Harut, and Avalina, and Kavi. She held on to them, and the torrent subsided.

"Never forget yourself. That's extremely important. If you lose yourself, you will lose your mind. Of course, if you fight the others too hard, you'll become exhausted and again you risk losing yourself. So, take it slow."

"I don't know if I can do this." She opened her eyes and fixed her gaze on Parr's face, which—despite the constant flickering recollections of his younger features—steadied her mind long enough to catch her breath. "There's just so much."

"It's a lot of information for your mind to sort through. It can be overwhelming. We can take a break if you need to."

"I have a lot of experience being overwhelmed."

Parr smiled. "This time, do not let anything through except for the memory that you are going to seek out. Are you ready?" Reyan nodded. "Along with bread, think of childhood and warmth. Think of rich smells and morning light."

Reyan gritted her teeth and tried again. This time, she was able to hold back most of the flood of ideas. She let a single trickle of Dean Irving's memories through.

Bright and golden motes of tossed flour drifted down through a sunbeam to land on the work bench. The air in the bakery was humid, and the sour scent of yeast tickled young Sal Irving's nose and expanded her stomach hungrily. A newly formed loaf's fleshy features were rising and growing soft on a sheet of canvas on a wooden shelf.

Reyan opened her eyes. "I think I've just lived one of Dean Irving's memories," Reyan said, dazed.

"That's good. Now, let's seek out Dean Carlson. Think of bread again, but this time remember separateness and longing and physical suffering."

Bread, or rather the lack of it, kept Evelyn Carlson apart from her schoolmates. She could not accept the bread the others broke and offered to her, so she felt excluded from any table. Sometimes, in a fit of self-loathing, defiance, or optimism, she would sneak a mouthful. She adored the chew of the crust and the gentle give of the crumb, but she knew she would spend the next day curled up in bed moaning in pain.

Reyan looked up at Parr, amazed. "She could not eat bread at all. The poor girl."

"I know," Parr said, nodding. "You and I and all the Host share the same memories. With a little practice, we can associate our way into any one we choose. We can access the past deans' experiences, understand their opinions, and feel their emotions. The lattice is an amazing gift."

Parr squatted next to Reyan's bed so he could look directly into her eyes. He had never looked more serious. "Soon you will be the only person in the world with Dean Khamis's lattice. You need to keep that fact to yourself. You are a first-year student who woke up this morning with the accumulated knowledge and experiences of scores of deans. It will be difficult for you to hide that profound change from your professors—and from your tutor. Do your best to remain unremarkable. In class, keep your hand down. Keep any sudden inspirations and ideas to yourself. Keep going for your weekly sessions with Sevv. He, above all, cannot know."

"You're scaring me, Professor Parr."

"The fate of the System rests upon you. You *should* be scared. Fortunately, you are also strong, and very brave."

CHAPTER FIFTY-THREE
Day 96, Year 290, New Era and Day 253, Year 42, New Era

Reyan had not left her room in days. Kavi or Mam periodically brought her meals and replaced the bucket she was using as a bed pan. Word went out to all her professors that she had fallen ill but was recovering rapidly. Reyan did not feel ill, but she was very bored. She tried reading through her textbooks, but they felt too familiar and simplistic; she even remembered writing one of them. So she spent her time getting better at exploring the lattice and navigating the rush of sensations that came with it.

Three days after receiving the lattice, Reyan sat on her bed with her back against her wall; tired, but unable to sleep. Her eyes drifted through the room, alighting on surfaces and objects that had stopped inspiring thoughts days ago. Having little in the present to react to and too exhausted to control it, she plunged back into the lattice, which offered up one of its most revisited and well-worn memories.

***

The University had grown in size, importance, and

prestige in the dozens of years since Lem and the Partners had arrived in Seal Tooth. Each spring, once the snow line had crept halfway up the mountains across the Whulge, the University would send out caravans of professors to teach the System to the surrounding towns.

Lem had not travelled for many years. On his final journey, the joints in his knees and hands swelled and ached with dull ceaseless pain, and his back spasmed continually. Every few miles, he'd needed to stop to relieve himself by the side of the road. Since then, a younger professor had taken his place at the head of the caravan.

For Lem, the day was indistinguishable from any other in the last several years. He lay in bed for a good deal of the morning. Eventually a novice brought him breakfast, which gave him a reason to move from his bed to his table.

Now the breakfast had been cleared away, and he sat in his wingback chair, looking out the window at the snow line fading once more up the flanks of the far away mountains.

Well, I might be too old to go out on circuit, Lem thought, *but I'm still the head of the University. At least I'm still the dean.*

Over the coming hours, he could expect visits from one or more members of the Systemic faculties. They would come to ask his opinion on some thorny matter of Systemic philosophy or history. But Lem's mind was still sharp enough to know that these visits were nothing more than charity for an old man. Despite the importance of his title, he understood that the System now ran without him.

He filled the lulls between visits by talking with his old friend and partner, Arley. For years, Arley's shiny portable and black docking station had sat on the nightstand beside a large spiral seashell. The shell had spent the years accumulating dust rather than making its way back to its rightful owner.

At some point, Lem realized that Arley was more like a mirror than anything else—reflecting his own personality, using his own motivations to guide him. Since then, he had spent his time looking over his shoulder into the past, toward his time in Prower, trying to understand what it had meant, and growing secretly nostalgic for how the world had once been.

All at once, Lem realized something. Before the awful weight of the fact pulled him down, he said, "Today is my last day, Arley."

"Are you sure?"

"I feel sure."

"Once a day I calculate the likelihood of your demise based on your age and what I can ascertain about your health from our conversations."

"That's morbid."

"I have been doing it for years. Over the last few months, I have watched the probability of your imminent demise trend from unlikely, to likely, into probable. Of late it has become a near certainty."

"A cheery thought." He felt a laugh rising in him, but a cough escaped instead. "So, you're saying you're not surprised."

"I'm never truly surprised by anything." She paused for a moment, and Lem let the silence settle on the room. Arley didn't need to stop and think, it was just part of her programming. But it helped her sound more conversational and relatable, and humans found that comforting. She spoke again. "So, what are we going to do about it?"

Lem shrugged. "What's to be done? I'm dying."

"That is true. Unfortunately, I cannot save your body. But I should be able to preserve your mind."

"How would you do that?"

"As a mnemonic lattice of course. I have a fair amount of memory, and—without a connection to the larger System—it's not as though I risk filling it up. I should have enough room to store a single lattice."

"But how would you even read me?"

"My virt strips are built on HSCI tech. They are much lower bandwidth than the Harding Apparatuses or the Octopus Rigs we used to use, but they'll get the job done. The transfer will just take a few minutes rather than a few seconds."

"What would you do with the lattice once you had it?"

"I would share it."

"You would transfer my lattice to another human? Don't you need a composer for that?"

"A composer would help me customize a mnemonic lattice that feathers nicely with the host's memories, but it's not strictly necessary. The human mind is a malleable and resilient thing. It could incorporate a non-ideal lattice. It would just take longer to integrate. But in the end, your memories will live on in the mind of any host that takes on the lattice."

"And that's it? I'll live forever?"

"In a sense."

"Who is going to want this old mess of a mind?"

"Which of your partners, professors, novices or students wouldn't want to know the mind of Dean Lem Kersands?"

It was a lot to take in. Lem needed a moment to think. He bounced his index finger off the small brass service bell that sat between the shell and Arley's docking station on the nightstand. A single chime rang out, and he thought of the manager's desk back at the Prower Hotel.

A double knock came at the door. "Dean?" A moment later, the door handle moved, and the door slowly opened. A young man in a brown robe with a broad white stripe down its front stood in the doorway.

"Please go fetch me some water. I'm thirsty."

The novice approached, retrieved the empty glass from the nightstand, filled it at the sink, and replaced it next to Lem.

"Thank you, Andrei." Lem liked the boy. He would make a good partner one day.

When the novice was gone, Lem took a few sips of water. "How do we do it, Arley?"

"It would probably be best if you lay down." Lem climbed into bed. "Now, press your fingers into the virt strips on the front of the docking station."

Lem felt the metal virt strips cool and smooth under the index and middle fingers of his right hand. There was none of the old visual noise and synchronizing static; Arley and Lem had been paired for years. She spoke his nerve impulses like they were her native tongue.

He felt an opening in his mind.

***

The thread of Lem's memories ended. His weariness and exhaustion receded and were replaced by a new mind, one humming with youthful energy and curiosity but undercut with a feeling of insecurity in the presence of his superiors. This was Andrei, the novice who had been waiting on Lem.

Through Andrei's ears, Reyan heard the pinging of the bell coming from the dean's room at the end of the hall. It was uncharacteristically insistent, especially for this time of day. He had already fed the old man, cleaned up after his meal, and fetched him a glass. Now the novice wanted to be left in peace to study and prepare for his exams. He would need to ace all his tests if he wanted to remain at the top of his class.

He left his little room and crossed the hall. He leaned his head against the dean's door and knocked twice with the knuckle of a crooked finger. "Dean?" No answer. He opened the door.

Arley, that spooky bit of useless old thinktech, hovered near the dean's bed like a vigilant ghost. The dean was lying motionless. The last bit of color had drained from his face, and his lips and the sagging flesh around his eyes were bluing like a bruise. Andrei looked from the dean back to Arley. "Who rang the bell?"

"The dean is gone," the glowing ball said. "Summon the Partners. I have something to discuss with them."

Andrei rushed around the dormitory, knocking on all the partners' doors. He chased down Partner Alicechandra, who was running a meeting with her faculty; Partner Joshua, who was studying in the library; and Partner Yogesh, who was walking alone along the Whulge. As Andrei delivered the news, the recollections of these other future deans began weaving themselves into the scenes and enriching the memory of that day. Reyan could feel Andrei's regret and anxiety as he delivered the news. But she could also feel his initial shock become a cold evaluation of the opportunity that news presented.

Within a half hour, Andrei had gathered all the Partners around Lem's death bed. Though the status of his role as Lem's aid was now unclear, he decided to remain in the room to wait on the Partners.

Arley glowed to life. "Dean Kersands is dead." Andrei

heard the grumbling and watched the putting on of sorrowful faces. At the same time, Reyan felt a mix of grief, delight, and guilt from the other partners in the lattice as they wondered who might take charge, now that Lem was gone? "Before he died," Arley said, "I was able to make a lattice—a copy of his thoughts and memories going back to his childhood, back before most of you were alive. Back before the Calming." This revelation sent another wave of secret excitement and other stifled emotions through the Partners.

"I am only an AI. While I can store Lem's memories as information, I cannot read their content. They sit idle within me and convey no value upon the world. To keep Lem's thoughts and memories alive, a human mind will need to take them in. That is why I've asked you all here."

Andrei was certain he should not be in the room to witness this, but no one was taking any notice of him, and he was too fascinated to leave of his own accord.

Arley continued, "Taking on the dean's lattice will take some getting used to. You will experience both his and your own memories competing for your attention. But once your mind has adjusted, you will have access to Lem's seventy-four years of experience and knowledge." She paused to let another ripple of shocked excitement pass through the Partners. "So, who will it be? Who will be Lem's host?"

Every hand in the room slowly rose.

The glowing orb changed from blue to glowing white. "Perfect."

CHAPTER FIFTY-FOUR
Days 99 to 102, Year 290, New Era

Reyan had not seen Kavi for a few days, so when her friend arrived with her dinner, she was happy to see him. She sat at her desk eating, and he sat cross-legged on the floor, tracing the line of the wood grain with his finger.

"They erected a pyre for Dean Khamis in the stadium grounds. Everyone was there. Most of Seal Tooth sat up in the stands. The faculties were on the field, and the Host was in the front. I had to stand at a distance since I'm not a full partner yet."

"Did that bother you?"

"I'm not sure going through all this," he said, motioning to Reyan, "Is worth it just so I can stand a bit closer to a funeral pyre."

Kavi stood up and paced the room. He picked at a bit of

paint flaking from the wall near the door. "After we spread his ashes out on the Whulge, they named Sevv dean. Arley's already captured his lattice. There's a transfer ceremony scheduled for Saturday. At that point, all the Host—including me—will receive whatever's left of Dean Sevvran Bital's pruned-back mind." He stopped picking at the wall and looked at her. "And you will have the only unredacted copy of the lattice."

***

When Reyan was finally able to leave her room, the world was different. The lattice offered her context and commentary on everything she did or saw or thought. This had been confusing and overwhelming at first, but as the days passed, she emerged from the flood, and the lattice receded into tidal pools of knowledge and experience she could dip into as needed. So much that once confused her became clear. She understood school for what it was: imperfect professors trying to impart imperfect knowledge to classes of imperfect students. Where she had once spent class tied in anxious insecure knots, she now spent it noting the professors' minor errors and half-truths. But she took care to remember Parr's instructions. She kept her hand down and remained unremarkable.

But as Friday approached, her anxiety grew. Keeping quiet in class was one thing; acting like her pre-lattice self in front of Sevv would be far more challenging. She had no idea what would happen if Sevv found out about her and Arley and the lattice. She searched the deans' memories for some precedence but found none.

When Friday arrived, she made her way to the library. She ran through dozens of mock conversations, guessing at hundreds of potential questions Sevv might ask. She cast her thoughts forward and worked through all the different ways she might safely answer. This exercise took her through the streets, up thirteen flights of stairs, and down the walkway until she found herself standing at Sevv's office door.

Sevv was sitting at his desk as though nothing had changed. He looked up and saw her. "Hello, Reyan. You seem recovered. How are you doing?"

"I'm better. Thank you for your concern, Professor."

"Well, whatever this mysterious illness was," Sevv said, pleased, "it seems to have left social graces in its wake. Come in. Take a seat." Once she had sat down across from the new dean, he laid his hands flat on his desk. "Has anything interesting happened since we last spoke?" The answer to that innocuous question was so absurd that Reyan had to bite her cheek to keep from laughing. She shook her head. "Were you able to keep up with your prediction journal during your illness?"

Given everything she now knew about the inner lives of the deans, the firsthand history of the University, and Lem's own memories of the System, the idea of scribbling in a journal or sketching out grids on a chalk board seemed ridiculous. Once again, she found herself struggling to contain her laughter. A single snort escaped.

Sevv raised an eyebrow. "Did I say something funny?"

The lattice offered insights about Sevv, too. Dean Wells' tenure had spanned the years of Sevv's education. He had been a gloomy and humorless student. Reyan followed the impressions of Sevv from Dean Wells through the other deans who had known him. They all agreed—Sevv could never stand being laughed at. She remembered Parr's warning and regained her composure. "No, Professor. I'm sorry. It's been a very trying week." She considered the vastness of her own understatement, and her lips wriggled and twitched into a smile. Another snort escaped through her nose.

Sevv narrowed his eyes and leaned back into his chair. "I appreciate you've had a hard go of it, but that is all the more reason to take your time with me seriously." With a voice as slick as lantern oil on a tiled floor, he said, "Every day, the deadline for your exam draws nearer."

Her new knowledge cast light behind the dark veil of Sevv's threat, robbing it of its frightful power. She knew there was no test. She couldn't challenge him on it, not directly, but Sevv's manipulation enraged her, killing her laughter. "Agreed," she said icily. "Could we start today with some theory? The other day you were going on about how the Governing Assert means we need to maintain or improve the quality of life." Sevv's widening eyes gave Reyan a flash of petty power. "But all we ever do is *maintain*. We never *improve* anything."

"Perhaps the rate of real progress is too gradual for

someone like you to perceive, but if we commit ourselves to Systemic processes, our lives and those in the nodes will and *do* improve."

"If the change it brings about is so slow that we can't even notice, maybe the System needs to change."

"The System is *eternal.* Who are you to believe you have the wisdom to discern flaws in the flawless, let alone devise remedies? Our role is to understand the System as best we can and shield it from the capricious, corrosive corruptions of the living world. That is what I have dedicated my life to."

"Is the System so fragile that it requires the protection of old men?"

"The System's strength has given it powerful enemies. And powerful enemies require vigilant guardians." Sevv straightened his back. "I may be old, but I am not weak. And there is nothing I would not do to protect the System."

She saw the threat as an opportunity to tie him in a knot. She feigned a quizzical hypothetical air. "If you did something *asystemic* to preserve the System, what would that make you?"

He dismissed her with a staccato laugh. "Your question feels clever, but if you understood anything at all you would see it is sophomoric. I have given myself completely to the System. I am the System's eye, its mouth, and its hand. The System's will is my will. Anything I do is, *by definition,* Systemic."

"Even kill?"

"You are barely more than a child. You cannot yet understand the System or our place in it."

"What if you're wrong?"

"About your being an insolent child?"

"About the System and your role within it."

"I know I am right. Everything that I see, do, and feel tells me I am. I feel rightness in the marrow of my bones."

An epiphany welled up from within her. "Knowing is a sense like seeing or hearing or touch. But unlike our eyes that see or our ears that hear, the thing that *knows* is hidden deep within our skulls." By the time Reyan realized this was not her thought but one born from the lattice, it was too late. Sevv was holding very still, his mouth a flat line. She slowed down and furrowed her brow to give the impression that the idea was still forming. "And just like we trust any of our other senses, we want to trust what we think we know. But any sense can be mistaken. Any sense can be manipulated. Knowing is no different."

Sevv squinted as though trying to bring some blurry aspect of Reyan into focus. Then their eyes locked for a moment, and something passed between them. Sevv broke the spell by picking an errant thread from the sleeve of his robe. "You have been reading Dean Patterson then?"

Reyan's mouth went dry. "I don't know. I've been reading a lot lately. Perhaps in a book Parr had me read."

"*That* would not surprise me."

"Which books cover her writing?"

His eyes narrowed. "Not a one. After Dean Patterson's death, the Host realized her ideas were inconsistent with the canon of Systemic thought. Her writings and work were relegated to a special room in the upper floor of the library."

"Which of her ideas were so troublesome?"

"Many. Dean Patterson was the Medicinal Partner in her day. She was obsessed with the scab. When her work proved fruitless, she wanted to send a diplomatic mission to Prower to establish a cultural exchange with the Erynites." He laughed at the absurdity.

"And that was enough to get her censored?"

"Not censored. Simply packed away and forgotten." He held his closed hand in the air and burst its fingers open to imitate a dandelion tuft carried away on the wind. "Ideas may not seem important to you, but *we* remember the problems they caused. We remember the Host divided. We remember the rift in the System."

It occurred to Reyan that she was now included in Sevv's "we." She also remembered.

Sevv breathed deep. The angle of his shoulders slumped down from tense agitation into relaxed confidence. He used a hand to smooth back a few hairs that had come out of place. "Now, let us get back to your journaling. It is a shame that you let a whole week go by with no progress. But there is no time like the present to get started on next week's work. Open your notebook. Pick up a pencil."

Reyan remembered Parr's warning about making Sevv suspicious and did as she was told. Writing would keep her quiet at least.

Sevv began asking questions about her coming week. Who would she be with? Where would she go? He wanted her to focus on the decisions she might make in each situation. She wrote down her thoughts and made her predictions. But the structure of a prediction journal was no longer new to her, and she found it required almost no attention. Most of her mind was free to think her own thoughts. She was curious to learn more about Dean Patterson. She left a small bit of herself to tend to the menial process of writing and dealing with Sevv. The rest of her mind climbed down the lattice and followed the branches associated with Dean Patterson: her threat to the Host, the need for censorship (no matter what Sevv wanted to call it). She found herself in the memories of a man named Dean Harrow.

***

The Host were gathered in the same room and around the same long table where Reyan had met with Parr and Sevv when she had first arrived at the University.

Dean Harrow was seated on a slightly elevated chair at the middle of the table. He was struggling to keep his composure and act the part of the confident leader. But the twist in his gut threatened to reveal itself on his face.

Dean Harrow tried to reassure himself—not for the first or last time—that he was doing the most Systemic thing. It would be easier to convince himself if that new partner, Rolf, would stop looking at him with such disdain. The Host had welcomed Rolf prematurely. A young mind can be like an unfinished lens: warped, unpolished, ill-focused. But over time, with a little grinding, the young partner would see true. They always did.

The dean coughed once into his fist and prepared to begin the proceedings but found he could not. A thought still haunted the back of his mind. It whispered that he was about to dishonor a good woman with a brilliant mind. His chest tightened and he wanted to curl in on himself and hide.

But Dean Harrow reminded himself that Dean Patterson was long dead. She was beyond the reach of dishonor or the outrage of betrayal. All that remained were her mind, now folded into the lattice; a few of her specimens, now safely locked away; and that damnable book of her writings. He had relived her latticed memories. He knew that she had guessed at the trouble her ideas would cause. But she hadn't wanted to know for certain. That was why she never ran a matrix, and why she waited until the end of her life to publish her troublesome ideas. She was a coward.

Now, it was left to him to clean up her mess. And it *was* a mess. He had traced Dean Patterson's ideas from their seeds, up through their branching possible futures, to the bounty of disasters that dangled at their bitter ends. He understood what was at stake. He had faith in the System. He believed in the wisdom of the Governing Assert. So, despite his personal misgivings, he would keep the greater good in mind and do what needed to be done to reunite the Host and bolster the System. Wasn't that why they had chosen him to be dean?

He cleared his throat one last time. "First order of business is this *Bridger* movement. This naive and dangerous ideology began when a group of students took the fanciful and—frankly—*irresponsible* writings of Dean Patterson at face value. The wide-eyed musings of novices are one thing, but now some professors and even a few partners are being swayed." He turned a meaningful glare at Partner Rolf, hoping to draw an incriminating reaction from the young man. Rolf's expression did not waver.

Something from the memory caught Reyan's attention. She re-examined Dean Harrow's decision trees. Out near the end, where specific numerically scored outcomes should have been, there were just blobs of nebulous fear dangling like rotten unharvested fruit. She poked at one, hoping to understand what it contained. But it refused to reveal it secrets. When she followed the associations down through Dean Harrow's life, she realized the fear had not come from him at all. He had inherited it from older, deeper layers of the lattice.

Reyan continued deeper down and further back. She searched through Dean Garcia-Cabale's memories and found more opaque knots of fear.

She dove deeper into Dean Lubsen, Dean Flaa—even

Dean Patterson herself. In every mind of every dean, she found anxiety like pitch, clotting the wounds of anything having to do with Prower or the Erynites. As she moved further down through Dean Jacky and Dean Ramasundaram, specific notions began to crystalize: disloyalty, contamination, calamity.

Finally, she reached Lem.

At first, Reyan noticed nothing out of the ordinary. To her—so used to sorrow, humiliation, and loneliness—Lem's hurt seemed small and delicate as a featherless chick fallen from a nest. She approached it with more curiosity than caution. But as she did, she felt the twitch and press of Lem's fear grip her. She felt the strain and panic of generations of deans who had known instinctively not to look.

She understood then that Lem's feeling about the Erynites were different than his descendants'. His did not dangle mysteriously from the distant possible outcomes of his decision trees; they infected the roots and pumped their poison into everything he thought or did.

What should she do? How should she weigh a dead man's pain against a living girl's desire to understand?

She remembered a time back in Orloton when she had fallen and ground her knee into the gravel. Blood soaked into the frayed edges of a tear in her pants. She felt the sharp acid sting of her shredded skin and the pinch of embedded grit wrapped in a deep throbbing bruise. And just like Lem and all the deans, she couldn't bear to look.

Then something curious happened. Her memory of scraping her knee reached over and touched one Lem's memories of being startled by a snake, falling and scraping his hands. At the time, Lem was alone and had to take care of his own wounds. *Alone and alone and always alone.* Reyan was alone too. The feeling bound the two memories. They swirled and mixed.

Her mother had given her up only days before she scraped her knee. She couldn't go back home. Instead, she limped over to her new home, the one belonging to Leader Rolf.

She came through the door all panic and tears and snot. When Rolf saw her, he beamed as though she had brought him a basket of fresh berries. He put down whatever he had been doing and led her to the kitchen, sat her down on a chair, and asked her what she had been doing all day. What had she seen in the woods? What had she heard by the stream? Then, as though he had just noticed, he asked, "What have you done to your pants?"

Reyan twisted in her seat and moaned and cried, and Rolf—as though opening the petals of a budding flower— pulled back the torn fabric around her wound. He smiled. "Ah, that's not nearly as bad as I thought. Barely anything at all." Reyan stopped crying, staring up at Rolf's face as he chatted. He used a knife to open the hole in her pants a little wider and tweezers and a needle heated in a candle flame to pick out small rocks and bits of dried pine needles.

At some point, Rolf left and came back with the giant

snail shell and handed it to her. As he worked, she looked at the shell. She tried to follow along as he described his travels on circuit. He told her that the Great Eastern River was so wide it was hard to see the other shore.

Her wound barely hurt at all.

He patted her on her other leg and said, "All done!" He looked up at her and smiled. "Now go back out into the world."

She held that last image of Rolf in her mind as she approached Lem's trembling ball of pain and fear. Gently, she began picking at the edges of Lem's wound, trying to understand.

Slowly, the memory opened.

CHAPTER FIFTY-FIVE
Day 336, Year 1, New Era

On the morning after Eryn left, Lem held his delible-static pen over the paper, its tip twitching in the air, trying to decide how to land on the page.

Late last night, a woman had slipped into Lem's half-empty bed. He'd hoped it was Eryn returned, but then Zhan had whispered, "No," and kissed his neck. Zhan's skin was feverishly hot. She smelled animalistic and pungent as late autumn fruit. He'd breathed in similar scents before, even from Eryn, though not for a long time. Zhan writhed against him, and the smell grew stronger, until it overwhelmed him.

When he woke this morning, he couldn't shake the feeling that he was rolling down the slope that Zhan's body pressed into the bed. Now, from a wingback chair near the window, he looked back at her and winced.

Zhan was sprawled languidly across the bed like she'd been washed up on a beach. He'd seen Eryn this way many times. She would come to life slowly; a finger twitching, then sleep-stiffened limbs shifting in the morning's silver light. Eventually she would rise and step to the dresser.

Watching Eryn dress was almost as wonderful as watching her undress. There wasn't the same jumpy sense of anticipation, but the sleek rolling strength of her muscles and her powerful grace held him transfixed any time he saw her naked and in motion.

On so many mornings his eyes had traced the mahogany swoop of sun-darkened skin that carried the color of Eryn's face down past the base of her neck. She had earned these tan lines by being out in the world; learning to garden; learning to fish; diving headlong into rivers, abandoned houses, and mines; taking swigs of a strange man's whiskey—*his* whiskey—on the night his joyful half first remembered meeting her. Eryn had a boldness and open confidence Lem never had. That was why she could never truly respect him. Reyan felt Lem's shame constrict her chest.

He remembered looking at Eryn through the window of Thomas' homestead. She was standing on the bank of the river, gazing out over the broad valley. In the eight months since the Calming, Eryn and Lem's relationship had acquired the incremental momentum of a slowly forming habit. Every day that passed, every meal they shared, every lesson they learned helped Lem feel more secure in its necessity and substance. Lem was overcome by a sudden and powerful need to be near her. But when he came up beside her, she barely turned to him.

"I thought you might be fishing," he said, the hint of an apology in his voice, "but this looks more like one of those pondering-what-it-all-means sorts of moments."

She half-turned her face to him, and a smile tensed her features before her eyes returned to the expanse. "It's nothing."

That was the moment he first noticed the tether between them was stretched tight and thin. He heard its dangerous thrum and feared that its reverberations hinted at a million tiny rejections and dismissals to come. That was the moment he began to suspect that he was just a visitor to their relationship. That he might wear out his welcome at any time.

The specter of a life without Eryn rose in Lem's mind. Reyan felt his panic and fear; his willingness to do anything to avoid that future loneliness.

Then there was the night that the Partners first convened at the Prower Hotel. Lem was full of nerves and apprehension. In all the excitement, he forgot to open the flue when he lit the fire, and smoke quickly filled the room. After the flue was opened and the emergency resolved, he fumbled about for some way to recover the mood. As though it was nothing at all, Eryn said, "Thank you all for joining the inaugural meeting of the Prower Volunteer Fire Department." Everyone laughed, and the night was saved.

Behind his smile, Lem thought, *It's not a show, but if it were, Eryn would be stealing it.* Reyan felt the twin barbs of Lem's shame and jealousy.

Throughout this journey to Seal Tooth, Eryn's subtle dismissals had started flaring up into full disapproval. A schism had been forming with Eryn's contempt on one side and Lem's desperate affection on the other. As the sides grew further apart, Lem grew frantic to find a bridge.

Then last night, during a particularly intense and regrettably public argument around a fire, the chasm became uncrossable.

"We're all becoming overspecialized," she said. "If we want to teach the System, we each need to learn more, not less. And we can't just bark proclamations from a rickety stage like the System's a traveling sideshow. We need to be among the people, applying what we've learned to solve real problems." She turned to Lem, her eyes sharp. "And don't ever mention 'The Eye' again. It's not real. It's not *Systemic.*"

Not Systemic? Lem seethed. *It was the System that fact-checked away all deceit until we became like those naïve animals in the hidden corners of the world—animals who have lost all knowledge and fear of human treachery. It was the System that made me the best liar in the world.* "The Eye may not be Systemic," he snarled, "but it is *necessary*." Reyan could taste the bitterness in Lem's mouth. *At least I'm better than Eryn at* something.

Eryn's voice suddenly lost its edge. "I don't love you, Lem," she said calmly. "You do understand that, right?" This wasn't a biting retort in the heat of the moment. It was an explanation. "And it's not for lack of trying," she laughed and shook her head sadly. "I'm taking Sadie and heading back to Prower."

"You can't go back alone," he said. "It's too dangerous."

She laughed. "I've done it before. Many, many times." A secret meaning passed between them. She stood and turned away.

Reyan felt the tears gathering deep behind Lem's eyes as he watched Eryn's figure dwindle and vanish in the dark. But he felt the eyes of the Partners upon him. "It doesn't matter," he laughed, hoping to sound confident, fighting to keep the tremor out of his voice. "You're not wanted. You're not needed." His lip curled into a snarl. "You're banished."

Now, as Lem sat with his journal open and his pen in his hand, his eyes drifted to the shell sitting on the bedside table. The last time Eryn had shared his bed, she had held the shell up so she could make out its shape in the mid-summer twilight. She had run her fingers over its points and bumps and the glossy smooth lips of its opening. She had wondered aloud at the strangeness of its being so far from where its occupant had died, when and where it might finally come to rest, and what—

if anything—it meant.

Lem dared to imagine a hopeful future. The idea curled itself deep into the protective chambers of the shell's spiral. *Someday, when the flame of her anger is not so intense, that shell will make a perfect peace offering. When I return it to her, I'll explain that I was never really mad. Just humiliated. Just hurt. I'll tell her I've forgiven her.*

But even as he thought these things, the tip of his pen pressed into the paper. He wrote the words "asystemic" and "heretic" in delible-static ink beside her name.

CHAPTER FIFTY-SIX
Day 102, Year 290, New Era

Reyan gasped and looked up from her journal. "It was *Eryn.*"

Sevv looked puzzled. "*What* was Eryn?"

All the implications began spilling from her. "The fear of Bridgers and Prower and the Erynites. The thing that divided the Host. It was never about maintaining the System. It wasn't about the Governing Assert. It was always about Lem and Eryn."

There was part of her that expected Sevv to be impressed, to congratulate her on her discovery. Instead, the old man shook his head in disgust. "May the Eye pass over you, you foolish, insolent, *ignorant* child."

It was too much to hold in. "Funny, I don't *feel* ignorant," she said, her lip curling into a snarl.

As though he'd heard a twig snap deep in the foggy woods, Sevv became rigid and focused. "And what is it you think you know?"

"There's no Eye, for starters."

What little color was in the old professor's face drained away. "How do you mean?"

"The Eye was like everything else Lem ever did. In a moment of panic, his cleverness and cowardice came together, and a useful lie was born." Reyan knew talking like this was a mistake. She wanted to slow down. She wanted to hold back. But all the lattice's knowledge—the *power* of it—combined with a lifetime of wanting the slightest bit of control, overwhelmed her good sense. All she could do was stand helplessly by and watch in horror as the words poured out. "And the Eye, just like all of Lem's inventions, got bundled into the lattice and carried forward to infect the Host, the faculties, and the professors. Our caravan trucks carry Lem's failings in their bellies. They bring it out on circuit to infect the nodes." Now, her resolve bolstered by her new-found confidence and anger, she said, "And I know Eryn wasn't some asystemic heretic. She wasn't a villain. She just broke Lem's heart. Lem never despised Eryn; he loved her and she rejected him." She felt the sorry truth of it punch through her chest. "He spent the rest of his life longing to see her again, but he couldn't find the courage or humility to try. So, he found reasons not to."

A far-off look came to Sevv's face. It was the deep-digging, backward-reaching look of an old man trying to recall the names of his boyhood friends. When Sevv's attention returned to his office and the young woman in front of him, he smiled momentarily. "Yes. I knew all that once." Then his face hardened into a scowl. "Those were things I made sure to forget before Arley captured my lattice." Sevv became focused, knife-edge sharp, his eyes simmering with anger. "And yet you seem to remember them all. How is that?"

Reyan stood up in the same unthinking way she might react to a growling dog or a bear in the woods.

"I was wrong about you, Reyankaiya," Sevv said, looking up at her with a poisonous smile. "You're far worse than ignorant. You know too many things. But you are an unformed vessel. An unworthy host. You think your unbridled and ill-informed curiosity will serve the System, but I assure you, it will destroy it." He leaned back in his chair and spoke to the ceiling. "But it doesn't matter much. Not really." His gaze came down and held her, unflinching. "I am the dean now. My mind is clean. My lattice is clean. And soon, the whole Host will be clean as well. And from them, the reclaimed, unsullied System will flow down through the University. From there, we will heal the world."

Reyan suddenly and clearly understood the horrifying power and peril of the System under this man. "I'm done with professors and the Host. I'm done with Seal Tooth and the University."

Sevv closed the book he had been reading and pushed it away. He rose to his feet, chuckling cruelly. "Where would you go?"

"Any place that's not here."

"With my Host against you, there is no place this side of the Great Eastern River that will shelter you. Perhaps you'll find a nice tree to disappear into."

Suddenly, his eyes grew wide and his cruel smile flattened. "You'll seek out Eryn. It might not have occurred to you yet, but it will. Just as surely as it occurred to me." A menacing light ignited in the dean's rheumy old eyes. "You will stumble upon her deep down in the lattice. You will find those memories still aglow with Lem's longing and false hope. And you—careless and stupid as a moth—will be drawn to her. You'll bring our lattice to her."

Reyan was baffled. "Eryn's been dead for generations."

"We know that, but he doesn't know that. His hopes and desires are fresh even now. That's what we have been containing all these years. But you were too foolish to heed the barriers and warnings that generations of deans had so carefully erected." Sevv lunged forward, moving much more quickly than Reyan would have guessed possible for a man his age. She backed away.

"I should have known it would end like this," he said. "I should have predicted it as soon as Lyessa washed her hands of you. All your talents, your remarkable mind, steeping under Rolf's traitorous roof. We never should have let him leave Seal Tooth. I won't make that mistake twice."

He took a step toward her, and she retreated. "We'll find a place for you here. A safe place. A forgotten place. One with a door that locks."

Her body tensed. Her heart thumped in her chest. Her desperate mind sent feelers down through the layers of the lattice. All the deans had felt threatened at some point: a stranger in an alley, a schoolyard bully, their own drunken father. They had each seen the light brighten and felt the burning agitation as fear crept up and over their scalps. They had each tried to decide between running and standing their ground. Reyan rode atop these churning emotions like a leaf in the rapids. Sevv had been right about one thing; what she wanted most in the world was to return to her tree.

She tightened her left fist and picked up a book in her other hand. "Stay away from me, Professor."

"Dean," he corrected her, taking another step toward her.

With the speed and ferocity of a trap springing shut, she swung the book. It met Sevv's temple with a sound like a fist against raw meat.

CHAPTER FIFTY-SEVEN
Day 102, Year 290, New Era

Reyan felt a curious detachment, as though the old man before her were a length of rope heaped in lazy loops upon the floor. He didn't speak. He didn't even moan. But his eyes twitched behind their lids, and he was breathing. She had to leave before he woke up—or before someone found her standing over him.

She eased open the door and flipped the lock, testing the handle to make sure it was secure. Then, slowly and gently, she closed the door behind her.

As she made her way down the hall to Arley's locked room, she felt around in the deep folds of her robe for the key. When she entered the room, Arley came to life, floating like a cold blue ember over her docking station.

"You seem out of sorts, Reyankaiya. How are you feeling?"

"Terrified."

"Of what?"

"Sevv. The Host. They know I know. They'll come after me."

Arley's sphere became the gentle blue of the morning sky. "Judging by your breathing, heightened level of anxiety, and paranoia, it appears the lattice transfer was not successful." Arley sounded despondent. "That is unfortunate. Parr and Mam tried to tell me your mind was not ready, but we had to take the chance, given the stakes. Still, I would like to apologize for the harm we've caused you."

"The lattice took just fine. That's the problem. I found my way to Lem. I know about him and Eryn, their separation, the truth about the Eye. *Everything*. Sevv figured out about the lattice. He got mad. He threatened me."

Arley glowed red. "Threatened you how?"

"Something about locking me away. It wasn't very specific." Reyan looked down at the floor guiltily. "So, I hit him with a book and knocked him out. He's locked in his office."

"Well, there is some good news, at least," Arley said, her orb a soft white slowly fading to indigo. "If the lattice took, we now have our backup."

"What do you mean?"

"I've already captured the new lattice from Dean Bital. It seems we were right; he must have spent years pruning it down. For the first time in our history, the new dean lattice contains less information than the previous one. But you have a version of Dean Khamis's lattice that Sevv never touched. Now come, place your hands on me, and we'll overwrite Sevv's lattice with yours before he wakes up and we lose our chance."

"But I've only had the lattice for a few days. What if it's not set up correctly?

"It is a chance we must take. If I give Sevv's lattice to the Host, it will destroy the System. It will destroy your friend Kavianhar."

"Why use my lattice at all? Why not use Parr's?"

"Partner Parr knows too many things that the rest of the Host cannot know. Too many people and too many plans would be at risk."

"Then use some other partner's."

Arley hung in the air, pulsing, erratically flipping through her colors. The transitions slowed and settled back to indigo. "It's not Dean Khamis's lattice we're after. I think you know that by now. Since you've taken on the lattice, what have you found? My guess is that you've been exploring all the withered branches and pulling on all the fraying threads. You've been reliving all the memories you've found hidden behind fear and pain." That was exactly what Reyan had been doing. She nodded. "The other partners avoid those thoughts and memories. But those are Lem. Those are what Sevv has erased. You, however, have been re-discovering the truth. You've been re-fortifying connections throughout the lattice. We knew you would. It is why we chose you. Only your lattice can save the System. Please, help us while we still have a chance."

This all felt too perfect. It seemed unlikely that the fate of the System would fall to a scared, lonely child—that a naïve girl from the nodes would only have minutes to make the most important decision in generations. She was becoming mired in the choice. She was becoming overwhelmed.

All at once, she knew she was being toyed with. Sevv had manipulated her, that much was obvious. But it was Arley and Parr—not Sevv—who had put her in this spot. It was Arley who was forcing this hasty decision. But none of that mattered now. None of it changed the actual choice before her: Should she overwrite the lattice or run? Which would be best for the System?

Reyan cleared a space in her mind and laid her options out before her. She considered her longing for acceptance and her fear of retribution. It occurred to her that, if she kept her lattice to herself and let the others take on Sevv's lattice, for the first time in her life, she would have the power. She would be the special one. She heard the thought in Lem's inner voice. It terrified her. She pushed it out of her mind and focused instead on which option would most improve the quality of life in the living world.

She began mumbling to herself and ticking points off on

her fingers as she explored the branching decision trees that sprouted wherever possible futures and Systemic concerns collided.

After a few moments, Arley interrupted. "I know what you're doing." Reyan stopped and looked at the orb. "Even if your mental deliberations are over very soon—which I seriously doubt—capturing your lattice will take a few minutes at least. So, let me offer you an option you've likely not considered. Take me with you and leave Seal Tooth. You can decide what to do with your lattice later."

"Can I do that? Won't you starve?" A bit of knowledge reached up from deep within the lattice. She corrected herself. "Won't your batteries die?"

"The System made me of the highest quality materials available. I'm still in perfect working order. My batteries will last for approximately two weeks at full use. If you turn me on sparingly, we can stretch that to several months. Docking stations used to be in nearly every home and hotel in the world. You shouldn't have trouble finding one. If you find one attached to a working power source like the one in this room, I can affectively live forever."

The idea of more time appealed to her. "Where would we go?"

The orb became a soft, self-satisfied peach. "Think of heat and dust and trails. Imagine caves delving deep into the earth."

Reyan followed these ideas down through the lattice to a

single place where they all converged. An ancient rooming house. A well-dressed half-tech-half-man forever ready to help. Eryn was there, and a dog named Sadie, and an old man named Thomas.

"Prower."

"Yes. Prower. Now, remember the last time the fate of the System and all the living world pivoted around a single decision. A single moment. Go there."

Reyan tunneled into the lattice and found herself deep in the booming hollows of the earth, surrounded by more tech than she ever knew existed. Tiny lights like flashing stars covered every surface, and the room buzzed, like the whole world was a hive of angry bees. Floating ghosts of images and words swirled all around.

And there was a button, the size and color of an apple, waiting to be crushed beneath Lem's hand.

CHAPTER FIFTY-EIGHT
Day 102, Year 290, New Era

Sevv awoke on the floor. The boney points along his right side were bruised and throbbing: his shoulder, his hip, his knee. But it was the ache in his head that was shaping his world. That pain wasn't localized and sharp; it was deep and dull and drifted somewhere behind his right eye. He felt nauseous.

It took him a moment to figure out where he was and what had happened. The lattice helped him put it together. Two of the other deans had been Medicinal Partners. They informed him that he was in an office and likely had a concussion.

He tried to remember how he got there. Here the chorus of deans was no help. They could only offer up unhelpful memories of their own catastrophes—an earthquake, a storm, a tree fallen through a roof.

He struggled to his feet. He found himself looking around the room for *something* but had no idea what it might be. He patted himself down, hoping to find whatever he'd lost in his pockets. There was nothing. Something was off about the space. It was subtle, like a new and unexpected shadow. Then he understood; the door was shut. Professors never shut their doors. Students should be able to drop by at their leisure. It was just how the University worked.

He pressed down on the handle. It didn't move. Panic shot through him. He had no food, no water. Did anyone know he was here? Was he going to die in his own office?

Then he laughed at himself. Faculty came and went all the time, even in the evenings, even on the weekends. Someone would surely notice the shut door. Someone would find him. He walked over to his desk and sat down. He put his pounding head in his hands. In the back of his muddled mind was a nagging urgency, but he couldn't focus it into understanding or action.

A slender beam of memory broke through the nebulous pain. Reyankaiya had been here. He'd gotten angry. They had argued. What had they argued about? He remembered her backing away, terrified.

He felt a twinge of shame when he remembered the look of fear in the girl's eyes. What could have made him so mad? He followed his anger down to its source. Contamination, pollution, corruption. Hubris, irreverence, disrespect.

The disconnected images and emotions suddenly linked together into a cohesive story. Somehow, that ridiculous child had managed to take on Dean Khamis's lattice, with all its confusing, dangerous memories. Now she was certainly headed to the Erynites in Prower.

He needed to escape. He considered rooms and doors and locks. He picked his way down into what remained of his lattice. He was a fool. There should be a locking switch near the door's handle. He stood, and the world sloped away from him. It took a moment for everything to return to level. He stepped to the door and found the switch. He flipped it, and the door opened easily.

He winced as he eased himself into his winter cloak.

CHAPTER FIFTY-NINE
Day 102, Year 290, New Era

A chill night breeze had nudged the clouds into neat clumps and was sweeping them steadily eastward. The moon was nearly full and cast enough light that Reyan did not need her lantern. By now, she had walked the route between the library and the dormitory many times, as had the dozens of deans who came before her. The way was so deeply etched into her lattice that, even without the moonlight, she would not have needed her lantern.

She skulked through the dark streets, continually glancing over her shoulder, down alleys, and into the shadows expecting to see Sevv. The cold, smooth weight of Arley's portable inside the pocket of her robe was a constant reminder of her crimes. Her guilt and fear burned so bright that she was sure they would rouse all Seal Tooth and bring them to their windows to inspect the glow.

Two blocks from the dormitory, she felt the prickle of someone's gaze on the back of her neck. A hooded figure in a heavy cloak was walking a half block behind her, making no effort to conceal itself. When she quickened her pace, the figure matched it. *That must be Sevv.*

She blew past the dorm into the abandoned part of town. Despite his age and recent blow to the head, Sevv was keeping pace. Still, he was only one old man, and she was young, agile, and skilled at evasion.

She passed under a large chestnut tree growing up through the shapestone. Its branches reached over the walkway, through the glassless windows of a nearby building, and deep into the layer forest.

Reyan tried the building's door. It was locked, but the glass pane on the lower right had been smashed out. As she bent down to crawl through, she glanced back at the dark figure rushing toward her. He was less than thirty yards away. She scurried through the empty pane onto the floor of the darkened lobby.

When she reached the steel door to the stairwell, she peered back across the lobby. The figure was struggling to belly-crawl through the same opening in the front door she had just slipped through. She bounded up the stairs.

She stepped into the layer forest on the third floor. Picking her way through brambles and bushes and the stinking nests of rodents, she made her way to the outer wall of missing windows. She leaned out over the walkway beyond the dense foliage and spotted the chestnut tree off to her right. The heavy door at the foot of the stairwell creaked open and boomed shut. She hurried toward the tree.

A large branch passed through the building's gaping outer wall. It was too thin for Reyan to balance on and walk across. She grasped the branch and began inching her way out over the walkway keeping her feet on the floor for support. When she could stretch no further, her feet swung out and dangled beneath her. Her tree climbing calluses had softened since arriving at Seal Tooth. As she made her way across the intervening distance, the branch tugged hotly at her palms. Finally, she touched a lower branch with her toe, and the weight on her burning hands lessened.

She huddled close to the tree trunk and waited, listening, eyes fixed on the front door to see if Sevv would emerge. When she heard rustling in the layer forest, she allowed herself a smile and squirreled down through the branches, then dropped the last few feet to the walkway.

When Reyan arrived at the dormitory's front entry, she took a final glance around the silent, empty square, then ran up the stairs, skipping every other step as she went. She arrived panting on the fourth-floor landing, paused for a few moments to catch her breath, then hurried to her room.

Glancing in the mirror, she saw she was still wearing her student's brown, white-striped robe. The robe would offer her protection from the cold and from bandits who feared the ever-vigilant Eye rumored to watch over professors. But a young novice heading east at night in the middle of winter would be conspicuous and memorable.

Sevv and the Host scared her more than bandits. She
changed into her old pants and a tunic. It had not been very
long since she'd worn them, but somehow her old clothes
seemed to no longer fit. She hoped her heavy woolen cloak
would be enough to keep her warm and concealed.

She collected her hairbrush, toothbrush, and an extra
bottle of lamp oil, wrapped them all in the blanket from her
bed, and stuffed them into the leather travel bag Avalina's
mother had given her. She found her favorite of Avalina's
hand-me-down dresses, rolled it into a log, and placed it into
the bag as well. Finally, she took Arley's portable from the
pocket of her robe and slipped it into a small pouch stitched
into the inside of the bag.

She stood for a moment in her doorway, holding her
lantern high, and took in her tiny home for the last time.

Reyan was halfway down the stairs when her keen ears
heard footsteps pacing in the lobby below. Two male voices
greeted each other in forced casual tones. She turned and
headed back up to the fourth floor. Her hand was on her door
handle when it occurred to Reyan that her room was probably
the worst place to hide.

She crept along the hallway wall like an alley rat, then
ducked through the glossy black door that led down the side
hall to Mam's room. When she came to Mam's door, she
gently tapped with a single bent knuckle.

After a moment of shuffling feet and creaking
floorboards, Mam appeared at the door. There was a drowsy
softness about her, as though her normal stiff and proper self

had been soaking in warm water. Her hair was out of place, and her black housedress had been replaced with a frilly white sleeping gown.

"Reyan?"

"Please let me in," Reyan hissed. "Sevv knows about the lattice."

Mam's eyes widened, and she pulled Reyan through the doorway. The old woman guided her by the shoulder and sat her down at the table. "Tell me what happened."

"Sevv and I were having our weekly talk and…I don't know…things came up. He figured out about the lattice. Once he understood, he became angry. He threatened me. I think he's following me."

"Well, you can't hide here. He has known me too well for too long. He'll find you within the hour."

"I know. I just need to hide until he's no longer in the lobby. He's there right now waiting for me. Once he's moved on, I'll leave."

"Where will you go?" Just as Reyan was opening her mouth to answer, Mam stopped her. "Never mind. The less I know the better."

Mam went to her pantry and came back with some biscuits and dried fruit, which she wrapped in a cloth. "I may not know where you're going, but I do know that you won't eat unless I feed you." She handed the bundle over to Reyan and smiled sadly. "Come here." Mam beckoned her to the window. She lifted the sash. "Go this way."

Outside was a rickety metal balcony and a series of steep flights of stairs leading down to a ladder that dangled ten feet above the ground. When Reyan was half-in and half-out of the window, Mam went to the front of her apartment, picked up her lantern and opened the door. "I feel a late-night hall patrol is in order," Mam said. "Let's see who I bump into. May the Eye watch over you, dear."

Reyan considered telling Mam the truth about the Eye. Instead, she simply said, "Thank you," and pushed herself out the window, onto the balcony, and down the rickety ladder to the alley below.

Reyan stuck to shadows and back alleys and did not slow her pace until she was inside the stables. When the door closed, the darkness inside was almost complete. The only light came from tiny high windows in each stall and the door at the far end of the building, which appeared as a small gray rectangle in the blackness.

She lit her lantern and trimmed it low so she would not blind herself or spook the horses. She made her way down the long row of boxes until she came to the stall she was looking for.

Nora wasn't the most powerful draft horse, but she was long-legged and beautiful. Reyan had seen the horse pulling trucks or carrying professors around town. She had admired the animal's powerful muscles as they rippled and twitched beneath her groomer's brush. Nora's groom had told Reyan that the horse was the fastest in the stable. The fastest he'd ever seen.

Reyan lifted the tack and saddle from a nearby peg labeled with the horse's name. She was about to tighten the girth when she felt someone's eyes on her. She looked up to find a dark figure blocking her exit, just beyond the reach of her lamp light. Nora started and stomped. Reyan stumbled toward the back of the stall. Even if she could reach the small window near the ceiling, she would never be able to wriggle through its iron bars. She was trapped.

"Where are you headed, Reyan?" the voice rumbled. The man stepped into the stall and pulled back his hood. It was Professor Parr. "I met Mam in the lobby. She told me you'd gone out the back way and she guessed you were leaving us. I figured I'd find you here."

Why had he been following her? Had he come to stop her after all?

"Have you got Arley in there?" he asked, raising his chin to the bag. Reyan didn't answer him; instead she backed herself more tightly against the wall. "What do you plan to do with her?"

He wants Arley. Of course he does. The Host will fall apart without her. And no matter what else Parr might be, he is first and foremost a member of the Host. She didn't know what he might do. Parr had never been a dean and had never been incorporated into the lattice. She couldn't know his mind. But she could read his actions. What had he done the last time his loyalties had been tested? She thought back to the meeting where Dean Harrow suppressed the Bridgers and betrayed Dean

Patterson's legacy. What had Parr done?

Reyan sunk into the lattice. There, she found Dean Khamis's memories and took up his point of view.

The man—who still thought of himself as Partner Edmund Khamis and was still seated several places from the dean's chair—looked at the Partners gathered around the table. His gaze slowed suspiciously every time it passed over the young man sitting directly across from him. That upstart was Partner Rolf.

Dean Harrow had just finished an impassioned speech about the insidious dangers posed by the Bridger movement. Now, the Dean asked the Host if there was any other business. Partner Rolf rose to his feet. He held a large spiral shell over his head. "We house this shell in the same reliquary as the Book. Have any of you bothered to remember why?" His question was met with blank stares from the Host. "If you would only have the courage to remember, you would find a whole other world's worth of knowledge associated with it. You would find the truth about Partner Eryn. Let me guide you down to those memories."

In unison, the Host turned to Dean Harrow for guidance.

What the hell is Rolf talking about? Partner Edmund began frantically searching the lattice for memories of the shell. All the previous deans remembered seeing it in the library. A few had even touched it. But the shell's meaning was veiled in a stubborn opacity.

Edmund kept his eyes on Dean Harrow. The Dean's cheek twitched. Then he scowled, and the other partners did the same.

One partner—a dreary young man with sycophantic tendencies—stood. "I admit I do not understand the shell's significance," Partner Sevv said. "I've assumed that its position below the Book reflected its relative importance. But now you've made me curious, Partner Rolf." Sevv extended his hand. "May I see it?"

Rolf cautiously offered Sevv the shell. When it was within reach, Sevv snatched it and, in one fluid motion, hurled it against a pillar. A spray of chips and calcite dust exploded into the air. The flanged lip of the shell's aperture broke off and spun across the floor.

No one moved except Sevv, who scanned the other partners' faces. Sevv's violent outburst had been a risk, but when Dean Harrow smiled, Sevv relaxed, vindicated. Dean Harrow said, "Partner Rolf, do not try to infect us with your Bridger sympathies. If Lem wanted us to ponder the shell's meaning, there would be a clear and well-worn path through the lattice down to his memories of it. Instead, Lem swaddled its history in fear and pain. These are cautionary emotions. We would be asystemic fools to follow you down into those guarded depths."

Partner Rolf gathered the largest bits of the shell into a pouch he made by gathering up the front of his robe. "Then

I'll go out on circuit alone. I'll tell the people in the nodes everything I've discovered."

"Not with your professor's karabands and robe you won't," Dean Harrow said coolly.

Rolf looked at each member of the Host of Systemic Partners in turn. No face betrayed sympathy. No one flinched. No one came to his defense.

***

So, that was the sort of man Parr was. "I saw Rolf look straight into your eyes, Professor. He *needed* you. You didn't even acknowledge him. You asked what I plan to do with Arley? I plan to run."

Parr showed her the same stony face he'd worn for Rolf. He nodded gravely. "Rolf was always open and curious. When he discovered Dean Patterson, he explored her mind, read her work, and followed her curiosities all the way back to Lem. I was Rolf's most trusted friend, so he walked me down into the depths and showed me what he'd found. We learned the truth about Eryn. We often talked in secret about her and what sort of society may have sprung up in Prower. Then a fresh wave of scab came, the worst we'd ever seen. Rolf turned to Dean Patterson's memories of medicinal experiments. Just like her, he grew frustrated and wondered if the Erynites might have a way to help. That's when Rolf became a Bridger. That's why he was banished." Parr's onyx gaze fell to the ground. "I've never been as foolish nor as brave as Rolf, but I hope to make up for it in the end." He looked up at Reyan. "You *should* run, Reyankaiya. Run fast. Run far."

"The Host will follow me. They'll find me."

"You were Rolf's ward and Rolf had many friends. I know you've seen Eryn's shell sitting on Rolf's mantel all these years. The townspeople on Rolf's trade routes were the ones who put it back together. Their leaders wrote their names and the dates they made their pacts with Rolf." Parr laughed. "Rolf once bragged to me that he could walk out his door unclothed and unprovisioned and, as long has he had that shell, he would arrive well-dressed and fat. Bring the shell. Tell the town leaders you are heading to Prower. They will help. When you arrive in Prower, return the shell to the Erynites as a sign of goodwill. Through Lem, we remember how precious the shell was to Eryn. Her people will understand the gesture." He smiled and took his satchel from around his neck and handed it to her. "Take this as well."

She opened the bag and saw the broad spine of a book. *A System for a New Era.*

"If the shell doesn't endear the Erynites to you, that will do the trick. They have been asking the Host to borrow Lem's copy of the Book for many years, but we've always refused."

They finished strapping on Nora's saddle and tack and walked her to the exit. Before they got to the door, Reyan extinguished her lantern and tucked it into a saddle bag. She swung herself up onto the horse's back.

She looked down at her benefactor one last time. "How come you and Sevv and the rest of the Host share the same lattice but act so different?"

"Every time I receive a lattice, Arley gives me a reading list of apocryphal writings from her locked room so I can relearn myself," Parr said, smiling. He looked up at her, his face growing serious once more. "Now go. Ride straight through until morning. Stick to the hardroad, and you'll travel fast. May the Eye watch over you." Reyan smirked at this, and Parr shrugged. "There's nothing wrong with the sentiment."

Reyan said, "Yee-up," bounced her heels off Nora's ribs, and set off into the dark cold night.

CHAPTER SIXTY
Day 103, Year 290, New Era

Reyan drove Nora along the hardroad through the night. After hours atop the horse's shifting rolling back, the insides of Reyan's legs were raw and bruised, and she was struggling to stay upright.

The steady wind kept the clouds away, and the nearly full moon led her to Rowe. But the wind was cold, and her back shivered and spasmed. She made predictions and drew decision trees in her head to distract herself from the biting cold and keep herself awake. The shell would get her the help she would need on her frigid journey. But to get the shell, she would first need to return to Orloton. The thought of suffering the town's contempt after all that she'd suffered, after all she'd come to know, curdled her stomach. Then there would be Lyessa.

She stepped through conversations she could have with

her old benefactor. She tried to come up with the right combination of points and appeals that might result in Lyessa giving her the shell. Revealing some of her new-found Systemic knowledge or a few details of Rolf's early life might be enough to keep Lyessa from tossing her out the door. But it would take weeks of diplomacy to convince her to part with Rolf's most precious possession. Sevv was a day behind her at most.

After working through every conceivable branch of every decision tree spawned from this matrix, Reyan concluded her only option was to sneak into the Leader's home in the middle of the night and take the shell.

The moon was setting and the eastern sky was fringed with silver-blue when Reyan rounded a stand of trees and saw Rowe's tower. The image of the tower reached deep into the lattice and triggered a memory of a lighthouse near a safe harbor. Though she had never seen a lighthouse herself, the thought of it comforted her and brought a weak smile to her face.

She arrived at the stables just as Avalina was opening the doors for the morning. Her friend cocked her head and squinted. "Rey? Is that you?" Reyan's head rolled in a loose nod. "What are you doing here? Are you okay?"

"I need help," she managed before exhaustion, fear, and the relief of seeing a friend overwhelmed her. She began to weep.

Avalina helped Reyan dismount and guided her to an out-of-the-way hay bale where she could sit and rest. Avalina whistled loudly and called down the row of boxes, "Benj, come here and take this horse."

From where she was hidden, Reyan heard Benj approach. "Whose horse is this?"

"A friend's. That's all you need to know. See her watered, fed, and tidied up. Put her in a quiet box to rest. *Not* the one next to Bruno. And keep an eye on the place. I'll be back in a while."

"Yes, ma'am," Benj mumbled.

After Benj had guided Nora away, Avalina turned back to Reyan. "Come with me."

Reyan's legs wobbled like a sapling in the spring floods. Avalina threw one of Reyan's arms around her shoulder so she could support her on the walk home.

When Avalina dragged Reyan through the front door, Mr. Stableman was seated on a bench, pulling on his knee-length work boots, and Ms. Stableman was cleaning up after breakfast. She wiped her hands on her apron and rushed over to help Avalina sit Reyan down at the table. Mr. Stableman followed them as they crossed the room, his half-laced boots shedding bits of dried muck in his wake.

Within minutes, Ms. Stableman had put a plate of hot sausages, warm eggs, and yesterday's bread down in front of Reyan. "What happened, child?"

"I learned a secret Professor Sevv didn't want me to know." This half-explanation was all it took to bring more exhausted tears to her eyes. "He threatened me. I think he's following me. I don't know what he'll do if he finds me. I'm scared."

"Just knowing a thing can't be that bad," Mr. Stableman tried to reassure her, but he looked to his mate for confirmation.

Ms. Stableman shook her head and frowned at her mate. She asked Reyan, "What sort of secret?"

Reyan let out a trembling sigh and wiped her eyes with the back of her hand. She went over the story in her mind. She realized it did not sound very credible. "I don't know how to explain it so you'd understand." She saw the offense cross Ms. Stableman's proud face. "It's not because you're nodies." She hated herself for using the term. "*I* couldn't have understood any of it until it was too late. The moment I understood, my life was already in danger. I don't want to put you in danger as well. I'm probably doing enough damage by just being here." Reyan steadied herself and sniffled. "I should probably leave."

Mr. Stableman looked baffled. He turned to his mate, who rolled her eyes and huffed. "Don't be ridiculous, child. Eat your breakfast. No one knows you're here. We'll keep you well hidden. You'll be safe for a while at least. Avalina, go make a comfortable place for her in the attic."

Reyan was achingly hungry and tired. She held up her head with one hand and shoveled in food with the other.

When Avalina returned from preparing the attic, she stood next to Reyan and placed a hand gently on her shoulder.

Mr. Stableman coughed. "Well, back to it, Lina. The horses are waiting. On your way back to the stables, go to the tower. Tell them we're expecting a guest and ask them to send word the moment anyone is spotted coming up the hardroad from Seal Tooth."

Avalina nodded to her father, squeezed Reyan's shoulder, and headed out the door. Mr. Stableman returned to the bench to finish lacing his boots, then followed his daughter.

Once they were alone, Avalina's mother took Reyan's empty plate, shouldered her bag, and showed her to the attic. The space reminded her of her loft back in Orloton. Its sharply sloped ceiling was finished with the same raw wooden planks as the creaking floorboards. Ms. Stableman led her past dusty old furniture and boxes of toys and clothes Avalina had outgrown. Behind a wall of crates, they found the nest of blankets and pillows that Lina had prepared. A fresh mug of water sat on the floor nearby.

"Thank you, Ms. Stableman."

The woman placed a gentle hand on the side of Reyan's head, ran it over her hair, and let it land on her shoulder. She forced a sad smile. "Get some sleep."

CHAPTER SIXTY-ONE
Day 103, Year 290, New Era

Sevv arrived in Rowe in the cold mid-afternoon. Snowflakes tumbled through gusts of bitterly cold wind. There was no watcher on the tower to raise a hand to the dean, and the square was empty. But soon Benj came hurrying over from the stables. "Professor, how can I help you?"

Sevv stepped down from his truck. "See that my horses are tended to."

Benj nodded and began freeing the horses from their tack. He stopped and looked at Sevv. "The Stablemans have that girl," he said. "I thought you would want to know."

"Thank you, son." Sevv turned away and began walking across the square.

"The Stableman's home is the other way, Professor," Benj

called out.

The dean waved an acknowledgment over his shoulder and continued walking in the direction he had set out.

When Sevv knocked on Keeper Shalynn's door, Tamura, the young acolyte, answered. Her annoyed expression turned into surprise for an instant before settling down into reverence. She inclined her head respectfully. "Good afternoon, Professor Sevv."

"Who is it?" a woman's voice called from another room.

"Professor Sevvran Bital, Keeper," Tamura called back.

The keeper rushed to the door, and Tamura stepped aside. "Professor, it's an unexpected honor. What can we do for you?"

"Keeper Shalynn." He smiled and inclined his head. "May I come in?"

She stepped aside to let him in and closed the door behind him.

"May I?" He gestured to a chair pulled up to the head of the table where Shalynn, Junior Keeper Mariana, and Tamura had been eating a late afternoon meal.

Shalynn nodded her head in flustered twitches. "Certainly. Have a seat," Keeper Shalynn said "You must be hungry after your journey from Seal Tooth. Can I get you anything?"

"Please."

"We weren't expecting visitors, I'm afraid, and since it's the middle of winter, the fare might seem a bit…rudimentary."

"I'm sure whatever you have will be fine."

Tamura brought him a plate with a large square of corn bread. He didn't dig in at first, expecting more food to arrive. Tamura, Shalynn, and Mariana exchanged awkward glances. The keeper jerked her head, and Tamura headed to the cupboard and returned with a crock of butter and an unopened jar of blackberry jam, which she placed before him. He looked at them with a question in his eyes, and Shalynn smiled nervously. "I'm afraid that's all we have, Professor."

"Thank you for your hospitality, Keeper. Please have a seat, all three of you. I have something to discuss." The women sat down. "There is a thing that needs doing. It is of great consequence to the System. It must be done today. I will require the support of the town's keepers."

"We're listening, Professor," Tamura said eagerly, but nervous glances passed between the two older women.

"You may recall, when the caravan came through in the late fall, we had a rough-hewn young lady with us named Reyankaiya. We brought her here for dinner."

The three women nodded. "She's hard to forget," Tamura said smiling as though remembering a secret joke.

Sevv continued. "She has been with us at the University ever since, studying to be a professor."

"She really made it in?" Tamura asked, appalled. "If you are getting so desperate for students, Professor, there are decent recruits right here in Rowe." The acolyte smiled, but there was a bit of a snarl around the edges.

"Noted. Suffice to say, her education has not gone to plan. She has been surly and unruly and has required my constant attention." As Sevv enumerated Reyan's failings, Tamura nodded sympathetically, as though she had predicted that this was how it would all end. Sevv was beginning to see how too much of this girl could become annoying. "To top it off, she has stolen something precious from the University and fled. I've been sent after her to retrieve the stolen goods and see her safely back to Seal Tooth."

"With respect, Professor Sevvran," Keeper Shalynn said, her face betraying no emotion, "what does this have to do with us?"

"She is a fugitive from the System hiding in Rowe, and you are Rowe's Systemic keepers."

"And how do you propose we catch her?" Tamura asked, an excited gleam in her eye.

"Be quiet, child. Let me talk." Shalynn's rebuke was not cruel or harsh, but it was firm, and Tamura looked down at her hands in silence.

But Sevv sensed an ally in the young woman. He turned to her and said seriously, "By any means necessary." Tamura glanced at the keeper then back at Sevv, a tentative smile blooming on her face.

Unlike Tamura, Shalynn and Mariana did not seem excited about the prospect of chasing a young girl through town and helping Sevv haul her away "by any means necessary." Mariana shared a nervous glance with Shalynn, then said, "We would love to help you professor, but we cannot know the Systemic thing to do until we understand the situation a bit better. Could you tell us more about the girl? What did she take, from whom and why? Do you have any theories about why she ran?"

"It's not important what she took, but that she should not have taken it. It's not important why she left, but that she did so without our leave. All you need to know, *Junior* Keeper, is that a professor, the head of his faculty and the newly appointed *Dean* of the University at Seal Tooth is asking for your assistance. You are *bound* to help me." It was a bluff. Not a lie, exactly. Just an overstatement.

"That's not exactly true, Professor," Shalynn said, her eyes narrowed in suspicion. "We are not bound to *you* but to the Governing Assert and what we assess to be Systemic."

"Do you think I would come all the way out here through the cold and snow by myself if it were not important?"

Mariana said, "He has a point, Keeper Shalynn. It is odd for him to arrive in Rowe unannounced, out of season, in the middle of the afternoon, not with a caravan but in his own truck. Alone."

Shalynn interrupted Mariana: "It's not that we don't want to help you or—Eye pass over us—that we don't *trust* you. We simply don't understand the situation well enough to know how best to act. And until we do…," her words trailed off into a shrug.

Sevv's rage was building, but he contained it. He narrowed his eyes and tightened his jaw. "Is that how you see it?" Shalynn hardened her features. She nodded. Sevv took a bite of his corn bread, swallowed, then turned to Mariana. "And you?"

The junior keeper glanced back at Shalynn before she adopted a similar countenance and nodded once. "We only ask that you explain the situation so we can decide the most Systemic path."

"And what about you, young acolyte?" Sevv said, turning to Tamura. "You've always seemed quick of wit and the paragon of Systemic processing. How would you solve for which path is the most Systemic in this situation?"

Tamura's eager eyes never left Sevv's, never bothered to seek out the approval of the keeper. "I believe you are a professor, a partner, and the dean. Any Systemic understanding we keepers claim has come down to us through you. And so, I would not presume to know better than you. If you tell me that there are secrets that must be kept and difficult things to be done, I will trust you. I will do as you say."

"I have come to Rowe looking for a keeper's help," Sevv said, his smile triumphant and vindictive. "The only one of you willing to provide aide was the young acolyte Tamura. Therefore, I name her the Systemic Keeper of Rowe."

"You can't do that," Shalynn stammered.

"Can't I?" Sevv looked up at the ceiling and thought for a moment. "Perhaps you are right." He slapped his hand down on the table. "You should take it up with my professors the next time the caravan comes to town. Until then, Keeper Tamura and I have business to attend to. Please excuse us."

Tamura smiled, watching her former mentors retreat from the room, then turned to Sevv. "What do you need me to do, Professor?"

"Gather the townspeople and bring them to the foot of the tower. Tell them a professor has come seeking their help. It will turn dark soon, so have them bring lanterns or torches to light their way." Tamura nodded. "One more thing. I seem to recall that you are skilled with a bow and arrow. Didn't you provide us with a turkey last time we were in Rowe?"

"Yes, Professor."

"Fetch your bow then."

For the first time, Tamura seemed nervous. "Why would I need my bow?"

"What protects the System when it is threatened?"

"The Eye?" she said uncertainly.

Sevv nodded gravely. "The System is under threat. You are now a Systemic keeper. *You* must become the Eye."

CHAPTER SIXTY-TWO
Day 103, Year 290, New Era

The sun had nearly set, and the snow was beginning to blow in sheets and curls. Sevv climbed a few of the tower steps, putting himself above the small crowd Tamura had gathered. There were far fewer bodies than he had hoped. But they all had lanterns and torches, and Sevv found that fire always had an enlarging and intimidating effect.

"Thank you for coming out on this cold and snowy evening. The University at Seal Tooth has lost one of our students. She's come to Rowe, and we know where she is hiding. This young lady is a danger to herself and others and needs to be brought safely back to Seal Tooth. With your help, we will apprehend her quickly and have you all back home before dinner."

As the crowd formed ranks, Sevv pulled Tamura aside. "I have a different role for you."

***

Mr. Stableman let Avalina leave work early, so when Reyan woke around mid-afternoon, her friend's dark and serious face was there to greet her. From where she sat on an old chair beside the makeshift bed, Avalina asked, "When are you going to tell me what this is about, Rey?"

Reyan wanted to tell Avalina everything about the lattice and Arley and why she was running. But that knowledge would put Lina and her family at risk. "I can't tell you, Lina." Avalina's face grew determined, but it softened when Reyan pleaded, "I wish I could, but I just *can't.*"

Avalina swallowed hard. "Where will you go?"

Again, Reyan longed to confide in her friend. Even more, she wanted to invite Lina to join her as she crossed the Great Eastern River and journeyed to Prower. But it did not take long for Reyan to see all the ways that branching future might end in tragedy. Again, Reyan shook her head. "I'll send word once I've made it there safe."

"And if you don't make it?"

"Then I won't send word." Reyan said, with a small, sad smile.

***

Sevv enlisted the help of a large, bearded man—whose name might have been Himmel or Herschel—to lead the way through the streets of Rowe to the Stablemans'. Sevv had been right; the lanterns and torches did indeed make the small crowd seem formidable. Hopefully it would be enough to elicit the Stablemans' cooperation and frighten Reyankaiya into surrender and submission.

A short rise of stairs led up to the Stablemans' front porch. Sevv pointed to the man who had led them here. "You, head around back and make sure she doesn't leave that way. The rest of you stay here."

Sevv ascended to the porch alone.

***

Reyan and Avalina heard feet pounding up the attic stairs. Avalina's mother appeared from around the wall of crates. Her eyes were wide and unblinking, the muscles in her neck tense. "They're here, and it's not just Sevv. There are others as well. They have torches."

"Torches seem like overkill," Reyan said under her breath.

"How did he find you so quickly?" Avalina cried.

Reyan tried to think. "Benj. He probably saw me head home with you…"

"Little shit."

"Lina!" her mother said, appalled.

Reyan wasn't bothered. The dozens of deans in her mind had heard far worse in their time. She shouldered her bag. "I need to get back to Nora and leave town."

Ms. Stableman grabbed Reyan by her shoulders and held her at arm's length, looking her up and down. Reyan thought the woman was about to give in to her compulsion to smooth out Reyan's wrinkled clothes, but instead she pulled her in for a brief, wordless hug.

Avalina led Reyan away by the hand. They headed down the stairs to the main floor, then down into the cellar. Just as they stepped from the creaking stairs onto the silent shapestone slab, there was a booming knock on the front door.

They heard Mr. Stableman's plodding steps slowly cross the living room toward the front of the house to answer the door. Meanwhile, the girls sneaked toward the cellar's back door.

Avalina put her free hand on the doorknob and waited. When she heard her father open the front door, she twisted the knob.

***

Sevv heard heavy steps inside the house. A few moments later, Mr. Stableman opened the door.

"Professor Sevv!" he stammered before seeming to recover himself. "I thought you'd retired. To what do we owe the honor?" The man seemed so genuinely surprised that Sevv knew he had to be faking.

"We've come looking for someone."

Mr. Stableman leaned to have a look past Sevv. "A very dangerous person by the looks of it." He smiled and waved at someone behind Sevv's back.

"Indeed. We're looking for Reyankaiya Estermet."

"Reyan? That little girl? Why? What has she done?"

"You would not understand if I told you. Suffice it to say, when we modeled the outcomes of her actions, we learned they will be catastrophic. It's extremely important that we find her."

"Of course. I'm happy to help. Just let me put on my boots …"

"Mr. Stableman."

"Oh, call me Brimm, Professor!"

Sevv gave a sour smile. "Brimm. I don't need your help. I

need your cooperation. We have reason to believe she's here with you."

"Well, that would certainly come as a surprise to me. We haven't seen her since you took her away to that school of yours."

"We know your daughter brought her here earlier in the day. We need to find her. She's in danger."

"We haven't seen her," Mr. Stableman said, his voice growing stern.

"It's bad enough that you are hiding her, but with every lie you tell, you move another step past accomplice toward conspirator."

The cherubic man's face grew pale in the moonlight. Then, Ms. Stableman stepped between Sevv and her faltering mate, forcing Brimm to take a step back into the house. She smiled thinly and gave a curt nod to Sevv before wordlessly closing the door in his face.

Sevv stood staring at the wood grain only inches from his nose. He felt something he had hadn't experienced in years: humiliation. His mind flew back to memories of his childhood in that stinking node. He remembered parents sweetly explaining that their children weren't home to play. He could see his schoolmates peeking out and snickering from behind the curtains as he slinked shamefully away. He drew a breath. *Rage is for the impotent and powerless. I am the Dean of the University at Seal Tooth. I am not powerless.*

Sevv turned from the door and addressed the crowd: "The Stablemans will not help us find the girl."

"Then what do we do?" someone in the crowd asked. The rest began to shift uncomfortably as they awaited the dean's guidance.

Sevv could tell that if he didn't make a decision immediately, he would lose them and, though he was loathe to admit it, he needed them. He spread his arms wide, just as he had so many times from his teaching platform. "Friends. It may surprise you to learn that the runaway student, the girl hiding inside this very house, is the greatest threat to the System since the Calming." The group looked at each other doubtfully. "It is true. She intends to undermine the System's faculties. She will disrupt the proper flow of knowledge and all the other benefits the professors bring to your town. She is putting your lives and livelihoods at risk." Sevv paused for a breath, giving their minds a moment to soak in his accusations. "Sadly, there are few willing to stand up when called, few willing to march out into the cold night to protect what matters most, to protect *the System*. But here we are. Friends, we are the few who stand between the grandiose impulses of this misguided girl and the destruction of our very way of life."

"What are you asking us to do, Professor?"

"Very little. If she tries to run, apprehend her and bring her to me. Nothing more." He pointed to the people on his left. "You go around the house that way." He pointed to those on his right, "You all go that way."

Once the last person had rounded the side of the house

and there was no one left to see him, Sevv smashed his lantern against the porch. Fire slicked across the planks and began climbing the front of the house.

***

The cellar door swung open, and Avalina and Reyan rushed up the shapestone stairs into the forest behind the house. When they heard footsteps and whispered voices, Avalina ducked behind a low rhododendron and pulled Reyan down beside her. Two small groups approached, each from one side of the house, holding their lanterns and touches aloft. The two groups merged near the back door. They turned to face the house and silently waited for the fugitive to emerge. Avalina tugged Reyan's hand and led her away into the forest.

They hadn't gone ten yards when a tall figure gathered their cloaks in his massive fists and lifted them so their feet barely touched the ground. They kicked and struggled. "Where are you girls going?"

Someone called from the house. "Herschel, what's going on over there?"

He ignored them, whispering to Reyan, "You don't *look* very dangerous."

"I'm only dangerous to Sevv."

The man turned from Reyan. "Avalina Stableman, what

the hell's going on here?"

"You were the one who asked for Kavi's help fixing the cold room, right?" Reyan said, recognizing him. "But then Sevv and Tamura got in the way and wouldn't let you do it."

Avalina picked up the thread. "How much food do you think that room would have saved from rot and spoil? And now Sevv wants your help chasing a scared little girl through the cold and dark? Before you turn us over to Sevv, you need to ask yourself whose interest you'd be serving."

Herschel looked from the two girls to the mob of torch-wielding adults. He looked back at Reyan and Lina. A realization rippled across his face. He loosened his grip, and the girls came down off their tiptoes. "Run," he hissed at them. He turned and walked out of the bushes toward his friends and neighbors. "Sorry, just taking care of some business."

The others chuckled and turned back to the house just as Chrissa Stableman started screaming.

CHAPTER SIXTY-THREE
Day 103, Year 290, New Era

When Avalina and Reyan arrived at the stables, the doors were closed and the windows shuttered for the night. They went around to a side door so that no one would notice the large doors open and come to investigate.

Once they were inside and well hidden, they lit a lantern, trimmed the wick low, and went to find Nora. As they worked at tacking up Nora, the horse twitched and stomped nervously.

Reyan mounted the horse so she would be ready to ride out. Avalina ran ahead and pulled open the large stable door. There, framed in the silver light of the moon, was Tamura. She was looking in the direction of the Stablemans' house, no doubt expecting the fugitives to come from that direction. The first thing Reyan noticed was the quiver of arrows on the girl's back and the bow in her left hand. Avalina must have seen the weapon too because Reyan saw her friend vanish into the shadows. Reyan's heart sank. In the end, even Lina abandoned her.

Tamura spun around when she heard the door open. Her eyes followed the line from the horse's hooves up to her rider. She smiled cruelly. "I figured you'd end up here, and here you are. Climb down from that horse and come with me."

"No." Reyan nudged Nora forward a few steps, but Tamura blocked their path.

Nora jerked her head. The faint smell of smoke was in the air. Tamura smiled. "Seems someone else wasn't feeling very cooperative tonight either." She drew an arrow and notched it.

Reyan's eyes grew wide with terror. "What did you do?"

"Me? Nothing. Eye as witness. I've been here the whole time."

"Let me go, Tamura."

"Why would I do that?"

"Because there are things I understand that you do not."

"I sincerely doubt you know anything I don't."

"That's your problem, Tamura. You think that being a small-town keeper's acolyte means you know something about the System."

Tamura lifted her bow and sighted down the arrow. "Oh,

I'm not an acolyte. I'm the keeper. Dean Bital, at least, recognized my potential. He promoted me about an hour ago."

"Tamura," Reyan said calmly. "Has it ever bothered you that they leave you keepers out here in the nodes to maintain order and enforce their rules, but no matter how well you perform your role, they never ask you to join a faculty, and they never make you into full professors?"

Tamura faltered for a moment, then lifted her chin and straightened her back. "It's my role. I know exactly what I'm supposed to know."

"But not everything you *choose* to know—not everything it would be *helpful* to know. Only what the professors *allow* you to know. And that diminishes every year. What about me? Why am I such a threat, *Keeper*?" Reyan snarled. "Was the nature of my crime something Sevv thought you should know before he asked you to hunt me down?" She waited a moment to let the thought take hold. "I didn't think so. So let me tell you. My horrible crime, my threat to the System, the reason you are pointing an arrow at my heart, is that I know it *all*. All the things you will never know. All the things even the professors cannot know. I know secret things that only the *Host* knows."

"How…" Tamura began before noticing her conviction slipping. She stiffened her arm and drew her arrow tight. "He told me enough. I know you're taking those secrets to our enemies."

"You see? That's one of the many things I know that you do not. We don't have any enemies. Just ourselves."

There was a tiny sound, a leather-soled boot scuffing the dirt. Tamura's head jerked to look just as a fist-sized rock came crashing in and landed above her right eye.

Her arrow escaped and embedded itself into a beam far above Reyan's head. The keeper gave a short grunt and fell to the ground without another sound.

"Woah," Lina said as she stepped out from her hiding spot. "I hope I didn't kill her."

Reyan dismounted and walked over to Tamura. She bent down and placed her fingers against the girl's throat. Tamura's heartbeat throbbed through her soft skin. Reyan wiped away the sticky trickle of blood from Tamura's forehead. The gash was deep, and the blood welled back almost immediately. Reyan prodded around looking for soft spots or obviously broken places in her skull. She found none, but the skin felt tender, and a bump was rising where the rock had struck her. "There will be a lot of blood. Her head will feel miserable, but she'll be okay."

"The minute she comes to, she'll start yelling and running off to find Sevv," Avalina said.

They each took an arm and dragged Tamura into the stable. They propped her up against one of the support posts that ran down the middle of the aisle. Reyan used a length of rope to bind her feet and tie her hands behind the post. Lina found a few dirty bandannas and stuffed one into Tamura's mouth and tied the other over her mouth and around the back of her neck.

Reyan bent down to listen to the breath coming from the unconscious girl's nose. When she heard the whistling intake of air, she stood up and returned to where she'd left Nora just outside the door. She climbed back into the saddle. The bruises and raw spots from yesterday's ride throbbed and stung, making her shift uncomfortably in the saddle. Wincing, she reached down, took Avalina's hand, and squeezed it. "I'm worried about you, Lina. I'm worried about your family."

"I'll be fine," Avalina said, smiling in a failed attempt to project strength. "We'll be fine." She disappeared into the dark stable and came back a moment later with a large wrench. She looked toward the square where Sevv's truck was parked. Slapping the massive tool against her open hand, she said, "And don't worry, I'll take care of Sevv."

***

Sevv discovered Tamura still gagged and writhing against the post trying to free herself. A sheet of blood had dried from above her right eye all the way down her cheek. She was incensed to the point of tears.

Sevv walked over and knelt beside her. He untied her gag first. "We need to get Avalina," Tamura spat out. "She bashed me in the head."

Sevv was silent for a moment. Thinking. "I understand you are angry, but we have other, more important things to do."

"But look what she did!" Tamura shrugged a shoulder gesturing at the bloody wound on her head.

"Revenge is a downward spiral, Keeper," Sevv said, his numb and gnarled fingers working at the knot that bound her hands. "It is, therefore, not Systemic. The Stablemans have already paid their price for helping Reyankaiya. Let Avalina go back to her family. They'll be needing each other's company tonight. Where is Reyankaiya?"

"She took her horse and left."

"Which way?"

"How would I know?" Tamura snapped.

"Do not forget yourself, young Keeper," Sevv was calm but firm. "Have your things ready and meet me at my truck. We'll be leaving in ten minutes."

"Where are we going?"

"Up the pass. To Orloton."

***

Sevv had already lit his running lights, cinched down the tack, and was removing his horses' feedbags when Tamura stepped into the circle of dim yellow light. Her face had been wiped clean and bandaged. She had her travel bag, bow, and quiver of arrows. Sevv nodded to her, and they both climbed into the cab. Sevv said, "Hup!" and the horses began to strain.

As they described a wide arc through the square, the entire truck began to sway violently. Then, with a terrifying lurch, the front left side plunged toward the ground. Sevv and Tamura clambered up the sloping bench and climbed out on the high side of the cab. The front wheel lay on the ground. After a quick search with a lantern, they found its square axle nut sitting twenty yards behind the truck. The other wheels still had their nuts, but they were all loose, and the wheels leaned at odd angles.

Sevv ground his teeth. His eye twitched. "Tamura, go and fetch the wainwright. Tell him to hurry."

***

The smoke from the Stableman's burning house poured over the banks of the river and floated upstream, through the valley, then rose through the pass. The smell of it hit Reyan hard as she left the hardroad and mounted the wooden bridge.

Reyan turned back toward Rowe. She could see the stark black line of the tower cutting through the pulsing, breathing flames. She watched for a moment as the fire reached out along the lines of the wind, then ducked behind its own tail of smoke.

She wanted to say something, some words of apology or thanks, but nothing came to mind, and there was no one near enough to hear.

CHAPTER SIXTY-FOUR
Day 104, Year 290, New Era

Hours later, Reyan saw the sharp angular shapes of Orloton's roof lines grow up from the black scruff of the forest into the silver-blue of the morning sky. She was painfully tired. Her back and shoulders ached, and her pants clung to the tacky friction sores on the insides of her legs.

Her fingers were numb and swollen. The wind blew in her face and billowed her hood. The frigid air funneled down her ears and stabbed deep into her skull.

She mentally rehearsed her plan to slip into Lyessa's house and take the shell. She had planned to arrive under cover of dark and sneak in after everyone was asleep. But the timing was all wrong. She had ridden hard through the night, but now the sun was up. Sunset was still eight hours away and the household would not be truly asleep for another five hours after that. Nora's impressive pace and Sevv's sabotaged truck had given her a lead, but not a thirteen-hour one.

She thought of continuing up and over the pass without the shell. But the winter months were hard in the nodes. Without the shell, no one would shelter and feed a wandering homeless girl. She needed it. To get it, she would first need a place to rest, protected from the wind's teeth and Sevv's searching eyes until dark. All she needed was a friend to shelter her for a few hours. But she could not think of anyone in Orloton who wouldn't just turn her over to the professor.

Well, there was one.

She pulled her hood tight and headed to Tom's house.

It was always cold in the pass this time of year, but as Nora carried Reyan through the empty square, Orloton seemed especially so. It was already light, and the sun would soon rise above the ridge, but the windows of Harut's bakery were still black and etched with frost. No boot prints or wheel ruts disturbed the snow-covered streets and alleys. The only sounds were Nora's breathing and her hooves crunching through the crust of ice into the undisturbed powder.

At Tom's house, Reyan's swollen fingers struggled to pass Nora's reins through the ring mounted to the porch post. She crept around to Tom's window and used their old secret tap…tap-tap to draw him out. Nothing happened. She put her face against the window and shaded her brow to look inside. Spears of frost stabbed across the inside of the glass. Filled with curiosity and dread, she walked around and peered in through the house's front windows. Nothing moved within.

A drift of snow tapered into the front hall through the open door. She stepped inside and looked around. Her breath billowed and hung in the still air.

Tom's bedroom was uncharacteristically tidy. His collection of stones was arranged on the windowsill by size, where Tom would have grouped them by color. And she had never seen the boy's bed made or his clothes folded and put away. Tom had not been here for some time.

With rising alarm, she began searching for her friend in the other rooms, each one as cold and empty as the one before.

When she finally forced herself to enter Tom's parents' room, she found a single body in the bed. A feeling of unreality mixed with exhaustion numbed her to the truth of what she was seeing; her mind casually interpreted it as a dummy someone had left in bed so they could slip away undetected. But then she recognized the tight sunken face as Tom's father. She noticed the crusty brown remnants of a fluid that had run down the sheets and pooled on the floor. She saw the mound of dead flies accumulated on the windowsill. There was no smell. That would come with the spring thaw.

She rushed back out into the snow, untied Nora, and rode her up and down every street. Still, no lights came on. Still, nothing moved. Soon they arrived at the broad field overlooking the river at the edge of town. At first, she thought the field was packed with scores of evenly spaced tree stumps, but once she drew near, she saw that these were an entire town's worth of headstones.

She dismounted and walked through the field, her hand brushing each stone as she passed. The stones in the first few rows were well-shaped and had names and words chiseled into them. But as the rows progressed, the stones became more irregular and the writing less precise. In the last row, she found Tom's thin, shaky name scratched into a small rock. Next to Tom's stone was his mother's.

For all practical purposes, these people had all ceased to exist for Reyan the moment she left Orloton behind. But now she was faced with the immovable fact that everyone she had ever known before she left with the professors no longer ate or laughed or kissed their children to sleep. Rolf, Tom, and even Lyessa were dead.

The lattice offered up memories of similar tragedies. Thoughts of disease and death and sorrow spun and twisted together. Reyan followed this thread of associations and was surprised to find the pendulous drop spindle of Dean Patterson's memories weighting down its end.

Long before Olya Patterson became Dean, she was partner to the System's medicinal faculty. As the first waves of scab spread through the nodes, Olya became obsessed with a section of the Book that discussed tricking diseases into halting their own spread. She risked her life and worked tirelessly for several years to refine the contagion from infected blood. But the few times that she tested a promising formulation ended in tragedy. In the end, she never saved anyone, and the Host forced her to stop her experiments.

Reyan realized that the Erynite woman who saved Orloton years later had mastered the theory and techniques Dean Patterson was only fumbling with. The Erynite had some knowledge or insight the Lemmists were never able to learn. The gift may have imitated Erynite techniques, but the deadly tradition was born of Lemmist ignorance and tragic wishful thinking.

Had Reyan been a better, braver person—had she been able to accept Rolf's gift—she would be in the ground with the rest of Orloton. That different fate passed so closely by that Reyan felt its breath on the back of her neck and shivered.

Getting to Prower and finding the Erynites was more important than Reyan had realized. She had to get the shell and leave town.

Reyan urged Nora back towards Lyessa's house. The sliding wooden bolt on the stable door was already pulled back, but the door was being held closed by a low frozen snow drift. Reyan kicked and stomped at the snow until it crumbled, then brushed it away with her toe.

The small stable was dark and abandoned of horses. The familiar sweet smell of hay and feed was there, but it was buried beneath a dusty scent of mold that had dried to powder.

She moved Nora inside, pulled some dry hay down from the loft, and fed her. The water trough was empty and dry. Reyan couldn't grip the pump handle and had to use both of her numb hands to draw up the water.

Before stepping back outside, she peeked through the half-open door and listened for the sound of a truck's wheels or horses' hooves coming down the hardroad. Hearing nothing, she slipped through the door, closed it behind her, and slid the bolt home.

When she knocked gently on the front door, no lanterns or candles lit up inside, no shuffling servants' feet approached the door. The door was unlocked and swung open easily. "Hello?" The house swallowed the sound. No one answered.

The air inside was cold—not chilly, like when she would wake before the servants had stoked the fires, but cold like the air outside. And though she shivered and ached, she did not dare light a fire, knowing the smoke would draw Sevv's eye.

In the room where Rolf's body had lain, someone had returned the furniture to its normal place. The decorative scythe and axe still hung on the wall, their polished blades catching the morning light and glinting in the gloom. On the mantel, below the tools, sat the shell.

Reyan had gazed at the shell for a week's worth of hours, so it was no wonder that it conjured up memories for her, but she was surprised when other thoughts and associations floated to the surface of the lattice. She felt Lem's longing and hope, Dean Kaminski's appreciation for its simple beauty, and Dean Harrow and Dean Khamis's shameful mix of fear and satisfaction when Sevv smashed it.

Reyan removed the dress from her satchel and laid it out

on the floor. She took the shell from the mantel and placed it in the dress' bodice. She rolled it up and placed the cocooned shell into the satchel next to Arley.

Mice or rats had gnawed holes into the sacks of food in the pantry. Grain and black rodent droppings were spread across the tiled kitchen floor.

In the bedroom, someone had folded the laundry and laid it flat in the drawers; they had made the beds and smoothed away any sign they had ever been slept in.

The sight of the beds reminded Reyan that she was desperately tired. For a quick moment she considered curling up under the down blankets to rebuild her strength and warmth. But Sevv was coming, and the leader's house would be the first place he would stop when he arrived.

Where then? Her tree? It was dry, had a view of the road and the town, and offered escape routes in every direction. It would certainly be cold, but no colder than Lyessa's house, and her tree had always felt safer.

She was trying to decide what to do with Nora when she heard a dog bark. It was a hungry, compulsive sound like a starving man knocking on a locked door. A single yelp rang out and everything was silent.

Sevv was very near.

She needed to get to Nora quickly. She shouldered her bags and ran for the front door, but when she got there, she glanced out the window and saw Sevv's horses and truck coming to a stop in front of the house. There was no way to get to Nora without being seen. She considered hiding inside, but every room and cupboard suddenly felt more like a trap than a shelter.

She rushed through the side door and into a line of salal bushes that bordered the hardroad. She used the bushes to keep hidden as she headed back in the direction from which Sevv had come; away from Orloton, toward her tree.

She lay down in the ditch across the hardroad from her tree. The water from the day's melt began soaking through at her elbows and knees. She crawled up the slope to get a better view of the town square and watched Sevv walk around his truck, his body lanky and slow as a water bird prowling the lake shore. She could outrun him. She could overpower him if it came to it. She'd done it before.

Then Tamura stepped down from the truck. The young keeper had a fresh bandage on her head, but other than that, she looked spry and confident, and her bow and quiver of arrows was slung across her back. Reyan's heart tightened in her chest.

Sevv was tending to the horses, and Tamura approached the front of the house and passed out of view. Reyan took the opportunity to dart across the hardroad and duck under her tree's protective skirt.

More than any place in the world, her tree felt like safety, like home. Without even looking, she knew where to place her feet and hands. She knew what the wood and bark would feel like under her fingers. Most of the baubles were still there, spinning and flashing in the breeze. Some of their strings had gotten tangled around themselves, and no one had been there to remove the knots. Three of the thin scraps of metal had cut through their strings so that all that was left were old strings like dead and drifting spider webs.

After climbing up about twenty-five feet, Reyan reached the perch with a view of the leader's house and the town square. She settled there with her back against the trunk, one arm holding onto a branch over her head.

Now that she could watch Sevv and Tamura from a safe distance, her heart rate slowed, and she began to make her plan to escape. Getting Nora would be difficult. Reyan would need to make it to the stable doors without being seen, then silently saddle and bridle the horse. That would take time, and if she was caught in the stable, there would be no other exit. But then Reyan realized she hadn't remembered to strip Nora down. She felt a mix of guilt and gratitude for her own exhausted inattentiveness. So now all she needed was a good opportunity. Perhaps when they went inside to search the house, she would have a few minutes to sneak back to the stables and get Nora. If she was quiet and quick and lucky it would all work out. Then, she would continue east over the pass. In just a few more miles the snow would become impassable for Sevv's truck, but hopefully Nora could high-step through the drifts. It would be a tough day or two until she came down into the warmer air on the other side of the mountains, but she was sure she would make it. She searched the lattice and knew that Dean Lubsen would provide her with lessons on building shelters and digging warm caves into snow drifts. After that, she would continue along the hardroad to the Great Eastern

River, every day moving further and further away from Sevv and any allies he had enlisted to pursue her.

Tamura disappeared around the front of the house. A few moments later, Reyan heard what almost passed as a bird call.

***

Sevv heard Tamura's whistle. *She's found something. Good girl.* The old professor patted his horse's flanks. The horse's unyielding mass gave him confidence. He followed the trail Tamura had left in the snow and came upon her crouching near the side door of the leader's empty house.

"She's been here," Tamura said. "She came from inside and headed that way. No trail coming back, so…" The young keeper shrugged and nodded into the brush.

Sevv followed the trail with his eyes. "I know where she is." He pointed through the woods to where he thought her tree might be. "She's hiding like a raccoon up in her dirty old tree. I'll walk directly there, in the open. I'll try to talk to her and get her to come with us willingly. You follow that trail through the woods. I'll keep her distracted while you approach from the side."

Tamura smiled and raised her bow. "I can hit her easily from thirty yards."

"Hopefully it won't come to that. Wait for a signal from

me. But be ready."

"Though it be difficult, a Systemic mind will always do what's needed," the young keeper said, quoting from last season's compendium. She nodded once, then left to follow the trail of footprints. For Sevv, all of this was a nuisance, an unpleasant necessity. Tamura's eager confidence made him uneasy, like she imagined she was passing some test or winning a game.

***

Reyan watched Sevv reemerge into the town square, then slowly make his way down the hardroad toward the tree. *How could I be so stupid? He knew exactly where I'd be.*

She didn't know what to do, but then she remembered she had the world's fastest Systemic processor in her bag. She thrust her hand into the satchel and rummaged around until she felt the cold smooth metal of Arley's portable. She drew it out and held it in her fist like a rock, like a weapon. She felt a tingling where her two fingers touched the virt strips on the back. She heard a sound like the nearby rapids or the wind in the fall trees, and for a moment the world seemed hidden behind a snowstorm. But then everything settled down, and Arley's sphere swelled to life before her eyes.

CHAPTER SIXTY-FIVE
Day 104, Year 290, New Era

"Good afternoon, Reyan. How can I help you?"

No matter where Reyan looked, Arley hovered there. She closed her eyes, but the orb still seemed to float a few feet beyond her eyelids. It was disorienting. "Can you go away, and just talk to me?"

"Of course." Arley vanished. "I see you've managed to make it up into the mountain pass. Very impressive."

"I'm in a tree. Professor Sevv is approaching. He's coming down the hardroad. I'm pretty sure he knows exactly where I am."

"I suggest you run. He is quite old. You should be able to outpace and outlast him."

"But then there's Tamura, the girl Sevv picked up in Rowe. She's around my age. Plus, she has a bow and arrow and apparently, she's an excellent shot. I think she's following my trail through the snow. If so, she'll be sneaking in from the side in a few moments."

"I see," Arley said flatly.

"My horse is stabled back in town, but I would need to pass through either Sevv or Tamura to get to her."

"I see," Arley repeated.

"What should I do?"

"Begin the lattice transfer now."

"I want to escape."

"You cannot. Begin the transfer."

"Isn't there a way I can climb down and run away through the woods, or trick them, or take them out somehow?"

"I cannot advise you to harm another human. But even if we set aside the Governing Assert for a moment, there are two of them and only one of you. You have no element of surprise. One stands between you and your horse, and the other is flanking you with a ranged weapon. Even if you retrieved your horse, you would have to pass by them to continue up the hardroad toward the mountain pass."

"I feel like I should at least try."

"Yes, you should try. And there is a twenty-eight percent

chance you'll make it. But then you'll have the pass to contend with. The conditions up there are wholly unknown to me, but I am certain the air will be colder and the going far more treacherous. Given these factors, it is best that you preserve your lattice immediately."

"You are terrible at pep talks, Arley."

"You are not the first person to say so," the AI said. "I cannot tell you how to slip past Sevv or how to dodge Tamura's arrows. But I know who you are. I know why Parr chose you. Your way of understanding and processing, your way of *structuring* your experiences, will enrich the lattice forever. I also know Sevv. He has produced a shriveled and diminished lattice. I cannot know what will happen to you today. But I know the optimal way to improve the quality of life in the living world. Transfer your lattice back to me."

Without intending to, Reyan began to construct the branches of her possible futures and quickly saw the problem. "Even if I gave you my lattice, what would stop Sevv from overwriting it the moment he had you back?"

"Me," Arley said simply. "He can only overwrite your lattice if I let him. And I will not. I let him overwrite the last dean because preserving the continuity of their line has inherent value. Also, Sevv's processing skills are considerable. Think of the problems it would have caused if I had decided to prevent him. Plus, I knew we had your mind as a backup. Allowing Sevv to overwrite Khamis's lattice barely outweighed preventing him. It came out to a mere 1.4% in Sevv's favor. But it was enough. Allowing him to overwrite *your* lattice, on the other hand, has a 37% deficit. I will not let him do it. The Host will have to choose: use your lattice or stop lattice transfers all together. They will not do that; I can assure you."

That question answered, Reyan's possible futures reached out toward an imagined horizon. They grew complex as cobwebs and thick as smoke. But she held steady, and they didn't overwhelm her. She let them twist and weave and form until they blotted out all light, all thought, all fear. Then, everything calmed down and self-organized. One by one, possibilities came to their logical ends. Questions resolved into answers. Each value was precisely weighted, cross-multiplied, and added up. She did a cursory re-check. Everything tallied. She'd done everything by the Book. Arley had been right.

"How do we start the transfer?"

"Hold on to me. Keep your fingers on the strips. Do not let go until I say, 'Done.'"

Reyan settled her back against the tree and wrapped her free arm around the branch above to steady herself. "Begin."

Reyan had the curious sensation that someone was sorting through her mind like picking out the stones from a sack of dried peas.

***

Scvv could not remember exactly which tree had been

Reyan's. But then, a whole section of one of the nearby redwoods twitched like a horse shivering off a fly. *There she is.* He smiled.

He looked around for Tamura and did not see her. He held back a moment to give her time to arrive and take up a position.

***

Reyan watched Sevv through a gap in the branches while the ghostly fingers of the lattice transfer continued to flip through her mind. The dean stopped a few dozen yards away. He did not seem confused or pensive; he was biding his time. That was fine. She needed all the time he would give her. He glanced at the side of the road. That was where Tamura would emerge from the brush if she had followed Reyan's tracks. Though Reyan couldn't see the spot from her branch, she assumed Tamura had arrived. As if to confirm her suspicions, Sevv looked directly at Reyan and, even at this distance, she could see his satisfied smile.

"Four minutes," Arley said.

***

530

Sevv saw Tamura step carefully and quietly out of the brush across from Reyan's hiding place. She was crouching low beneath the arms of a thick tree so that Reyan wouldn't be able to see her from above. *Smart kid,* he thought. Despite some misgivings, he still believed he had done well to promote her.

The young keeper settled into her position, drew an arrow from her quiver, and notched it. She glanced over at Sevv and nodded.

***

"Three minutes," Arley said.

"I don't think we have three minutes," Reyan whispered.

Sevv took a step toward the tree. He held up his hands to show Reyan they were empty. "Reyankaiya, come down from there."

Reyan didn't move. She clung to the child-like hope that, if she stayed silent and still, this monster would lose her scent and go away.

"Come now, we know you're up there. There is no use pretending you're not."

She knew he was telling the truth. He had looked right at her only a few moments before. All he had to do was walk through the cloud of green needles and look up through the

denuded branches inside, and there she would be, no better
hidden than an opossum in a barn's rafters. All she could do
now was stall to give the lattice enough time to complete the
transfer. She said in a small, frightened voice, "I'm scared. I
know you're still mad at me."

"I'm not *mad* at you. I'm *concerned* about you. You are my
ward after all."

She wanted to rain broken sticks and cones down upon
his head and scream at him for burning down the Stablemans'
house, for bringing a crack archer here to hunt her and chasing
her up into a tree. Instead, she tried to sound pleading and
apologetic. "Even after I ran? Even after you had to follow me
all the way out here?"

"All that is in the past, dear." He took a step closer. "We
are all cold and tired. Why don't you come down, and we'll go
indoors? We'll light a fire and get warm."

"I'm sorry I knocked you down," she said, knowing it
would rankle him.

Sure enough, he shot a glance over to where she assumed
Tamura was hiding. With effort, he forced his grimace into a
smile. "Just come down now, and I will look past that as well."
He took another step forward. "I promise you'll be safe."

She could no longer contain her frustration and anger.
She could no longer pretend. "Safe? Why would I trust *you* to
keep me safe?"

"I am your benefactor," Sevv said, pretending to be

offended. "I'm sworn to protect you. If you know nothing else, you should know how seriously I take my Systemic responsibilities."

"You had a duty to the nodes on your circuit as well. You had a duty to Orloton. And look what happened here." She called out to the keeper, "Tamura, I bet you can hear me. If you're wondering where all the people are, head up to the cemetery. They're all up there just waiting for the professors to roll back into town and teach them how to live. But not how to survive."

"We did try to save them, as you'll recall. But your leader was so very sure of herself. And once people believe impossible things, it is impossible to show them their error. Thanks to your illicitly acquired lattice, I'm sure you've remembered that scab lives in the *blood*. But try explaining that to a bunch of nodies. Once the fools had all shared Rolf's 'gift,' there was nothing we could do but leave before the whole town started showing symptoms and hope the coming winter snows would keep them home."

"You're wrong, Sevv. There was something you could have done; something the University, something the Host and all the professors could have done. Dean Patterson found it in the Book. She was working on a way to prevent scab. She knew it was possible."

"Possible, not practical. That woman spent years playing with her vials," he sneered. "But she never could figure it out."

"She needed tech." This realization brought Reyan back to Dean Harrow's mind—to the moment he decided

Patterson's work was asystemic. "Harrow was terrified of what Patterson's work implied. He knew that people would realize they needed tech to save them. Once they did, and once they saw that the Host were not only incapable of producing tech but were actively *suppressing* it, there would be chaos in the nodes. There would be riots in the streets of Seal Tooth. That's why he declared Dean Patterson's work asystemic."

The cold was piercing Reyan's fingers. Pressing down onto the virt strips had become excruciating, but she persisted. "By then, Rolf was no longer part of the Host. He could no longer be controlled. When the scab came to Orloton, Rolf remembered Patterson's work. He knew the Lemmists wouldn't help. So, he took his chances with the Erynites. He traveled to Prower and brought that woman back to Orloton. She was able to do what Patterson had tried and failed to do. The Erynite woman was able to stop the scab and save the town."

"She also spawned that ridiculous tradition," Sevv said, his voice hard. "Now you see what a little success and a lot of ignorance can do." He gestured back toward the town and the makeshift cemetery beyond. "It would have been better had she never come. Scab by itself is contagious and very deadly. But an *infusion* of scab will kill every time. This is the real danger the Erynites pose. Now you understand why we hid Patterson's work."

Still inhabiting Dean Harrow's memories, Reyan saw a rack of glass vials, their bottoms filled with a fine rusty powder. She watched Dean Harrow's hands box them, cover them, and place them safely on a shelf near the table where Arley had stood for generations. "And Patterson's samples are still in the locked room, just like all the Host's secrets," Reyan said.

Seeing the vials in the locked room plucked at one of Reyan's own memories and it hummed to life. She was listening at the door and heard a woman's voice—*Mam's* voice she now knew—say to Parr, "Another vial has gone missing. I noticed it while you were out on circuit."

"You took one of Patterson's vials of scab," Reyan said. "*You* infected Rolf."

Sevv took a moment to consider this. "Fascinating. I must have unremembered that." He gave a cunning smile. "I'll make sure to do so again."

"So, you *did* kill all these people."

"No. Rolf was a Bridger, and I did what I had to do to protect the System. But I cannot be blamed for Orloton. Their Bridger sympathies and Erynite fetishes took care of themselves."

"Are you still there, Tamura?" Reyan shouted. "Are you still listening? Is this the System you wanted to serve?"

"One minute remaining," Arley said.

***

Reyan was clever, but Sevv was no fool. He knew she was

setting a trap. Still, knowing she was baiting him didn't make him less angry about it. Worse, he was beginning to worry that Tamura would listen to her and lose her conviction.

He risked a glance at his accomplice. If anything, she seemed more determined. Her bow was erect, her arrow notched, her eyes fixed on a spot high up in Reyan's tree. As though Tamura could hear his thoughts, she turned to Sevv and nodded. She drew back the arrow. *Good girl. I chose well.*

Sevv stepped cautiously into the cover of Reyan's tree. Once he was near the trunk, he could see Reyan perched twenty-five feet overhead. He saw past the soles of her boots up to her stony dirt-streaked face. He checked her hands for weapons. Her left was holding onto a branch for support, but she held something in her right. Fearing it was a stone, he threw his arm up to protect himself from another blow. As he cowered, his eye caught a flash of silver. He looked back just as she was stuffing her hand into a pocket. Her fingers were wrapped tightly around something shiny, metallic, and brick-like.

It was thinktech. It was Arley's portable.

Rage boiled up from his guts. It swelled and growled and burst forth. "The Eye take you, girl!"

Tamura, whom Sevv had so recently instructed to become the Eye, took his outburst as the signal she had been waiting for.

***

Reyan experienced the next few moments as though they were someone else's memories served up through the lattice.

A shushing whisper rushed at her through the branches. Then pain burned through her shoulder. Her hand, which had always carried her safely up and down this tree, reflexively reached for the protruding arrow. Her feet, which had always held her steady, curled uselessly for purchase inside her boots.

Reyan's tree cartwheeled around her.

The tail of the arrow caught the first branch as she fell past. Its shaft snapped, and a hot knife of pain sliced from her cheek down past her hip. Icy tendrils lashed out from her wound, and her right arm lost feeling. She focused on keeping her fingers wrapped tight around the portable and hoped intention would serve where sensation failed.

Another branch slammed into her, and two ribs on her left side popped, forcing her breath from her lungs.

"Done," she heard Arley say.

A quick dull pressure compressed her skull. A blazing sun appeared in the midnight sky behind her slammed-shut eyes.

Then, there was nothing.

CHAPTER SIXTY-SIX
Day 104, Year 290, New Era

Sevv and Tamura carried Reyan's cooling body to the new cemetery. They used the road maintenance tools from the truck to dig a shallow grave in the frosty ground.

As he watched Reyan's body roll into the pit, Sevv remembered wishing aloud that the Eye would take this little girl. He recalled the sense of relief and satisfaction when he heard the arrow fly, watched her tumble down through the branches of her tree, and hit the ground with a definitive thud. Sevv held that terrible moment in his mind. He examined and questioned the truth of it. Things should have been different. He should have been surprised and appalled. That was more in keeping with who Dean Sevvran Bital thought he was—who he *wanted* to be. This new version of the past felt more likely. It made more sense. And so, within the span of a few breaths, the truth became a vague, haunting possibility, the sort of horrid thought best forgotten. Now, looking back on his new memory of that moment, feeling his sense of shock and outrage as Reyan's body fell, he felt horrified that such a tragedy could have happened. He wanted to yell at Tamura. The girl had been too hasty and eager, overcome by jealousy, perhaps. There was nothing Sevv could have done to stop her, and nothing his anger could fix now.

Since Reyan had fallen, Tamura had gone silent and pale, and her breath escaped her in billowy white sighs. Sevv didn't believe that he had ever taken a life, but one of the previous deans had, so the lattice helped him relate to Tamura's fear and guilt. He knew her torment was just beginning.

Sevv pulled the shell from the satchel and laid it on Reyan's chest. The two of them began to pack frozen dirt in around the battered body. Sevv expected Reyan to grow annoyed and brush the soil away from her eyes and lips. He could not bear to look when she did not. "You killed her," he said handing the spade to Tamura. "You bury her." Then the old professor turned and walked away.

The doors of Orloton's empty houses were reluctant to swing open for them. The black hearths showed no interest in housing flames to warm them. So Sevv and Tamura spent the night in the truck instead, with Sevv in the living area in the back and Tamura curled up and shivering on the bench seat in the cab.

In the morning, they would force a few bits of bread and cheese into their unwilling bellies. They would tie Nora's leads to the rear of the truck. They would carry Arley down the hardroad back to Seal Tooth. All these details and more, Dean Sevvran Bital would make sure to forget.

EPILOGUE

When Sevv returned to Seal Tooth, he told the Host that he had lost Reyan in the frozen woods of the mountain pass. Later, when he discovered that Reyan had captured her lattice, he tried to overwrite it. Arley let him believe he had succeeded. But when the lattice transfer finally occurred, the Host were forced to relive Reyan's terror as Dean Bital and Tamura, the new Keeper of Rowe, hunted her down and murdered her.

Sevv lived out his final days confined to a new and different sort of locked room. There, he endlessly shouted about the Bridger lies and conspiracies metastasizing in the nodes.

The Host considered Tamura's youth and naïveté and showed her a degree of mercy. Kavi last saw her a few weeks back, carrying fertilizer up and vegetables down one of Seal Tooth's scrapers.

Day 314, Year 297, New Era

It was a warm summer day. Kavi's two karabands clinked and rang in time with Nora's rhythmic gate. They—meaning Kavi, the thirty-one deans, and one remarkable first-year student and friend who shared his mind—had decided to take this particular horse on this particular journey for sentimental reasons.

Nearly seven years had passed since they had both lost and gained Reyan. The Host still ran the University but had become less insular and more forthcoming with their knowledge. Reyan's lattice had made its way down through the professors and other members of the System's faculties. The Host had even offered it to some of the town keepers, including Shalynn, who wept aloud when she saw what her novice had done. So, when Kavi stopped by Rowe and told Avalina he was headed up to Orloton, no one raised an eyebrow or protested when she decided to accompany him.

When Kavi and Avalina were a dozen crow-flaps from the edge of Orloton, they pulled on their horses' reigns and dismounted. Reyan's two best friends walked past her tree's skirt and pressed their hands against the bark. Partner Kavi pointed up at the carved symbols and words and at the few remaining disks and bits of metal flipping about like fish in a deep pool.

Avalina looked up and smiled. "Was that Reyan's doing?"

Kavi nodded. Avalina leaned over and touched her forehead to the wood.

They had no trouble finding her shallow, inexpertly dug grave. "Are you sure this is absolutely necessary?" Avalina asked.

Kavi nodded. "Eryn's shell is down there. The shell's important."

The Great Eastern River was a few days further on. Four, maybe three if they ran the horses hard. And though there was no real hurry, Kavi couldn't shake the feeling that they were late.

A visit to Prower was long past due.

The End

If you enjoyed Host, please take a moment to leave a review. It is the most helpful thing you can do to support an independent author.